One More Song to Sing

Center Point
Large Print

**This Large Print Book carries the
Seal of Approval of N.A.V.H.**

One More Song to Sing

Lindsay Harrel

CENTER POINT LARGE PRINT
THORNDIKE, MAINE

The text of this Large Print edition is unabridged.
In other aspects, this book may vary
from the original edition.
Printed in the United States of America
on permanent paper.
Set in 16-point Times New Roman type.

ISBN: 978-1-68324-646-6

Library of Congress Cataloging-in-Publication Data

Names: Harrel, Lindsay, author.
Title: One more song to sing / Lindsay Harrel.
Description: Center Point large print edition. | Thorndike, Maine :
    Center Point Large Print, 2018.
Identifiers: LCCN 2017046258 | ISBN 9781683246466
    (hardcover : alk. paper)
Subjects: LCSH: Large type books. | GSAFD: Christian fiction. |
    Love stories.
Classification: LCC PS3608.A729 O54 2018 | DDC 813/.6—dc23
LC record available at https://lccn.loc.gov/2017046258

In loving memory of my mother,
Sandy Lynn Walker. Mom, I love you up,
down, around, and back again.
You were and always will be my inspiration.

1

**Civic Center Music Hall, Oklahoma City
Twenty-three years and nine months ago**

One song is all it will take to change my life forever.

I primp my brown curls in the dressing room mirror and apply bright-red to my lips. I wish they were fuller like Sally May's, but I guess I gotta work with what the good Lord gave me.

Everyone else has their mamas fussin' over them. Mine's nowhere to be found, but maybe that's better.

With a twist and a firm jerk, I flatten my denim shirt. I tried ironing it this morning but was liable to catch something on fire. And Mama wasn't home to help. Big surprise.

I won't look in the mirror again. It can't change anything about how well I sing or play guitar.

Besides, today nothing's getting me down.

"Marie Culloway?" A stagehand with a clipboard scans the room where about ten of us wait our turn.

I raise my hand.

She nods my direction. "You're on in two."

I scurry out the dressing room door and follow the stagehand to the backstage area. It's

7

hard to see but I can sure hear. The audience is lovin' some girl from Tulsa who belts out Patty Loveless's "Chains." They've probably never heard of little old Red, Oklahoma. Why would they, when everyone who leaves never claims they're from there, and everyone who stays never goes anywhere else?

This is only the second time I've been more than twenty miles away. And now here I am, at the Oklahoma City Amateur Singing Competition. Who knows? Maybe I'll actually win this thing, get a chance to go to Nashville and meet Trisha Yearwood herself. That might be the start of my career. Then I can get out of Red for good. Out of Red . . . and away from Mama.

I strap on my guitar and twiddle my thumbs as I bounce, waiting, the cheers and whistles from the audience filling me up. Maybe they'll do that for me soon. Maybe Mama will emerge from whatever watering hole she's found and do the same.

The music ends and Little Miss Tulsa flounces past me in the wings, a wicked grin on her lips. "Beat that."

I inhale deeply and try to think of something nice to say. But my mind is blank, and the stage-hand pushes me out onstage. The lights blind me for a minute, and the smell of popcorn and oil hits me square in the nose.

"Here's Marie Culloway from Red, Oklahoma, singin' Dolly Parton's 'Jolene.'"

The crowd applauds, and I start strumming. This feels like breathing, holding a guitar to my chest and bursting out in song. It's what I do all those nights I'm alone in our trailer, when Mama leaves for "work" and doesn't come home till morning. It's what I do when I feel like crying.

Guess it's what I do with most of the scattered moments of my fifteen-year-old life.

The crowd hushes as I twirl out the melody, a simple tune that's somehow big enough to fill up this auditorium packed with more than three thousand people. Then a commotion rises, but I'm too lost in the music to figure out what it is. Finally, I look up.

A little girl with pigtails sits in the front row. Her eyes are wide, and she's looking off to my left.

I can't keep myself from following her gaze as I pluck out the chords.

And there's Mama, on my stage, doing some sort of interpretive dance, a beer raised in her hand. She's wearing a miniskirt and tight shirt that's got the top two buttons undone, and her tattered overcoat lies on the floor. Her red hair poofs over itself like a beacon for everyone in the crowd.

Oh, Mama. My heart pounds out my defeat.

Our eyes connect and she races toward me, grabs

the mic, and sputters and wails, "Jo-leeeeeeene. Jo-leeeeeeene." She looks at me and splays her toothy grin. Her blue eyes are slightly sunken into her skull, but that never stops me from thinkin' she's pretty. Except right now.

Right now, she's just the death of my career before it even starts.

I can't keep playing, so I stop then and there and leave the polished stage.

Mama's still swaying back and forth, shouting out the last lines to the crowd, having a grand old time.

Hot tears poke the back of my eyes as I reach my cloth case and stuff my guitar inside. My hair falls in my face, and I yank it back, securing it with a rubber band that's on my wrist. How can she do this to me? She knows I worked hard.

"Mariiiiiiie!" She stumbles backstage, a broad male stagehand assisting her. "Get off-a me!" She pushes the stagehand away.

He shrugs, drops Mama's coat on the ground, and leaves.

I take off down the hallway, out the back door, into the biting January cold. There's no reason to stick around till the end of the competition. I won't be meeting Trisha Yearwood anytime soon. Maybe never. I won't ever escape this life.

My boots crunch the snow coating the ground as I head for the car, the music hall forever behind me. And then, in my direct path, a tiny pink flower peeks out from the white covering. How has it survived the harsh winter?

Mama wobbles past me. Her heel slams down on the flower, smashing it back into the snow.

I jerk my head up.

Mama's still holding her beer and throws her free hand on her hip. "Why you runnin' away from me?"

I bite my lip to keep from screaming. The taste of blood meets my tongue. "Never mind, Mama. Let's just go."

"No, girl. I asked you a question. Answer me."

A few stragglers in the parking lot stare at us as they pass by. How I wish I could imagine we were just a mother and daughter out to enjoy the day. I thought Mama came to support me, but I suspect she only wanted to blow the twenty bucks they gave me just for showin' up.

A fire boils in my belly. Usually I can stuff it down, but today it bubbles up. "Fine. You wanna know why I ran away? You embarrassed me up there, Mama." Tears roll down my cheeks, and I let them. "You ruined my chances of going to Nashville, meeting Trisha, actually going some-where and being somebody."

She pouts. "I thought you'd like singin' with your old mama."

She's not old by any means, only sixteen years older than me, since she had me so young. But she likes to say that to get pity. I point in her face. "I would have if you hadn't been drunk as a skunk. Again."

She grabs my finger and twists.

I cry out and pull my hand to my chest. My whole body trembles.

Mama snarls. "You think you're better than me. You're ashamed of me. Well, guess what, girl? You're stuck with me. And you're stuck in Red. You ain't never gonna leave. It's who you are. You and me, we're the same. You just don't know it yet."

The fire inside bursts like a volcano. I scream, "I'm nothing like you. If I ever have a daughter, I won't embarrass her in front of thousands of people. I'll do what's best for her. I'll take care of her and love her, like you've never done for me!"

For a second, it looks as though she'll slap me. That wouldn't be new. But instead, she gets real close to me and lowers her voice. Her teeth chatter. "You're a Culloway. You're always gonna be a Culloway. Culloways ain't nothing special. And Culloways most definitely ain't cut out to be mothers."

I turn and run away from Mama, away from what seems at every turn to be my destiny.

Whether I want it to be or not.

2

Nashville, Present Day

No matter how undeserving, Olivia Lovett was the queen of grasping for second chances.

She took the clipboard from the receptionist and headed for a seat in the corner of the partially filled waiting room. A quiet hum vibrated in the air, which smelled of lavender. To Olivia's left, a wall fountain trickled canned tranquility. Just overhead, the local meteorologist filled a forty-inch television screen as she forecasted sunny skies on this autumn Monday in Nashville.

Olivia prayed the forecast was metaphoric as well as physical. She needed a miracle. *I'm out of options after this, Lord.*

Sinking into a black leather chair, Olivia set her oversized purse on the seat next to her.

With her sunglasses still over her eyes, she took a quick survey of the room.

The half-dozen or so fellow patients flipped through magazines, fiddled with their phones, or jittered their knees while staring at the clinically white walls. All except one woman, who studied Olivia.

Olivia flashed a quick smile and looked down

at the clipboard in her hands, staring at the name at the top.

Dr. Peter Fancy, Otolaryngologist. How many times had she seen that title as she sat in waiting rooms like this one? But maybe Dr. Fancy was the answer to her prayers.

She pulled the pen from the top of the board and scrawled her name across the page: Marie Cull—seriously? Twenty-three years as Olivia Lovett, and her old identity sometimes came creeping out when least expected.

Perhaps it was because her subconscious knew what this week was, despite all her attempts to distract herself.

She scratched out the error and wrote *Olivia Lovett* with a flourish. Despite disclosing her name on these forms, she'd been assured the utmost confidentiality by the office manager.

"Excuse me."

She glanced up to see the woman who'd been gaping at her now standing over her, something clutched in her hands.

"Yes?" Olivia held in the sigh threatening to escape her lungs. This woman must have recognized her. Would she be the next "mysterious source" leaking Olivia's desperation to the tabloids?

"I hate to bother you. I'm here with my sister"—the woman aimed her finger at a mousy lady with a bandage over her throat—"getting her checked out after her surgery last week." The sweater the woman wore pulled flecks of gray from her eyes, granting her the appearance of innocence.

Olivia instantly tasted remorse over being so cynical. She lowered her sunglasses. "That's nice of you."

The woman's mouth formed an *O*. "I thought it was you. Wow, Olivia Lovett, as I live and breathe." One hand fluttered to her chest.

Olivia held out her hand. "It's nice to meet you . . . ?"

"Stephanie. Stephanie Little." She took Olivia's hand and pumped it like a water well handle.

"Nice to meet you, Stephanie."

Stephanie lowered herself onto the chair across from Olivia, held up a pen and a Target receipt. "Could you sign an autograph real quick? Sorry about the receipt. It's all I could find in my purse."

The familiar ache hit Olivia between the eyes, but she smiled wide in spite of it. "Of course I can. Anything for my fans." Those that still existed anyway. She reached for the pen.

"I've always wanted to be a singer like you someday."

Poor Stephanie didn't know what she was saying. Putting one's heart out there in the music, night after night, took something from a person. Olivia never minded giving it—but it stung when her label had dropped her the instant she was no longer useful to them.

But she'd be useful again. She had to be.

Olivia took a deep breath and—thanks to years of practice—kept her grin in place. "Isn't that the sweetest thing?" She scribbled a personalized message to Stephanie and handed the pen and receipt back to her. "Here you are."

"Oh, thank you." Stephanie held the receipt as if it was a treasure. She studied Olivia's signature for a moment. Then her head popped up and she leaned in, looking around as if about to share a secret. "Are you here to get your voice fixed? Will you be singing again soon?"

Olivia picked up the pen from her clipboard and ground the sides of her middle finger and thumb against it. "Guess we'll see, won't we?"

However much she was tempted to think of this as her last shot, life still had meaning with or without her voice. If this didn't work, she'd get back up again, throw herself into working toward a new dream.

Because, with a past like hers, the only place Olivia Lovett could move was forward.

"Ms. Smith?" A nursing assistant emerged from behind the large oak door. Her white hair was pulled back into a severe bun, forcing the wrinkles at the edges of her eyes upward.

"Here." Olivia patted Stephanie's knee. "You take care now, okay, hon?"

Stephanie nodded and returned to her sister. She showed her the receipt, and they examined it together.

Olivia stood, taking her bag and the clipboard with her.

The nursing assistant led her to a back room and told her the doctor would be right with her. In here the air seemed thinner, closing in on her as her chest tightened. Olivia settled into a lime-green chair, and a replica of the larynx caught her eye. She could identify the hyoid bone, windpipe, vessels, muscles, and vocal cords. It would be amazing if she couldn't after all she'd been through.

A knock sounded at the door, and a man walked in. He wore brown slacks and a button-up shirt with a colorful bow tie. His salt-and-pepper hair was a bit tousled. "I'm Dr. Fancy." He held out his hand and shook hers, a spark of recognition lighting his eyes. "How can I help you?"

Olivia leaned forward. "Thank you for taking the time to meet with me, doctor. I won't sugar-coat things. I'm here because I want to sing again."

"I see." The doctor tapped his pen against his knee. He tilted his head. "I'm not going to pretend I don't know who you are. I'm a big fan, in fact."

"Thank you."

"I'd heard the rumors you had to stop singing because of cysts. But that was a few years ago. Why are you coming to me now?"

Recalling the story always reminded her how desperate for success she'd been—how she'd ruined the only thing she'd ever been good at. "As you probably know, I was performing almost every day, and my manager was adding tour dates like crazy. So when I started to notice the pain, I just shoved it away."

"That's a common occurrence with career performers like yourself."

A fact that didn't comfort her. She should have known better. "By the time I finally saw a doctor about it, she told me I needed rest. That might have cured it if I'd listened."

"But you didn't, I presume."

"No. I didn't." Olivia moved her hair to the front of her shoulder and fingered a large chunk, the blonde hair split on several strands. "Finally, it was too much. I had to take some time off. My label agreed to give me a month, but it wasn't enough. I could barely sing a middle C when I came back."

"So you didn't have phonomicrosurgery?"

"I actually did have the surgery. Three months ago. I know what you're thinking. 'Why wait so long?' " She often wondered that herself. What if she'd pressed onward, not allowed depression to set in and take hold, found a way to sing again before her fans moved on to the next big thing? "I guess that doesn't matter much now, because here we are. A friend and I are starting a new venture, and it'd be helpful if I could sing again. But the surgery and three months of vocal therapy haven't gotten me anywhere. I need a second opinion."

"If the surgery didn't work, I'm not sure what else is left to try."

"Please, doctor. An acquaintance recommended you, said you have innovative new methods that are changing the field of otolaryngology. There's got to be something you can do." The old, familiar cry pounded in Olivia's chest, begged for release. "I need this."

Dr. Fancy sighed and rubbed his chin. "All right. I'll take a look. But no promises."

"That's all I can ask for." Because it was quite possible her luck had finally run out.

How had it come to this, singing in a backwoods joint that felt more like a prison courtyard than the concert hall of Ellie's dreams?

The Lizard Lounge was definitely a far cry from the Grand Ole Opry.

Any minute now, those two guys near the bar would break out into a brawl. Beer flying, popcorn on the floor, and no one, not a soul, would hear her song.

Ellie adjusted the mic. "How y'all doing tonight?"

Who was she kidding? No one was going to answer her. Besides the men pacing and eyeing each other, the only other people in the lounge included a couple making out on a tattered couch in the corner; Sam, the burly bartender; and one older guy hunched over at the counter, nursing yet another beer. The mixed smell of buffalo wings and sewage—probably from that overflowing toilet in the ladies room across the way—stained the stale air.

Ellie stood partially in the dark, thanks to one broken neon light overhead. Not exactly how she'd imagined spending her Monday nights every week. But it was a paycheck. And she needed groceries. A girl could only survive on Ramen noodles for so long.

She nestled her guitar against her body, strummed, and launched into an acoustic version of "Sweet Home Alabama." Something familiar, easy. Ellie closed her eyes, pretended she stood on the edge of a stadium stage before a rapt audience, playing her own songs, pulling from somewhere deep. Finally being somebody.

And instead of a bunch of drunks who couldn't care less, her long-lost mama would be sitting in the front row, cheering her on.

A burp rang out from the man at the bar.

Ellie tapped her foot, but it stuck to the

concrete floor, then sounded like ripping Velcro as she moved it up and down. She wrapped up the song. "Y'all have any requests?"

"Dinner with you." The bartender flung his white rag across the counter and winked at her.

Smirking, she shook her head. Sam was the only reason she felt safe coming to the seedier side of Nashville.

"No, with me." One of the pacers took a sluggish step toward the stage. He swayed.

"Now, boys, I'm flattered." Ellie winked back at Sam. "But seeing as you both have wedding rings on, I'm thinking your wives wouldn't be too keen on that idea." Like she had time to date anyway, what with scraping together hundreds of dollars for rent every month, writing her music, and working thirty hours a week at the diner.

But maybe someday, once she made it big.

The girl on the couch came up for air. "How 'bout something by Taylor Swift?"

Of course. She got that request at least once a night, if not more. "Sure. Here's an old one."

As Ellie plucked the notes and sang "Teardrops on My Guitar," the heavy door at the front opened, and a few leaves that had fallen from the tree outside blew in.

A middle-aged man in black pants and a shirt with rolled-up sleeves pushed his way inside. His silver watch reflected one of the lights and flashed in Ellie's eyes.

Hmm. Not the kind of customer who normally frequented the Lizard Lounge.

He plopped onto a stool, said something to Sam. Then he turned to face Ellie, one elbow on the bar.

A lump formed in Ellie's throat at the intensity of his gaze, but somehow she pushed the tune through.

When her set was up, she packed away her guitar. Sam had kicked out the two brawlers several songs ago, and the couple on the couch had left in the middle of her last song. The disheveled elderly man had lapsed into some stage of beer slumber. The last guy who'd strolled in still sat at the bar, ale in hand.

Sam flipped on the radio, and the low tones of Tim McGraw whooshed into the room, seeping into Ellie's bones. Her shoulders relaxed as she strode to the bar and leaned her guitar case against the counter.

Sam poured her a Coke. "On the house."

Ellie hunkered down onto a barstool a few seats away from the man. She felt his eyes follow her. "Thank you." She snatched up the glass and drank, chasing away her yawn. Oh, it felt good to sit.

Sam's eyebrows knit together. "You doing okay?" He opened the cash register and handed a twenty to Ellie.

Andrew Jackson mocked her as she clutched the bill in her fist.

"Thanks, Sam." The money wouldn't go far, but it was something. Just thinking about her dwindling bank account soured the Coke in her mouth. "And yeah, I'm okay. Just . . . tired."

"You still working four-a.m. shifts at Lulu's?"

"Yep."

Maybe it was her imagination . . . but was the man at the counter listening to their conversation?

She lowered her voice. "I pull double shifts when I can." Working at the diner definitely wasn't her dream job, but the tips were decent and the customers polite.

"I'm worried about you." Sam's bushy eyebrows slid together. He shook his finger in her face. "You need to take better care of yourself."

"I don't have a choice, Sam. Gotta pay the bills." She held up the cash. "As much as I love performing, this ain't gonna cut it."

Sam grunted as he gathered a few dirty glasses and appetizer plates from the counter and stacked them.

She handed him her empty glass, then kneaded her neck. Mmm, a bubble bath sounded nice right about now. Yeah right. The second she got back to her tiny apartment, she'd collapse on her bed, fully clothed, as usual.

"How long have you been singing?" The guy with the nice watch finally spoke up.

Ellie straightened at the question. "As long as I can remember." Yep, since Daddy had given her his old guitar and she'd used it to become her true self.

The thought of Daddy pinched her gut. Oh, how she missed him, even if he'd never been around much. There was a difference between him being gone working in the city and being gone forever.

"I like what I heard." The man slid off his stool, held out his hand. "Rob Jenkins."

She hesitated, then shook his hand. "Ellie Van—I mean, Ellie Evans." Would she ever get used to using Grandma's maiden name? But VanRisseghem was too complicated a last name for someone looking to strike it famous one day. Nobody would be able to spell it right on Google.

"Nice to meet you, Ellie." The man leaned against the counter. His cologne floated between them. It smelled like something they'd sell inside the fragrance department at Dillard's.

"Just what is it you do, Mr. Jenkins?" Sam leaned over the bar, his protective instinct clearly flaring.

Ellie stifled a giggle.

Mr. Jenkins didn't look bothered. He settled back on his stool. "I book the talent at

Bernadette's Café for open mic nights and other performances."

Sweet applesauce. Bernadette's? The upscale restaurant on Broadway with the black-and-white awning? Rumor was music label execs were regulars there, and open mic nights were filled months in advance on an audition basis. In fact, she'd submitted her tape for consideration a few times last year.

But something didn't make sense. "Why would anyone come to the Lizard Lounge looking for talent? No offense, Sam." After months playing this joint, she'd never even seen a businessman here, much less a booking manager.

Still, Mr. Jenkins did have that executive air about him, as if he hung out with rich people all the time. And he was confident. The gray at his temples spoke of someone not ashamed of who he was and where he'd come from. "I don't normally come to this side of the tracks but was down this way for a personal matter and heard you from outside. Decided to check it out. And I wasn't disappointed."

What could she say to that? "I—"

"You have your own songs you can play?"

"Yes. Absolutely. Yes, sir."

Mr. Jenkins reached into his pocket and pulled out a business card. "Here. Why don't you stop by? We have a good crowd on Friday nights, and

I've got a last-minute cancellation this week. You interested?"

"That would be amazing." But wait. Hadn't she agreed to take Jason's shift that night at Lulu's? "I'll have to check my work schedule, but I'd love to play if I'm free." She'd beg her coworkers to switch with her if need be, do whatever it took to get the night off. Maybe Lena could get out of her Friday night class and cover for her.

"Let me know as soon as possible. I need to fill the slot, and there are lots of artists who would be happy to take it."

"I will. Most definitely."

Sam filled a new patron's shot glass, then glanced back at Mr. Jenkins. "Wouldn't happen to know anyone in the industry by the name of Marie Culloway, would you?"

Ellie's eyes widened. Why hadn't she thought to ask the same question? Maybe because every time she did, people shook their heads.

Kind of like Mr. Jenkins was doing now. "No, that name doesn't sound familiar. Who is she?"

Sam opened his mouth to speak again, but Ellie swooped in. "Just someone from my past I'd like to reconnect with."

No, not just someone. Her mother. The one who'd left a newborn Ellie with a teenaged father and his parents and had run off to Nashville to become a singer.

All she had to go on was what her dad's parents knew about her mom—that she and Daddy were from different towns, had a one-night stand after some amateur singing competition, and were in high school when Ellie was born.

Daddy had kept everything else a secret from Ellie and his parents, saying it was "for the best." Then, two years ago, he'd died in a senseless car accident, taking any other information with him to the grave.

Mr. Jenkins rubbed his chin. "You let me know if you're free on Friday, and I'll ask around about this Culloway woman. Might be that someone I know knows her." He slapped a twenty on the counter to pay his bill. "You have a card so I can call if I get any information?"

"Yeah, of course." Ellie fumbled through the pouch on her guitar case till she found her stack of business cards. The cheap paper felt rough beneath her fingertips as she handed one to Mr. Jenkins. "Thanks."

"Great. I'll be in touch." Mr. Jenkins rose from his stool and walked out the door.

The wind howled through the cracks as he left, sweeping away the cobwebs in her heart that had grown thick around an emotion she'd nearly forgotten.

Hope.

3

Three thirty in the morning had arrived earlier than usual.

And now, four hours later, Ellie forced down a yawn as she scurried behind the counter at Lulu's Diner toward the coffee. With a shaking hand, she snatched the oversized pot and poured the black liquid into four red mugs. Coffee splashed over the sides of the last one, onto the black-and-white-tiled counter. She longed to gulp down a mug herself but had barely made it here on time this morning. With seven tables, she likely wouldn't have a chance for any wake-up juice for a long while.

But that was all fine. Because her big break was around the corner. She could feel it. The encounter with Rob Jenkins last night seemed random—but she knew better than to believe in coincidence. Maybe God cared what happened to her after all.

"Ellie, table eight's order is up. Didn't you hear Martin?"

At her boss's gruff voice, she jumped and nearly dropped the pot. "Sorry, Mr. Morgan." With a quick shove, she slid the pot back into the coffee maker. "Let me deliver these to table five, and I'll get right on it."

He sighed. "All right. And I need to talk to you today before you leave."

Was that good or bad? She nodded, placed the mugs onto a tray, and steadied her hand as she maneuvered past two other servers and on toward table five.

The diner speakers usually played a mix of the greats, and at this moment, Tammy's "Stand by Your Man" added an extra kick to Ellie's step. Maybe someday she'd join the legends in soothing the edges of someone else's frayed soul.

"Here y'all are." This early in the morning, her cheery voice sounded like the chirping of an annoying bird. Ellie set the tray on table five, where four college students sat, two wearing Belmont University College of Law sweatshirts. She delivered their coffee without spilling another drop. Whew. Now to get the food for table eight. Ellie took the quickest path through the crowded diner. The din of chatter and clanging silverware mixed with the Charlie Daniels Band and swirled around her.

When she reached the food bar, the order was nowhere to be found.

Her roommate and fellow waitress, Lena, swept past her to snatch a few muffins from the pastry case. Her short black hair was pulled low into pigtails. "I delivered it for you." She kept her voice quiet. "Mr. Morgan isn't in a good mood today."

"Thanks." What would Ellie do without Lena's watching her back? And why was she having so much trouble keeping up today? It's not like she hadn't been serving for the last few years, ever since coming to Nashville. Must just be distraction over the exciting possibilities her future held. She bent toward Lena. "By the way, do you have class on—?"

"Table three, order's up!" Martin shouted and slid three plates of food across the gleaming silver bar between the kitchen and the area behind the front counter.

"Never mind, I'll ask you about it later." Ellie darted forward and piled the plates onto a tray. She lifted it and spun to face table three, where a trio of men in business suits sipped on their coffee. Wouldn't it be strange if Rob Jenkins was among them? But no, they were strangers she'd never seen before. As Ellie approached, she couldn't help but overhear their conversation.

"I had another newbie try to give me his CD yesterday. He was a nurse monitoring me after my colonoscopy, of all things." The large man sat with his back to Ellie, and his shoulders bounced as he guffawed.

Ellie stepped forward to deliver their food but stopped. Maybe she could learn a few things—these guys were obviously industry professionals.

"Will they never learn? There are proper

31

procedures for these things." Another man pushed his glasses up the bridge of his nose and pressed his lips together.

"Oh, lighten up, Zeb." The third gentleman, who faced Ellie's way, folded his hands in front of him. "They're just kids looking for their big break. I agree it's nice if they would follow protocol—"

"Tony, you bleeding heart. You'd give a contract to every Tom, Dick, or Harry you met on the street." The large man waved his hand in the air. "You know the statistics—how few make it, how many merely perfect the art of waitressing instead. But every performer thinks he'll be the one to break the mold. He's convinced himself it isn't about who you know—which we know it is—but talent. All artists think their big break is around the corner."

Ellie had just said those words to herself not minutes ago . . .

"How foolishly naïve." Zeb noticed Ellie standing there and raised his eyebrows. "Are you going to keep eavesdropping or give us our food?"

If cheeks could turn as red as the dirt in Oklahoma, Ellie's must be close. She stumbled closer. "I—"

A kid darted in front of her at the last second.

Ellie tried to stop, and lost her balance. The whole top of her body shot forward.

The tray flew through the air in slow motion—eggs, bacon, biscuits and gravy, the works—and the plates landed face down on the ground.

All, that is, except for one, which splatted on the back of the large man. His black suit dripped with yellow and gray.

Ellie felt like a buck about to be shot as the man turned and glared at her.

All sound seemed to have halted in the café except for a few *oooh*s and a burst of applause from some jerk in the crowd.

"I am so sorry. So sorry."

The man stood slowly, his two companions silent. His eyes bulged out of their sockets, like they might be rockets about to take off into outer space. His bulbous nose resembled that of a clown's. But unlike a clown, he offered no hint of a smile.

Mr. Morgan ran from the kitchen, beer belly jiggling in step with his apology. "Mr. Granger, I apologize profusely for this."

Wait, Granger, as in Granger Records? No, no, no. Ellie groaned.

A fellow server bustled from the kitchen with towels.

Ellie stood there, blinking.

Mr. Morgan snapped his head up and glowered. "Ellie, get the mop and clean up this mess."

"Right. Sorry." She turned on her heel and ran toward the cleaning supply closet. Where was the mop? It wasn't where they normally kept it. The room spun, and she sank to her knees on the linoleum.

"Ell." Lena's voice sounded distant. Her friend appeared. "C'mon, focus on me. It's okay. Just breathe."

With Lena squeezing her hand, Ellie managed to slow her breathing. Her eyes felt heavy, and all she wanted to do was curl up in a ball and die. Granger Records was the number one recording label in Nashville, and she'd just served breakfast all over its owner, the most powerful man on Music Row.

Lena patted her back. "I'll get the mop. You stay here and relax. It'll be okay." She left.

Mr. Morgan appeared in the doorway. "Ms. Evans, I need to speak with you in my office. Now."

She stared at him for a second before stumbling to her feet and trudging after him.

When they reached his tiny office, which smelled of stale donuts and something like refried beans, he plopped into his chair and indicated she should sit across the desk from him.

Ellie lowered herself and folded her hands in her lap. She stared at her blue sneakers, which were still splattered with dots of gravy. "I just wanted to say how sorry—"

"I didn't bring you here for an apology. I know

you wouldn't intentionally drop that food on Mr. Granger." Mr. Morgan leaned forward on his beefy forearms. "But the fact of the matter is you did. I managed to soothe him by offering him free breakfast for a year, but that's . . ."

Ellie picked at her cuticles. Oh, why didn't he just spit it out? Was he going to dock her pay to cover those breakfasts? Make her work extra shifts? She didn't have enough time for her songwriting and gigs as it was, but she needed this job. "I'll do whatever it takes to make up for this, Mr. Morgan."

"I'd wanted to talk to you about your performance lately anyway. You're often distracted, overly tired."

"I'll do better. I've just been playing a lot more lately." But that was no excuse. "I'll . . . do better."

"I was already going to cut your hours, put you on probation. But now I have to let you go. Can't have my customers thinking we run anything but a first-rate establishment here."

Oh, come on. "It's just a diner." At the taken-aback look on his face, she knew she should shut her mouth but couldn't stop the words from flowing. "Servers drop food. That's just what happens."

"They may drop food occasionally, but when they drop it on John Granger, they get fired."

One mistake, and she was done for. Okay,

maybe not just one, but still. This couldn't happen. Not when her bank account had dwindled to pennies.

It was ironic, really. She'd prayed to be seen. And today, she'd been seen all right—seen making a complete and utter fool of herself. Guess it was true what they said. She should be careful what she wished for.

She stood quietly and untied her white apron with *Lulu's* scrolled across the front. Ellie gulped down the lump in her throat. If she'd been any sort of normal person, her eyes would be littered with tears right now. But ever since Daddy died . . . Ellie pushed the thought aside and straightened. "Thank you for the opportunity to work here, Mr. Morgan. I appreciate it."

Then she turned slowly on her heel and headed out the back door, toward a future that suddenly seemed very uncertain.

4

The news had the power to wreck her—if she let it.

Olivia swerved her red sedan into the last available spot in front of Bernadette's Café, one of Nashville's premier hotspots for country music singers and songwriters trying to make it big. Her days of standing in line, hoping to make it onto the open mic night list, seemed so long ago, yet the memories popped fresh at the front of her mind.

She pulled down the car visor and flipped open the mirror. Did the disappointment show in her eyes? The last thing she wanted was for Andrew to see her as anything but professional. She couldn't handle his questions or his pity.

Olivia swiped at the mascara smudges that still lingered from her phone chat with Dr. Fancy. After a thorough assessment of her X-rays from Monday's visit, he'd made it clear—there was nothing more he could do. Her voice was a lost cause, at least when it came to singing.

And to make matters much, much worse, her insurance had called this morning. They'd denied her appeal, said they wouldn't cover the cost of her surgery and therapy like she'd been sure they would.

Bad news piled on bad news—and on today of all days.

To others, it was a normal Wednesday at the end of September. But to her, it was the day her world had changed forever, twenty-three years ago. The day she'd do anything to avoid, because it reminded her of what she'd had to do only a few weeks later. Reminded her of how it'd felt to rip her own heart from her chest and, somehow, go on living.

Olivia blew out a steadying breath and stepped from her car. Gnarled leaves crunched beneath her boots as she headed toward the front door of the café. A brilliant blue covered the sky, and the sun warmed her face despite the brisk autumn breeze. How could the whole world look so clean and fresh when hers was old and used up?

But no. She had her new business venture to make life exciting again. She couldn't forget that.

Olivia pulled open the door and stepped inside the classy café. The smell of tomatoes and herbs mingled with that of barbecue sauce, brewing warmth in her belly. *Rachel must be cooking up a storm for tonight's writers night.* Olivia would go say hi after her meeting.

She strode past a line of plush crimson booths toward the sound crew, who unraveled microphone and guitar cords.

The light from the windows created spotlights

on the floor. One crewmember spoke into the microphone on the stand in the middle of the small stage. "Testing, one, two. Testing, one, two."

"Hey, y'all." She lifted her hand as she passed.

"Hey, Liv. How you doing today?" Jimmy, an audio tech with a bushy beard, grinned from the sound booth.

"Fine, just fine." The lie slipped through her teeth. But it's not like she could just blurt out the truth anyway. "I've got a meeting, and I'm a few minutes late."

They murmured their goodbyes, and she headed toward the back, where Bernadette let Andrew and Olivia hold auditions for their label.

Several artists already gathered in the corridor, strumming guitars and mouthing lyrics. When they saw her, they straightened.

She remembered that spark of anguish and excitement when she would audition, wondering if she would get her big break. Of course, for her, the anguish had been the result of more than just nerves. She'd left behind one dream—an impossible one—to pursue something else, a failed attempt to rid her life of the sorrow she faced each and every night before drifting off to sleep.

Olivia cleared her throat. "Thanks for coming. We'll be with you shortly. I can't wait to hear what y'all have for us today." She moved past them toward the audition room.

Inside, Andrew sat behind a six-foot folding table, wearing slacks and a button-up dress shirt. He pored over a stack of papers and tapped his pen repeatedly against his other hand. His short brown hair was perfectly gelled, and he wore his long-sleeved shirt buttoned without a wrinkle, his tie not a millimeter askew. Simply put, he looked every bit the Music Row executive he used to be before she'd convinced him to join her in this venture.

"Sorry I'm late." Olivia slid into the seat next to him. "We ready?" Maybe if they could get moving without a lot of chitchat, Andrew wouldn't have time to notice her puffy eyes. In the ten years she'd known him, he'd always seemed to observe things like that.

Andrew looked up. "Bernadette's crew came and set up everything we need." He indicated the tiny stage in the corner, where a guitar amp and a single microphone stand decorated the otherwise bare room.

"Great." Olivia took a swig of the sweet tea that sat in front of her, and it went down smoothly. "Should I call in the first artist?"

"Hang on a sec."

Had he noticed? She didn't want to talk about it yet. Maybe never. After all, she hadn't told anyone she was visiting the doctor, hoping beyond hope for another chance. "What?"

His warm brown eyes made her squirm. He

put his hand over hers for a brief moment and squeezed. "I hope we find the one today."

"Me too." Especially since this was something like their tenth audition and they hadn't found any prospects yet.

They'd agreed to start small, with one artist, until they had the funds to successfully sign more. Didn't want to bite off more than they could chew, what with the risky nature of starting a new record label.

Andrew steered her attention back to the stack of papers. "I'm almost done finalizing some of the finer details with our lawyer, which means we'll be able to move more quickly once we select an artist."

She'd discovered in their brief partnership that Andrew was extremely meticulous—almost to a ridiculous level. Some might complain that he moved slowly, but it was a relief to know every *t* had been crossed, every *i* dotted. "Oh, and I've been busy scouting locations for our future office."

The news that everything was coming together should electrify her, bring her to life with gratitude. Radiant Records wouldn't be possible without Andrew's business acumen, Music Row know-how, and connections. But she'd secretly hoped to be their first artist, make a comeback, and finally reach Hall of Fame status. "That's fabulous." Her voice fell flat.

"What's going on with you?" He furrowed his brow.

Here it went. "Nothing. I'm great."

"Liar."

"Not now, okay?"

Andrew pushed his thick-rimmed glasses up the bridge of his nose. "But later."

Fine. "Later."

Andrew nodded. "All right, then. You ready to hear some singin'?"

A laugh bubbled in her throat despite everything. "You know, whenever you try to sound southern, your Florida shows. You'd think after twenty years in Music City, you would've figured out the twang by now."

"Guess you can take the boy out of Florida . . ."

Olivia stood and grinned. "Guess so." She peeked at a clipboard on the table, walked to the door, and opened it. "Cindy James?"

A petite redhead in a jean jacket charged the door. "Right here!" She swung her guitar case as she bounced toward Olivia. They shook hands. "It's such an honor to meet you, Ms. Lovett."

"You too, Cindy. Follow me." She closed the door behind her and moved back toward the table.

Andrew stuck out his hand. "Andrew Grant, president of Radiant Records. Thank you for coming today. You can set up right there and start whenever you're ready."

Olivia settled into her chair and studied Cindy. The girl's smile took up a large portion of her face, and she was stunning, just the sort of pure beauty that would look right at home gracing the cover of *Country Music Today* and other magazines. Given the girl's youthful enthusiasm, Olivia put Cindy at around twenty-one. Still so young—though five years older than Marie Culloway when she'd found her way to Music City over two decades ago, broken and in desperate need of fixing. And yet, somehow, she'd transformed herself into Olivia Lovett.

But she couldn't think of that, especially today.

Cindy played her guitar, a swift melody that filled the room, loud and proud. Then her voice joined the fray, and Olivia closed her eyes to listen. Cindy's singing blended together spunk and sweetness. It tapped the edge of Olivia's soul.

Olivia sighed. Cindy was good—very good—but she wasn't the one. Olivia's soul needed a good stirring, not just a tap.

Cindy finished her song and left, grinning.

Andrew turned to Olivia, then leaned back in his chair. "I think she's got great potential, don't you?" He patted the papers in front of him. "She's got a fabulous demo and a large following already."

"We don't need great potential. We need someone who's all in."

"What does that mean?"

Olivia jumped up and paced. "I don't know. Someone who feels the music with everything she has. Who lives and breathes her music. Who breaks off a part of her heart and hands it to the audience on a platter with every performance. Not just someone who sings well."

Andrew sighed and ran his hands through his short hair. "I get that, Liv, but we also have to be practical. We don't just need an artist. We need a performer, someone who will wow the crowd. Cindy's got that spark."

"But she's missing something else. I'm telling you, she's not the one. And besides, didn't you quit at Lucky because they'd only sign the next starry-eyed country pop wannabe? I thought you wanted more."

"That's true. And I trust you, I really do. I wouldn't have gone into business with you if I didn't. But do you think . . . ?"

Olivia halted in her steps. "Do I think what?"

"I'm just saying. This is the tenth audition we've held. And it's not as if we make appointments with just anyone. We've pre-filtered each for sound, quality, and platform. Yet you haven't been interested in a single one."

"So? They haven't been right for this label."

"Will anyone but Olivia Lovett be right for this label?" He said it quietly, but the intensity in his eyes socked Olivia's gut.

Because he was right.

It was time to move on. Yes, she'd wanted to come back to singing, but creating the label was her dream now. The past was the past, and she couldn't change it. But she could still build a future, something that would last.

And she had to have the right artist to make that happen.

Cindy James wasn't it. Olivia could feel it with everything she had. She squared her jaw, glanced at her list, and moved toward the door. "Austin Bentley? Come on in."

Sometimes, this whole dream seemed ridiculously impossible.

But maybe that was just the tired talking. After a long day of fruitless job searching—who knew that most of the jobs for the upcoming holiday season had already been filled?—her bed sounded like the best place in the world.

Ellie opened the door to her worn-down apartment building. The threadbare gray carpet muffled the shuffling of her feet as she made her way to the mailboxes. She'd avoided it—and her bills—long enough. How was she going to pay her half of the rent with no job? The gigs she played paid pennies. And then there were gigs like the upcoming one at Bernadette's, which didn't pay at all. At least she didn't have to find someone to cover her shift on Friday now. She was free as a bird—and as unemployed as one too.

Of course, she'd been in such a rush to get started on her job search today that she'd forgotten her phone at home. Which had meant she hadn't called Rob Jenkins yet to let him know she was available on Friday. She should have called yesterday, but she'd spent the day spilling her emotions across her guitar strings after Mr. Morgan let her go. And it was probably too late to call tonight. Hopefully the offer still stood when she called tomorrow.

She pulled her keys from her pocket, inserted one into her mail slot, and drew out a stack of Lena's and her mail. Overhead, the dim lights hummed. After closing the mailbox and retrieving her keys, she turned and trudged up the stairs, each one groaning beneath her weight. Ellie yawned and rubbed the corner of her right eye. Finally, she reached her third-floor apartment.

The *3* on *3C* listed slightly to the right, and the paint on the orange metal door peeled in random places.

Ellie unlocked the door and walked inside.

Just ahead, the dinky TV blared out a greeting. Lena must have left it on but was nowhere in sight.

Ellie turned left and, in two steps, arrived at her room. She flicked on the light. Her green comforter lay askew, and stacks of papers were scattered on her floor.

Yeah, it wasn't much of a system, but at least it kept her songs organized. She plopped onto her bed, mail in hand.

Ellie sorted and stopped when she saw *The Bluebird Café* on the return label of one envelope. One thin envelope. She dropped the rest of the pile and ripped it open.

Ms. Evans, thank you for auditioning for our Sunday writers night. As you know, competition is fierce, and we could only choose a handful of those who auditioned. We hope you will try again in the future.

Ellie groaned.

"Bad news?"

Ellie looked up.

Lena crossed her arms and leaned against the doorframe. She wore striped pajama pants and a tank top. "What's that?"

"Got a no from the 'Bird. No biggie." Except this was the third time. And if she couldn't make it at the 'Bird, how could she ever expect to get a contract with a major label someday? Not that it was her only option. It's just that so many country greats had gotten their start there, and Ellie had hoped to be one of them.

"Sorry, friend." Lena joined her sitting on the bed.

Ellie sifted the paper between her fingers. "Guess I should have expected it. Only the best of the best get to play there for writers night."

Had her mama ever made it that far?

Ugh, she was too tired for questions like that. She refocused on Lena.

Lena bumped her shoulder against Ellie's. "I think you *are* one of the best, hands down."

Ellie smiled. An art history student at Belmont University, Lena was as tone-deaf as they came. They'd met at Lulu's Diner and clicked instantly despite the fact Lena knew nothing about music and Ellie knew nothing about art. " 'Cause you're so knowledgeable and all that."

Lena threw her lips into a fake pout. "I know what I like, and I like your music."

A weight hung on Ellie's heart. She waved the letter in the air. "Too bad not everyone agrees with you." Though Rob Jenkins seemed to. That was something, wasn't it?

"They should." Lena snatched the letter and ripped it in half. "What have you been up to today?"

"I was out looking for jobs. No luck."

"That's not a very fun way to spend your birthday."

Ellie frowned. She glanced at the calendar over her desk.

Lena bit her lip. "Your birthday *is* September twenty-eighth, isn't it?"

"Yes." Had she been so busy she'd forgotten her own birthday? Wow. But Daddy had always made a huge deal out of them, even when he wasn't home. And now that he was gone . . .

Ellie stood, walked to her window, and opened it. She stared at the full moon, partially eclipsed by the neon lights of the bowling alley across the street. The evening breeze chilled her arms, and the freshness stung her cheeks, a reminder that there was more to the world than her little seven-by-seven bedroom. But on nights like this, when her dreams felt so far away, it was hard to believe that she wasn't forgotten somehow in the big scheme of things.

Even harder to believe that God had a plan.

"You all right?"

Ellie spun.

Lena cocked her head.

What was she thinking? Ellie wasn't forgotten. She had a good friend in Lena. And she had Grandma and Grandpa, her dad's parents, who'd probably left a voicemail wishing Ellie a happy birthday. Ellie rubbed her arms, then turned and closed the window. "I will be."

"If you're up for it, I wanted to give you your gift. Well, it's not necessarily a physical thing. More like an experience. But I think you're gonna like—"

"Lena, I love you, but just spit it out." Ellie let herself grin as she settled back onto the bed.

"How would you feel about—ready for this? A *Full House* marathon?" Lena wagged her eyebrows. "I know it's your favorite."

Yes, there'd always been something enchanting about a show featuring a huge family, especially to a young girl with no siblings, a dad who was frequently away in Oklahoma City, and grandparents in their forties who worked. Ellie used to spend hours watching taped reruns.

She poked Lena in the ribs. "You'd do that for me? I thought Kimmy Gibbler annoyed you to no end."

"I'll sacrifice my time to watch it with you."

"C'mon, you know you love Uncle Jesse."

"I confess, he makes the show much more enjoyable." Lena sighed dramatically. "So what do you say? I bought all the necessary junk food for a girls' night in."

"After the day I just had, that sounds incredible." Ellie crushed her in a hug. "Just let me change into my pajamas, and I'll meet you on the couch in a few."

"I'll go make some popcorn." Lena bounced up from the bed and headed for the door.

"Lena?"

Her roommate turned.

"Thanks. It means a lot to have a friend like you."

"Cut. It. Out." She motioned like Uncle Joey would and screwed up her face in a smirk.

"Have mercy." Ellie giggled and threw a pillow at her. "Now get outta here."

"How rude." Lena winked and left, her laughter trailing behind her.

Ellie changed into her pajamas, then grabbed her phone off the side table.

Yep, there was a voicemail from Grandma and Grandpa.

Ellie held the phone to her ear.

"Ellie Bellie, we wanted to call and say happy birthday." Her grandpa's voice soothed her soul. "And now you're forcing me to talk to a machine. Guess that's 'cause you're busy bringin' lots of people joy through your music. We couldn't be prouder of you and how you shine for Jesus."

Oh, Grandpa. Ellie's eyes burned.

"Okay, now it's my turn." Grandma's voice took over, and a laugh pushed from Ellie's throat. "Darlin', we hope you have a very special day. You deserve it. Call us when you can, so your old grandparents don't worry too much, all right? Love you, sugar."

Ellie disconnected from the voicemail and sighed. Her grandparents had always supported her dream to come out here, even when her own daddy hadn't. Of course, he'd always praised her for her talent. He just hadn't wanted her being disappointed by rejection.

51

She flipped to her phone's email app and scrolled through her messages—mostly discounts and offers from various retailers. But she stopped at one that had been sent this afternoon. She hadn't talked to James Gilbert since Daddy's funeral. Why would her dad's best friend be writing to her now?

Ellie, I hope this note finds you well. Your grandmother gave me your email address. I trust that was all right with you. I would have called but wanted to give you time to think before I caught you unaware.

I know you went off to Nashville to pursue your dreams. That takes great courage. I'm sure your father would be so proud of you. However, if it's not everything you'd hoped it would be, that's okay too.

In addition to several business ventures, I am the director of a string of music studios where junior high and high school students all over Oklahoma can take private and group lessons. Unfortunately, our guitar teacher at the Marlow location decided to leave us without giving much notice. I have students scheduled to come in this week and can postpone one lesson, but would like to avoid postponing more than that. Since Marlow is not that large of a town, I think it will likely be difficult to find someone qualified to take over as quickly as I need them to.

That's where you come in. Ellie, if you're interested, I'd like to give you the guitar-teaching position. I am aware that you do not have a degree, but you're very talented and passionate about music. Those things matter more to me than a piece of paper. However, if you accept my offer, I'd like to pay for you to attend college and get a degree, if that's something that interests you. It's the least I can do for Ben's daughter. He was so proud of you, and I think this is something he would want for you.

The studio is located just up the road from your grandparents' house. We could discuss a transfer to one of my other studios in the future, if you decide to attend school.

I know this all probably seems over-whelming, and I understand. But, given my current situation, I'd need you out here by Saturday at the latest. Please give me a call tomorrow, so we can chat about all of this and I can answer any questions you may have.

-James

Wow. Ellie blinked. What an incredible offer. She'd always thought of college and teaching as a solid backup plan, one she'd consider if her time in Nashville didn't go as she hoped. But she'd only been here two years, and Nashville was a ten-year town. Could she really give up and go home already?

Still, it was such a great opportunity. If she turned James down now, who was to say she'd ever get the chance with him again?

And she definitely couldn't count on achieving her dream here. Mr. Granger's words replayed in her mind: *"But every performer thinks he'll be the one to break the mold. He's convinced himself it isn't about who you know—which we know it is—but talent. All artists think their big break is around the corner."*

Was she a fool to hope she wouldn't be just another statistic?

Of course, she was here for more than fame. She'd come to find her mama. But with every dead end she'd hit so far, even that seemed like a foolish dream.

The smell of popcorn wafted from the kitchen, and the *Full House* theme song rang out from the television. Ellie set her phone down. Right now, she wouldn't think about this anymore.

Instead, she'd enjoy the last fleeting hours of her twenty-third birthday.

• • •

This day could officially go down as one of the worst ever. After the chat with the doctor, the call from her insurance company, and a failed attempt to find the first artist for Radiant Records, Olivia couldn't face going home to an empty house.

Not yet.

Her heels clicked on the gleaming wood floor as she walked away from Andrew and the audition room. She hurried through the door of Bernadette's kitchen, which was dominated by counter space and top-of-the-line stainless steel appliances. Steam hit her face.

Her best friend, Rachel, leaned over a pot of tomato bisque, waving her hand over the soup as if to better smell her creation. Her brown hair was tucked into a bun at the base of her head, tiny pieces askew.

Italian spices tickled Olivia's nose.

On another counter, fresh cuts of filet mignon sat ready for seasoning.

Olivia approached Rachel. "How's it going?"

Three or four servers in black pants and dark-purple shirts bustled around the kitchen. A college-aged brunette squeezed past Olivia, muttering her apologies. A young man with cropped hair scooped ice into a glass and placed it and a bottle of sparkling water on a tray.

"Busy night." Rachel's brows furrowed as

she tested the bisque. "Needs more oregano."

Olivia snagged a spoon from the counter. She sidled up to Rachel and dipped it into the soup. "If you need help, you just holler, and I'll throw on an apron." She lifted the spoon to her lips, and the tangy soup danced down her throat. "Tastes great to me."

"The day I ask you for help in my kitchen is the day I croak." Rachel cocked a hip. "You take a seat on the other side of the island, far away from the food."

Her friend knew her well. Olivia laughed and set the spoon in the sink. "The offer still stands." She sank onto a four-legged stool. It squeaked as she hooked her boots over the lowest rungs.

Rachel sprinkled more oregano into the pot, then served up a bowl of soup and slid it across the counter toward Olivia. She began to protest, but Rachel gave her the same look she pummeled her kids with when they misbehaved. "You need to eat. Put some meat on those bones."

"Yeah, yeah, so you've been telling me for fifteen years."

Rachel grabbed a spatula and stirred the contents of a metal bowl. "Maybe if you'd start listening, I'd shut up." The corner of her mouth lifted. "Besides, I'm sick of going out on the town with you and feeling like Dumbo next to a Disney princess."

Olivia snatched a roll from the breadbasket on

the edge of the counter and broke it in half. She dragged it through her soup. "You hush. You're gorgeous and you know it. Matt's lucky to have such a hot wife."

Rachel grabbed a bag of chocolate chips, measured them out, and folded them into the batter. Then she spooned the mixture into a round cake pan. "If anything ain't beautiful, it's because of the three children I gave him." She stopped and grimaced. "I'm sorry, honey. Didn't mean to touch on a sore subject, especially today."

A pang twirled in Olivia's stomach. Rachel was a wonderful mother. How did she manage to do that—keep a lovely home, stay sexy for her husband, and work a full-time job amazingly well?

Oh yeah, and have time for Olivia and her troubles?

Apparently some people were born with the nurturing gene.

And others weren't.

"It's all right."

Music from open mic night rolled in waves under the kitchen door from the main part of the restaurant and occasionally burst through whenever a server barged in. Maybe the next great thing was performing at this very moment—but Olivia couldn't sit and listen to one more song tonight.

"How did auditions go?"

Olivia let out a staccato laugh. "You read my mind." She dunked the bread in her bowl with her spoon. It disappeared in the waves of soup but bobbed to the surface again. "We listened to fifteen artists, and not one caught our interest."

"Our?"

"Okay, none caught *my* interest. I think there were about three or four that caught Andrew's." Olivia pushed the soup aside and put her elbows on the counter. "He's getting real frustrated with me."

Rachel sauntered to the fridge and bent over, rummaging for a moment. She emerged with a bag of cherries and set them on the counter. "Do you blame him?"

"I can't very well start a recording label with someone who doesn't turn my head." Why did no one seem to understand that?

"No, that's true." With a flourish born of practice, Rachel poured together sugar and cornstarch. "So what are you going to do about it?"

Olivia shrugged. "Guess we go back to square one. Keep auditioning. Keep visiting cafés, hoping to find the perfect artist. Rob invited us here on Friday. Said he had some hot talent coming in." She massaged her temples. "Sometimes I just wonder if it's ever gonna happen."

"Maybe your standards are set at perfection."

"When I was in the biz . . ."

"And that's the problem, isn't it?" Rachel lit a flame under her cooktop and placed a pot on top. She poured in some sort of juice. Faint popping sounds flicked from the pot. "Times have changed, even in the few years since you've been out. The biz isn't the same anymore. The artists aren't the same now as when you started. Everything's more pop, more show, and less about that thing that sears you in the gut."

"I know that, but—"

"You think you hide it well, but I know you want to make a comeback."

"That's what Andrew said too." How had they both seen through her carefully disguised façade? Not that she'd meant to be secretive. But some hopes went so deep if she exposed them to the world, she'd either be talked out of them or realize they'd never come true.

Of course, Rachel had always been there for her. In fact, she was the only one who knew the whole truth about Olivia and who she'd been in the past. No reason to keep the most recent news from her.

Olivia inhaled sharply and her lips trembled. "I've been working with several doctors, seeing if my voice will ever heal. Even had surgery."

"What? When?"

"Remember this summer when I went to New York for a week?"

"Yes. I was so jealous that you'd be shopping Fifth Avenue without me. Are you telling me you went there for surgery instead? Did anyone go with you? Who took care of you?" She threw her hand on a hip. "And why didn't you tell me?"

Olivia winced. "One of the best vocal surgeons in the country practices in New York. I went alone and stayed in a hotel to recover." She hung her head. "It was awful, and yes, I should have told you. I'm sorry I didn't. I . . . I guess I was embarrassed. Part of me knew it was absurd to try to get back what I'd had. But it didn't work, despite three months of therapy afterward."

Rachel's eyes welled with tears. "Oh, honey."

If Rachel started crying, Olivia was sure to join her. "I saw another doctor on Monday. Today I got a call confirming my voice will never be the same. And that's not even the worst thing about all of this."

Her friend started toward Olivia and wrapped her in a hug. "I'm so desperately sorry."

Olivia buried her face in Rachel's shoulder. A burning smell caught her attention. "Rach!"

"Oh no." Rachel flew back to the stove. She made quick work of salvaging her dessert, then wiped under her eyes. "Go on. What's the worst part?"

Olivia sighed. "I spent a lot of money in my

recovery attempts. I've completely depleted my savings and don't have my share of the funds to start the label."

"Oh, Liv. Are you going to be okay? Do you need some money to cover any of your expenses this month?"

Good old Rach. "I get enough each month through residuals to cover my living expenses, and I paid off my mortgage several years ago. My savings were from the last advance I received before everything went haywire with my voice."

Rachel was quiet for a moment. "Why would you risk that money?"

"I thought my insurance would kick in and reimburse me, but apparently not. I just found that out today too."

"Ouch. What rotten news. Does Andrew know?"

"No." If he did, would he dump her as a business partner? Sure, they'd been friends for a decade, but he was first and foremost a businessman. "We agreed to an equal partnership, and I don't want to give him any reason to doubt I'll keep my word. I'll just have to raise more funds through investors or something."

Though that added a whole other layer of complication to their business.

"Would he be able to front the extra money if you asked?"

Olivia shook her head. "He's put nearly all his

savings toward this, except Grace's college fund and an emergency fund he won't touch. And we both agreed not to take out personal or business loans for this venture. That was one condition he had for agreeing to this partnership in the first place." She hauled the bowl of soup back in front of her and ladled some into her mouth.

It flowed down, cold and mushy. Just like her dreams—once hot and vibrant, liquid gold. Now . . . She needed to get some rest. Maybe everything would look brighter in the morning. "I'd better go. I've bugged you long enough." Olivia eased off the stool.

"Don't be silly." Rachel stirred her cherry sauce, set her spoon on the counter, wiped her hands on her apron, and headed to the fridge. She came back carrying a clear to-go box holding a beautiful chocolate cupcake topped with ganache and two raspberries. "This is for you. I know it's a hard day, even without all the other stuff going on."

Olivia wrapped her friend in another hug. She whispered into Rachel's hair, afraid that speaking too loudly would be the end of the composure Olivia had tried so hard to keep from the moment she'd awoken and seen September 28 on the calendar. "Thank you."

Olivia left the café through the side door, cupcake in tow. She kept it safe as she drove to her modest three-bedroom home—small for a lot of former country artists, but still too big for one woman and two crazy golden retrievers.

She juggled her purse and the cupcake as she unlocked the front door and walked inside.

Chloe immediately attacked her legs with licks. Pascal whined and jumped up to sniff the cupcake.

"Down, boy."

The dogs immediately began playing with each other as Olivia walked to her kitchen and set everything down on the island.

The kitchen smelled like pumpkin, not because of any baking skills she possessed, but because she'd picked out the most autumn-y Glade PlugIn she could find.

A stack of letters sat on the edge of the counter, and the top one—from the Oklahoma Department of Corrections—screamed at her. She'd ignored it long enough. How had Mama gotten her address? It wasn't listed in the phonebook. Olivia had made sure of that.

She grabbed the letter from the top of the stack, slipped her finger under the flap, and snatched the single page from inside. Her eyes scanned the paragraph written in chicken scratch.

Mama was getting out. Soon.

Olivia couldn't deal with this now. Not today of all days. She dumped the letter in the garbage.

If only the past were as easy to dispose of.

She went to the refrigerator and poured herself

a glass of milk. Olivia set the cupcake on a small white plate, grabbed a fork, and moved toward the oak table large enough for eight. Why did she torture herself with buying things that were bigger than she needed? It's not like she'd ever have a family. She'd given up any chance of that a long time ago.

With quiet precision, she slid her fork into the cupcake, careful to snag a raspberry. The first bite had to be the best, because that's how her life had been. She'd had happiness for a brief moment twenty-three years ago. But she'd not been fit to receive such a gift. Never would, due to who she was and where she came from. The letter in the garbage reminded her of that.

She lifted the fork as a toast. "Happy birthday, baby girl, wherever you are. I pray you are happy and loved, that your daddy's taking good care of you. I hope all your dreams are comin' true."

And, Lord, watch over her since I never could.

Olivia savored every bite of the delicious flavor until the cupcake was gone and her tears were spent.

5

Ellie burrowed down in her blue corduroy jacket. Wind whipped against her legs. It wasn't normally this chilly in September. Still, she should have checked the weather report before heading out for a walk this morning. But she'd needed to clear her head, figure out whether she should leave Nashville or stay.

She glanced up. Across the street, Bernadette's was bathed in light from the rising sun. The front windows gleamed but emanated darkness, all employees long gone after a night of listening to good music and serving good food. Had her subconscious led her here?

Glancing both ways, Ellie hurried across the two-lane street. Since Bernadette's sat just off Broadway, it was tucked away from the main foot traffic bustling around the corner. For the moment, Ellie was alone, the brick building looming before her, no sound but that of distant cars passing. She placed her hand on the glass and squinted as she peered inside.

Booths lined the walls. Tables with overturned chairs on top were scattered throughout the diner. There, at the front of the room, the stage beckoned her.

It didn't look so scary from out here, and Ellie

could almost see herself up there tomorrow night, grinning, strumming her guitar, singing with abandon.

But she could just as easily picture herself teaching at a studio in Marlow, helping others learn the art of performing.

So which one was right? And what did her wishy-washiness say about the strength of her dreams?

"You casin' the joint?"

Ellie jumped back and twirled.

An attractive guy with short blond curls and intense green eyes stood to her right. A lazy grin spread across his face, and his reddish scruff caught the morning light. He had a guitar case slung across his shoulders.

"Of course not." Ellie turned and started in the direction of her apartment.

"Hey, I was just kidding."

She stole a glance behind her.

The guy leaned against the bricks, hands tucked into his pockets. His brown jacket hung open to reveal a royal-blue shirt with Nashville Community Center emblazoned across the front.

Ellie puffed out a breath. "I was on a walk and didn't mean to end up here." She probably shouldn't be talking to a stranger. But growing up in a small town, her first instinct was to be friendly. Although something about him seemed familiar . . .

"Quite the mystery." The guy's eyes twinkled. "Name's Nick." He stuck out his hand.

"Ellie." She placed her and in his and shook. "Have we met before?"

"I've seen you at the songwriter's association. You're friends with Jenny Bruno and Logan Daly, right?"

She nodded.

"I've hung out with them before. Logan lives in the same apartment complex as I do." He rubbed his hands together and blew into them. "Say, if I'm cold, you're probably freezing. Can I walk you home?"

He had a welcoming face, and chatting might keep her mind off her current situation. Maybe she'd let him keep her company part of the way. Ellie turned south and they started strolling. "Do you work at the community center?" She waved a finger at his shirt.

"I volunteer there. Used to play a little basketball in high school."

"Where was high school?"

"Tyler, Texas."

She feigned shock. "Oh no. You aren't a Longhorns fan, are you?"

"In fact, I am." He tilted his chin, and his eyes glittered with mischief. "What of it?"

"I don't think I can associate with you. I'm a Sooners girl through and through. Oklahoman, born and bred." And even though she was from dinky Marlow—population 4,662—she'd always be proud of her roots.

"Ah, should have known."

"What's that supposed to mean?" Despite the weight of the decision she had to make, Ellie tried out a grin. It settled on her lips.

"You've just got that look about you."

She stopped, threw her hands on her hips. "Again I ask, what does that mean?" It felt good to rib him, to forget everything else for a moment.

"Never mind. I don't want to bring the wrath of a Sooners fan upon me."

She play-punched him in the arm, then immediately stuffed her hands in her pockets. It felt so natural to be around this guy, but that didn't mean she had to flirt with him. "How long have you been in Nashville?"

"Just over ten years. But part of that time I was in school too."

Wow. "You perform as well as write songs?"

"I do."

And look, even after a decade, he hadn't given up. If Ellie was in the same place in eight years, would she be kicking herself for not taking James's offer?

Nick cleared his throat. "What about you?"

"Only two. I left home on my twenty-first birthday." That day had been so frightening, but so invigorating as well. "Before that, I was attending community college and dreaming of moving out here. But then my dad died—" Her lips clamped shut. What was it about Nick that made her such a chatterbox? She glanced at him to gauge his response, but he kept looking right at her—didn't avert his eyes like some did when she mentioned her tragedy. "That's when I decided to save up and move here."

"I'm sorry about your dad."

"Thanks."

They walked in silence for a bit. Every so often the breeze would bring a flurry of leaves to their feet.

"Where do you work, Ellie?"

She kicked a rock. "You mean, where *did* I work?"

"Did?"

"Yep. Just got fired two days ago."

He groaned. "I'm sorry."

"That's twice now you've apologized for things that aren't your fault," Ellie teased.

"We aren't off to a fabulous start, are we?" They passed a number of businesses on Broadway, and he stopped in front of a tiny coffee shop. He hesitated. "How about some coffee?"

"Oh. Um, I don't have my wallet."

"My treat."

Ellie looked past him, toward the warmth of the coffee shop—the warmth of more conversation with a guy who intrigued her and made her feel comfortable at the same time. But today wasn't a day for comfort. It was a day for decisions. She pulled her jacket tighter. "I'd better get home. Thanks for keeping me company."

"Okay, sure." Nick folded his arms across his chest, looking troubled.

Oh man, she'd hurt his feelings. She should explain. "You're nice to offer. But I'm kind of a mess. You probably don't want to be anywhere near me right now."

"I don't know about that." A slow smile spread across his face.

Oy. What was it about him that made it so hard to focus? She rubbed her forehead. "I've got a lot to figure out. Like whether I'm moving back to Oklahoma tomorrow. You know, life-changing choices like that." The wind picked up around her.

"I've heard some of your stuff at our songwriter meetings. You've got talent." Nick shrugged. "Maybe you shouldn't give up just yet."

Something inside her burst. "Who said I'm giving up?"

"You said you were moving home. I just assumed. Sorry." He grimaced. "And that makes three times saying *sorry*. I'm on a roll, apparently. I'd say sorry for that, but . . ."

Laughter bubbled from her. She couldn't help it. This guy was plain adorable. "All right, one cup of coffee can't hurt, I guess."

He pumped his fist in the air, then opened the door for her.

A bell tinkled overhead, and the anticipated heat smoothed over her cheeks as she entered. The sweet smell of cinnamon and lattes melted the frost in her fingertips. She gave Nick her order and slipped into a chair at a small corner table, where she could see the street alive with pedestrians headed to work.

Nick sat down across the table and slid a pumpkin spice latte to her.

She leaned over and inhaled the spicy goodness. After taking a sip from the oversized mug, she let the flavor seep into her taste buds. Ellie's gaze wandered the shop.

A couple in the corner snuggled close, sharing a Danish and laughing as if telling secrets.

Nick lifted his own mug and waited patiently, as if sensing she needed a moment to herself.

"Thanks for the coffee. I don't normally agree to drink with a guy I've sorta-kinda just met."

"I don't normally buy coffee for a girl I've sorta-kinda just met."

She searched for the tease she'd seen in his eyes before, but it was nowhere in sight. A shiver ran up her spine, and she sucked down a gulp. "About me possibly moving—I've been here two years and haven't gotten any breaks." In her performing or in finding her mom. "Feels like I'm hitting a wall, you know?"

regularly. . . . Wait. "Nick, as in Nick Perry?" He was a big deal in local singer-songwriter circles, had a good following, and played the 'Bird all the time. He didn't have a record deal yet, but rumor had it he was on the brink of something good. "I can't believe I didn't recognize you."

His cheeks tinged and he sipped his drink and shrugged. "No reason you should."

"Right."

Maybe this wasn't a chance meeting at all, given the choice she had to make. Who better to ask for advice than someone who knew the industry and was fighting for the same dream she was?

God, did you arrange this?

Ellie fidgeted in her seat. "About Bernadette's. I'm not sure I'm gonna do it."

"Why not?"

"I got a great job offer back home. It's for a music studio. I'd get to teach guitar. And the director said he'd pay for me to attend college, if I'd like."

"That's definitely a great opportunity." Nick drummed his fingers along the edge of his cup.

"I know."

"But is that your dream?"

"It could be."

"I'm not asking what you could make yourself want in the future. I'm asking what you want right now."

73

"What if what I want right now never happens?"

Nick was silent a moment. "It won't happen if you leave."

"That's true. But it won't necessarily happen if I stay either." What if, after all this trying, the truth she'd been fighting against forever finally settled into her soul? What if she really didn't have what it took to stand out? And what if she wasn't supposed to find her mom?

Or worse—what if she found her . . . and her mom left again?

"But it might happen. If you go, it definitely won't." Nick shifted in his seat. "Look, Ellie. I can't tell you what to do, and I wouldn't presume to understand your situation. I can only tell you what *I* would do."

"I'd like to hear that."

He nodded. "We all know Nashville is a ten-year town. I've been at this longer than ten years and still haven't hit my big break." He cocked his head. "But I believe it's coming. I'm trusting God to make it happen just like he wants it to. Doesn't mean I haven't had those times I wanted to quit. But what if your big break is just around the corner and you quit before it happens?"

He spoke about trusting God as if it came as naturally as breathing. Maybe he was a fellow believer.

The idea sent an unexpected thrill through her.

She refocused on what he was saying. "It's just such a risk to take."

"Tell me this. What made you decide to pack up everything and move here?"

"Like I said, this has been my dream nearly my whole life."

"Right, but why not come out when high school ended? Why did you wait till you were twenty-one?"

"I was saving up. And to be honest, I was scared to come."

"But you came. Why?" Nick's prompting was like a breeze, gently rustling the leaves of a tree, applying just enough pressure to help the branches create a beautiful dance.

"My dad died."

"How did that play into your decision?"

She pictured Daddy leaning over his guitar, teaching her the chords during one of his infrequent visits home to Grandma and Grandpa's house. The answer clicked in Ellie's brain. "My dad was such a talented musician, but he had me when he was a teenager. It changed all his plans. Instead of being able to come to Nashville when he was young, he was busy getting a college degree and working, so he could send money home to take care of me." He'd said he'd never regretted the way his life had turned out, but he'd also had no clue he'd die at thirty-eight. "His death taught me that life was too short to wait around and not go after my dreams."

And it had instilled in her the sudden need to find her mother.

"What's changed?"

The question hovered in the air like the steam from Ellie's coffee. "Nothing. Nothing's changed." This was still her dream, no matter how difficult it would be to achieve. The thought brought instant relief. "I'm not ready to throw in the towel—not by a long shot."

"Good. I'm glad to hear it. And not just for your own sake."

"Oh?" Ellie lifted her left eyebrow.

"I'm secretly happy I'll get to see you again. Although, I guess now it's not a secret."

A blush spread across Ellie's cheeks. "You're such a blabber-mouth."

Nick laughed. "That I am." He checked his watch. "Oh man. I've got to get to the community center."

Already? Was he going to leave without asking for her number? Maybe it was her turn to make a move. "I think, to be fair, I owe you a therapy session. You know, to repay you for giving me one."

"Yeah?" Nick scratched the back of his head, and his eyes communicated his pleasure.

"Sure." Ellie tried to act nonchalant. She pulled out her phone. "What's your number?"

He rattled it off to her, then leaned in for a quick hug. His curls tickled her forehead. "I'll see you soon, I hope." Nick pulled back and winked at her, then headed out the door, casting one last look at her before exiting.

Ellie's wide smile likely broadcast her joy to everyone around her, but at the moment, she didn't care how goofy she appeared.

She checked the time on her phone. Nine a.m. She needed to call James Gilbert, thank him profusely, and decline his generous offer. And then she'd call Rob Jenkins and officially accept the slot at Bernadette's tomorrow night, if he hadn't already given it away. After that, she could hit the streets looking for work. Maybe she needed to take a page from Nick's book and trust that God truly had it handled.

Her phone buzzed in her hand. Looks like she had a voicemail—she must have missed a call while chatting with Nick. The number didn't register in her mind. She lifted the phone to her ear.

"Ellie, this is Rob Jenkins. I asked around for you and found someone who might know Marie Culloway. Let's chat after you sing on Friday night. I'm assuming you're not crazy enough to turn down a slot at Bernadette's, so unless I hear differently from you, I'll see you at six thirty. Bye for now."

Ellie drained the rest of her latte, rushed out into the beautiful fall weather, and embraced the breeze.

6

Today was a new day. Tonight, a new night.

Olivia crossed her legs beneath the round booth she and Andrew shared at Bernadette's. She checked her watch. Five minutes until open mic night started. She fingered the laminated menu, then set it down in front of her. "Maybe we'll finally find the one."

Andrew laid his menu on top of hers, then removed his thick black frames and rubbed the bridge of his nose. "Let's hope so."

"You still upset with me?" They both faced the stage, and she nudged him with her elbow.

"No, just tired. Grace had a flat tire last night on her way home from cheer and needed help changing it. But the spare was also flat, so we had to wait for a tow truck."

"Ah, you're such a good dad." Andrew would drop anything for his sixteen-year-old daughter. He talked about her all the time, so proud. But he never spoke of his ex-wife—and Olivia never asked. Sometimes people had to keep things buried for their own sanity.

A server approached their table, grabbing her pen from its perch above her ear. "What can I get you folks tonight?" A small tattoo on her wrist snagged Olivia's attention. It looked like a bird of some sort—a dove, maybe.

"I'll have the prime rib, medium, please." Andrew handed the young woman his menu. "Liv?"

In the background, someone tuned a guitar and the sound flowed through the speakers.

Olivia leaned forward, so the server could hear her. "My name is Olivia, and I know the chef. Tell her to surprise me."

"You got it." The server scurried away.

Olivia turned in her seat to observe the rest of the café. It was packed, with every table filled and a line forming outside. A handful of executives from other labels were scattered throughout the room, along with nervous musicians with guitars, professionals drinking martinis, and coeds psyching up their performer friends. Servers bustled in between the tables, carrying food and drinks.

Olivia sipped her Diet Coke as Rob Jenkins approached their table.

"Olivia, Andrew, pleasure to see you again." Rob extended his hand and shook Andrew's. He leaned down to hug Olivia.

"How are you, Rob?" Olivia flashed her pearly whites. An old friend, Rob had been on the lookout for fresh talent that might interest her and Andrew. "Got a great lineup for us tonight, I hope?"

"Nothing but the best." Rob prodded her over in the booth and slid in next to her. Now she was sitting right next to Andrew. His leg was warm against hers. Had they ever sat this close? She shifted.

Rob placed his arm along the back of the booth. "I'm very excited about two acts in particular. One's pretty new—hasn't sung here before—but she's something else. Found her playing over at the Lizard Lounge."

Andrew sipped his tea. "We're not really interested in amateurs."

"Who said she was an amateur?"

A current of annoyance ran between the two men. Where had that come from?

Olivia cleared her throat and angled her body back toward Rob. "I can't wait to see this act. If you say she's good, we trust you." Even though Andrew clearly didn't. "What about the other?"

"Thanks for your vote of confidence, Olivia." Rob emphasized her name. "The other act is brilliant. Great performer, great musician, great songs. He's got quite the following around town. Name's Nick Perry. Heard of him?"

Andrew perked up. "Of course. But rumor was he was signing with Clear Creek."

"Nah, the execs over there wanted him bad, and they had a few meetings with him. But apparently he's holding out for the right offer." Rob issued a smirk.

Andrew harrumphed. He prided himself on keeping a close pulse on the industry. "Remind me who his manager is."

"Doesn't have one yet. Again, holding out for the right offer."

"So is the kid arrogant or just picky?"

"I could ask the same about you."

Their tossed words volleyed back and forth, like a tense game of ping-pong. What was with them tonight?

Rob eased out of the booth and rubbed Olivia's shoulder. "Let me know what you think." He winked and walked toward the sound booth.

"Oh, brother." Andrew's whisper escaped just under his breath.

"What?" Olivia scooted back toward the edge of the booth, and the leather groaned with her movement. "Why are you so uptight?" Rob had always been a flirt—had even asked Olivia out a few times over the years, which she'd politely declined—but why should Andrew care?

"Forget it." He pulled a folder from his brief-case and opened it. "While we have a few moments, let's go over the numbers we need for start-up again. When are you planning to cut me a check for your half?"

A weight settled in Olivia's stomach. Time to come clean about the fact she didn't have the funds anymore, that she'd spent them on her surgery instead. She opened her—

"Ladies and gentlemen, welcome to Friday night at Bernadette's." Chelsea Treadway, Bernadette's emcee, stood on the little stage.

Thank you, Chelsea.

"We've got a fantastic lineup for you tonight, so sit back and enjoy. First up, we've got Mindy Edwards."

A tall, wiry girl climbed onstage and began strumming. The café filled with a haunting tune that made Olivia want to run home, climb under the covers, and sleep with the lights on.

She glanced at Andrew, who thumbed through his folder. Good, he wasn't into this either.

The server brought their food in the middle of Mindy's set and placed a plate of chicken spaghetti in front of Olivia. The ultimate comfort food. Rachel was clearly still worried about her.

Olivia tucked into the food, twirling the noodles around her fork. Tantalizing spices soothed her the way Mindy's song, unfortunately, didn't.

Mindy's set ended and Olivia and Andrew applauded politely.

She leaned close to him to whisper but caught a hint of his spicy cologne. Was it new? Olivia pushed the thought from her mind. "Let's hope the next one makes you at least look up from your pile of papers."

Andrew chuckled, but his eyes gazed down into hers and stirred something inside her. For a second, they simply stared at each other.

What was this? Olivia laughed nervously, then moved back to eating her spaghetti. Much safer to ignore whatever was going on with Andrew right now and focus on why they were here.

"Thanks for playing for us, Mindy. All right, folks, this next singer-songwriter is Ellie Evans. It's her first time playing at Bernadette's, so please give her a nice welcome."

Quiet applause filled the room as a petite girl with shoulder-length brown curls made her way to the stage, guitar gripped in her hands. Her sneakers squeaked on the clean tile, and her faded jeans and plain T-shirt gave her a down-home feel. Not exactly star material, but one never knew what lay beneath the surface.

Olivia sat back, threaded spaghetti through her fork, and waited.

"Thank y'all for the kind welcome."

Her soft tone wrapped itself around Olivia's heart and squeezed.

"It's a pleasure to play here." Ellie settled onto a stool, plucked out a few notes, and began to strum. Her guitar playing was simple but straightforward and calming. She leaned into the mic on the stand, eyes closed, clearly feeling the music. Something about her seemed so familiar, and yet Olivia couldn't recall ever meeting her.

Then Ellie's singing came flowing through the speakers. It was strong but not overwhelming, as if it could break but wouldn't. And the lyrics—about loss and loneliness but also hope—stole Olivia's breath.

A feeling she had tamped down for years snuck up inside and pushed tears from the corners of her eyes.

The girl finished her tune, and a quiet hush filled the café. After a moment, applause swept over the room.

Ellie's eyes widened, as if she had no idea that she'd just mesmerized a crowd of some of the harshest critics in the industry.

This girl, she was like magic, drawing out the poison from Olivia's wounds, healing them with her voice and purity and . . . well, faith.

Olivia leaned toward Andrew's ear. "She's the one."

They didn't hate her.

In fact, they cheered Ellie off the stage. Her hands trembled as she removed her guitar from around her neck and headed toward the back of the restaurant, where Lena stood hooting and whistling.

Guests smiled at her and shouted their appreciation for her music as she passed.

And there was Nick leaning against the bar, a cowboy hat covering his curls. She hadn't seen him before her set.

"Great job, Ellie."

A thrill of pleasure tossed in her stomach. "Thanks."

"Don't know how I'm going to follow that act."

"I'm sure you'll do awesome." Ellie fiddled with the knobs on her guitar.

Nick grinned and opened his mouth to respond.

"Nicky!" A girl in tall cowgirl boots, tight jeans, and an off-the-shoulder shirt sidled up to Nick and threw her arm around his waist. Her eyelids sparkled with perfectly applied glitter eye shadow, and her tan skin radiated with bronzer.

"Hey, Lynette." Nick squeezed the girl around her shoulders. "Ellie, this is Lynette. Lynette, Ellie."

Lynette eyed Ellie and smacked her gum. "I'm Nicky's biggest fan."

"Oh?" She looked like more than that, holding onto Nick for dear life. How could Ellie have been so stupid yesterday, thinking Nick was interested in her? He had probably just seen someone in need of encouragement, and being a nice guy, took pity on her. Ellie averted her eyes and waved at Lena. "Break a leg, Nick. I've gotta go. Nice meeting you, Lynette."

Before he could say another word, she turned, strode to the back, and slid into the empty chair across from Lena. She sheathed her guitar in its case and set it beside her.

Lena had ordered her a lemonade. Ellie took a sip. Her lips puckered. She took a deep breath. The fact that Nick most likely had a girlfriend would not affect her mood. Nope, it wouldn't.

"You were awesome, girl." Lena gave her a thumbs-up. "So glad my class was canceled and I got to come."

"Thanks. It was so nice having you here." She was still reeling. People had actually seemed to enjoy her music. And she'd loved singing it. When the lyrics had spilled from her mouth, the moment had almost seemed ordained. Like she was supposed to be here.

For a split second, a breath, she'd been seen.

She scanned the room for Rob Jenkins. She'd yet to find him and ask him about his lead on Marie Culloway. Who knew? Maybe it was her lucky night and he'd really know something helpful.

The emcee—Chelsea, was it?—got up and introduced Nick.

He walked onstage, so calm and collected, and had the whole crowd clapping within two verses.

Lena leaned closer. "I saw him talking to you. You know him? He's hot."

Ellie shrugged. "We met briefly yesterday. And I've seen him at songwriter meetings before that."

Nick sang with ease and spirit. His lyrics were fun yet catchy, and his hand flew across the arm of the guitar as he gave an amazing performance.

If he could gear up such a small crowd in one minute flat, imagine what he could do in an arena with thousands.

She sucked down her lemonade as he played song after song. Didn't surprise her he'd been given one of the longer slots. He was that good.

Across the room, she spotted Mr. Jenkins. He said something in Chelsea's ear and then headed down the hallway.

Ellie slid out of her chair. "I'll be back." She hurried after him, but Mr. Jenkins had disappeared.

Perhaps he'd gone into the restroom. Would it be weird and stalker-ish to wait out here for him?

"Excuse me, Ms. Evans?"

Ellie turned and had to steady herself. Olivia Lovett stood before her. Olivia. Lovett. It was silly to be star-struck after two years in Nashville, but this was different. She was one of the best, her brilliance dimmed much too soon. "H-hi."

Ms. Lovett extended her hand. "My name is—"

"Oh, I know who you are." Oops, she'd interrupted. "Please, Ms. Lovett, call me Ellie."

Ms. Lovett smiled. "Only if you call me Olivia."

Ellie nodded. She stuck her hands in the back pockets of her jeans and rocked on the heels of her sneakers. Suddenly the whole place felt very warm—like Oklahoma-in-the-dead-of-summer kind of warm. "I just want to say what an honor it is to meet you. You were one of my daddy's favorite singers. It was always Dolly, Trisha, Martina, Faith, and you on a constant loop around our house. I was so sad when you retired."

Olivia's smile sank, then turned back up right quick. "Thank you, Ellie. That's kind of you to say. I was a little sad myself."

"You were always such a role model too, with the whole purity thing." Knowing an amazing star like Olivia Lovett was saving herself for marriage had made it much easier for Ellie and her friends to commit to do the same. "And your faith has always inspired me."

"That's sweet." Olivia's shoulders straightened and her lips flattened. She motioned to a bench in the hall. "Do you have a minute to sit with me? There's something I'd like to discuss."

There was? "Okay." Ellie sat. She moved her hands to her lap, then slid them down to rest on the bench beside her legs.

"It's been my dream for a while now to start my own record label. I've been searching for the perfect artist to sign."

That was exciting and made sense. Olivia had been too good to walk away from the industry altogether.

"I really liked what I heard from you tonight."

Did Ellie need a Q-Tip? It had sounded like Olivia Lovett liked her music. Impossible.

"I wanted to find out whether you're in talks with any other labels at this time. And if not, would you be interested in auditioning for us?"

Sweet applesauce. "No. Yes." Ellie gripped the edge of the bench till her fingers went numb. *Snap out of it, Ellie.* She released her hold. "I mean, no, I'm not talking with any other labels right now. And yes, of course I'd be interested."

"Perfect. Do you have a manager we should speak with?"

"It's just me."

"No problem. If my business partner agrees, maybe we can set up an audition sometime next week?"

"Sure. I mean, yes. Of course."

"Good." Olivia stood and brushed off her black pants. "I know I interrupted your retreat to the restroom, and I need to get back out there. It was great to meet you, Ellie. I'm assuming Rob Jenkins has your contact information?"

Ellie found her voice. "Yes, he does. Speaking of Mr. Jenkins, have you seen him? I have something to talk to him about."

Olivia's hand flowed in the air like a fairy godmother flicking her wand. "Oh, he's around here somewhere. I'll talk with my business partner and call about that audition, all right now?"

As Olivia returned to the main dining area, Ellie let out a tiny squeal. Hopefully the sound hadn't carried out past the hallway, but she couldn't contain her joy.

Even if Olivia didn't call or Ellie totally bombed the audition, this encounter proved one thing—there was nowhere she'd rather be right now than in Nashville. Turning down James's offer had been the right thing. *Thank You, God.*

Ellie rose from the bench and headed back toward the open café, and her gaze locked onto Rob Jenkins. Maybe tonight would hold even more good news for her if his information panned out.

The man had propped himself against the far wall, chatting once again with the emcee. As Ellie approached, he said something to Chelsea and walked toward Ellie. "Wonderful job up there."

"Thank you. And thanks again for inviting me to play. Good things are already coming from it."

"I saw you chatting with Olivia. She's looking for new artists for her label, you know."

"We spoke a little about that." This time, Ellie held in the screech threatening to escape from her.

"Good, good." Rob scanned the crowd. "I've

got to grab an associate before he leaves. I'll definitely be calling you when I have future openings here. You were a hit."

"That'd be great." Ellie bit her lip and screwed up her courage. "Before you go, you said you had some information for me? About Marie Culloway."

"Right, right. Look, it's nothing solid, but I figured it's a lead, right?"

Ellie's heart plummeted. "So you didn't find someone who knows her?"

"Didn't say that. I'm just saying my information is thirdhand. I asked around, and a business contact of mine—he's pretty high up on the food chain—said he thinks he's heard that name associated with Olivia Lovett."

Seriously? "What does that mean? Associated with her?"

"I figure it means she knows your friend Marie."

"But you don't know for sure."

"No. I didn't ask. Thought you'd want to do that."

Olivia Lovett. The woman who might want to meet with Ellie and discuss her career. God sure worked in mysterious ways.

Maybe this was the beginning of something good—something life-changing.

Maybe today it wasn't just the crowd who'd seen her. Maybe God finally had too.

• • •

Yes sir, she'd found the one. Now to convince Andrew.

There was something about that girl. Olivia just couldn't put her finger on what. Perhaps it was the humility, the fact that Ellie had no idea the kind of treasure she was.

Olivia approached the booth where Andrew sat chatting with a young man. No one played up front, which meant it was intermission. She smiled as she slid in next to them.

"Olivia, this is Nick Perry." Andrew nodded toward the young man, who grinned and stuck out his hand in greeting.

"Nice to meet you, Nick."

"Likewise, ma'am."

"He just finished his set, while you were out of the room."

Andrew said it casually, but she knew him well enough. He was upset with her for going after Ellie when Olivia should have been watching the other artists play. But she'd been so moved, she couldn't wait to speak with her. Probably made Olivia look desperate, and maybe she'd come on too strong. She just couldn't shake the feeling that Ellie was special. "I'm sorry I missed it." Olivia twirled the straw in her soda. "But what I heard was great."

"That's all right. I gave Mr. Grant my demo."

"We'll be in touch, Nick. Thanks." Andrew

shook the guy's hand again before Nick left their table. Then Andrew looked pointedly at Olivia. "What was so urgent that you had to miss the full performance of what could be our new label's first artist?"

"Settle down, Andrew. I was following my own instinct." She sipped her soda, but it tasted watered down. Olivia flagged the server for a refill.

The corner of Andrew's mouth quirked. "And what was that?"

"I told you. I think Ellie Evans may be the one to launch our label." Of course, she'd run off before Andrew had had a real chance to respond. "Her performance . . . it hit me here." She put her hand over her heart.

"She was good, I'll give you that." Andrew cut into his prime rib, which must have been cold by then. He always got too excited and busy to eat. "But you heard Chelsea. She's never played here before. I've never heard of her. What do we know about her except that she hit you in the heart?"

"What else is there to know?" Olivia bit the inside of her cheek. "Isn't how an artist's songs touch people the biggest factor?"

Andrew forked a slice of steak and waved it in the air. "There's a lot more to succeeding in this business than that. You were in it. You know."

Olivia's mind took her back to the interviews,

the wining and dining, the flirting with radio hosts for more airtime, the grueling hours of building a fan base. She loved her fans, but sometimes not what it took to get them. Still, she'd been able to keep her nose fairly clean. "Guess I'd like to protect our artists from some of that if we can."

"That may be a naïve hope." He chewed slowly, swallowed, then took a drink of his tea. "Now, Nick Perry, he's got what it takes. His songs are catchy but real, his performance on fire, and his fans loyal. Did you see the line of girls outside hoping to get in? He's one of the only males in the lineup tonight. I'm shocked no one's picked him up yet. We should swoop in soon. I asked him for a meeting next week."

"But what about Ellie?" Sure, she didn't have the big star appeal Nick Perry might have, but she was raw and honest—and the world needed that.

Olivia needed that.

"Maybe we can entertain the thought of her later, when her career's more established. I think Nick might be the one to start our label off right. He seemed eager to discuss the possibility." Andrew slid a CD across the table. "Listen to his demo, will you?"

"I told Ellie we might want to audition her next week."

Andrew lifted his eyebrows. "I wish you hadn't.

We shouldn't waste our time listening to people we wouldn't really consider at this time. It's not fair to them or us."

Olivia sighed. Maybe Andrew was right. After all, he knew what it took to survive in this industry from an executive perspective, and if he didn't see them succeeding with Ellie, then why not go with the sure thing—or as close to a sure thing as anyone could get in Nashville? "Of course I'll take a listen." She stuffed Nick's CD in her purse.

"You ready to call it a night, or do you want to stay for the rest? I took a look at the lineup, and I think it's all artists we've listened to and decided against."

She should check in with Rachel, thank her again for the cupcake. "I'll stay for a bit. You go home if you want."

"I'll call you tomorrow about scheduling an appointment with Nick." Andrew gathered his files and tucked them into his briefcase.

"Sounds good."

Andrew headed for the door.

Olivia spun her fork in what was left of her spaghetti. But there was no comfort in cold, limp food. No comfort for the disappointment that threatened to bubble up and out of her.

Andrew was right. Wasn't he?

She eased out of the booth, and something caught her eye.

Ellie sat in the corner, talking with a gray-headed man. Her big doe eyes—and her smile—widened as they chatted.

Who was this guy? Olivia should leave well enough alone, but she couldn't stop herself from walking in their direction.

What was wrong with her? Ellie could talk to whomever she wanted.

But what if it was another label trying to recruit her? Despite Andrew's dismissal of Ellie as a candidate, Olivia had to know. She maneuvered through the café, greeting people as she went.

The man turned.

Olivia inhaled.

Donny Green.

She should have known. She picked up the pace, dodging servers and threading her way through the room. She approached the pair without flinching. "Ellie, I see you've met Donny." The slimeball.

Donny swiveled his head, and his eyes pierced Olivia. He had a nasty reputation of hooking young artists with his lies and leading the performers astray. He'd tried it with Olivia all those years ago, and if it hadn't been for her upbringing, Olivia would never have figured him out till it was too late. Guess Mama taught her something good after all.

Ellie looked between the two, confusion darkening her face.

Olivia pulled her lips into a fake smile. "I forgot to give you my card earlier, Ellie." She reached in her purse and pulled one out. "I'll call you to come audition for me and my business partner next week." Who cared what Andrew said. She couldn't let Ellie be drawn in by this guy. She seemed too innocent to know any better.

As the card left her hand, Olivia pummeled herself mentally. It wasn't her usual move to horn in like this. But she couldn't help the protective instinct that flared up inside when she saw this girl.

Ellie stared at the card in awe. "Thank you so much, Ms. Lovett." Her cheeks glowed a deep pink.

Donny reached into his tweed jacket and pulled out a card of his own. "I'll be calling too, but here's my contact info if you have any questions in the meantime." He winked at Ellie and stood. "Olivia, always a pleasure." He snatched her hand and kissed it before she could do anything to stop him.

Olivia jerked her hand away and twisted from him. "Have a nice night, Ellie. It was great meeting you."

"Oh, you too."

She strode toward the door. Maybe she could catch Andrew before he left. He'd probably been delayed by some old business associates on the way out. She pushed open the door and stepped into the night.

A street lamp illuminated the sidewalk and parking lot. The crowd out front had dissipated, and crickets chirped, hidden in the dark somewhere.

Olivia scanned the lot. Ah, there.

Andrew unlocked his Acura and threw his briefcase inside. The dinging from his open door split the air.

"Andrew, wait!" She scrambled around a few parked cars to try to catch up with him. How would she convince him to take another look at Ellie?

He shut his car and walked toward her. "Liv? What's wrong?"

Oh, her tone had sounded a bit panicked, hadn't it? Why was this so all-fired important?

The label had to succeed, that's all. It had nothing to do with Ellie herself. Ellie was just the means to success. Right?

C'mon, Olivia, think. "We could theoretically launch the label with two artists, couldn't we?"

He took a moment to answer. "Perhaps, if we got a bit more funding from investors. But you know as well as I do that every artist we sign costs money. So it's best to begin slowly."

Oh. "Right." She *did* know that. The excitement of the moment was just getting to her.

Andrew cocked his head, seemed to consider

her. His eyes softened. "You really think this girl has potential, don't you?"

"Yes. I really do." Olivia couldn't figure out why. But her instincts had never failed her before. Even when that meant doing something hard.

He ran his hand through his hair, paced for a moment, then stopped. "All right. How about you take some time over the next few weeks to get to know Ms. Evans some more? Help her get some small gigs to see how she does, if she's got what it takes to make it in this biz, that kind of thing. We need to make sure whoever we choose can hack it in interviews and in front of any crowd we throw their way."

But what if Donny Green moved in on Ellie before Olivia got her signed? Then again, Ellie seemed like the kind of girl who was loyal. If Olivia mentored her, she wouldn't be likely to turn away and run to someone else. At least Olivia didn't think so. Was she crazy for basing such assumptions on five minutes of talking?

She chewed her lip. "That seems fair. What about your guy?"

"I'll schedule a meeting and full audition with Nick, and you and I can discuss the two of them as soon as we have more information."

"All right." Olivia stared at the ground. Her boot tapped the asphalt like a drummer *rat-tat-tatt*ing.

"Liv."

Her head shot up at his gentle tone and the light touch on her arm. "Yeah?"

"It's going to be all right. We'll find the best artist for our label, and we'll start off successfully."

"I know." Especially if they had Ellie. She could be their ticket to the top. What's more, Olivia had the strangest feeling that meeting Ellie was no coincidence. This girl, somehow, was going to change Olivia's life forever.

7

Olivia's nerves wound tight around her muscles. She fiddled with the cloth napkin on the table. A breeze rolled through The Robin's Nest, a small outdoor café and one of her favorite spots in Nashville. Other customers filled the tables surrounding Olivia's. She tuned out their conversations, while the smell of fresh oranges and fried bacon drifted under her nose.

The bangles on her wrist clinked together as she tucked her hair behind her ear, waiting for Ellie to arrive.

Olivia was a professional. She'd been in plenty of high-pressure situations with some of the biggest label execs in the industry before. So why should one girl make her stomach quiver? But her gut reminded her this was different than all those times on stage or in closed-door meetings.

This may very well be her last shot to make her mark on the world.

And what if she was staking her last shot on the wrong person? After all, Ellie was an unknown. Maybe Olivia's gut had been wrong last night.

That's why this meeting was so important. She needed to know who Ellie really was, down deep. Not that that could normally be achieved in an hour-long meeting, but Olivia prided herself on being a good judge of character. *Lord, help me to know if she's the right fit for our label.*

"Sorry I'm late." Ellie slid onto the chair across from Olivia, curls windswept. "It's a pleasure to see you again, Ms. Lovett."

"Call me Olivia, please." Olivia sat up straighter. "I'm just glad you could make it on such short notice."

"When Olivia Lovett says she wants to do brunch, you jump outta bed and do whatever it takes to make it." The girl fingered the glossy menu. "I just had a bit of trouble finding the place. I'd never heard of it before."

"Once you've lived here as long as I have, you find the gems. They're tucked away all over the city." Olivia folded her hands on the table. "In fact, I view finding good artists in much the same way. Why don't you go ahead and look over the menu, and then I'll tell you why I called."

"All right." Ellie perused her options. She looked up, brown eyes piercing Olivia. "Are the eggs Benedict any good?"

"Delicious, as is everything here."

A waitress with a pink streak in her hair headed their way. "Welcome to The Robin's Nest. What can I get y'all this morning?"

"I'll have the spinach frittata, please." Olivia gestured across the table. "Ellie?"

"Eggs Benedict would be great, thanks."

The waitress collected the menus. "Coming right up."

Ellie turned her attention back to Olivia, her whole body rigid.

Ellie's nerves made Olivia relax and smile. "As I mentioned last night, I liked what I heard from you. I spoke with my business partner, Andrew Grant, and we decided I should meet with you on my own and see if you might be a good fit for our label. This is just an informal time for us to get to know each other."

Ellie gave a tentative smile. "That sounds great." She took a sip of water.

"How long have you been at this?"

"I've been singing since I was young, mostly at my small church in Oklahoma."

"Ah, I thought I detected an accent. Us Oklahoma girls gotta stick together, am I right?"

"For sure." Ellie laughed.

"You mentioned church. Is your faith important to you?" Even though she'd failed God so miserably, Olivia couldn't imagine being in this music scene without him.

"It is. I wouldn't have survived the last few years without Jesus by my side." The girl became quiet. "I don't always understand why God lets certain things happen. But I still believe things happen for a reason. Like coming out here. It's been . . ."

"Harder than you thought?"

"Yeah."

"I remember that feeling. Wondering if you'll ever make it. If the next connection will be a dead end or the thing that will make all the difference."

"That's exactly how I feel. How long did it take you?"

"Seven years."

"Wow. I feel silly complaining about two."

Olivia shrugged. "It's different for all of us. I had a lot of growing up to do when I first got here. I was only sixteen, you know."

"Really? Your parents let you come?"

"My daddy was never in the picture. And I suspect my mama was happy to have only herself to think about again." Wow. Why was she telling this to Ellie? This meeting was supposed to be about getting to know Ellie, not the other way around.

Ellie's eyebrows scrunched together, and she stared at the table. "My mama wasn't in the picture either. I've never met her."

A quiet fell over the table, and for a moment, Olivia had the strangest urge to pull Ellie close, stroke her hair, and tell her it'd be all right— almost like a mother might, although that had never been her personal experience. The thought came quickly and struck her in the very core of her heart. Since when did she have any sort of maternal instinct? But mentoring required many of the same intentions, so maybe she shouldn't be surprised.

Ellie moved her gaze back to Olivia. "Like I said last night, my daddy and I used to listen to your albums together."

Olivia studied the girl. "You used to? Was I replaced by someone better—much hipper, younger?" Her mouth slipped into a wry grin.

Ellie's eyes clouded for a moment. Her chin trembled. "No. He died a few years ago. A drunk driver hit him on his way home from work."

"I'm so sorry." Is that what drove the desperation that seemed to lurk beneath the surface of this girl's soul? Ellie was genuine, but that meant something deeper than fame inspired her. Olivia should know. It's why she had come to Nashville all those years ago. To prove that, even if she couldn't be who she wanted to be, she could be somebody. Do something important. "Is that why you're here?"

"Sorta." A strange look came over Ellie's face. "I also—" But she pressed her lips together, as if unsure whether to continue.

"Here's your food, y'all." The waitress slid platters in front of Olivia and Ellie. "Anything else?"

Olivia shook her head. "No, thank you."

The waitress nodded and left.

Ellie lifted her fork and cut into her eggs.

Looked like she was done discussing her dad.

Olivia took a bite of her frittata. The cheese and herbs blended together in perfection with a sharpness she appreciated. "Would you like to hear more about our label?"

Ellie's eyes lit up as she seemed to mentally shake away the blues trying to strangle her. "Absolutely."

"Radiant Records is in the infant stage—in other words, we're a startup. I want you to know what you'd be getting into if you were to join us." Olivia set her fork down. "But Andrew is a real professional. He was vice president of the Lucky label for the last five years before stepping down to join me. So he's the best of the best."

"He looks a little intimidating from afar." Ellie's eyes widened, and her hand flew to her mouth. "I'm sorry. I shouldn't have said that."

Olivia laughed and waved off Ellie's comment. "Your honesty is refreshing. And if I didn't know Andrew so well, I might be tempted to think the same thing. Andrew and I are looking to create a label where artists feel nurtured. We want to back away from the glitz and glamour. Country music is meant to be simpler than all that. In many ways it's going the same direction as pop music, and it can be hard to tell the difference between the two. We want to allow our artists to flourish but also keep those qualities that make country music unique."

A pigeon landed nearby and walked toward their table.

Ellie shooed it away with her foot. "I couldn't agree more. Whenever I take requests, I'm asked to play something by the latest tween sensation. My grandma and grandpa raised me to really value the roots of country music: faith, family, America, and love." She chuckled. "And of course, if you don't occasionally sing about your dog, your pickup, and your achy-breaky heart, it ain't country music either."

"Yes!" Olivia leaned back in her seat. She had that eerie sense again—the one that felt an automatic kinship with this girl. But maybe Ellie just reminded Olivia of herself. Whatever it was, something about her made Olivia want to be transparent. "Andrew and I have been searching for our first artist for a while now. Until I heard you, I was beginning to think the perfect artist didn't exist."

Ellie's fork clattered against her plate. "What are you saying?"

All her earlier doubts of just minutes ago had seeped away with Ellie's presence—her honesty and authenticity. "I'm saying that I think you're perfect for our label. But I still need to convince my business partner." Olivia reached for Ellie's hand. The action surprised Olivia, unprofessional as it was. And yet, something about it felt right. "Look, darlin', I think you're great. I think you can go the distance. And I want to walk through it with you. Don't waste your time on two-bit thieves like Donny Green, the producer you met last night. You are special."

Ellie's lower lip trembled. "Do you really think so?"

"I do." Olivia released her hand. "Like I said, we just need to convince Andrew that you're perfect. Thing is, he's got his eye on another performer. Nick Perry. You know him?"

"I met him earlier this week." Ellie stared at her plate. "He's an amazing performer. No offense to your instincts, but why in the world would you think I'd be a better choice than he is?"

"Ellie, look at me."

Ellie lifted her chin.

All around them, servers bustled and plates clanged, but Olivia zeroed in on the extremely talented girl in front of her. The one who truly didn't see how amazing she was. "I don't think it. I know it. I'm sure Mr. Perry is quite talented. But there's something about you I can't put my finger on. I just know you're a good fit for this label. The perfect fit. You're gonna help me prove it."

"How?"

"I want to see how you do singing for a few different crowds, and I've got a great opportunity to start. I attend Koinonia Nashville Church. You know it?"

"The megachurch on the outskirts of town?"

"Yep, that's the one. The first service is televised every Sunday. Sometimes I help the music pastor find talent for offertory and special music. I got a call from him an hour ago, and it just so happens the woman scheduled to sing tomorrow is sick. If you're free, I'll tell Pastor Neal I have the perfect stand-in."

"T-tomorrow?"

"That's right." Olivia tilted her head. "You think you can handle that?"

A string of emotions flew across Ellie's face, but determination finally took their place. "Yes."

Good. Her instincts about this girl had been right. And it was only a matter of time before Andrew realized it too.

Olivia Lovett thought she was special.

Ellie shook her head and laughed in disbelief as she trudged up the stairs to her Saturday afternoon song-feedback workshop. The former star's words echoed in her mind: *"Look, darlin', I think you're great. I think you can go the distance."* And not only did she think that, but she wanted to invest time in Ellie and help her get there.

Ellie had gone to the meeting hoping to ask about Marie Culloway, but when she'd started to, something in her had balked. She hadn't had time to analyze her hesitancy yet. There were

111

more immediate things to do today, like prepare to wow the crowd at Olivia's church—Olivia included. And Ellie knew just how to do it.

As she entered the meeting room, she scanned those already seated in clusters and located Jenny and Logan. She waved and maneuvered through the group of about twenty aspiring artists.

"Hey, Ellie."

The voice stopped her in her tracks and she turned to find Nick Perry sitting two feet away, tuning his guitar. "Nick. What's up?" Then she scrunched her nose. "I've never seen you in this workshop before." They both attended the monthly guest speaker night, but weekly workshops were divided based on skill and experience—and Nick far exceeded her in both categories.

"I'm normally in the later one." A.k.a. the advanced songwriter's section—the one a song-writer had to receive an invite to be able to attend. And this guy was her competition for a spot on the label. Did she really stand a chance?

Yes, because Olivia's instincts meant something. And today Ellie was choosing hope instead of doubt.

She fingered the strap of her guitar case. Even though Nick was being cool, meeting his girlfriend last night had been so . . . awkward. "What are you doing here today?"

"They asked me to help out the teacher for this class." Nick strummed his guitar, the picture of calm. "The assistant couldn't make it. Flu or something."

"Oh." Ellie shifted her stance. Did he know they were potential competitors for Olivia's label? How much had he been told? "Cool." She glanced at her friends.

Jenny's eyebrows were raised in interest.

"I've gotta go set up." She hurried away before Nick could answer and dropped onto the open chair next to Jenny.

Logan barely glanced up but nodded his greeting as he continued to tune his guitar. Jenny's boyfriend was a lot quieter than Jenny herself.

Ellie turned to Jenny and raised her hand to stop her friend from asking the question clearly on the edge of her lips. "The answer is yes, I know Nick Perry."

Her friend pushed aside her notebook and leaned in, strawberry perfume so thick Ellie had to stop herself from coughing. "He and Logan are friends. He's hot." She didn't seem to care that she'd just complimented another guy's looks in front of Logan.

He remained oblivious, focused on a riff.

"Are you guys just friends or what?"

"I'd barely even call us friends. More like acquaintances." Ellie unzipped her case and

113

whipped out her guitar, along with her auto tuner. She had only a few minutes until class began, and she needed every moment to gather her courage. Because today she'd do something she hadn't done for several months—not since she'd been thoroughly embarrassed in a private critique session.

But a public critique was her only option today, and she had to get someone's opinion on the song she planned to sing at Olivia's church tomorrow. Her megachurch. The service that was televised.

Ellie's hands slipped on the chords, and she took a moment to wipe the sweat from them.

"Cute. You're nervous. I think you do like him." Jenny nudged her.

Sure, she'd let her friend think that. Ellie wasn't ready to share her news with anyone just yet. Speaking the words out loud—"Olivia Lovett wants *me*"—might somehow jinx the whole thing.

"All right, class, welcome." Their instructor, Bill, headed to the front of the room. He reminded Ellie of the character from those *Where's Waldo?* books—long, lanky, and even wearing a red-and-white-striped sweater.

Instantly, guitars quieted, as did their owners.

"I've got Nick Perry assisting me today, so feel free to ask him questions during our breakout session later on."

"You gonna ask him any questions, girl?" Jenny's whisper filled Ellie's ear.

Ellie rolled her eyes and stuck out her tongue at her friend's teasing.

Bill continued. "Today, as usual, we'll start off with some public critiques. Remember, this is a chance for you to get feedback from your instructors as well as your peers. This is a safe zone, so don't be afraid to try something new. Any volunteers?"

Before she could consider the nerves creeping up in her belly, Ellie raised her hand.

"Ellie, thanks for volunteering. Why don't you come up here and play us your latest?"

While Jenny gawked, Ellie rose, gripped her guitar tight, and made her way up front.

Rows and rows of eyes stared back at her.

There would be way more tomorrow, so she had to move past it and get this right. She forced a smile to her lips. "Today I'd like your opinion on my song 'The Light of Your Eyes.'" She soon lost herself in the song—one that reminded her that, no matter what the day held, she could always come back to the light and find peace. She'd put everything into this song, had written it on the second anniversary of her dad's death. It moved her, and she could only pray it also moved those who would listen tomorrow.

When she finished the song, everyone

applauded politely. She scanned the group and found herself looking for Nick's approval.

He smiled at her, but something troubling rested in his eyes.

Ellie looked down at her shoes. A tiny bit of mud was crusted on one of her laces.

Bill joined her. "Thanks for playing, Ellie. All right, what did y'all think?"

Classmates called out encouragement—one liked the lyrics, one the sense of peace, one her voice. One said he didn't understand why she'd chosen certain phrasing, but admitted it could just be him. This was good. Very good.

Bill turned to her. Here was the part where he'd tell her this song was ready to perform. Her toes curled. "Like others have said, you have a way with lyrics, Ellie. You're a poet at heart."

She blushed. "Thank you."

"But I found the chord progressions to be fairly basic. Not only that, but the song stayed kind of flat throughout—no surge of energy, nothing to excite me. I got bored after the first thirty seconds." Bill's words slapped her in the face. Her breathing sped up as she listened to him detail several other problem areas. "Keep working. It's not ready just yet."

Ellie nodded and, without saying another word, fumbled her way back to her seat. A few others volunteered for critiques and played their songs, but Ellie couldn't focus. All she could hear, over and over, were Bill's words—*"Not ready."*

What other song could she sing? She mentally flipped through all the songs she'd written. Nothing had quite the snap she needed, not for something this huge. Ellie tugged on her sleeves and stared at her notebook, willing inspiration to come.

Someone tapped her on the shoulder, and Ellie jumped. She hadn't noticed, but classmates were breaking off in groups and helping each other. The public critiques were over. Ellie looked up.

Nick towered over her. "Want some help on that song?"

She'd meant to quietly sneak out of the room at this point in the class, but something in Nick's voice stopped her. It wasn't pity she heard, but compassion and real interest. And as much as she hated to admit it, she needed help—plain and simple. "Okay."

The chair groaned as Nick plopped down. He set his guitar case on the floor and leaned forward. "I didn't agree completely with Bill."

"You didn't?"

"First, the lyrics were awesome. I felt them here." He raised his hand to cover his heart. "Second, I think the chord progressions matched the simplicity of the emotions you're expressing in the song, so I thought they worked great."

"Really?"

"Really." Nick smiled and dimples rose to

the surface of his cheeks. Oh, she had to stop blushing every time he looked at her that way. He had a girlfriend, after all.

What were they talking about? Oh yeah. Her song. She snatched up her pen, hovering it over the page. "So what did you agree with?"

"I think we could change up the bridge and maybe the second chorus. But it's not going to take much."

"That's good, because I'm planning to sing this tomorrow."

"Then let's get to work."

8

The congregation of Koinonia Nashville Church must have been bigger than the entire population of her hometown—at least, that's how it seemed.

People milled in the aisles of the massive auditorium, and Ellie was dwarfed by the sheer size of it all. With its two balconies, fifty-foot ceilings, and stadium seating for thousands, the place reverberated with energy. Two huge screens hung on either side of the stage, and cameramen were poised throughout the lower aisles, ready to broadcast the service once it began. Chris Tomlin's voice filtered through the room from the speakers, singing about the wonder of creation.

If only she could cling to the safety and familiarity of her guitar in this moment, but it was onstage waiting for her to play. And Ellie would be up there soon. She knew her song backward and forward, had spent the rest of yesterday practicing. Nick's advice had been solid, and when they'd finished class, he'd grinned. *"I think you've got a winner on your hands, Ell."*

Ell. Something about the way he'd said the nickname—well, it was cute. But she couldn't think about that now. Or ever.

Ellie lowered herself onto the third-row seat that had been reserved for her, conveniently located so she could slip out and backstage just before the offertory prayer.

"Good morning, Ellie." Olivia approached from the other end of the row. She looked amazing, as always, in a flattering pair of jeans, brown knee-high boots, a blouse, and a scarf. Her blonde hair shimmered under the lights.

Ellie had worn her best outfit and still felt like a hick next to Olivia. "Morning."

"Do you mind if I join you?" Upon the shake of Ellie's head, Olivia sat next to her. "How did your mic check go?"

"Great. Pastor Neal is really nice."

"Yes, I've known him for years. He and his wife, Debbie, are the sweetest people." Someone called Olivia's name, and she glanced over her shoulder. She held up her hand and then turned back to Ellie. "There's someone I'd like you to meet."

A man—wait, wasn't that Mr. Grant?—walked down the aisle toward them, a high-school-aged blonde following behind. He must attend church here as well.

Olivia stood and scooted out of the row once more. She gave both of them a quick hug and then motioned to Ellie. "Andrew, Grace, this is Ellie Evans."

Ellie rose and moved into the aisle toward

them, not missing the private glance Olivia gave to Andrew, almost like a visual nudge.

"Ellie, this is my business partner, Andrew Grant, and his daughter, Grace."

Ellie pulled her hands from her pockets—when had she stuck them there?—and held her right one out. "Nice to meet you."

"You too, Ellie." Andrew seemed to study her from behind his glasses.

Grace nodded shyly.

Andrew trained his eye on Ellie and Olivia's seats. "Can we join you?"

"Of course." Olivia led them back to their seats and they all sat.

Andrew leaned forward to address Ellie. "I'm very much looking forward to hearing you sing again. Will you be performing something original?"

"Yes." She should say more, but his scrutiny thickened her tongue.

"Good, good." He whispered something in Olivia's ear.

She looked at him and nodded.

What had he said? Was it about her?

Stop being paranoid, Ellie. She reached into her purse to silence her phone. A text from Grandma—yes, she'd finally learned how to send one—caught Ellie off guard.

Praying for peace and a steady hand as you play for him, and him alone.

Oh, Grandma. She was right, as usual. Ellie was getting caught up in all the details, but God had already worked it all out on his own, right? After all, she was here, singing for Olivia Lovett, in a bigger venue than Ellie had ever played before. She recalled her conversation with Grandma last night, her sweet encouragement seeping through the screen straight to her heart: *God's led you here. You just gotta take the next step, is all. Don't worry about the rest.*

Even if all this led to nothing, she'd met Olivia for a reason. Ellie had to believe that. Who knew? Marie Culloway could be that reason. Ellie just had to find the perfect opportunity to ask about her—and this time, Ellie wouldn't hesitate.

The pastor got onstage and welcomed the audience. Then the praise band took over and asked the crowd to stand.

The sound of thousands rustling to their feet, in anticipation of praising their Lord together— Ellie loved it.

When they all sang as one, peace settled over her soul, just like Grandma had prayed for her. Yes, whatever came, this would be all right.

After a few songs, the lead guitarist gave them permission to sit again. As he plucked out a chord progression, he prayed.

Ellie listened to the music, let it flood her soul.

Then the guitarist began to sing, and Ellie's stomach dropped.

"Just a closer walk with thee . . ."

No, not now. Not today. Not moments before she had to get up there and perform. It was a more modern version of the song, but it sounded the same as it did that day. How could he be singing this song—the one that still had power over her, not because of the lyrics or spiritual impact behind it, but because of the memories it held?

"Grant it, Jesus, is my plea."

Her mind flitted back to an auditorium very different than this one. It'd been small, had a rough wooden cross at the back.

"Daily walking close to thee . . ."

She'd played her heart out.

"Let it be, dear Lord, let it be."

But it hadn't mattered. In the end—

"Ellie, time to go." Olivia's whisper broke through her memories.

Ellie stood, gripping the seat in front of her to steady herself. She straightened and trekked to the door leading backstage. She could do this. She'd just push the past from her mind, the significance of that memory, that day when she'd been invisible. Today, she'd change all that. The world would see Ellie Evans for the first time— and they would love her.

Oh, how she hoped and prayed they'd love her.

She wound her way through the backstage area and arrived at her entry point. She turned on her battery pack and stuck her ear buds in, so she'd be able to hear the monitors.

Peace, Lord. Please.

But her soul still rumbled, mired in the past.

The band ended the song, and the guitarist prayed again, this time for the offering they were about to take. As he prayed, the others quietly unplugged and walked off backstage.

Ellie moved quickly and picked up her guitar, the one that had been with her through thick and thin. She cocooned it in her arms, wrapping the strap snug around her shoulder.

The prayer ended and the guitarist left the stage.

And then it was only Ellie, standing in the bright lights of the stage, where she'd always longed to be.

She exhaled slowly, then moved closer to the microphone stand. Everything up here was shiny, new. Her trembling hands fell into the familiar motion as she strummed.

All she could see were the people in the first few rows. A baby cried somewhere in the distance. Someone coughed. But none of that mattered. Ellie could do this.

She opened her mouth and sang, the words coming to her as if on a breeze. Natural. She felt the meaning of the words down in her toes.

Then a man in the front row stood. Turned. Walked down the aisle toward the doors.

Ellie faltered. Her heart skipped a beat.

Six feet tall, thin, broad shoulders, he looked like . . . but it couldn't be. Daddy was gone.

And he'd never had time for her performances anyway, not even the ones he'd promised to be at.

She stopped singing, and her hands quit playing, as if they had a mind of their own. Ellie tried to choke out the words to finish the song, but she just couldn't. "I'm sorry." She whispered the words into the microphone, unplugged her guitar, and ran backstage, past a few sound guys, past the band members who stood watching her, past the pastor who waited to come back out to give his sermon.

And there, in the middle of some abandoned hallway, she hunkered down against the wall, pulled her knees into her chest, and begged God for tears.

"I'll be right back." Olivia whispered in Andrew's ear before slipping out of the pew and heading up the aisle toward the backstage entrance. What in the world had happened? One minute, Ellie was churning out something raw, beautiful. The next she'd frozen. Perhaps she'd gotten a bad case of stage fright. But that would be odd, since she'd been doing so well.

There must be more to this story.

The pastor spoke, his words muffled as Olivia reached backstage. The praise band guys shuffled past her, nodding and filing out the door to the auditorium. Olivia maneuvered through the carpeted hall until she rounded the corner and halted at a sight that tore at her heart.

Ellie sat, back against the wall, knees up, face buried in her arms. Her hair was splayed around her shoulders.

Oh, the poor girl. Olivia walked into the dressing room, where she was met with the heavy smell of hairspray. She located a Kleenex box, snatched a few tissues, returned to Ellie, and sank down next to her.

Ellie straightened, startled. Surprisingly, her eyes were completely dry. "I'm so sorry. I blew it, didn't I?"

Olivia handed her the tissues anyway. "Don't worry. No one will remember this come tomorrow." Except they probably would. The Nashville music scene was a tight-knit community. She'd have to work double-hard to convince Andrew to sign Ellie now. But the girl didn't need to hear that. She needed comfort.

Above them, an air vent came on and drowned out the silence.

"What happened out there? Seemed like more than a typical bout of nerves."

"How did you know?" Ellie tucked her lips under her teeth.

Olivia shrugged. "Call it a hunch." She straightened her legs in front of her and crossed her boots at the ankles. "What's going on?"

Ellie stared at the tissues in her hands. "I was thinking about the last time I sang in church. My dad . . . he said he'd come. But he never showed. I kept waiting for him to open the door, to walk in and hear my solo. He'd promised to make it that time."

"He didn't usually show up for your performances?"

"It wasn't his fault. He just wasn't around." Ellie balled up the tissues, then smoothed them out on her knee. "My grandma and grandpa kinda raised me. My dad had me young, but they didn't want him to miss out on college. We lived in a small town, and there wasn't much opportunity for him to go to school. So he went to Oklahoma University, which is about an hour away. Then he got a job there in Oklahoma City and came home whenever he could."

Olivia's first instinct was to berate the man. How could he abandon a daughter like Ellie to live his life elsewhere? But with her own past, she had no room to judge anybody. "Why didn't you go live with your daddy?"

One of Ellie's shoulders lifted, then lowered. "He used to talk about it. 'Someday, you'll come to the big city. How'd you like that?' But as I got older, he changed his mind, I guess. Said I should grow up in a small town, where there's less crime and I'd be safer. Plus he worked a lot and said I was better off with Grandma, who was a teacher and off in the afternoons and summertime."

Olivia put her arm around Ellie. This girl was burrowing her way into Olivia's soul, and Olivia couldn't help herself. "I'm sorry."

Ellie shredded a piece of one of the tissues, separating it from the rest. "It's all right. I grew up knowing lots of love anyway. Grandma and Grandpa are special people, that's for sure. I don't have any room in my heart for resentment. I know my daddy loved me. Whenever we were together, he'd make a special day of it." Her voice shuddered.

"That's why today was so rough, huh?"

The girl nodded, ripping away another piece from the same tissue. "Someone in the front row stood, and for a second, even though it made no sense, I thought it was him."

Olivia squeezed the girl's shoulders, then pulled her arm back. "I'm sure he'd be here if he could. And I'll bet he was listening from heaven."

"I like to think so." Ellie let the pieces of tissue fall to the ground. "You know the worst part?"

"What's that?"

"I can't cry."

"About what?"

"Anything. Not since his funeral. It's like my body decided it'd had enough and was moving forward. I'm a freak. A normal person would be a blubbering mess right now."

"You are not a freak. People deal with grief in different ways."

Ellie's nose wrinkled and she half-shrugged, as if she didn't believe Olivia. She looked lost in thought. Then the reverie cleared from her eyes, and she looked up. "And then there's my mama . . ."

Olivia's heart skipped a beat. That's right, Ellie had said her mom left when she was little. "What about her?"

"Every time I sing, I can't help but wonder if she's out there, listening."

A question broke through Olivia's better judgment, and she couldn't keep from speaking. "Do you hate her for leaving?"

Ellie studied Olivia, as if sensing something deeper behind her question. "My dad said she left because she was young and scared. I guess I do wonder if I was the reason. But no, I don't hate her."

Olivia released a breath she didn't know she'd been holding. It sounded like she had a lot in common with Ellie's mama.

"You know, I want to share my music with the world. But some part of me also wants to become famous, so my mama will see me for the first time—and maybe she'll regret leaving."

"Maybe she already regrets it. Or is at least saddened by it." Why was Olivia continuing this conversation? She was treading on dangerous ground. But she had to let her thoughts fly. They'd been trapped inside for so long.

"Then why wouldn't she have ever tried to find me?"

"Perhaps she thinks you're truly better off without her. Her leaving could have nothing to do with who you are and everything to do with keeping you safe."

Ellie's lips puckered into a frown. "Maybe."

And when spoken out loud, not for the first time . . . Did Olivia really believe her own intentions, all those years ago, were as pure as she'd always told herself?

Or had she left her own precious daughter behind for far more selfish reasons?

In the distance, a door opened, letting in part of the pastor's sermon.

Ellie looked up, her vulnerable eyes shining like jewels. "I have a question."

"Anything."

"I came to Nashville to play my music, but also to find my mom."

"She's here?"

Ellie tilted her head, watching Olivia. "I think so. I was wondering—"

Andrew appeared from around the corner. "There you ladies are. Everything okay back here?"

This fiasco was not going to make Ellie very attractive to Andrew as a performer. But to Olivia, it only made her more real. She jumped up and extended her hand to Ellie, wearing a pasted-on smile. "Everything's dandy. Right, Ellie?"

Ellie looked troubled but nodded. She took Olivia's hand and stood.

Olivia's heart thumped in her chest. She couldn't shrug off the feeling that, while Ellie was special, she might just be Olivia's undoing. But that was silly.

Wasn't it?

9

Twenty-three years and seven months ago

It's been eight weeks since Mama ruined my chances to see Trisha Yearwood.

Eight weeks of strumming on my guitar in my room, afraid to see what kind of mood she's in. She's been worse lately, if that's possible. I've heard whispers around town that she's involved in something shady. Folks don't think I can hear when they say such things, but my ears work just fine.

Today, I sit up in bed like usual, ready to go to school. My head swims and my stomach hurts worse than it did yesterday. It's been doing that this whole last week. Most mornings I can ignore it.

But right now, I run to the bathroom and empty last night's dinner into the toilet.

What's wrong with me? After several minutes, I crawl to my bed and climb in. I pull the phone from its cradle and dial Bette's number. She answers.

"It's me."

"Why you callin' so early? Need a ride to school again?"

"I'm not going today. Threw up this morning.

Can you get my homework and bring it over this afternoon, so I don't get behind?" If my music doesn't work out, school's the only thing that will get me out of Red, Oklahoma.

"Of course I'll get your work for you." Bette pauses. "Sorry you don't feel good. You have the flu or something?"

"Not sure. I haven't been around anyone who's sick. Maybe I'm just tired." Come to think of it, the last few weeks have been exhausting. I've gone to bed by eight every night and haven't felt like hanging out with friends. Bette's noticed.

"Marie, you don't think . . . ?"

"What?"

"Well . . ." My friend, who normally could talk the ear off an elephant, doesn't say anything for an eternity. "Have you had your time of the month yet?"

My head throbs. "I don't know. It's been awhile, I guess."

"What if you're pregnant?"

I sit up straight, and the phone base crashes to the floor. Leaning over, I pick it up and set everything to rights. "I can't be."

But I can.

I was stupid. There had been Mama's embarrassing me after the performance, and the anger I had toward her, and then there was Ben, another performer in the competition. When

I stood in the crowd and heard him sing, his voice mesmerized my heart and my soul, and I knew I had to meet him. He took me out for a burger, and he was so cute and sweet. He just *got* me, and I hadn't had someone get me in such a long time. We drove in his Mustang to nowhere in particular and talked till the sun sank low.

And so, when he kissed me, I couldn't help myself. I wanted to feel connected to someone. The only thing that mattered in that moment was getting as far away from Mama as possible.

Far away from Mama—and how she said I'd never escape my fate as a Culloway.

I groan. "What do I do?"

"I'll bring you a test when I drop your stuff by this afternoon, all right? It's probably nothing. You're probably fine."

It's not nothing. And I'm not fine. I know it.

This can't be happening. But why wouldn't it happen to me? All the bad things do.

I stare at the test strip in my hand and stifle a cry. It's true. I'm pregnant. At fifteen. Just like Mama was. Just like her mama was.

I'm no better than them. Why, God? I tried to be a good girl and listen to the preacher on TV and stay away from sins. But they found me in spite of it all. And now what?

I place my hand on my flat stomach. But flat for how long? This changes everything. Instead of being the one who got out of Red, I'll just be another who stays, trying to make ends meet. Maybe find a boy to marry me someday. Course, who'd want to marry someone saddled with a baby?

Oh no, I have to tell Ben. But I can't do that to him. He's seventeen, almost a senior. He's planning to go to college. From what he told me, his parents are lovely people. He's their only kid. They'd be so mad at him if they found out he was gonna be a father. Maybe he never has to know. It's not like he lives anywhere near here anyway. Why should both our lives be ruined?

"Marie? What you doin' in there, girl? Open this door now."

I know I should hide this from Mama. But she'll find out sooner or later. I rise slowly from the bathroom floor and walk to the door, leaving the test on the counter. Flinging open the door, I nudge past her.

"What's this?"

I ignore her, heading to my room.

A rough hand grabs my arm, squeezes hard, and yanks me around. Mama waves the test in front of my face, her own red and splotchy from her afternoon drinks. "You're pregnant, girl? Thought you were smarter than that."

"I did too." Somehow, my voice isn't shaking. Somehow, God's keeping me calm. I did this, yes. I made a mistake. But this doesn't have to be the end of everything I care about. I don't have to end up like Mama, do I?

And then she laughs. It's the kind of screeching laugh I imagine a hyena makes just before it takes a bite into some poor, unsuspecting prey. "I always knew you were good for nothin'. And here you had this high-and-mighty attitude, thinking you was better than me."

I lick my lips and turn to leave again, but her hand keeps a firm grip on my arm. "Let go." A new fear snakes through me. What if she takes me to the doctor, makes me get rid of my baby, like Ruthie's mama did to her? Well, I won't do it. I'll leave before I let her do that to me.

But her lips flatten into a grim line, and she nods. "Well, at least you'll start earning your keep around here. You get a decent bit of money for being a mom on welfare."

How can this be my life? How can I raise a baby here, with her?

I'll figure it out. I have to. Just like I've figured out everything my whole life. Mama won't ruin this baby, not like she tried to ruin me. I'll protect her, my baby—my hand presses against my stomach again. Yes, I'm sure my baby's a her.

A little girl. Some part of me wants to be excited for what's ahead.

But that part is snuffed out right quick as my mama pulls a cigarette from her pocket, lights it, and blows smoke in my face.

10

The room was dark. Ellie squinted from the stage. Where had everyone gone? Why was no one there to hear her?

Then a spotlight lit the floor, where the audience should have been. Nothing remained but emptiness. She could see the grains of the wood. In the quiet space—where at least fifty people had just been—footsteps echoed.

Could it be? Had she finally come?

Ellie laid down her guitar and stepped from the stage. Almost mechanically, she walked toward the dot of light.

Someone else approached from the other side.

Was she finally going to meet her mom?

A tall figure with long hair stood in the shadows.

Ellie couldn't tell much about her, but as Ellie moved closer, it felt like . . . like she knew her somehow. She entered the circle of light. "Mom?"

The figure shook her head, raised her hands, turned away, and began to flee.

"Wait!"

But the figure didn't stop.

Ellie followed the woman out of the café onto the strangely empty street, into the night.

An owl hooted somewhere in the distance.

The figure's long blonde hair bounced behind her as she ran. But under a streetlight, she turned and Ellie saw her face.

It couldn't be . . .

Ellie sat up straight in bed, sweat streaking the back of her neck. Her breath came in spurts, and she shook her head, cleared the sleep from her eyes.

Man, that dream had seemed so real.

But that was impossible.

She rolled over and willed her brain to shut off, to not think about the dream anymore. But all she could see in the dark of her mind was Olivia standing there, illuminated by the light, eyes wide as if she'd been caught doing something she shouldn't have.

Ellie pedaled the stationary bike at the university gym, feeling sticky in her tank top and yoga pants.

Beside her, Lena gripped the handlebars of her own bike, leaning forward and pedaling hard. They both panted, though Lena was clearly working much harder than Ellie. Her friend's lean body glistened with sweat.

Music blared from speakers above them, and about ten televisions mounted around the room flickered different images. Weights clanged and people groaned as they lifted.

All the noises distracted her from her own physical pain—and the dream she'd had this morning. It replayed over and over in her mind.

"That was a nasty hill." Lena sat up straight and continued to move her feet.

Ellie copied her motions. "Totally." Despite the band holding back her hair, a few frizzy tendrils fell in her face. She swatted them away.

Lena took a swig from her water bottle. "When was the last time you came to the gym?"

"Considering I don't have a membership and you had to get me in on one of your buddy passes, I'm not sure." Ellie's calves burned. She lowered the resistance on her bike.

Whew, that was better.

Walking around Nashville kept her mostly trim, but her muscles were straining.

"You should try to get a job here. Then you could work out for free with me."

"Oh, so I can feel like I'm going to die every day?" Ellie pushed out a laugh. "But that's a good idea. I'll check online to see if they're hiring. No one else seems to be."

"You'll figure something out."

Fortunately, just yesterday Grandma and Grandpa had sent her a belated but much-too-generous birthday check in the mail—enough to tide her over for weeks, or even a few months if she tightened her belt. They were too good to her.

The stud in Lena's nose glinted under the

fluorescent lights. "I'll bet being in better shape would help you to sing better."

"How's that?"

"It'd make it easier to hold notes longer and stuff." Lena fiddled with some controls on the bike and stopped pedaling. "Time for a cool down. You want to come stretch?"

Ellie nodded and slid from the bike. Ouch. "Why in the world did I let you convince me this was a good idea?"

Lena wiped a towel across her brow, then led Ellie to a row of six blue mats in front of a wall-size mirror. "You had been cooped up in that apartment for days. You needed to get out." She lowered herself onto the mat and laid flat on her back.

Ellie followed. "Trying to live down the embarrassment from Sunday, I guess. And writing some new material." She wasn't going to let one setback keep her down. Staring up at the ceiling, Ellie waited for the tension to leave her frame, imagining each droplet of sweat expelling a tiny bit of it from her body. "How have your classes been going?"

"Good. I can't believe there are only a few weeks left until midterms." Lena stretched her arms above her head and exhaled slowly.

Ellie copied her. "Time definitely is flying by." Had it really been a week since she'd met her singing idol, Olivia Lovett?

Lena pulled her right knee into her chest. "Speaking of holidays, Mom wanted me to invite you over for Thanksgiving if you don't have plans. It's ridiculously early to be thinking about that, but Mom wants her RSVP list like six weeks in advance, so she has time to plan."

"Ha. Thanks for the invite. I'll be there." Ellie glanced at her friend. "Is your mom going to invite over the latest string of romantic possibilities?"

Lena rolled her eyes, switched legs. "Probably. It's like she thinks I'm an old maid at twenty-two."

"She just wants you to be happy, I'm sure."

"No, she wants to pick out a rich husband for me from among her friends' sons." Lena gritted her teeth and folded one leg across her body to stretch her lower back. "She's always bugging me to move back home and out of our 'scary apartment.' She doesn't seem to get the fact I want a different life than hers. Mom still won't accept that I plan to move to Europe and pursue my art after school is done. She's always tried to turn me into some little princess. At least she has Ava. She's a willing victim."

"Your sister definitely is Miss Priss." Ellie sat up and leaned forward to touch her toes. "But your mom will come around eventually."

"You don't know her like I do. When I chopped my hair and got this"—she pointed to the nose ring—"you'd have thought I'd murdered some-one."

"At least you have a mom." She hadn't meant for that thought to slip out. "Sorry. That was a stupid thing to say."

Lena smacked her forehead as she sat up. "Duh, I'm so dumb. I realize it's hard for you. Any progress on finding yours?"

"I haven't asked Olivia if she knows her yet." Ellie had tried but couldn't. The words got stuck in her throat.

Next to them, a guy climbed on the treadmill, and it whirred to life. Soon he was running, his footsteps pounding in Ellie's ears.

"Why don't you ask? What are you waiting for?"

Ellie twisted the top off her water bottle and took a sip. The condensation on the plastic slicked under her fingers. "To be honest, I'm not sure." She tugged her knees into her chest. "I've started to ask her two times already. I can't figure out why I stop."

Lena maneuvered her towel over her short hair. "Didn't you come here because you wanted to find her?"

"Yeah, but look. I have a wonderful grandma, who's been like a mom to me. Maybe I don't need anyone else. I was fine with that my whole life. Why do I care so much now?" When Daddy had died, a fire for the truth had lit inside of her. Because if she didn't have a mom, that meant she was an orphan. At twenty-one. Something about that was difficult to process. So she'd set out to find out more—and when it turned out her search led her here, a place she'd wanted to come anyway, to pursue her dream—it had seemed like providence. Destiny.

But then why did she feel this hesitation deep in her soul? Why could her lips not form the question when she was with Olivia?

"Come on. Let's keep talking outside." Lena motioned toward the door, and they threaded their way through the crowd of college students.

Two girls, with perfect makeup and not a drop of perspiration on them, stood near the free weights, eyeing a few buff guys.

Ellie and Lena reached the cubby-type lockers near the front desk, where they gathered their things. As they left the building, the crisp breeze lifted the humidity that clung to Ellie's skin.

"Sorry, that just seemed like the kind of conversation we should have in private." Lena turned to Ellie. "You have a right to know where you came from. Why your mom left."

"But my dad must have had his reasons for never telling me, right? I mean, if he'd wanted me to know . . ."

"You can't assume that. Maybe he always intended to tell you. You know, eventually. But then he died before he could. Or maybe he was just waiting for you to ask."

"Could be." *Is that it, God?* Ellie pulled her hair from its binding, and it fell around her shoulders. She scooped it back up and piled it in another messy bun at the top of her head. "I've just been thinking about it a lot since this morning."

"What happened this morning?"

"I had a crazy dream." Ellie's tennis shoes felt tight, and she flexed her toes. "I had just finished singing, and there was a full crowd. Suddenly, everyone was gone, except one person. I got closer and closer to her. With everything in me, I thought, 'I've finally found her.' But then she ran away."

"Bet that didn't feel too good. Were you mad at her?" Lena leaned forward, seemingly engrossed in Ellie's story.

"No, that's the thing. I just felt . . . desperate. Like I was so close to knowing her identity. But it was just a stupid dream, right?"

"I don't know about that. Dreams can reveal our strongest desires."

If that was true, why hadn't she asked Olivia about Marie Culloway yet? The air turned chilly, and Ellie wrapped her fingers around her arms.

"How did it end?"

They started walking toward Lena's car.

"That's where it gets weird. But maybe it

means that dreams don't always have a meaning. Sometimes they're just a bunch of random thoughts thrown together."

"What happened?" With a click of her key fob, Lena unlocked her Prius, and they both climbed inside.

Ellie pictured that moment when the figure had turned. "It's ridiculous. The person I thought was my mom was Olivia."

"I don't think that's ridiculous."

"Clearly she's not my mom. Why in the world would I dream she was?"

"She's been a big influence in your life lately. Like a mentor, really. So perhaps you want your mom to be someone like her—all-around awesome."

Understanding dawned in Ellie's mind. "She is pretty great, isn't she? What would it be like to be the daughter of someone like her? Not the woman . . ."

"Who you're afraid is really your mother?"

She stared at her friend. "What do you mean?" But she knew.

"Right now, you don't have a clue who your mother is. You want to find out, but you're scared. Because what if your mom is . . ."

"An awful human being?"

"Well, she did abandon you." Lena grimaced. "Sorry, that sounded harsh."

"But you're right." Ellie's mother had left.

Daddy had reasoned it away, but maybe he'd just been protecting Ellie from the truth.

"I guess you have to decide if knowing the truth is worth the risk."

Yeah.

And until she figured out what she really wanted, she wouldn't be saying a word about Marie Culloway to anyone—especially Olivia.

Surely the third time really was the charm. Either that or Olivia was in trouble.

She straightened her blazer and picked a stray piece of lint from the lapel as she waited in the bright lobby of Warner & Sons Investment Capital Corp. She and Johnny had been friends for years. He was sure to see how great of an investment opportunity Radiant Records was and want to get in on the ground floor.

Of course, that's what she'd thought about Larry and Antonio, and look how those meetings had panned out. And then there was Chuck, whom she still couldn't reach via phone. His secretary said he was out of the country and his plans were indefinite.

Olivia crossed her legs and smoothed her dress pants as she glanced around the lobby. The red walls spoke of power, while the lush potted plants in the corners served to make visitors feel welcome. A very Johnny move. He'd built this company from the ground up, just like she and Andrew were trying to do. Perhaps he'd appreciate their initiative.

After all, at one time, the name Olivia Lovett meant something in this town.

"Ms. Lovett?" The brunette receptionist moved aside her hands-free phone headset.

Olivia stood. "Yes?"

"Mr. Warner will see you now."

"Wonderful." Olivia took her briefcase in hand and walked down the hallway toward Johnny's office. It would have been nice to meet somewhere less formal, maybe a coffee shop or restaurant, but Johnny was a busy man. When she got to the large cherry wood door, Olivia knocked.

"Come in."

She entered to find her friend sitting behind an ornate desk, eyes on his computer screen. Floor-to-ceiling windows covered nearly all of the wall space, granting a beautiful view of downtown Nashville from the seventh floor.

Johnny looked up and cracked a smile, the weathered lines on his tan face increasing. "Olivia dear, how are you?" He stood to greet her, and she walked into his open arms, throwing a kiss onto his right cheek. His jacket smelled of peppermint, like always.

"I'm fabulous, Johnny." Olivia moved to the other side of his desk and took a seat in his visitor's chair. She had to remain calm, not let her desperation show. Her insurance was still refusing to reimburse her for her surgeries and therapy sessions. If she didn't secure her half of the finances, then their record label would fail before it'd begun. She couldn't let that happen, especially since she'd found Ellie. "How're Nancy and the kids?"

Johnny settled onto his desk chair again and picked up a framed photo. He turned it so she could see. "Nancy's still running the country club fundraisers. The kids are getting older and wiser, I guess. Seth's a senior in college, and as you know, Thomas and Jude are here working for me."

"That must be such fun."

"It is, it is." Johnny set the picture back in its place and steepled his fingers in front of him. "But that's not what you're here to talk about, is it?"

Olivia's insides squirmed, but she couldn't let her nerves show—even to an old friend. She had to portray the confident businesswoman now, no matter how she felt inside. "No, it's not." She pulled their business plan from her briefcase and slid it across the table toward Johnny. "I don't know if you've heard, but Andrew Grant and I are starting up a new label."

Johnny reached for the glasses hanging around his neck and slid them up the bridge of his nose. Then he took the portfolio in hand. "I'd heard rumors that you wanted to get back into the business, yes."

"Right." Olivia continued to talk, while he flipped through the plan. "Andrew and I know the ropes—from both sides, performer and business executive—so we have a unique angle going into this."

"Then I'm sure you've done your research and found that start-up record labels are having a difficult time succeeding in the long-term?"

She'd anticipated his concern. "Of course there will always be trouble with startups, but we feel we have exactly what it takes to succeed." To illustrate her points, she directed him to a few specific pages in the document he held.

He was quiet for a few moments—so quiet Olivia could hear murmurs from the office next door.

It sounded as if someone was watching a tournament or game of some sort. The person's voice alternated between cheering and disappointed shouting.

Olivia's pulse kept time as she waited for Johnny to respond. *Favor, Lord. I know I screwed up by using the seed money on my voice. But I also know you can make this work if you desire it.*

"What exactly are you asking of me, Olivia?" Johnny's voice had changed from warm to slightly cool. His business voice.

"I'm searching for investors to back our venture." The answer sounded far too simple and abrupt, but what else could she say?

"I see. And how much are you asking?"

She swallowed her anxiety and attempted to keep her voice steady, then named her price. "I came to you because I know you're always looking for exciting, new opportunities. Andrew and I are positive we can make a go of this, given our combined experience and connections in the country music world. A successful go."

Johnny removed his glasses and rubbed his temples. "Olivia, I have to be honest with you. You've been out of the game for a while. Your connections can't be what they once were. The business has changed drastically, even in the last few years. You know I love you like family, but I can't hand over the amount of money you're asking. I can't even hand over half of that."

He acted like she'd been out of the business for decades instead of a handful of years. Time to lay it on thick—whatever it took. "Look, Johnny. I can appreciate your line of thinking here. But even though things have changed in the industry, I still know it. I've kept up with the latest industry news, am friends with a lot of people, and can make this a success. What's more, I have an artist I'm confident can be the next star."

Johnny studied her. "Who might that be?"

"Her name is Ellie Evans, and, Johnny, let me tell you—"

"Isn't that the girl who left the stage early at Koinonia on Sunday?"

How did he know that? He'd never attended church a day in his life. "She had an emotional reaction to—"

"Doesn't matter, Olivia. I'm not an expert in the music industry, but I do know that artists shouldn't let their emotions get the better of them. If you say the girl's got talent, I believe you. However, if she's not a professional, there's no way I want my money backing her."

Olivia inhaled and nodded. Tears pricked the back of her eyes, but she held them in.

If she couldn't get Johnny Warner, someone who was like a surrogate uncle, to give her money, then what chance did she have of getting any investors, especially this last-minute?

"I understand." She stood. "Thanks for your time."

Johnny stroked his mustache. "Tell you what. If you can prove to me this girl has what it takes, I'll do what I can to help you find the right investor."

"Thank you. That would be great." But after years of friendship, Olivia knew virtually nothing could change Johnny's mind once it was made up.

Still, it was kind of him to say it.

Olivia hugged him again, took her business plan from his hands, and shoved it back in her briefcase. She made her way into the hall, down the elevator, and out toward the parking garage to retrieve her car. What was she thinking? Why had she ever thought she could do this—be a businesswoman, succeed where so many had failed? Sure, she'd been a country star once upon a time, but those days were long gone.

Would she always be poor Marie Culloway, trapped in generations of failure?

Her phone buzzed inside her purse, and she groaned.

What if it was Andrew? Her friend would be able to hear defeat in her voice right away. Maybe he'd even figure out that she didn't have the funds she'd promised to get this venture off the ground.

Olivia hit Ignore without looking at the screen and kept walking toward her car.

The sooner she faced the truth, the better off she'd be. Her career had come and gone. End of story.

The buzz of her phone indicated a voicemail. From Ellie.

Wait. Olivia was thinking about this all wrong. It wasn't about *her* anymore. Instead, she could be a part of making someone else's dream a reality. And despite the way Ellie had messed up on Sunday, she was still that person—someone

Olivia could help guide through this sticky business.

And somehow, that idea tasted nearly as sweet as the thought of her own comeback.

11

Second chances might actually exist.

Ellie braced herself against the wind as she stepped off the bus and headed toward the recording studio address Olivia had given her. She tightened her grip on the guitar strap that hugged her torso. Orange and red leaves swirled on the sidewalk, and Johnny Cash belted a tune from a nearby restaurant gearing up for the lunchtime crowd. Ellie spotted the address she was looking for and opened the heavy doors.

The studio wasn't much to look at on the outside, but once inside she could see why Olivia had chosen it. The lobby floors glistened with polish, and exotic fish danced in a large aquarium in the corner. No one was in the lobby to greet Ellie, but she quickly found the signage for the room she needed and headed down the corridor, located the right door, and opened it to reveal a small recording booth.

Olivia waved her in. "Good to see you, Ellie."

"I didn't know you'd be here." But she was glad for it. Ever since she'd opened up to Olivia, Ellie didn't feel so intimidated by the former singer's presence. In fact, in many ways, it had a calming effect—almost like Olivia was nurturing and caring for Ellie.

"I can't stay for the whole thing but wanted to get you settled, make introductions, things like that." Olivia gestured around the dim room. Behind her, a middle-aged guy sat at a soundboard and set of computers, headphones on, adjusting levels and getting things ready for Ellie's session. Next to him, a pizza box lay open, a few slices still waiting to be devoured.

"That's fine. So you said on the phone you want me to lay three tracks?"

Olivia plopped onto a stool and motioned for Ellie to take a seat across from her. "Do as many as you can in the few hours you're here. But yes, three would be ideal. As I said yesterday, try to give a good sampling of your original work—a ballad, something upbeat, and then maybe something in between."

Ellie nodded. If only she had a pen and paper to write this down. But what she'd prepared would work fine. She just needed to relax. "It's really nice of you to help me out like this."

"It's nothing. Grady here owes me a favor, and he had some time open up. Even if our label can't take you on, you need a good demo to get quality gigs."

"You mean my self-made demo from my dinosaur laptop didn't do the trick?" Ellie forced out a laugh and kneaded a knot at the base of her neck.

Olivia's mouth crinkled at the corners. "Hopefully you won't need this demo for long, but in case it takes some time to convince Andrew to let me sign you or it doesn't work out, this gives you a way to get some backup singing gigs and more prestigious open-mic nights around town."

She didn't deserve Olivia's generosity. "Why are you doing this? I mean, if you don't end up signing me . . ."

"What's in it for me?"

Ellie swallowed hard, nodded. "Yeah."

"I told you, Ellie. I believe in you. And I know how many times I almost gave up. It would have been nice to have a little help along the way."

"Thank—"

"Let's get this show on the road." A gruff voice barked from behind Olivia. The audio engineer tapped his pen on the desk. He'd moved the headphones down around his neck, and his hair held an indention where they'd been.

"All right, Grady, don't get your knickers in a knot." Olivia stood. "Ellie Evans, meet Grady O'Brien."

Ellie stuck out her hand, and the guy crushed her fingers as he looked her up and down with a wary eye. She glanced at the studio on the other side of the glass, where a microphone sat next to a stool. Simple, but all she really needed. "How does this work?"

Grady rolled his eyes. "Olivia, did you bring me a green one?"

Olivia patted him on the back. "You be nice, Grady." She checked her watch. "I've gotta go. Ellie, don't worry. His bark is worse than his bite. Make me proud."

Ellie nodded as Olivia left. How did she have it all together? Olivia was so polished, so easy around people. Ellie didn't have the same charisma and charm. All she knew was she loved music and that it had the power to move her.

But it also had the power to get her where she wanted to go. And she'd do anything to become like Olivia—a country music dynamo. Time to shed the meek country mouse and take charge, in spite of her flub-up last Sunday.

She pulled her guitar from its case, fumbling only a little despite her clammy hands.

Grady watched her with an amused look—or was that a sneer?

She pulled her shoulders back. "Should I head on in there?"

"Be my guest." Grady eased back in his chair and watched her every move.

She approached the stool.

A cord snaked its way across the room.

Ellie leaned over, snatched it, and plugged in her guitar. Then she sat on the stool.

A music stand loomed in front of her. A pair of headphones hung on the edge.

She slid them over her hair onto her ears. With a quick flick of her wrist, she adjusted the microphone, so it sat right in front of her lips. She was ready to rock.

Now what? She took off the headphones, set her guitar down, and walked back to the engineer's booth. "Am I supposed to play and sing at the same time? Or are you recording the tracks separately?"

"Look who thinks she knows everything there is to know about recording." Grady spun his pen between his thumb and middle finger.

Ellie's cheeks flamed. She'd never said that. "I . . ."

"By the way, you can just talk into the mic out there, and I'll hear you in here. No need to come trouncing in here every time you need to ask a question."

Why was he being so mean? Yeah, this was her first time. So what? But she'd dealt with rowdy customers and jerks her whole life, first at the bowling alley where she'd worked in high school, then playing the Lizard Lounge and other such establishments. She could handle Grady O'Brien. Ellie rose to her full five-foot-two-inch height. "Thanks for the information. So. Play at the same time or separate tracks?"

Grady pursed his lips, but something akin to respect rippled in his eyes. "Let's go for a live-recorded sound, since we've only got a few hours. I find that newbies do better with that anyway. Most aren't used to singing without the comfort of their guitars in their hands."

Ellie nodded and zoomed back to her seat on the stool. Inside, her heart hammered, but she took three long breaths to calm herself. This was no different than playing in her room. She couldn't think about what this demo would or wouldn't mean for her career. All she had to do was play.

"Whenever you're ready."

She launched into her upbeat number. When she finished, she peered through the glass, trying to find Grady's eyes. A glare kept her from seeing him.

"Again." Grady's voice cut into her headphones through the silence.

She swallowed, nodded. Five more times she played that song. She expected to hear "again" for a sixth time.

"Next song."

Her heart gave a little fist bump to her chest. "Improvement."

A chuckle came through her headphones.

She played through the next two songs several times each, until Grady was satisfied.

"All right, time's up. My next appointment is here." Grady's voice had grown softer over the course of their session.

Ellie's fingers ached from playing, but her voice felt strong and powerful. She glanced at the clock above the glass. Two hours had flown by—and she'd loved every minute, once she'd decided to ignore Grady.

And for some reason, he'd seemed to admire that.

She packed up her guitar and headed back through the door.

Grady stood and stretched. "You did good, kid. Olivia was right to like you."

"She did do well." From the corner of the room stepped a woman not much older than Ellie—but instead of Ellie's rumpled jean jacket and Chucks, she wore a crisp blouse and stylish skirt. Something about her seemed familiar.

"Th-thank you." She should be bold. Ellie stuck out her hand. "Ellie Evans."

The girl shook her hand. "Nice to meet you. I'm Kacie Hayes."

Ah, so that's how Ellie knew her. "You just signed with Monument, didn't you?"

The girl smiled, and her white teeth sparkled. "I did. Grady here is helping produce my first album. And I'm getting a tour set up for the spring. It's all very exciting."

What would it be like to be Kacie Hayes? She had everything Ellie wanted. "Congrats."

"You know, Ellie, I'll be looking for some backup singers for my tour." Kacie pulled a business card from her purse and extended it. "Why don't you send me your demo once Grady's done producing it? I'll share it with my manager and see what he thinks. I liked your sound."

"Sweet applesauce. Thank you. I will."

"Great." Kacie nodded toward the room. "Guess I'd better get in there." She waved and swooped through the door.

Ellie watched her for a moment, then shook herself from a daze. She thanked Grady and headed back outside. She didn't know what tomorrow held, but today had been a victory. Small, perhaps, but a victory all the same.

12

It was time to come clean.

Olivia pulled up to Andrew's house but couldn't bring herself to go in just yet. She sat in her car, letting the heat from the vents warm her. Tall elms lined the street on either side and wrought-iron black lampposts rose up to meet them. A lawnmower whirred in the background—a neighbor perfecting his winter grass, green despite the approaching season. Sunlight poked through the clouds, giving no true indication of whether this would be a sunny day . . . or a dreary one.

But for Olivia's part, she knew. This morning she had to tell Andrew she had no money to offer for her part of their venture. Even after another week of searching for investors, showing off Ellie's demo to any friends who would listen, a bunch of noes still rang in her ears.

How could today be anything but dreary?

Gathering her courage, she shut off her car, opened her door, and pulled the two drinks from her cup holders. The cold seeped into her cheeks, but the warmth from the cups saved her hands from the chill as she made her way up Andrew's front walk toward his two-story brick home. Once there, she rang his doorbell with her elbow.

A few moments later, Andrew opened the door. He wore sweatpants and a tight white undershirt that showed off his sculpted chest and biceps. "You're early." His normally gelled hair was rumpled.

Is this what he looked like when he'd just rolled out of bed?

Adorable.

She shook the thought away. "Am I? Sorry. The Starbucks line must have gone faster than usual."

"It's no problem." Andrew motioned her inside, and Olivia stepped through the doorway.

The delicate scent of cinnamon greeted her, and her stomach growled in response. Until they officially launched their label and leased a space, they'd taken to meeting in Andrew's living room three times a week. Olivia brought the coffee, and Andrew provided the breakfast.

She handed him his latte.

He took the lid off and inhaled deeply. "Ah. Nothing like the smell of coffee to wake me up in the morning."

Olivia settled onto a chair at the small kitchen table. "As if you need that. You have a teenaged daughter." A daughter who had clearly decorated this place. Every time Olivia stopped by, she was amazed at the fact Andrew Grant had allowed Grace to put up pink wallpaper in the kitchen alcove, line the windows with lacy curtains, and keep a crystal vase with flowers as a permanent fixture on the table.

Andrew settled his hip against the kitchen counter and placed the lid back on his coffee before taking a swig. "True enough. She likes to blast her music in the bathroom at six a.m."

"I can't even imagine." Except she had. So many times. Olivia cleared her throat. Time to get this over with. "So I have something I really need to talk to you about."

Andrew slid onto the chair across from her. It squeaked on the hardwood floor. "First, how are things going with Ellie? Are you still feeling the same about her?"

"Like she's the one? Yes." Olivia sipped her caramel apple spice. She lowered the drink and traced the *Olivia* scrawled in the barista's cursive across the cup. "Things are good. The demo was a success. I've helped her get more gigs. She's done very well."

"Better than she did at the church, I hope." Andrew stared at Olivia. His eyes bored into her, as if he could sense something was wrong.

"I told you the story behind that. I've moved past it, and so should you."

"Hard to do when I'm courting a professional like Nick Perry." Andrew leaned back in his seat and tapped the table. "Did I tell you I got him booked at Lorenzo's?"

Olivia nearly choked on her cider. "You didn't."

Andrew stood and headed to his cupboard. "I did." He pulled a cup down and filled it with water from his fridge dispenser, then slid it across the table to Olivia.

"Thanks." She took a drink of water, the cider still burning the back of her throat.

"I think it's time to talk about signing him, Olivia. He's ready. We're ready."

How could she tell him they weren't ready, because they only had half the funds they were supposed to have? She'd messed up big time, thinking she could fix this on her own. Not only was she risking her own future—her own dreams—but that of her good friend too.

A good friend, who looked much too attractive staring at her like he was, sitting in his pajamas, his light-brown chest hair poking from beneath his V neck. "Um, could you go change before we chat? I'm not used to you wearing something like that."

Andrew cocked his head. "Oh, you prefer Andrew Grant, the boardroom exec?"

"Not necessarily. I just don't need to be talking to Andrew Grant, the sexy pajama model." Oh my, had those words really just come out of her mouth? She was seriously flustered—and no, it didn't have anything to do with how casual he looked. And how much she liked the more casual vibe he was giving off around her lately.

No, it had everything to do with the fact that

she was about to drop a bomb on their friendship. The thought sobered her.

Andrew grinned and stood. "All right, I'll throw on some real clothes. Be right back. Go ahead and cut yourself a slice of coffee cake if you want. It's in the oven on Warm."

He slipped down the hall, and Olivia set her head in her hands. She couldn't do this to him— maybe there was another way.

But hadn't she been racking her brain for another way for over a week? She'd been selfish to risk the label seed money on the off chance she could sing again. Now she had to face the consequences.

Yes, you've racked your brain . . . but have you prayed?

The thought nudged against her conscience. Sure, she'd offered a desperate prayer in Johnny Warner's office—and a few more before that— but when he said no, she figured she should stop bothering God with this. He'd already given her so many second chances. She didn't deserve more.

Still . . . "Okay, God. If anyone can fix this, it's you. But if you choose not to, would you please give me the strength to tell Andrew the truth?"

Olivia sat there a moment longer and blew out a breath. She stood and walked to the oven, slipped a pair of oven mitts onto her hands, and took out the coffee cake. Mmm. She could almost taste the treat now. Though would she really be able to enjoy it, knowing how much pain she was about to inflict upon its creator?

On the table, her phone jangled in her purse.

She plopped the cake on the stovetop, got rid of the oven mitts, and hurried over.

The caller ID showed a restricted number.

"Hello?"

"Olivia? This is Chuck Bernstein."

"Chuck. So good to hear from you." When she'd been making the rounds looking for investors, she'd never heard back from the producer of her old label. She knew he'd left the record industry to start his own investment firm, and had contacted him to see if he'd want to invest a little money. Olivia had begun to suspect his secretary never gave him her message. "How are you?"

"Good, good. Listen, I know I'm calling early, but I'm leaving for Europe in an hour."

"Wow. Business must be good."

"It is. Very good."

Something like hope fluttered in Olivia's chest. She glanced down the hallway, not sure if she wanted Andrew to overhear. "Congratulations." Olivia strode to the door, opened it, and stepped out into the cold.

"Thanks." She could picture her white-haired

friend waving her comment off. "I'm calling you because I heard that you're starting a record label."

"I am." Her toes began to grow cold within her boots, so she paced up and down Andrew's driveway. "I left a message with Linda last week."

"Yes, I'm sorry about that. Your message got buried in a pile the size of Texas."

"That's okay." Maybe he was simply calling to apologize. He'd always been a considerate man. Probably didn't want to leave her hanging.

"I want to invest."

She stopped in her tracks. "What? You're kidding."

"Not a bit."

A hovering cloud in the sky moved away from Olivia, and the sunlight filtered down around her. "Don't you want to see a business plan, hear a demo of the first artists we're considering? Something?"

"Anything you touch is gold, and I want in." Then he told her the amount he wanted to invest, and she nearly dropped to her knees.

"You're sure?" Olivia's breaths came in sputters.

"Send over a contract, and I'll have the funds wired into your label's account this week."

They exchanged more details, and Olivia hung up. She barely registered the fact that her teeth chattered as she went back inside Andrew's house. God had given her a miracle after all. A pure miracle.

She still had to convince Andrew that Ellie was right for the label—but after what had just happened, that was a piece of cake. Her mouth quirked. A piece of coffee cake.

Wait, he'd said he had booked Nick at Lorenzo's, right? Olivia checked her watch. It wasn't too early to call.

"Hello?"

"Steve Lorenzo, as I live and breathe. This is Olivia Lovett."

"Olivia! How is the new business venture coming along?"

"Andrew and I are really excited about it. Actually, I was hoping you could do me a favor." Olivia paced. "An artist we are hoping to sign is already playing in your showcase next week—Andrew arranged it. Any chance you could open a spot for one more that night?"

Steve sighed. "We filled those spots months ago. The only reason we were able to squeeze in Andrew's guy was due to a cancellation."

Would asking for one more tiny miracle be pushing her luck? *Please, God?* "Now, Steve, you know I'm not one to nag. But if you could even squeeze her in for one song—that's only three minutes—I'd owe you."

"I'm sorry, but—"

"I'll get Rachel to make you some of those cream puffs you love."

"That's not fair."

"And I'll convince some of my friends in the industry to visit your mom's assisted care facility, like we did a few years back. You'll be the favorite son."

"Until Ma decides to change her mind again." A groan came through the line. "You're impossible to say no to, Olivia. Fine. I'll make sure your act gets one song."

"You're amazing."

"Yeah, yeah. Just make sure I get a double batch of those cream puffs. And try to get Josie Monroe. She's Ma's new favorite."

"You got it." Olivia hung up and couldn't keep the grin from overtaking her face. She walked back toward the kitchen, where Andrew sat in business-casual wear, his hair combed, not a lock out of place.

"I thought you'd left but saw your purse. Everything all right?" He slid his last bite of coffee cake into his mouth.

"Better than all right." Olivia sat on the chair next to him and pulled it up close. "What if I told you that I just secured us enough funding to sign not one but two artists to our label right away? It means we'll have to take on an investor, but—"

"I'd say I could kiss you."

The comment broke Olivia's focus for a

moment. She stared at Andrew, noticed a crumb of coffee cake at the corner of his mouth. A nervous guffaw pushed its way through her throat. "Not only that, but I got Ellie booked at Lorenzo's the same night as Nick."

"Seriously?" Andrew's eyes held respect—and something else Olivia didn't want to examine.

She couldn't entertain thoughts of Andrew like that. They had too much staked on their business partnership to explore anything more. "Yes."

"You're sure about Ellie?"

"I am. And you're sure about Nick?"

"Yes." Andrew adjusted his glasses. "All right, let's do it. Let's sign them both."

Olivia squealed and threw her arms around his neck, then pecked a kiss onto his cheek. "This is the best day ever."

Andrew pulled back and stared at her. "Hey now. I said I could kiss you, not the other way around."

Olivia smirked. "Maybe some other time, Mr. Grant. Right now, we have a couple of artists to make very happy."

"We have to wait for our lawyer to draw up the contracts and all that. Don't get ahead of yourself."

"I'm not. I'm just . . . delighted." Olivia settled back onto her chair. It was happening. They'd found the artists who would help get their label off the ground.

"I hope they're both as successful as we're anticipating."

Was that a bit of challenge in Andrew's voice? "Oh, they will be." Olivia took a piece of her hair, twirled it between her fingers, and looked off to the side, feigning nonchalance. "Of course, my artist will be more successful than yours. But I won't say, 'I told you so.'"

"Oh, really?" Andrew leaned forward in his seat. Playful fire sparked in his eyes. "How about a friendly wager?"

"I'm listening."

"We see whose artist is most successful. Whoever wins, the other gets a prize. Sound fun?"

"Uh-uh. I'm not agreeing to anything till I hear all the conditions."

"Atta girl." Andrew's hands flew as he talked. "How about whoever can get their artist on *Nashville Insider* first wins."

The nationally syndicated television talk show would be a tough gig to land, but with more training and maybe a hit single, Ellie could do it. And the fact Olivia knew the host from her own appearances on the set couldn't hurt. "What does the winner get?"

"Hmm. If I win, you have to go camping with Grace and me next summer."

He'd been trying to get Olivia to go camping with them for the last several years. And she wasn't exactly the outdoorsy type.

But she was confident in Ellie. She wouldn't need to brave the woods and worry about sleeping among the bears and mosquitoes.

"All right, and if I win, you have to get up and sing karaoke. My choice of time and place." Imagining straight-laced Andrew singing onstage made her giggle. She'd pick a really hilarious song for him too, like Shania Twain's "Man! I Feel Like a Woman" or something equally as embarrassing.

"I can live with those terms."

She stuck out her hand. "Then you have yourself a wager, Mr. Grant."

He pulled her closer to him and looked into her eyes with a mischievous gleam in his. "You're on, Ms. Lovett. You're on."

13

"Ladies and gentleman, the library will be closing in fifteen minutes." The intercom squawked in the expansive room where Ellie perused the last in a stack of magazines she'd found in the periodical section. "Please make your final selections and head to the front checkout stations before that time."

All around her, library patrons sat at rows of long tables, several short lamps sitting atop each one. Some people gathered their backpacks and books. Others still typed furiously on their laptops. The white columns of the main branch of the Nashville Public Library lined the room and ended in great arches above her head. A chandelier sparkled from the center, reflecting the late afternoon sun through the huge windows on either side of the room.

Ellie turned the page of the latest issue of *American Songwriter* magazine and continued reading about rising star Keith Johnson and how his hit singles had shaped several other songwriters' styles over the last year. When she finished the article, she closed the magazine and smiled. She may not have a lot of money in her pocket, but life was good. Without time spent working at the diner, she'd been able to write three new songs in the last week. They still needed tweaking and finessing, but it felt awesome to let the words flow from her pen like they hadn't in a while.

"Fancy seeing you here." Nick stood at her side, a backpack and his guitar flung over his shoulders. He had a beanie tugged over his curls.

She hadn't seen him since that day in class two and a half weeks ago when he'd helped her perfect her song. He'd been so sweet and encouraging. She'd thought about calling him up, buying him a cup of coffee to thank him— but his girlfriend probably wouldn't approve of that.

"Same to you. What are you up to?" She gathered the pile of magazines into her arms.

"Just getting some books to read in my free time." Nick picked up the last magazine and looked over the cover. "You studying?" He handed it to Ellie.

"Of course. I've gotta become as good at songwriting as somebody I know."

A nearby student with bloodshot eyes shushed them, running two hands through her unkempt hair like a crazy scientist.

Nick nodded toward the stairs, and Ellie grabbed her purse.

She placed the magazines on a re-shelving cart and met him at the top of the stairs, then directed his attention back toward Miss Intense. "Someone must be studying for midterms. I can't believe it's already the middle of October."

"Yep. Halloween is right around the corner." They descended the stairs and walked through the lobby. Nick held the front door open for Ellie, and she slid past him and into the fading daylight.

The square outside the library was filled with stone benches, patches of newly mown green grass, and a small garden—a peaceful place to sit and ponder life, if it hadn't been so chilly out. It was well below the seventy-degree temps they usually enjoyed this time of year.

She shivered and pulled her jacket tighter around her shoulders.

Nick eyed her. "Where are you parked?"

"I don't have a car. My bus stop is just over there." She burrowed her hands into her coat, but the pockets were well worn and didn't do much to keep her warm.

"You want a ride?"

"I can't inconvenience you like that."

"I don't mind." Nick pulled out a set of keys and jangled them in front of her. "Where are you going?"

"Home." She told him the crossroads.

He frowned. "That's the opposite side of town as I was headed—and I do need to be somewhat on time. But tell you what. If you're not busy,

I have a quick stop to make first. It's kind of a tough one, though. You can stay in the car if you want."

"What kind of stop?"

"Just performing a set. But for a bit of an unusual crowd."

"I'm used to unusual." She thought back to her last Lizard Lounge audience and smiled. "But I don't want to get in the way."

"You wouldn't be. In fact, I'd love to spend some time with you."

She liked the sound of that—too much. After all, he had a girlfriend.

Ellie weighed her options. She had a ton of work to do on her songs, plus an audition with Kacie Hayes to prep for. But Nick's car sounded a lot more comfortable and inviting than the bus.

"If you don't think it would bother Lynette."

"Lynette?" Nick laughed and gave her a strange look. "Oh, she won't mind."

"All right."

Nick led her to a small pickup with peeling blue paint.

She peered through the window. "Is there a place for your guitar?"

"I'll just throw it in back."

She stared at him in horror.

He chuckled. "Kidding. There's just enough space between us for it."

"I was about to smack you. My guitar may be old, but it's family."

He unlocked his door, climbed in, reached across, and swung hers open. "Was it your mom's or dad's?"

"Dad's." She climbed in next to him. The truck smelled like pine, and Ellie spied the reason—an air freshener shaped like a tree—hanging from the rearview mirror. "My mom left after I was born."

"Oh, that's rough." Nick started the truck, and it sputtered to life. John Denver blared from the speakers, and Nick turned the volume down.

"Wow, you like the old stuff." Ellie set her purse at her feet and put on her seatbelt. "And don't worry. I'm fine with it. My mom, I mean." As fine as someone could be who had moved here partially to track her down.

Nick aimed half the vents at Ellie.

Cool air blasted her for a moment and then slowly turned warmer.

"Let me know if you get too hot."

Finally, heat poured out, and she held up her hands to relish the feel. The way Nick took care of her—well, he was a good friend.

Friend. Just a friend. Her heart had better fall in line with her brain soon, or she'd have trouble on her hands.

She cleared her throat. "So tell me more about yourself, Nick Perry."

He pulled out of the parking lot and headed west. "What do you want to know?"

She shrugged. "The basics."

"I was born on a cold, windy night—"

"Ha-ha." His guitar slid toward her, and her hand darted out to steady it. "You know what I mean."

"Oh, right." He leaned back in his seat, arms at attention. How could he appear relaxed and alert at the same time? "Not much to tell. Oldest of six kids. Parents were busy all the time. Came to Nashville to attend Belmont, decided to stay."

"What did you major in?"

"Commercial Music, with emphases in performance and songwriting."

"Wow." See, she really couldn't compete with this guy. But for the first time, instead of feeling inadequate and slightly jealous of him, Ellie felt happy for him. It certainly was his time to get a record deal and move forward in his career—even if that meant it wasn't hers.

"I came out here and have been playing ever since. My family is pretty supportive, even though my parents often ask me when I'm going to get a real job." Nick tugged off his beanie and rustled his curls absently. "I tell them I can't imagine working a nine-to-five, even if that means scraping to make ends meet. Just isn't me and wouldn't be true to my dreams."

"I know what you mean. I was super close to leaving that day we met, but that wouldn't have been true to *my* dreams." Ellie stuck the edge of her thumbnail in her mouth.

"I remember." Nick pulled up to a red stoplight. "I'm really glad you didn't leave." He reached across and took hold of her free hand.

She glanced up, and her eyes locked with his. Ellie swallowed, hard. She pulled her hand away. "I'm not sure your girlfriend would appreciate that."

Nick's brow wrinkled. "Girlfriend? I don't have a girlfriend."

"But that night at Bernadette's. Lynette. The girl who claimed to be your biggest fan. I thought . . ."

The light turned green and Nick pulled into a large parking lot. He kept the motor idling and turned to face her. "Lynette is literally the president of my fan club. One she started. She's kind of crazy yet sweet. But she is most definitely not my girlfriend."

Words strung together shouldn't have the power to make her heart thud. She nibbled her lips to keep from grinning, then changed the subject. "Where are you taking me?"

He turned off the truck and pointed to a sign.

She looked at Nick. He couldn't be serious.

But, clearly, he was. "I told you, you can stay in the car if you want."

• • •

"Oh, Nick." Ellie's whisper got lost in the big room filled with toys and child-sized tables.

Against one wall, a little girl read on a bright-green couch. Every now and then, the corners of her eyes would crinkle, and a grin would spread across her face, revealing a few missing teeth. At a table across the room, two boys, probably about ten or eleven years old, played checkers. The red and black pieces scraped across the board when they moved them. Other kids scattered about the room played with a variety of dolls, GI Joes, and LEGOs.

It all seemed so normal.

Except for the scarf on the little girl's bald head. And the wheelchairs where the boys sat playing checkers. And the IVs that dripped, monitors that beeped, and floors that reeked of bleach and wax.

The smells reminded her of Daddy's last days, when he was in a coma from the car accident and she didn't know whether he'd live or die.

She stood there, frozen.

Nick grabbed Ellie's hand and squeezed.

A tingle shot up her arm. They walked farther into the room.

One little boy, maybe seven, looked up from his video game. His glasses took up most of his face. "Nick!" He dropped the video game controller.

Other kids echoed the cry, and the few adult volunteers in the room waved in greeting.

Nick laughed and approached the boy. "Brian, what's up, my man?" He leaned over and shot him a gentle high-five. He continued around the room, saying hi to the other children.

Obviously, he'd been here before. Many times.

"Is that your girlfriend?" Brian stared at Ellie, his blue eyes, like sapphires, piercing her heart.

"No, she's a friend. Her name is Ellie."

Ellie waved, a knot in her throat.

The kids smiled back at her.

"Can you all say hi and make her feel welcome?"

"Yeah." The little chatterboxes giggled and whispered—loudly—in response to Nick's introduction. Was . . . was it possible that some of them might actually die? Daddy had been young at thirty-eight, but that was nothing compared with these little angels.

"Nick?" The girl with the book on the couch scrunched her nose and smiled. "Are you gonna sing for us?"

"I sure am, Cindy Lou Who." Nick pulled the guitar case from his back, unzipped it, removed the guitar, and positioned it with the strap over his shoulder.

The kids cheered, and the ones on the floor scooted closer.

Someone pressed against Ellie.

"Will you come sit with me?" Brian stared up at her.

If she could cry, she'd need a whole fleet of buckets to catch the tears. "Of course I will, honey."

The boy snatched her hand and dragged her to the ground. Well, tried to drag. He plopped onto the floor, and she followed suit, sitting cross-legged beside him.

A tiny girl crawled into her lap just as Nick sat on a stool in front and began to strum. The girl's purple scarf tickled Ellie's nose, and it was all Ellie could do not to crush her in a bear hug.

Nick started with "The Wheels on the Bus."

Ellie did the motions with the kids.

Their movements may have been slower, and some couldn't do them at all, but they had fun.

Then he switched to "Twinkle, Twinkle, Little Star" and other kid favorites.

A few times, Ellie caught him staring at her.

He ended the last song and stood. "Do you guys want to know a secret?"

"Yeah!" A chorus of sweet shouts rang out.

"My friend Ellie here is also a singer."

The little girl whipped around, her eyes wide as inflated balloons. "You are?" Her voice floated before Ellie in awe.

Ellie brought her nose to the girl's. "I am."

With a giggle, the girl buried her face in Ellie's shirt.

Brian turned to her, tugged on her sleeve. "Will you sing a song for us right now?"

How could she refuse those eyes? "Sure. What would you like to hear?"

" 'Jesus Loves Me.' " He blinked, so innocent.

She swallowed, smiled. "You got it." Ellie nudged the tiny girl from her lap, then rose from the floor and dusted off the seat of her pants. Nick glanced at her, and she swallowed again. When she got to him, she turned to face the children.

He plucked out the melody, then strummed, slow.

"Jesus loves me, this I know, for the Bible tells me so."

Nick's strong baritone joined hers in the room—and in the crevices of her soul. "Little ones to Him belong."

"They are weak, but He is strong." Ellie closed her eyes. The sound was better than anything she'd heard on the Nashville stage.

This wasn't a performance like that. It was . . . different.

When they finished, Ellie glanced at Brian, and his grin became a beacon.

"All right, guys, thanks for letting us sing for you. I'll be back next week, okay?" Nick removed his guitar and set it in its case.

Ellie moved back to Brian and knelt. She wrapped her arms around him and buried her nose in his peach fuzz. He smelled like crayons and cherry cough syrup, and she could feel his bones beneath her hands. Oh, this poor child.

"Thanks for singing. That's my favorite song."

Her throat felt warm. "You're so welcome. Maybe I can come back with Nick sometime. What do you say?" She pulled back.

He bobbed his head. "I'd love it."

As hard as it had been to come into this room, it was even harder to leave.

Nick led her out the front entrance and toward his pickup.

She climbed in without a word, her chest tightening with every moment.

Nick hopped onto the driver's seat and fired up the engine. He turned the heater knob up a notch, then glanced sideways at her. "You did great in there."

"Thanks." She paused. "That was my first time in a hospital since my dad died."

Nick groaned, and his forehead sank until it touched the wheel. "I'm such an idiot, asking you to go there. I didn't even think about that."

"No, it was nice. Hard but nice. To see their faces, to know that I helped bring them a little happiness to brighten their days." Especially since no one knew how many days they had left. "It just was great to perform for someone else, instead of performing to try to reach some goal. They inspired me."

"They're amazing kids, aren't they?" Nick's voice was soft. "I started going there regularly when one of the kids from the community center—Tommy—got cancer and was placed there."

"Who are you, Nick Perry?"

"What do you mean?"

She reached tentatively for his hand.

He grasped it tightly.

Ellie looked up into his eyes. "You're like a saint or something. First the community center, then the hospital. And you've been so kind to me."

"That part isn't so hard." Nick's thumb stroked her hand. "But I'm no saint. I've got a lot of trash buried in my past. Stuff I want to leave there. It reminds me of who I used to be. Who I don't ever want to be again. And how God's changed me."

The way he was talking, she knew the answer but had to ask. "So you're a believer?"

"I am."

"Good." Because she couldn't deny she was falling for him fast, and knowing they had faith built on the same foundation . . .

"Yeah. Good." Nick's hand moved to her cheek. He fingered a strand of her hair. Blood whooshed in her ears as he leaned toward her.

Trisha Yearwood's "How Do I Live" suddenly punctuated the air.

Ellie straightened. What a moment for her phone to ring. "I should get that." While she fumbled through her purse, Nick's phone jingled from the center console.

Ellie grabbed her phone and stared at Olivia's name on the screen. "It's Olivia."

Nick looked at his phone. "Andrew."

Sweet applesauce. This was it. The moment of truth. Nick snatched Ellie's hand and answered his phone.

Ellie punched the Accept button on hers. "Hello?"

"Ellie, hi. I've got some exciting news."

"You do?"

"I'm calling to officially ask you to join Radiant Records."

14

Ellie fidgeted in the booth at Lorenzo's, listening to another local artist sing about first kisses. It had been a whole week since Olivia had offered her a contract with the recording label, and Olivia and Andrew were still working with their legal team to finalize the paperwork. So officially, Ellie couldn't yet announce her new status as a signed recording artist.

Unofficially, though, she and Nick, who had also been offered a contract, were the artists that Olivia and Andrew had chosen to represent their hopes and dreams. Ellie couldn't—wouldn't—disappoint them.

And performing at Lorenzo's was a good step toward proving her worth. She and Nick would both play for the prestigious crowd, filled with other execs, producers, and promoters—people who could get them and their music in front of larger audiences. Olivia had already pointed out industry professionals who could help them get on radio shows and tours, and their albums in more stores.

No pressure or anything.

The artist ended her set, and the audience applauded.

The emcee, Trix McGinty, who had spiked

hair and long dangling earrings, approached the stage. "Thanks again for coming out tonight, y'all. We'll take fifteen before we hear our last set for the evening."

The establishment was not as upscale as Bernadette's, but everyone who was anyone in country music played here at some point. It was like the 'Bird, but a bit larger. But unlike the 'Bird, it didn't offer open mic nights, where just anyone could play.

"Earth to Ellie." Nick nudged her with his elbow as he slid across the rounded booth toward her.

Light music filtered through the speakers, and all around them people laughed and chatted.

"Sorry. Just distracted."

"Nervous?" Nick fingered the corner of a menu. A brown cowboy hat rode low over his eyes.

She had the sudden urge to steal it from him and run her fingers through his curls. They'd been spending a lot of time together this last week, though almost always in the company of Olivia and Andrew. Being the two initial artists on a record label would likely throw them together fairly often.

Not that she really had a problem with that. There hadn't been a replay of their almost-kiss, but she couldn't help hoping for a repeat—and follow-through.

"Aren't you?" Ellie raised an eyebrow his direction. Her throat felt like sandpaper, so she took a sip of water.

Nick shrugged. "It's no different than any other place."

"Don't you ever get nervous?" Would she eventually get to that point?

"Maybe a little." Nick fiddled with his fork, turning it over and scraping the prongs against the table lightly. "I've practiced and done what I need to do. Guess I figure I'll let God do the rest."

Why couldn't she be more like that? "I always feel one step away from failure. Like it doesn't matter how much I practice—I can always mess up. And I have before."

"I'm not saying I've never messed up. Done my fair share of that. But why bother worrying about things that may never happen?"

Hmm. "Just preparing for the worst, I guess."

"I say prepare for the best and deal with disappointments as they come." Nick set the fork down. "Of course, that's a lot easier said than done, right?"

"Definitely." Especially when she'd already had so many.

"You know, you're an amazing performer. You've only been here two years and already caught the eye of one of the legends of country music. And you've been offered a contract with a record label. Why do you doubt yourself so much?"

"It's really easy to see my own faults, I guess."

"Mine are plenty clear to me too, believe me." Nick entwined his fingers with hers and squeezed. "You're gonna do great."

She couldn't help her heart from two-stepping inside her chest. "You too."

"How about we go out after this and celebrate?"

Olivia and Andrew approached the table before she could respond to Nick's question.

She dropped his hand and pushed against Nick. "Scoot." They shifted toward the middle of the booth, so Olivia and Andrew could join them.

Olivia moved her long hair over one shoulder and leaned in. "How y'all feeling?"

"Great." Nick piped up.

"Awesome. Nick, you'll be on first and play three songs. Then, Ellie, it'll be your turn. As you know, we could only get you in a one-song slot, but you'll close out the evening, which will be perfect."

Both nodded in reply.

They chatted about the schedule for the week. "We're planning a formal press conference once it's time to announce you as our artists, but we'll need to be strategic about the timing." Andrew adjusted his glasses, then pointed to the stage, where Trix signaled them and grabbed the microphone from its stand. "Looks like it's about that time." Andrew got up, so Nick could scoot out of the booth.

Nick strapped on his guitar and tuned it just offstage.

The emcee nodded to the guys in the back sound booth and flipped on the mic. "All right, we're back with more sounds from your favorite local artists. Up next is a real treat. Put your hands together for Nick Perry."

The crowd applauded as Nick took the stage, and a few girls in the front row whistled.

Nick plugged in his guitar and started to play. His voice filled the room.

It was way too easy to get lost in the sweetness of his tone, the deep brown of his eyes. Of course, all the women seemed to love watching him too. And though Ellie waited for him to turn his eyes to her, he stayed focused on all the other ladies in the crowd.

Something murky brewed in her stomach—and it had nothing to do with her nerves.

Olivia patted her leg.

Ellie jumped at the touch.

"You ready for this?"

With a tight smile, Ellie nodded. "Nick's a hard act to follow."

"Just remember, you're your own act. You can't compare yourself to anyone else."

"Right." If only she could remember to apply that principle to every aspect of her life.

Nick finished his second song, and Ellie stood. She grabbed her guitar and threw the strap over her shoulder, then waited in an alcove near the stage, letting the music from Nick's guitar wash over her. With the lights dimmed and her own guitar in hand, she could finally relax. This was her chance to shine.

It was the end of something and the beginning of something else. The start of her journey to become someone—someone Daddy would be proud of, someone her mom might finally see. The performer God had made her to be. After all, he'd led her to this moment, hadn't he? Now she had to follow through.

Nick's third song ended, and the crowd erupted into cheers.

The girls in front grinned up at Nick. "Encore! Encore!" They wiggled their hips, and Ellie couldn't help but wonder if Nick liked what he was seeing. If he'd get bored with a girl like Ellie eventually.

Stop it, Ellie. Just focus.

Soon the entire establishment shouted in unison. "Encore!"

Ellie could see the interest on several pro-moters' faces. One table from the influential Providence Group leaned in and spoke in low tones. They looked back at Nick.

In a few short songs, Nick had clearly solidified his future. Her Nick was going to be a star.

Whoa, what was she doing, assigning a personal pronoun to his name? Sure, they'd become friends, and sure, he'd held her hand, and sure, he'd looked at her in ways that made her want to melt, but he wasn't *her* Nick. Not yet anyway. But maybe someday . . .

Man, she was a hot mess.

Trix returned to the stage. "Thanks, Nick, for that great performance. Sounds like the audience would like to hear more from you. That all right?"

Nick flashed a smile and pulled the cowboy hat from his head. "Of course, Trix. Thanks for asking." He threw the hat into the crowd, and the girls in the front row rushed to snatch it midair.

They cheered, and he launched into another song. Then another. Then another.

The girls squealed—and he crooned right to them.

Ellie's stomach fell into her toes. The lights grew dimmer and dimmer. Nick shone more and more.

And Ellie sank into the shadows.

Trix stepped back onstage.

Ellie shook out her fingertips and breathed deep. This was it.

"Thanks for that, Nick." She waved her hand in

front of her face. "It's definitely a little warmer in here now than it was thirty minutes ago."

The girls in front hooted again—didn't they know any other sound than *woo?*—and Nick grinned. He was enjoying all the female attention, wasn't he? But what guy wouldn't?

"And thanks for coming out tonight, ladies and gents. It's been a great night, and we hope you enjoyed the show. Come back next week, same time, same place, for a batch of new artists."

Wait, what?

The lights came back up, and people in the audience stood, beginning to head out the door into the wind that twirled the leaves outside.

What had happened? Ellie stood there, numb, all the adrenaline that had built having nowhere to go.

Nick looked at her, stricken. He jumped from the stage and made his way toward her, but was intercepted by his adoring fans.

Ellie trudged back to her guitar case, unhooked her guitar from around her shoulders, and laid it in the foam-padded coffin. It was fine. Fine. She'd have other opportunities to play. This didn't mean anything.

Except . . . this wasn't the first time, was it? That she'd been ready to sing and there'd been no one to hear her. No one willing to hear her.

Her gaze scanned the room for Olivia and Andrew. They'd know what next steps to take.

"Ellie?" Nick's voice pierced through her thoughts.

"Great job up there." She picked up her guitar case and moved toward Andrew and Olivia's booth.

"Wait." He snagged her elbow and turned her to face him. "I didn't know that they'd cut the evening short, without you getting to play. Otherwise I'd never have kept playing."

"Of course you would have. And you should have. You're good, Nick. You can't disappoint your fans." Ellie tried to force a smile to her face but had a feeling it fell flat.

"Ell—"

"It's okay." She pushed her hair from her eyes. "I've gotta go." Ellie headed toward the restroom, where he couldn't follow her. She gawked at herself in the mirror above the sinks. A face that was, according to Olivia, "painted for the stage" stared back at her—bright rouged cheeks, lined lips, blackened eyelashes. Up close, she only looked like a clown.

Ellie yanked the faucet knob up, wet a paper towel, and scrubbed her face till not a speck of makeup was left.

"Nick did great, didn't he?"

"Hmm?" Olivia averted her gaze from the direction Ellie had run several minutes ago.

Andrew touched her elbow. "Nick. He did

great." His eyebrows knit together. "It's a shame Ellie didn't get to play, though."

"Indeed." Olivia scanned the room and saw the emcee was no longer talking to patrons. She exited the booth. "Be right back." The heels of her boots hit the ground, and she maneuvered through the dispersing crowd toward Trix, who was helping the sound crew wind cables and put equipment away.

The girl smiled as Olivia approached. "It was a pleasure to have you in the audience tonight, Ms. Lovett. I'm a big fan."

Olivia shook her extended hand, but only as a courtesy. "It was great being here. A lot of wonderful talent." She paused. "What happened up there? You had one more singer in the lineup for tonight."

Trix shrugged as she laid a microphone in its designated case. "That Nick guy had a great vibe going on. I could tell the promoters were interested in him. Just thought I'd do him a solid."

Olivia clenched her fists at her side but kept her voice calm. "I understand. But what about Ellie Evans? She came prepared to play."

"That's show biz." Trix snapped the microphone case shut.

"I spoke with Steve, and he fit Ellie in as a favor to me."

Trix's face turned red. "Oh, I'm so sorry. I had no idea. Please don't tell him." She brushed her hand through her hair. "I need this job."

Olivia's chest released some of the tension it'd been holding. This girl hadn't meant any harm. And Ellie was going to have to get used to disappointment in this industry.

"I won't. Let's just throw her in the lineup next week and make sure she plays, all right?"

Trix nodded like a bobblehead doll. "Yes, ma'am. Definitely."

Olivia turned to leave but halted. "One more thing."

"Anything."

"Keep the lights on."

"The lights?" Trix glanced around, then shrugged. "Yeah, okay."

Olivia walked back to Andrew. "I'm going to go find Ellie."

Andrew checked his watch. "You need me to stick around?"

"No, that's all right. I'll call you tomorrow."

"All right. If I head home now, I'll catch Grace before she hits the sack."

"Have fun." Without waiting for a reply, she hightailed it down the hall toward the bathroom—the only logical place for Ellie to be hiding out. She pushed through the doorway and found the girl gazing at herself in the mirror, her cheeks pale and a stain-ridden paper towel in her hand. "Rough night?" Olivia leaned against the wall just inside the door.

Ellie crumpled the towel and tossed it into the garbage. "Nick did great, didn't he? He's such an awesome performer. I'm happy for him." Her voice pinged with a high-pitched cheeriness that sounded forced.

"I didn't come here to talk about him."

Ellie wrapped her arms around her middle and stared at the ground.

Olivia gave her a hug. "I came to make sure you were all right."

Ellie shuddered and burrowed her face into Olivia's shoulder. Something about the way the girl fit in her arms—it just felt natural. Like Olivia was meant to help her along this journey.

With a squeeze, Olivia pulled back and smoothed Ellie's hair down. "Buck up. I've got a surprise for you."

"What is it?" The toe of Ellie's boot scuffed against the ground.

"You'll see." Olivia took her hand and led her through the doorway, down the hallway, and into the now-empty dining room. Everyone had cleared out quickly, moving on to their next activity. But Olivia's next activity was here. This was important for her, for Ellie.

The sound and light board beckoned to Olivia. She dimmed the house lights and pulled up other lights that bathed the stage in a soft glow. Trix had left a single microphone on a stand, as well as a plug for Ellie's guitar. "Time to play."

The girl's hand sneaked up to her hair and snagged a curly strand, tugging it downward, upward, downward like a Slinky. "Play?"

"Yep. You didn't get a chance tonight, but you should have. So go. Play."

"But . . ."

Olivia covered the distance between them, crossed her arms. Time for a little tough love. "But what?"

"But no one is here."

"So now I'm no one, am I?"

"You know what I mean."

Man, Ellie needed to snap out of this. The sooner, the better.

"No, I *don't* know what you mean. Whether there's one person listening or thousands, you should play your best. You can change the whole world if the right person is listening." Olivia softened her tone. "I'll see you. And God's here too—the most important audience. Let that be enough."

Ellie chewed her lip, debate playing across her features. Then, she moved the guitar case over her head, laid it on the table, unzipped it, and pulled her instrument from inside. With no sound, she headed to the stage, slipped the cord into the bottom of her guitar, and sat on the stool. "What should I play?"

"Something from the heart." Olivia lowered herself onto a chair, front and center. Ellie needed this, to be reminded of the gift she possessed.

Ellie leaned over her guitar and plucked the strings, and it seemed like medicine to the girl's soul. Slowly, all the tension leaked from Ellie's shoulders, her heart written on her face. She barely stood five feet tall, but her stature—all that she was—loomed over Olivia. There was something hauntingly familiar about the melody. Had she played it for Olivia before?

The girl opened her mouth and began to sing.

Something unlocked inside Olivia, and her jaw dropped. Because the words were from a singing competition long ago, where Olivia—Marie—had been enthralled by a talented boy.

Her palms grew sweaty, though she sat in a cool darkness. Olivia closed her eyes. Pinpricks of light dotted the back of her lids. She felt the overwhelming need to hurl.

How did Ellie know that song?

Olivia opened her eyes again, studied Ellie's features as she sang: her nose, a button; her lips, like rose petals; her eyes, green with brown flecks, just like—

No.

No.

Just . . . impossible.

She was mistaken. There was some other explanation.

Ellie finished the song and smiled sweetly.

The air hung still as the last note reverberated from the guitar. Neither said a word. Ellie just looked at her. She didn't even seem to need a reaction from Olivia—as if she'd learned, in that moment, to just be.

Olivia hated to disturb the silence, but she couldn't go another second thinking . . . wondering . . . She clapped furiously, her palms slapping against each other, tingling, numb. "Breathtaking." Olivia choked on her own word. "How did it feel?"

"Amazing." Ellie set her guitar on the stand and walked off the stage toward Olivia. She leaned over and hugged her, the rosy scent of her shampoo meeting Olivia's nose.

"Sit for a moment, will you?"

Ellie sank onto the chair across from Olivia.

"That's a new song. Did you write it?"

Ellie's eyes widened. "You said to play something from the heart, so I did. The song . . . well, I've tweaked it some, but it's something my daddy used to sing to me when I was growing up. I think he wrote it."

A murmur of concern pulsed through Olivia's blood. "Don't worry, hon, you're not in trouble. I was just curious." How to broach the next subject? "I'd love to know a little more about your daddy, if it's not too painful to talk about."

"Really? I don't mind. What do you want to know?"

Olivia waved her hand in the air, trying desperately to appear casual. "Oh, just the little things. What was his name? Where did he grow up? Just wondering if we ever crossed paths. You know, since he was a songwriter and we're both from Oklahoma."

"Oh, right." Ellie sat up straighter and folded her hands on the table. "His name was Ben VanRisseghem, and he was from a small town— Marlow, Oklahoma." Ellie smiled. "That's where I lived with my grandma and grandpa when Daddy moved to Oklahoma City to attend school and work. It's just an hour away." Ellie kept talking, moving her hands, telling stories about her daddy.

But all Olivia could focus on were those dreaded words: *Ben VanRisseghem* and *Marlow, Oklahoma.*

It couldn't be true. Ellie couldn't be her daughter. God wouldn't let this happen. It would be cruel. He knew how hard it had been to let her go.

Yet the more she watched the girl, the more she saw Ben in nearly every movement—and especially in her eyes. How had she never noticed before?

And oh. Ben. He'd died. A pang rent her heart. She'd only known him a little while, but the interactions between them had proven him to be one of the most decent people she'd ever met.

She never would have left Ellie with him if she hadn't believed that to be true.

Get it together, Olivia. It didn't matter how much she wished this hadn't happened. It had. Her daughter had found her. And what in the world was she supposed to do now?

Did she continue on as if nothing had changed—being part of Ellie's life but not claiming her as a daughter? After all, she'd promised Ben all those years ago that she wouldn't make a reappearance in their daughter's life. But Ben was gone now, God rest his soul. And Ellie had come to Nashville in part to find her mom.

To find Olivia.

What if . . . could she let herself imagine it? What if she told Ellie the truth? Would she want nothing to do with her, or would her daughter understand? What if this was the last year Olivia had to spend September 28 alone in her house, eating a cupcake in honor of her precious girl's birthday? What if the rest of the September 28s for the entirety of her life could be spent with Ellie—celebrating what had been found?

"Olivia?"

Ellie's voice tore through Olivia's thoughts. She couldn't say anything, could only stare.

Because the way Ellie sat there—hand on her hip, head cocked—the other half of Ellie's heritage was clear. Her shortness, her shoulders, her long torso . . .

Before they belonged to Ellie, they'd belonged to Jeanine Culloway.

And no matter how much Olivia wanted to be part of her daughter's life, there was no way in the world she was letting Mama sink her claws into Ellie.

15

Twenty-three years ago

I've never been more in love in my life.

How can I love a person who screams constantly and isn't comforted by anything? I don't know how it's possible, but I do. I love my daughter with every breath my soul lets in, lets out.

But love isn't enough.

Whenever my two-week-old baby balls up her fists and her face turns red from the cries, I want to cry myself. I'm only sixteen—what do I know about being a mom? I don't know how to console my baby girl. I try to get her to eat from me, but she won't have any of that. I try changing her diaper, and she wriggles and writhes. I try just holding her, but she doesn't seem to want me.

And Mama will just stand there, shaking her head at me, smirking. Then she'll close herself in her room and crank up her soaps on the TV, leaving me to figure this out myself.

I guess that's fair. I got myself in this mess. I should've been smarter.

In a way, I don't regret it. Because then my daughter wouldn't be here. In other ways, though, I just want to be sixteen again, with only myself to worry about.

I stomp around with my baby in my arms, trying to soothe her. "It's okay, Baby. Mama's here, Baby."

Baby. That's all I can come up with for a name. Because a name brands you forever. A name defines who you are. And much as I love my baby, I can't bring myself to give her the wrong name.

Anything ending in Culloway is the wrong name.

The other day, I got desperate, thinking maybe she was dying on account of she wouldn't stop screaming. I took Baby to the little clinic a few towns over, and they told me she was colicky. The doc gave me some medicine and told me to rub her belly. It isn't working.

It's eight p.m., and I can't remember the last time I slept. Or that Baby slept. She's crying and I'm crying, and all I can think is, "God, why have you left me on my own?" I just want a little peace, so I bounce and bounce Baby, then set her on my bed—laughably covered with a pale-pink bed-spread, as if I'm still a little innocent girl. Maybe she'll miraculously go to sleep on her own.

She screams even louder.

So I scream back. "Shut up! Please, shut up! Go to sleep! Can't you hear yourself? Why are you crying? Why?"

I sink to the floor and sob. I sob for all the not knowing, for all the screams—but most of all, because just now, I sound like the one person I've vowed never to become.

Mama.

She's screamed at me plenty of times, like I just screamed at Baby.

How did this happen? How did I become her?

Her words from the festival nine months ago drift back to me: *You're a Culloway. You're always gonna be a Culloway. Culloways ain't nothing special. And Culloways most definitely ain't cut out to be mothers.*

God, no. It can't be true. I may not have wanted to get pregnant, but now Baby is here and I'm her mama. Me. I can change. Be a different sort of Culloway.

I hear Mama entertaining a gentleman in the room next to me. I cover my ears but can't drown out the squeaking of the bed, the drunk laughter.

And Baby keeps on crying.

Who am I kidding? Being different just ain't in my blood.

And then, the solution comes to me. But I can't. Can I?

I sit up on my knees, peer over the side of my bed, and stare at this precious little life. I don't want to ruin her, like Mama ruined me. I want to give her more than Mama gave me. I don't want to turn her into the next Culloway daughter, destined to be ruined by her mama.

And the only way that won't happen is if she isn't a Culloway.

But can I do it? Can I let her go?

I stand, almost mechanical. I begin to pack the few outfits I have for Baby—hand-me-downs from Bette's older sister—and stuff them into a grocery bag I find lying in the corner of my room. I pull down my own suitcase and jam all my clothes inside. I run out to Mama's car and pop the trunk, throwing in my guitar and everything else I own. It's not much.

Then I go get Baby. "We're going for a ride."

And we drive all the way to Marlow, Oklahoma. I only know Ben's address because I looked him up in the phonebook. The night we met, he told me stories about his parents. His daddy, strong and quiet but loving. His mama, sweet and kind, a proper Christian lady who wears nice slacks and pearls.

Baby will be loved. And she won't have to grow up cursed. Maybe she'll have a chance here, far away from me.

I pull her from her car seat, cradle her against my chest, and walk to Ben's front door.

It's late, but a light's on inside.

I ring the doorbell.

Ben appears. He's tall and as handsome as the night we met. A little stubble is growing on his chin. He looks surprised to see me. "Marie."

"Hi, Ben." I bounce Baby. I can't spit out anything else.

His eyebrows knit together. "What are you doing here? I haven't heard from you in a long time. You never told me where you live." He eyes Baby. "And who is this? Your sister or something?"

"Ben, this is your daughter." The words just tumble out.

Baby whimpers but doesn't scream—as if she understands the importance of this moment.

Ben freezes. "My what?"

"Daughter."

"But . . . how?"

"You know how."

Ben's face scrunches, and he steps out of the house, closes the door. "I know but . . . we were careful. And . . . why are you just now telling me this?" He runs his hands over his cheeks.

My instinct is to turn and run, to figure something else out. But I know what I have to do. My voice is calm. Somehow calm. "Ben, I didn't tell you because I didn't want to ruin your life. You've got so much going for you. But Baby needs you."

"What do you mean, needs me?" Ben stops pacing. "You need money? Is that it? I'll go get everything I have in my wallet right now. I have more in savings. We can get it in the morning."

He begins to leave, but I reach out to stop him. "No, Ben. She needs *you*."

He shrugs off my arm, paces, as if that will solve something.

I stay quiet, while he thinks.

Baby fights against my hold, and her face begins to redden.

"We should get married."

Married? I hadn't thought of that. Maybe that would solve all the problems.

But no, she'd still be near me, and even if my last name changed, I'd still bear the Culloway name, down deep. I'd still carry the scars. Maybe if she never knows me, she'll escape the same fate. I won't have a chance to hurt her like Mama's hurt me.

And Mama won't be able to find her.

"We can't. I'm leaving."

"Where you going? You're just gonna show up, tell me I have a daughter, and then leave? I may be young, but I know how to man up when I need to. I . . . I want to be in her life."

"I'm glad." I shove Baby into his arms, and her whimpering stops. See? This is how it has to be. "I can't do this, Ben. I can't ruin her."

"What are you talking about?"

I run to the car and pull out the grocery bag of clothes, a few diapers. Then I unbuckle the car seat, and I drop it all at Ben's feet. "It's not much, but it's all I have."

I turn to leave, and he yells my name. "Don't you dare leave this baby with me. Don't you love her even a little?"

"You don't understand." My lip trembles. "I'm leaving *because* I love her."

"That doesn't make any sense."

"Maybe not to you. Because you're good people, Ben. You'll love her right and not like a Culloway would."

"I don't get it." Ben grips my arm and makes me face him. "Come inside, and we'll talk this out. My parents . . . they'll know what to do."

I shake my head, tears finally drenching my cheeks. I can barely see Baby's face, but I do see she's content in her daddy's arms. That's all I need to know. "I couldn't get her to stop screaming, not for one second. But look at her now."

"Marie, listen to me. You can't go. I'll just come find you. There's no point in leaving."

"You won't be able to find me. I'm running away, and I'm not coming back. And I'm changing my name, so don't try to look for me. Please. I want . . . I want her to have the best kind of life. If I'm in it, she won't." I let myself reach out and stroke her cheek for the final time. It's feather-soft against my fingertip. I want to tell her how much I love her. But actions speak louder than words. "You don't have to worry, Ben. I promise I won't interfere. You'll never have to see my face again." I pull from his grasp and race to my car, locking myself inside. I start the engine before I can stop myself.

Ben pounds on my window. "Marie!"

I hear his muffled cries through the glass, and my own cries join his. I throw the car into Reverse and leave his driveway as quickly as I can.

Rocks crunch beneath the tires.

The last thing I see is him standing there, half in the light, half in the shadows, Baby nestled in his arms, peaceful at last.

I point Mama's car toward Nashville—and I don't look back.

16

A loud noise from the kitchen snapped Ellie to attention in bed. She glanced at the clock. Only five a.m., though Lena could be up for a number of school- or work-related reasons. Ellie tried to snuggle back under her sheets, but they were twisted around her legs, and her pillow was soaked. Had she had the dream again? She couldn't remember.

Another sound from the kitchen echoed down the hall, this time accompanied by some bright language from Lena.

Ellie might as well get up too, since she wasn't going to be able to go back to sleep. With a sigh, she stood, and as soon as her feet hit the cold floor, she hurried to grab a pair of socks. She fluffed her hair and yawned, then plodded out of her room toward the kitchen.

Lena sat reading a textbook at the kitchen table, only a small lamp on the counter bringing any light to the room. Dressed in her flannel pajamas, she leaned over a bowl of cereal.

"Kinda hard to read with no light, isn't it?" Ellie shuffled to the coffee maker, a Keurig Lena's parents had given her for Christmas last year.

Lena's eyes flitted up and back down to her

book. "You're up early. And for your information, I've got plenty of light."

"You're gonna strain your eyes."

"Okay, Mom."

"Ha-ha." Ellie twirled the silver revolving rack filled with K-Cups, skimmed the surface of several as they passed.

"I hope I didn't wake you up. The stupid table must have moved in the middle of the night and failed to inform my toe about it." Lena flipped a page in her text.

How she could read about art history and carry on a conversation at the same time was beyond Ellie. Especially this early. Morning people.

Ellie chose a medium roast and pulled the pod from the rack. She flicked on the Keurig—should have done that first—and leaned against the counter as she waited for the water to heat. "I think I might have had that dream again." Her subconscious was obviously twisted in knots, if her sheets were any indication.

"Have you decided whether to keep looking for your mom?"

"No. I haven't had much time to think about it."

"You sure that's why you haven't made a decision yet?"

Ellie lifted the Keurig lid and slid the K-Cup inside. She shut the lid, placed a mug underneath the spout, and hit the button to start brewing. "It's too early to be thinking about this."

"It's never too early for self-reflection. But I'll let you off the hook for now." As Lena crunched her last bite of cereal, she closed her textbook. "It sounds like you did really great last night at that café. Lorenzo's, was it?"

Ellie pulled her steaming mug from the Keurig and set it on the counter. "What do you mean? I didn't get to play." She turned to the fridge and pulled out the half and half. Almost gone. She'd have to see if she had enough money to go shopping today. Olivia had told her there would be a small advance coming after the contract process was complete—there was currently some hold-up with legal—but Ellie didn't know how long till it would hit her bank account. And besides, she had to make it last since she still couldn't find a steady job—and the money Grandma and Grandpa had sent was being stretched to the max.

"Really? Then what's the video from?"

Ellie stirred the coffee and cream with a spoon and wrinkled her nose. "What video?" She sipped the liquid, and it warmed her insides as it slid down.

Lena stared at her as if she had horns growing from her head. "The one that's all over the web. Of you. Playing."

The mug suddenly felt very heavy in her hands.

Ellie walked to the table and sat down. "I don't know what you're talking about."

"I swear, Ellie, do you live under a rock?" Lena stood and waltzed to the sofa, then pulled her laptop from her bag. She opened the lid and typed in something on the screen. Then she set it in front of Ellie. "There's a video of you playing at Lorenzo's—see, it's titled "Ellie Evans Plays Lorenzo's"—and it's gotten thousands of hits already. You've been tagged in the video like a bazillion times in retweets and shares. Doesn't your phone notify you whenever you're mentioned?"

Ellie stared at the screen, where a YouTube video thumbnail showed her sitting on a stool. "My phone was dead last night when I got to Lorenzo's, and I guess I forgot to charge it and turn it back on." She leaned in and studied the frame. Sure enough, it was her on the Lorenzo's stage, when she'd played for Olivia. But how . . . ?

"I have to go finish getting ready. Watch the video if you want. It's really good." Lena leaned over and gave Ellie a quick hug. "Things are finally happening. See? What did I tell ya?"

Ellie could only stare at the screen as her friend left the room. She hit Play.

The sound of her guitar and her own voice lifted and filled the room. The emotion that flitted across her face . . . well, it reminded her how she had felt in that moment. Like playing for Olivia—and God—was enough. Like nothing else mattered but remembering Daddy and that God had given her a gift and she was so happy to be able to use it.

But Olivia hadn't taped this. Ellie would have seen her. Besides, the angle seemed to indicate it had been taped from farther back than Olivia had been sitting. Who would have taped it and put it up online? Whose YouTube account was this? She searched for the owner of the video—and froze.

Nick's face grinned at her from the tiny thumbnail picture next to the account name, "Nick Perry, Official." She pulled up another tab and scrambled to her Facebook page, searched for Nick's. He'd shared the video at nine p.m. last night on his page, which had thousands of followers—apparently loyal followers. The post read: "Y'all, this here is Ellie Evans, an upcoming singer and songwriter. Isn't she something else? If you like it, share the love!" She navigated to his Twitter account, where he'd written something similar.

Heat crept through her veins, and it had nothing to do with her coffee. Whether they were just friends or something more, this was one of the nicest things anyone had ever done for her.

Because, in an instant when she hadn't been trying at all, someone had seen the real Ellie.

17

Much as Olivia had looked forward to this moment, dread and confusion muddied the pleasure she should have felt. She'd lain awake all Wednesday night long after the revelation at Lorenzo's. And now, two days later, she was no closer to figuring out how to handle the Ellie situation.

Olivia checked the address again on the brick office complex. Yes, this was it. The office Andrew wanted to lease. Apparently, there was a great deal on the table, and they needed to swoop in quickly before someone else took it.

She walked into the foyer, where a large concrete fountain spurted water in an arc. Olivia felt the spray as she breezed toward the elevators.

A few doctors in scrubs stepped from the opening elevator doors and nodded their greeting.

Olivia got on and punched the button for level seven. The doors rolled shut, and she waited.

A ding indicated she'd arrived at the right floor.

Olivia stepped from the elevator and found Office Suite 703 to her right. She opened the brown door and found Andrew standing at a huge secretary's desk just ahead.

He held some documents in his hand, studying them, his hip propped against the desk.

"Hey."

He looked up, and a huge grin lit his face. "What do you think?"

She glanced around. The office was simple enough and came furnished—a nice thing, so they wouldn't have to use their precious capital to decorate. The small lobby held a few potted plants and some plush waiting-room chairs. The walls were painted a rich burgundy with cream-colored trim. The art hanging on the walls was subtle but stylish. "So far so good."

"Let me show you the rest." Andrew hurried down the hall, and she followed. Off the main corridor was a small kitchen, a conference room with a large oak table for twelve, a copy-and-supply room, and an office with a view of the building across the street. "I figured this could be my office."

"Great."

Andrew looked so excited, but Olivia's heart wasn't in it. How could it be, when every other second Ellie's face crashed into her mind? The way she smiled Ben's smile back at her, the way her eyes lit up, the way . . .

She had to focus. Olivia grasped her purse handle tightly as she trailed Andrew to the final door at the end of the hallway.

He paused, as if for dramatic effect. "And

this . . . this could be your office if you want it, Liv." Andrew pushed open the door and led Olivia inside. He flicked on the light, and she gasped. Though the space was smaller than the first office, the panorama behind the desk was stunning.

She walked to the window and stared out at a green park with gentle, rolling hills—a golf course, complete with walking paths and a sparkling pond. "It's beautiful." Her fingers grazed the glass, and something warm lit in her heart. She turned. "Thank you."

He shrugged, cheeks red, and shoved his right hand into his pocket. "I looked at several office locations, but I know how much you like a good view. When I saw this, I thought it was perfect."

"You were right." She sat down on the office chair and swiveled it to face the park. People filled the benches, and a few golf carts whizzed by. That would soon change when the November and December winds started blowing in—and maybe with it, some snow. She tried to imagine the landscape coated in the white stuff. It would be gorgeous.

"Let's sign the lease papers right now, then, if you're sure."

She pulled her gaze from the window.

Andrew held up the documents he'd been skimming through earlier. He placed them on the desk in front of her, pulled a pen from his pocket, and held it out to her.

"Where do I sign?"

He came around the desk and hovered over her shoulder. Close. A shiver ran up her spine.

Andrew flipped to the third page and indicated where she should place her signature. "It's for a three-year lease, which I know might be a little risky, considering we're a startup. But with Ellie and Nick in our pockets—well, I just have a really good feeling."

Three years? Olivia nearly groaned. "I can't. I have to think." She couldn't move forward without being completely honest with Andrew. But she couldn't do that until she'd been honest with Ellie. Although doing *that* would almost certainly put Ellie in Mama's path whenever Mama inevitably got out of prison. And Olivia couldn't allow that either.

Her head hurt.

"If you really like this one, you need to sign, or we'll lose it."

"I understand." Olivia set the pen down. "But I'm not ready."

"Why?"

"There's just a lot to think about."

"Are we talking about the office space—or something else?"

Olivia's only response was silence. What could she say?

Andrew pulled a chair over and sank down beside her. "What's going on, Liv? Are you having second thoughts? Because once we sign the contracts with Ellie and Nick on Monday, we're in business. It'll be official. We'll have obligations, and we can't take those lightly. So I need to know—are you still sure about this?"

"Yes. No. I don't know."

Andrew's staccato laugh of disbelief cut her. "Which is it? You approached me with this idea, remember? I walked away from a lot of money and a comfortable job to take this risk with you."

"You misunderstand me." Olivia rubbed her forehead. "I'm still sure about the label. Just not about signing Ellie."

"What are you talking about? This is very unlike the woman who told me, in no uncertain terms, that Ellie Evans was the next big thing."

"She is. But maybe we aren't the label for her." She wasn't ready to tell Andrew everything, but she had to warn him. What if she told Ellie the truth and Ellie didn't want to be part of Radiant Records? Or what if she kept the secret to protect her daughter—but then being around her, working with her in close proximity, was too much? Her daughter needed a mentor she could count on. Olivia couldn't possibly be that person anymore, could she?

Andrew took a step back and held up his hands. "I don't know where this is coming from, but I can admit when I'm wrong. The success of that YouTube video proves the girl has what it takes. You were right to want her." He cocked his head. "Did something happen?"

"She didn't do anything wrong, if that's what you mean." Olivia stood and moved to the window again. Her breath fogged the glass in front of her. "I can't sign anything right now, Andrew. I'm sorry. I just need time to figure out what to do."

She felt him walk up behind her, and she could see his reflection in the window. He scratched his head. "Is something else going on? You're acting very strange."

She sniffed back her tears. "No, everything's fine."

He reached up and touched her shoulder. "If there's something wrong—"

Olivia whirled. "Nothing's wrong." She cringed at the way her voice sounded. None of this was Andrew's fault. It was all hers.

"You're holding something back. I know you better than you think." Now his speech was tinged with frustration, and open annoyance played across his features. "If we're going to run a business together, we should be able to trust each other one hundred percent."

"Then trust me right now." Olivia edged past him, grabbing her purse from the desk. "I have to go." Papers scattered to and fro. She bent to pick them up, tossing them back onto the desk, then hurried toward the door.

Andrew cursed under his breath. "I can't wait forever, Olivia."

She paused at the doorway, rotated to stare at her friend. She had the eerie sensation he wasn't just talking about the label.

He clenched a crumpled paper in his hand.

"I'm sorry." Olivia fled down the hall, down the elevator, out the front doors, toward her car. She climbed inside, fired up the engine, placed her hands on the steering wheel—and realized she had nowhere to go.

There was nowhere the past couldn't reach.

And that settled it.

Ellie could never find out the truth. Olivia couldn't saddle her with the old Culloway scars. Because once a Culloway, always a Culloway. Even if you changed your name, ran away, became a star, and tried to live a new life.

Olivia was living proof.

18

Someone needed to tell the sun that today wasn't a day for shining.

Olivia rolled over in her bed, away from the window allowing in streams of bliss from the outside world. She buried her head beneath her mountain of satiny pillows. Her left foot peeked out from the covers, but she didn't have the strength to pull it back in. All the worry over Ellie and the semi-fight with Andrew had led to a head cold that had developed overnight and given Olivia an excellent excuse to stay right here for the whole weekend.

A wet tongue met her toes.

Olivia unburied her head and squinted into the light.

Two sets of brown eyes met her gaze.

"Chloe, Pascal, go lay down."

Pascal's tongue wagged out in response, and he barked. Chloe rounded the foot of the bed to get closer to Olivia's head.

Olivia darted her hand out into open air and rubbed the dog between the eyes. "You're my faithful girl."

Suddenly, Chloe's ears perked up, and Pascal growled. They both darted into the living room.

Probably heard a truck outside. Olivia pulled

her hands and feet back under the comforter, ready to disappear in sleep again—if only she could avoid the dreams.

"Yoo-hoo!"

"Rach?" Olivia uncovered her eyes once more as her friend rounded the corner into her room, followed by two eager dogs eyeing the food bag Rachel held. "What are you doing here?"

"You said you were feeling under the weather yesterday when you canceled our chick-flick marathon, so I brought you some of my home-made chicken noodle soup."

"You're sweet, but I'm not hungry."

Rachel flung her purse onto a chair by Olivia's vanity, then set the bag of food on Olivia's bedside table. She pulled a to-go soup container from the sack, along with homemade rolls and a plastic spoon.

The smell wafted from the container, and Olivia's stomach rumbled.

Rachel eyed her. "Really? When was the last time you ate?"

"Two days ago." The exact amount of time she'd been lying in this bed, only getting up to do her business and grab water from the fridge.

Rachel took off her jean jacket and placed it over the arm of the chair that held her purse. She rolled up her sleeves and pulled her short brown hair into a ponytail. "Oh! I almost forgot." Her friend leaned over her purse—her "Mary Poppins bag," as she affectionately called it, given its huge nature and the fact that she kept everything but Elvis's golden microphone inside—and pulled out a few magazines. "Thought you might be getting bored." She plopped the magazines on the bed next to Olivia. Then she settled into the chair and stared at her. "All right, spill. What's going on?"

The dogs huddled at her friend's feet. The traitors.

"What do you mean?" Olivia shifted her gaze to the ceiling, where her fan gyrated slowly. If she watched long enough, maybe it could hypnotize her and take her far away from here. "I'm just under the weather, like you said."

"The Olivia Lovett I know—the one I've known for fifteen years—has never been laid up sick."

Olivia kept watching the fan go round and round. The sameness of it soothed her. "I'm allowed to be sick every now and then, Rach."

"I'm not saying you've never been sick. Just that you've never let something like a minor cold stop you from doing what you wanted to do—and unless I'm mistaken, girls' night was totally your idea."

"It was, but—"

"I mean, remember that time you had the flu and still insisted on performing at the Opry? You nearly puked as soon as you made it off that stage, but nothing was going to stop you from getting up there in the first place. So don't tell me that puffy eyes and a stuffy nose are really what kept you from enjoying my fabulous company last night."

"Give me a break, will you? I'm just sick." A cough rolled from her tongue as if her body was trying to prove her point.

The fan began clacking, off its rocker for a moment, but then found its groove again and smoothed out.

"Stop it. Sit up and look at me, Olivia."

"All right, all right." Olivia sighed and pulled her eyes from the ceiling. She eased herself up and rested against the pillows.

Rachel's eyes radiated concern.

"What do you want from me?"

"How about the truth?" Rachel scooted the chair closer. "Something ain't right, and I'm not leaving here till I know what it is."

Olivia couldn't say it. If she did, it'd be real. But if she couldn't talk to Rachel about it, she couldn't talk to anyone. And maybe she needed to talk to someone. After all, she couldn't ignore the truth forever. She inhaled a trembling breath. "You know Ellie?"

Rachel leaned back in the chair, folded her arms. "Of course. The next Olivia Lovett."

If only she understood how close to the truth that statement was.

"We offered her a spot on the label last week. The contract has not been signed yet, which is good. Because I'm thinking about pulling the offer." It was the only thing she could do, wasn't it? She'd make sure Ellie found a home with another label—would call in every favor she had to do so. But she just couldn't risk Ellie finding out the truth and being linked with Olivia. She was too sweet—she might actually believe Mama's pity stories.

"Why in the world would you do that?" Rachel opened the Ziploc she'd brought and pulled out a roll. "Here, eat."

Olivia took the bread obediently and fingered it, turning it over and over in her hand. "I realized I can't work with her."

"But I thought she was perfect."

"So did I." Oh, Olivia just longed to slide under the covers again. But Rachel would never let her. "Rach, I found something out the other day."

"Spit it out. What?"

Olivia couldn't speak for a moment. "Ellie . . . is my daughter."

"She is?" The blush on Rachel's cheeks brightened, while the rest of her skin paled.

Olivia detailed the events of the night at Lorenzo's. "It was the most frightening moment of my life. At first, I thought she'd figure it out right away, that she'd walk out of my life before I could explain. And then I was scared that she *would* ask me to explain." She absently pulled the roll in half, then set it down on the bed. "But despite the fear, I know for sure now that I did the right thing all those years ago."

Rachel's eyebrows knit together. "What makes you say that?"

"Ellie turned out amazing. She wouldn't have if I'd raised her." For years, the question had haunted Olivia. Had she really run off for the good of Ellie . . . or the good of Olivia? Now, she had her answer—and it was a relief. "I mean, look at her. She's beautiful and strong and motivated."

Chloe sat up, and Rachel petted her golden coat. "Olivia, you are also beautiful and strong and motivated. I think Ellie gets those traits from you."

"No." Olivia shook her head. She grabbed a strand of her hair and tugged as she wound it around her index finger. "She is the way she is because she was raised by Ben and his family." Her voice rose as she spoke. "Not by me and mine."

Pascal whimpered at Rachel's feet.

Rachel soothed him and waited several seconds to speak. "You can't change the past anyway. I'm not trying to question your decision back then. But you can't let your old thinking affect the decision you make now. You're not the same person you were."

Some nights, when Olivia was young, old Mrs. Robbins from down the street would take her to church when Mama was too drunk to say no. The Sunday school teachers liked to recite the verse about being a new creation in Christ—becoming someone different. But Olivia had tried that, and now she knew it was a bunch of baloney, at least for her.

She'd always be Marie Culloway, deep down.

"But my old thinking is right. I was never cut out to be that girl's mother. And I'm still not." Suddenly, the room stifled her. Olivia threw back the covers. "I would have ruined her then, and I'll ruin her now."

"And just how would you do that? You're a competent, wonderful woman, not a sixteen-year-old kid controlled by fear of her mother."

"Okay, maybe *I* wouldn't ruin her, but being associated with me would. I can't tell her the truth, because of my mother."

"Why not?"

"Mama's getting out of prison soon. She'll come here, and she'll find out about Ellie, and she'll do who knows what to her. Ellie's too naïve. I can just see it now—she'll start caring about Mama, then Mama will ask her for money, and that'll be the beginning of the end. She'll crush my baby girl." Like she'd crushed Marie.

Rachel frowned. "First off, the likelihood of all that happening is super-slim. Second, Ellie is an adult. Don't you think you should treat her like one and tell her the truth? Let her decide who gets to be in her life, on her terms."

"You don't know my mama. Give her an inch, and she'll beat you senseless with a yardstick." Olivia stood and headed for the connecting bathroom, leaving Rachel in the bedroom. She threw water on her face. The shocking cold seeped into her pores, and she braced herself against the counter.

"Olivia." Rachel's gentle voice lifted from the doorway.

Olivia turned.

Her friend stood there, flanked by the dogs. "Don't you think maybe God's giving you an opportunity here?"

"An opportunity for what?" She hated how her voice squeaked out. She cleared her throat.

"To put your regret in the past."

"I don't regret my decision." Olivia moved back into the bedroom, walked to her closet, and began picking out her outfit for the day. Lying there in peace was no longer an option. She'd already missed church. She might as well get some work done. At least hit the grocery store. Something, anything, to quit thinking about this.

"Are you kidding me?" Rachel had—surprise, surprise—followed her. "I see the regret in your eyes every year on September twenty-eighth. Even now, I see it."

"Lay off, okay, Rach?" Olivia yanked a sweater from its hanger.

Rachel quieted.

Olivia saw the hurt in her eyes. An apology sat on Olivia's tongue, but no. She was right. Rachel needed to stop pushing.

"All right. I'll go." Rachel headed to the chair to grab her jacket. She put it on unhurriedly, no anger in her motions. Then she looked up, and her eyes pierced Olivia. "But you can't avoid the past forever. It's come to your doorstep. And there's a reason for it. Olivia, you're going to have to tell Ellie the truth—before she finds out some other way."

19

The next day, Olivia left Ronnie's Bakery and Café with a dozen chocolate chip cookies she planned to eat in one sitting.

Dusk was falling as she walked toward her car. A slight chill hung in the atmosphere. Children's laughter rang from the park across the street. Olivia opened her car door and lingered. Did she really want to head to a house empty of all but two dogs? Maybe the fresh air would do her some good.

She dropped the cookies and her purse into the front seat and locked up. Olivia turned and crossed the street, taking a path that led through the trees toward a playground. Crickets were beginning to chirp. Old-fashioned black lampposts illuminated the trail. She passed the occasional dog-walker or older couple in jogging suits, but otherwise was alone.

It seemed the laughter came from the other side of the park. There appeared to be some sort of festival going on. It wouldn't hurt to check it out and possibly would help get her mind off of things. She'd prayed about the Ellie decision yesterday after Rachel left and all of today, but was no closer to an answer. Did she tell her daughter the truth or leave things be?

And then there was Andrew. The last three days of uncertainty had already been unfair to him. Olivia had reached for the phone several times to call him and then changed her mind. What excuse did she have for her behavior, short of telling him the complete truth? But she couldn't put him off forever, not when they had a business to run.

At least she'd patched things up with Rachel. Her friend still believed Olivia needed to come clean with Ellie, but she'd agreed to leave it alone for a while.

Olivia arrived at a clearing and found herself on the outskirts of a small fair. There was a bounce house in the shape of a castle and a huge inflatable slide. Shrieks of delight flew from all directions. Carts of food and drinks—popcorn, hot chocolate, churros, hot dogs, pizza, coffee— were stationed every few yards. Booths lined the path through the festival and touted carnival-like games, from a spinning fortune wheel to a dunking booth and a milk bottle toss.

A tiny girl wearing a tiara ran past Olivia on one side. The girl was followed by a miniature pirate, who drew his plastic sword and shouted at the princess to walk the plank.

What in the world?

Oh. It was Halloween. How could she have forgotten? And how had she not noticed that all the children were wearing costumes?

As a girl, she'd adored the holiday. Most kids loved it for the candy, but that wasn't what had appealed to Olivia. The costumes were her favorite part.

She stuffed her hands in her jacket pockets and continued walking through the festival.

Of course, she'd never had a new costume like so many other kids. Sometimes, she'd make her own from things she found around the house. Others were hand-me-downs from one of Bette's sisters. But that hadn't made a difference. She still loved playing dress-up.

The fact that she could become someone else entirely for one night—that had been what mattered.

A young dad walked toward her, holding the hand of a wriggling Hulk.

The child wrenched away and tugged at his mask.

The dad crouched down and helped him take it off. "You don't want to leave it on?"

The boy looked about five. He threw his arms over his chest. "I don't like it. It's hot and itchy, and I can't see or breathe good."

"You don't have to wear your mask if you don't want to. I guess you'll just have to take it off and be the Incredible Teddy instead."

"Yeah, that's who I am. The Incredible Teddy!"

"Can I tell you something?" The father leaned forward as if sharing a secret.

"What?"

"I like the Incredible Teddy much better anyway."

Olivia stopped, and a gasp whooshed from her lungs. The words—they were flint striking steel, lighting something in her conscience.

For twenty-three years, she'd been wearing a mask. Just like when she was a girl, the grown-up her had loved pretending she was someone else.

But now, with Ellie reentering her life, Olivia was forced to consider peeling off the mask. Was it possible that her mask was hot and itchy and didn't allow her to see things as they really were? Had the mask of Olivia Lovett started to suffocate her without her even realizing it?

The young boy pumped his fist in the air. Then he skipped down the path mask-free.

Could that be her, if she was brave enough to follow?

Lord, what do I do? Rachel is the only one who knows the whole truth. Do I unveil myself to Ellie? And is it time to let Andrew see the woman behind the mask? We have to work together, and there's no other way to explain my behavior than to let him in on my past—some of it, at least.

Do I need to give him a glimpse at Marie Culloway?

20

Apologizing to a friend was hard to swallow. But hopefully the apology would go down easier with homemade lasagna, garlic bread, and a bottle of Chardonnay.

Olivia lowered the oven door a tad and observed her creation. Fragrant Italian spices greeted her. But the cheese wasn't quite melted, and Andrew would be here soon. Hmm, maybe five more minutes at an increased temperature would do the trick—or so she guessed with her limited cooking experience. She flipped the knob to a higher setting.

Pascal nudged up beside her as she closed the door.

"Back, boy. You don't wanna get burned." Olivia untied the orange apron from around her waist and pulled it over her head, careful not to muss her hair. She hung the apron on a hook in the pantry and lit a pumpkin candle on the counter, then leaned over to inhale the sweet scent.

How would she start this conversation? How much should she say? She'd have to keep praying for clarity throughout the evening and hope it came.

The doorbell chimed, and the dogs barked, bounding toward the door.

"It's just Andrew." Olivia followed them to the door. "Sit." They obeyed, though reluctantly, and she opened the door.

Andrew stood there, hands in pockets, worrying his lip.

The poor guy. She'd put him through a lot and tested their friendship in the process. But tonight was about repairing their relationship and moving forward. "Hey."

He looked up. "Hey."

"Thanks for agreeing to come over."

"We need to talk."

"That we do." She swung the door wider. "Come on in."

He stepped through and shrugged off his tan overcoat, hanging it on Olivia's oak coat rack, to reveal jeans and a brown sweater that perfectly complemented his eyes. She couldn't help but notice the trim figure he cut—all those salads and days at the gym had done him lots of favors.

Focus, Olivia.

"Um, let's go in the kitchen."

"All right." He leaned over to pet Chloe and Pascal, who crowded around his legs. "But first I have to greet my adoring fans."

She eased out a laugh. "They do seem to like you." She headed toward the kitchen. "I have a surprise."

He followed. "Wow, did you actually cook something?"

She donned her black kitchen mitts. "I did indeed."

"You must really be trying to butter me up."

"Ha-ha." With a swift flip of her hair behind her shoulder, Olivia tugged open the oven. Steam smacked her in the face, and she coughed—then groaned as she eyed the lasagna. She pulled it from the belly of the oven and plopped it onto the counter, staring at her once-perfect creation. The cheese looked black and possibly inedible.

Andrew walked up behind her. "Maybe you're not trying to butter me up after all. You're trying to kill me."

Olivia pushed out a laugh and stripped the mitts from her hands, snatching a nearby fork from the counter. "I just might if you keep saying things like that." She aimed it at his heart. "I don't know what happened."

"Looks like you flipped the broiler on."

Of course she had. At least she still had the bread . . . but wait. She'd forgotten to pull it out of the freezer, hadn't she? And didn't it take something like twenty to thirty minutes to heat up? Olivia slumped against the counter and put her head in her hands. "This is why I don't even try." Some start to her apology.

Andrew eased her hands from her face and tilted her chin up, so she had to look him right in the eyes.

Oh my, he was close. She could smell his

shampoo—something citrusy. Why couldn't she seem to get her head on straight around him lately?

"Olivia, it's not the end of the world. Look." He released her, grabbed a spatula, and peeled some of the cheese off the top. The red sauce and the edge of a noodle appeared to be unharmed by the oven's harsh temperature. "It's still edible underneath. Sometimes you have to scrape away the yuck to get to the good stuff."

She let his words sink in.

And suddenly, she couldn't go another moment without telling him how she was feeling. "Andrew, I'm sorry."

"It's just food."

"No. I'm sorry." She emphasized each word.

"I know." He lowered the spatula, then turned to her. "Tell me what's going on. I'm more than your business partner. I'm your friend. You can tell me anything."

No, as sweet as he was, she couldn't tell him *anything*—she couldn't tell him the whole truth. But some part of the truth was better than nothing. It was time to give him a glimpse under her mask. She held out her hand. "Okay."

He took it firmly in his, and they stood connected like that for a few moments. She broke their gaze first and led him into her living room.

The dogs followed them.

Olivia sank down onto her plush green sofa,

and Andrew lowered himself at an angle, so he faced her. She pulled her hand out of his and into her lap.

Chloe settled onto the oversized dog bed in the corner, and Pascal curled on the floor at Olivia's feet.

Time for her to talk. She took a deep breath. "I wouldn't want anyone else as a partner in all of this."

"That's a relief to hear."

She nodded and, despite the heat coming from a vent near her feet, Olivia gathered her yellow sweater tighter around her. "I was having a rough day last Friday. I've been having a rough month, actually."

"Why? What's going on?"

"Some stuff from my past came up. Hurtful stuff." She'd start fairly easy. "Remember this summer when I took a vacation?"

He nodded.

"I really underwent surgery on my vocal chords. To see if I could get my voice back."

He leaned forward. "Why didn't you tell me?" His sudden movement roused Pascal, who grabbed a ball and brought it to Andrew's lap. Andrew tossed it down the hallway absently, and a joyful dog bounded after it.

"I didn't tell anyone at the time. Not even Rachel. Guess I figured if it failed, I was no worse off and at least I'd have tried. And no one would know about my failure." She tucked her hands inside the ends of her sweater sleeves. "But the surgery didn't work."

"Oh, Liv. I'm sorry."

She shrugged. "I've made my peace with it, mostly. It's just . . . life doesn't look the way I always thought it would at this point. For so long, my career was on this trajectory toward major success. And then, boom, I fell on my rump—and there was no amount of hard work I could do to change the outcome. So, I had to get a new dream." She reached for Andrew's fingers again. "You helped me make that a reality."

"I've been happy to do it." Andrew scooted closer. "You know I care about you."

The look in his eyes—oh. He did care, didn't he? Too much. She'd wondered over the years, and what she wouldn't give to explore the new feelings caressing her soul, to let him hold her hand, maybe kiss her. But how could she be with him and not tell him the truth, especially when he had a daughter of his own? He'd never understand. Especially now that she knew her daughter's identity.

Olivia bit her lip. "And I care about you too. You're such a good friend to me." She made sure to stress the word *friend*. She tried to pull her hand back into her lap, but his thumb edged over the ridges in her knuckles, his touch feather-light—and she couldn't.

"How else did you always imagine your life to be, Olivia?" His gaze was intense. "Did you always think . . . maybe you'd marry? Have children?"

His tone was so hopeful. But she had to tell him the truth. "Andrew, I can't have kids."

He looked taken aback. "I'm sorry, I shouldn't have presumed that—"

"That came out wrong. What I mean is I shouldn't have kids. Not with a family history like mine."

His eyebrows knit together in confusion. "Do you have some genetic predisposition toward a disease or something?"

"Nothing like that." Olivia stood. "I'll be right back." She walked down the hall to her bedroom, opened her nightstand drawer, and found the letter—the one she'd thrown away a month ago, then forced herself to snatch back out and keep. A penance of sorts, her burden to always bear. Hers, not Ellie's. Olivia inhaled sharply, then headed back to Andrew. She handed him the letter and sat.

He adjusted his glasses. "I don't understand. Why do you have a letter from the Oklahoma Department of Corrections?"

"Because she found me."

Even after moving to a new unlisted address, somehow Jeanine Culloway had located her all the way from prison.

"Who?"

Olivia snagged a long piece of hair and twisted it between her fingers. "My mama."

"She's in prison?"

She nodded. "Go ahead. Open the letter."

Andrew set it on the coffee table in front of them. "Just tell me."

Here goes nothing. "I ran away from home when I was sixteen. Came here to start fresh. Changed my name and everything. When I finally started getting playtime on the radio and such, my mama recognized my voice and contacted me. Gushed about how proud she was of me and all that."

"That's good, isn't it?"

"If she'd meant it." Olivia snatched the letter again and pulled it from the envelope. She waved it in the air. "You know what this is? A plea for money. That's all I am to her. The only reason she hasn't shown up on my doorstep is because she got arrested years back for some shady drug deals, prostitution, and who knows what else." She dropped the letter, and it floated into her lap. Now her breath came short, in spurts. Thinking about it literally hurt her chest. "And that's not all. She says she's been a model prisoner, so she might be getting out soon . . ." It complicated everything, the Mama factor.

Andrew contemplated her. He gently took the letter and placed it out of sight. "It sounds like you must have had quite the childhood."

"Not sure I could even call it that." Olivia rubbed the bridge of her nose. She hadn't meant to go all woe-is-me on him. "Anyway, now you know why I could never have kids."

"Why, because you had a bad mother?"

"No." Her voice grew soft. "Because I'd end up just like her if I had a child of my own."

"That's ridiculous."

"You don't get it." Olivia stood. "How about that lasagna now?" She stood and tried to walk around him to the kitchen.

Andrew snatched her wrist, rubbing his thumb over her pulse, which beat wildly. He rose to face her. "You are your own person. You don't have to be your mother."

"I can't take that chance. Ever. I can't negatively affect a child's life by being in it."

"Negatively affect—? But I've seen how you are with Ellie."

Panic clawed at her chest. He couldn't have figured it out—could he? "So?" She choked the word out.

"You're amazing with her. You give her confidence, and I have no doubt you'll shape her into the star she was born to be."

How much should she say? "But—"

"But nothing. She needs you. If anything, having a bad mother seems to have made you into someone who would make a great mom yourself. You're a fabulous mentor to that girl."

What do you think, God? Could I mentor her? If I did, would it ruin her like I would if I mothered her? If I have the careful boundary of mentorship set up between Ellie and me, there won't be the deeper expectations associated with being a mother, right?

Rachel's warning about telling Ellie the truth flickered back to haunt her conscience.

No. Her friend had meant well, but couldn't she see? As Olivia Lovett, Olivia could offer Ellie much more than she could as Marie Culloway. And she could protect her from Mama by keeping her at arm's length.

This was her answer. It was best for all of them. Ellie would get one of the two things she came to Nashville for—a music career—and Olivia would get to watch Ellie mature into the beautiful young woman and artist she was always meant to be.

And Mama would be none the wiser, especially if, by some miracle, she remained locked in a prison cell several states away.

Despite a twinge of warning pinching the corner of her soul, Olivia made her decision.

"Thank you for your confidence in me." Olivia threw her arms around Andrew's neck and squeezed tightly. "Now, when will those contracts be ready to sign? We have a label to launch."

21

"What do you think?" Ellie stepped out of the dressing room at Charming Charlie, a hip clothing and jewelry boutique she never would have set foot in alone. It was a good thing Olivia had volunteered to help her shop for the photo shoot tomorrow.

Olivia sat cross-legged on the bench across from Ellie. She tilted her head. "Twirl."

Ellie felt slightly ridiculous in the blue-and-white polka-dot dress but obeyed. She held out her arms and spun, trying not to trip over her feet. "Do you think it's really me?" The dress, while cute, seemed something more befitting a fashionable person like Lena, or Olivia herself—not Ellie, whose usual fare consisted of flannel and worn-out jeans.

"I think it's lovely." Olivia rose and approached Ellie. She adjusted the dress's collar and stepped back. "Hang on a second." In three quick steps, she left Ellie standing there.

The moment of quiet was actually a welcome thing. Since signing the contract late last week, life had been a whirlwind of activity.

Ellie pulled her phone from her purse and snapped a selfie in the mirror. Then she dashed off a quick text to Grandma. *I don't even recognize myself.*

A reply came fast. *I do. You're the same beautiful girl who knocked out her front two teeth with binoculars when she was six. The one who skinned her knees playing football with the boys and didn't care. You're just a little more grown-up now. And more lovely every day.*

Oh, Grandma. Ellie hugged the phone to her chest. How she missed Grandma and Grandpa.

Olivia returned, holding a chunky yellow necklace. She handed it to Ellie. "Tell me this won't look fabulous."

Ellie put her phone away and fingered the necklace. "I wouldn't know. I'm not exactly a fashionista."

"Now hush. You have a style all your own." She spun Ellie halfway around, then placed the necklace around Ellie's neck.

The beads hung heavy against her throat.

Olivia fluffed Ellie's hair, then steered her to a mirror outside the dressing room. "See? Fabulous."

Wow. The girl staring back at her exuded confidence and class, without being prissy or arrogant. She touched her reflection.

The reflection moved with her.

Yep, it was her, all right. "You certainly have a gift."

Olivia squeezed her shoulders. Some sort

of emotion—longing, maybe?—flashed over Olivia's features, but it was gone in an instant. "So do you, and it's my job to make sure you look the part of country's next sweetheart. I think this outfit will be perfect for the first part of your shoot."

Ellie turned to look the real Olivia, not her reflection, in the face. "I have to get more than one outfit?"

"Of course, silly. Go try on that green shirt with the jeans I picked out for you. Oooh, and pair it with that long black necklace."

Ellie headed back inside and did as Olivia asked.

Olivia fussed over her some more, and then they left for another store. Eventually, they landed at Starbucks, all the while discussing what to expect from the photo shoot, Ellie's latest songs, and the upcoming press conference to announce and officially launch the new label.

"I won't have to do anything but stand there and look pretty, right?" Ellie adjusted her wooden chair forward.

It scraped against the coffee shop floor.

"Exactly. You and Nick will be behind Andrew and me as we make the announcement for the press. Then you'll just interact with people at the launch party afterward."

"I think I can handle that." She snuggled her fingers around her pumpkin spice latte.

Olivia sipped her drink. "You'll be in the lime-light a lot. You know that, right? You'll be doing lots of interviews, impromptu singing, shows—as much as we can get for you."

"Oh, I know. I think the thought of all of it overwhelms me a bit, but like you've told me, I should just take it one day, one event, at a time."

"Precisely."

Behind Ellie, a barista called someone's name. Soft jazz floated from the speakers—one of the few places in Nashville not playing country music.

It reminded her of another coffee shop, not too long ago, where a handsome near-stranger had bought her a drink.

What was she going to do about Nick Perry?

"I have a question." Ellie blurted the words before she could snatch them back. What was she thinking? It was completely unprofessional to ask her employer for love advice. "Never mind."

"Go ahead. Ask away."

"It's about Nick." Ellie checked Olivia's reaction.

Olivia watched her.

Not for the first time, Ellie felt like there was something her mentor was holding back. "I don't really have an older female in my life to ask."

She raised an eyebrow. "I'm not that old."

Ellie felt her cheeks warm. "I didn't mean—"

"Relax. I'm teasing you. But what about your grandma?"

"Oh, I can't talk to my grandma about guys. Never could. She's the sweetest woman, but it would just feel weird."

"It's fine, Ellie. Really." Olivia's lips lifted, but something in her smile faltered. "What about Nick?"

"I'm not sure what to think of him. One minute it seems like maybe he's interested in me—but the next, it's like I'm competing with a thousand cheering fans."

"He's a good-looking, talented guy. He will likely spend his career surrounded by a thousand cheering fans. More than that, probably." Olivia tapped her fingers on the table. "I'm guessing you like him?"

"I'm crazy about him." She'd never admitted it out loud. But, yep, it was true.

"Does he know that?"

"I'm not positive."

"Has he ever said he's interested in you?"

"Not in those exact words." Ellie peeled the corner of the brown cardboard holder around her cup. "He did ask me to hang out a few weeks ago, but he could have meant as friends."

"That's true."

Olivia's answers weren't helping. Couldn't she just tell Ellie what to do? "I don't really have time for dating right now, do I?" Because maybe she didn't need the complication in her life, when things were finally going her way. She especially didn't need drama with Nick, the only other artist on her label. What if they dated and then broke up? The fallout would be horrible.

She should take a page from Olivia's playbook. "You never dated when you were my age. I remember how you inspired me—you said you were waiting to find the right guy, and you didn't want to date a bunch of frogs to find him."

Olivia shifted in her seat, almost as if she was uncomfortable.

But she'd said those things, hadn't she?

"How do you know Nick isn't the right guy? Are there red flags?"

"He's pretty close to perfect, actually. Other than the fact he attracts any female within a ten-yard radius." She laughed, but it came out sounding sour. Another sip of sweetness from her cup chased it away.

"From what I've seen, he's a great guy. I wouldn't follow my example, Ellie. Look at me these days, without a prince in sight. Do you want this to be you when you're nearly forty?"

"I'd like to settle down eventually. But I have to focus on my career. Don't I?"

Olivia shrugged. "Only you can decide what's most important in your life. All I can say is don't base your decisions on those that anyone else made. Especially me." She checked her watch.

"I'm sorry, girl. I've gotta cut this short. I have another meeting across town in twenty minutes."

"Okay." They both stood, put on their jackets, and headed for the door, tossing their cups in the garbage on their way out. A breeze whipped Ellie's hair but then let up. She turned to Olivia. "Thanks for today." Then, without thinking, she hugged Olivia. When she realized what she was doing, she tried to pull back, but Olivia held on tightly.

Olivia finally released her and swiped at her face.

Was that a tear? Strange.

"Oh, I've still got the clothing bags in my car. Do you want me to bring them to the shoot, or do you want to take them home?" Olivia shifted her keys from one hand to the other.

"You can bring them to the shoot if you don't mind. It's easier than me carrying them on the bus."

"Do you need a ride?"

"No, I don't mind taking the bus. I'd make you late."

Olivia hesitated, then nodded, waved, and ducked into her car.

Ellie headed down the sidewalk, determined to ignore the wind. It blew dead leaves across her path as she walked north toward the nearest bus stop. What a great day. Even though Olivia had acted a little odd at the coffee shop, it had been so wonderful to get her advice about Nick. To go shopping with her. To sit and have coffee. To bury herself in a hug, where she felt so cared for and safe.

Is this what it would have been like to have a mom? Ellie had admitted to Lena she was afraid her mom was actually a horrible person, but what if her fears were wrong? What if her mom were an amazing person like Olivia? Maybe she'd been searching for Ellie all these years. Maybe Daddy had known it and denied her mom access to Ellie. If he had, her grandparents didn't know anything about it.

God, I'm driving myself crazy with the what-ifs. If there was a way for me to know the truth, you'd show me. Wouldn't you?

A swirl of emotions followed one burnt-orange leaf down the sidewalk. The leaf skipped across the street and got caught in a short wrought-iron gate.

Ellie waited for a car to pass and then crossed the road. She bent and picked up the leaf, then peered past the gate into a cemetery.

Some invisible force beckoned her inside. And given what she'd just prayed . . .

Walking through the gate, she twirled the leaf in her hand and let it go. It bounced and swept its way along the dirt path in front of her, and she chased it.

The branches of hibernating trees hung over

the pathway, and headstones surrounded her. Occasionally she passed someone kneeling over a grave, crying or placing flowers there.

She was nuts. What was she doing, pursuing a leaf into a cemetery? But something inside her couldn't shake the feeling that God was leading her. She followed on, until the leaf pranced off the path upward to a large slope in the grass.

It stopped on a small grave.

Ellie walked toward the grave, almost afraid of what she'd see.

The headstone was blank, except for one word: *Father.*

Ellie sank to her knees. Who lay here, she didn't know, but right now, she'd pretend. If she couldn't talk to her dad in this life, maybe she'd imagine she could talk to him in the next. "Daddy? It's me. I miss you. I don't know if God tells you the awesome things that happen after you leave, but if you didn't know, I got a record deal. I'm pretty blessed." She changed positions, shifting to her rear and sitting cross-legged. "I've got this amazing mentor, and you won't believe who it is. Olivia Lovett. I know, right? She's as awesome in person as she was on the stage. And she's got me thinking about my mom."

She ran her fingertips over the soft grass beneath her. "Even though Grandpa, Grandma, and you were always enough for me, I think a part of me always wanted to know more about her. After you died, something in me became desperate to find out. I just . . . I don't want you to feel like I'm betraying you or something. You were a great dad, and I am confident you loved me, in spite of you being gone a lot. But I don't have that same assurance about my mom."

She sighed. "I wish you'd told me who she was. Why didn't you?"

Ellie stopped talking, listened—wishing beyond hope that Daddy would walk over, open his arms, and answer all her questions.

"A girl should have a right to know if she wants to. Maybe, if you were still alive, I wouldn't feel the need as much." The wind picked up and howled around her. "But maybe I still would. And I think that's okay."

Ellie looked at the ground, surprised to find clods of soft dirt in her fists, strands of grass still attached. She couldn't stand not knowing anymore. Her subconscious appeared to be telling her that much.

And that meant she must follow the only lead she had, however flimsy.

"I'm going to ask Olivia if she knows Marie Culloway."

She dropped the clods back onto the grave. Patting her hands on top of the dirt, she smoothed out the ground as best she could. Then she wiped her hands on her jeans, pulled her phone from her pocket, and dialed Olivia's number while the draft chilled her wet cheeks. She'd rather ask in person, but she might lose her nerve before she saw Olivia again.

Her mentor answered after two rings. "Hi, Ellie. Did you need a ride after all?"

"No, thank you." Ellie cleared her throat, trying to act normal. "I had . . . I had a question."

"Okay, shoot."

"It's going to sound weird." Ellie pulled her knees in to her chest. "Do . . . do you know someone named Marie Culloway?"

Olivia gripped the steering wheel as she sat in traffic during rush hour.

Ellie's voice filtered over her car's Bluetooth system.

Why would her daughter be asking her that? Did she think every performer knew everyone in Nashville, or did she suspect the truth?

The light turned green, but the cars in front of her barely moved, gridlocked.

"Olivia?"

"I'm here."

The silver Honda Civic in front of Olivia finally progressed, and she rammed her foot down on the gas pedal—only to slam the brakes when the other car came to an abrupt stop.

Olivia's heart pounded, and not because of her near car accident.

She'd decided not to reveal her original identity, so that she could sign Ellie to the label and do all she could to make her a success, but she'd never thought about what to do if Ellie asked her for the truth point-blank. The likelihood had been so slim—and yet, here they were.

"No, that name doesn't sound familiar. Why?" The lie slipped out, but Olivia couldn't bring herself to correct it.

A sigh came across the phone line. "She's my mom. I just thought . . . someone told me you might know her, that's all."

Who would have said that? Surely not Rachel. Perhaps Olivia's first manager, the only other person in Nashville who'd known her true identity?

It's me. The words simply wouldn't form. Fear held them inside.

What was she going to do?

She was flustered, needed time to think. This one lie didn't have to ruin anything.

The Honda shot forward, leaving wide open space in front of Olivia.

"I've gotta run. See you soon." She eased off the freeway, determined to leave the conversation behind for now.

Just until she could figure out what to do.

22

Her daughter was so beautiful.

Olivia couldn't help but stare as Ellie held her guitar and flashed the photographer a smile. Hopefully the camera could capture her essence. Despite how the world had changed, people still longed for genuine connection. And Ellie could give them that.

Ironic that she was the daughter of a liar.

Olivia shoved the thought away. She didn't have time to think about what she'd told Ellie yesterday. After all, she had a label to launch.

She stood in a 1,500-square-foot indoor area they'd rented for the day, Ellie's shoot going full force at one end, Andrew observing Nick's at the other. Floor-to-ceiling windows lined one wall of the studio, and movable partitions allowed photo assistants to change and create space as needed. Olivia had chosen the photographers carefully, insisting they pay top dollar for the best she'd ever worked with in the business.

She checked her watch. The graphic designer was supposed to meet Andrew and her to discuss the promotional materials he'd be creating once he received the images from the photo shoot. Had he arrived yet? Olivia scanned the room and saw him talking with Andrew.

She walked toward them.

Someone grabbed her elbow. "Liv."

Olivia turned. "Rachel?"

Her friend stood next to the food table.

"What are you doing here?"

"Didn't Andrew tell you? He asked me to cater lunch for everyone."

"No, I didn't know."

She hadn't seen her best friend in a week and a half. They'd texted some, but it was probably obvious to Rachel that Olivia had been avoiding her.

And now that Olivia had not only kept the truth from Ellie but flat-out lied to her, she really had no desire to be anywhere near her overly perceptive friend.

Time to play it cool. "Good to see you."

"Something's happened, hasn't it?" Rachel arched an eyebrow as she arranged a stack of muffins on the table.

"Things are busy."

"I don't mean with the label. I mean with Ellie."

"Oh. Right." Guilt invaded her airway. She had to get away. "I was on my way to see Andrew when you grabbed me. Better go."

"Liv."

"I'd rather not talk about this here." The room wasn't that large. Someone might overhear them.

Rachel removed a tray of mini quiches from a warming bag and began setting them one by one onto a round tray. Her lips tightened.

"Fine." She'd find out eventually anyway. Olivia lowered her voice. "Ellie asked me yesterday if I knew Marie Culloway. I said no."

"Oh, Olivia."

"I know, it sounds bad. She caught me off guard."

"You have to fix this."

The smell of egg and cheese made her nauseous. There was merit to Rachel's words. Olivia knew it was wrong to lie.

God had been niggling at her conscience all day.

But she also had no clue how to tell Ellie she'd lied without telling her the rest—and she'd already determined that telling her the full truth might be more harmful than helpful to her daughter.

Thankfully, Ellie didn't seem to suspect anything, so there was no rush.

Though that didn't keep Olivia's mind from spiraling.

"I appreciate the concern, but I have it handled."

"But—"

"Liv, can we talk to you for a second?" Andrew approached, the graphic designer trailing him. "Sorry to interrupt."

Rachel shrugged. "That's all right. We can finish our conversation later."

Olivia threw out a weak smile. "We don't have to. Everything is okay."

Or it would be if she could only focus on the task at hand and keep putting one foot in front of the other.

23

Finally, they'd arrived at this day.

Olivia visited the soundboard crew at Bernadette's for the third time. "Everything ready?"

Jimmy looked up from his scrutiny of the controls. "Sound system is a go."

"Perfect. Your team rocks."

She bustled toward the edge of the room, where several tables were filled with refreshments—everything from pimiento crackers to bacon-wrapped scallops, lobster salad, and potato pancakes with some sort of sour cream topping, not to mention a whole range of chocolate and fruity desserts. Rachel had outdone herself. And Olivia owed her big time—especially with the way Olivia had treated her friend over the whole Ellie-secret situation. Things were still awkward, given Rachel's belief that Olivia needed to come clean to her daughter.

It had been nine days since Ellie had asked her if she knew Marie Culloway. Olivia had come to terms with the idea she'd probably done the right thing, even if it required telling a lie. Above all, she wanted to protect Ellie.

Is that really true?

She pushed the thought away.

"Everything looks great." Andrew had snuck up on her and now stood at her side. He cut a handsome figure in his three-piece suit.

A nervous energy spun between them.

Olivia swallowed hard. "Bernadette and her crew have done a fabulous job."

"Indeed. Are Ellie and Nick here yet?"

"I'll go get them. You can start letting the crowd in if you'd like."

"Sounds good." Andrew touched her elbow. "And you look beautiful, by the way." He kissed her cheek, lingered, then headed toward the front doors.

Olivia couldn't stop the grin from spreading on her face as she walked down the hall to fetch their two artists. Since divulging her past to Andrew—well, part of it—they'd felt much closer the last few weeks. And she had to admit she liked it.

She opened the door to the back room and found Ellie and Nick standing there, chatting. Nick looked the part of a handsome, young cowboy, wearing jeans, a blazer, and a Stetson. Ellie was gorgeous in her new green blouse and jean skirt, complemented by boots and white jewelry. Her arms were folded over her chest, and a small smile played on her lips. Olivia almost hated to interrupt them.

When Ellie had asked Olivia for advice last week, Olivia had nearly frozen in fear—

especially when she'd said something about Olivia inspiring her. But then she'd remembered what Andrew had said about being a mentor. Mentors gave advice. She could do that. She just had to make sure Ellie knew Olivia wasn't perfect and definitely wasn't someone to emulate.

She cleared her throat. "Ready to make your debut into the world of signed recording artists?"

They both jumped at Olivia's greeting, and turned to look at her.

Nick recovered quickly. "Sure are."

Ellie bobbed her head in agreement. "Let's do this."

"Come on, then." Olivia swiveled to indicate they should walk through the door before her.

Nick adjusted the hat on his head and motioned to Ellie. "After you."

"I'll be there in a sec."

"All right." He winked and walked down the hallway toward the main part of the restaurant.

The sound of voices and soft country tunes filtered through the hall.

Ellie turned to Olivia. "I said yes."

"To what?"

"He asked me out again. For real this time. You know, not just as friends. And I wouldn't have had the courage to agree except for your advice."

Olivia swallowed a lump in her throat. Her daughter had taken what she'd said and considered it. Pride swept through her heart like a gentle tide. "Let me know how it goes."

"I will."

Olivia took her hand for a moment and squeezed. "Now, let's go announce to the world who the next stars of country music are gonna be."

Ellie looked at her with those trusting eyes. "I'm ready."

"I know you are. I wouldn't have signed you if I didn't think so."

They headed down the hall and turned right into the main area.

Olivia inhaled. So many familiar—and unfamiliar—faces.

At least a hundred people crowded into the restaurant. Members of the press, some with notepads and recorders, some with cameras, stood in the roped-off area up front, where all the normal tables and chairs had been cleared away. Others, who Olivia and Andrew had invited—promoters, producers, and country music elite—roamed the rest of the restaurant, already claiming seats at the red booths lining the walls. There were a few no-shows, but that was to be expected at any event.

As she maneuvered through the crowd with Ellie, Olivia offered quick greetings to various people, leaning in for cheek kisses and hugs. She introduced Ellie briefly, letting them know they'd have a chance to mingle with her more after the press conference was over.

Andrew and Nick waited up front for Olivia and Ellie to join them onstage. A podium with a microphone had been placed there.

Olivia caught Andrew's eye, and he nodded. Showtime. She led Ellie onstage.

Ellie and Nick stood slightly upstage and to the right of Olivia and Andrew, who stood behind the podium.

Jimmy stopped the calm undertones of music trickling through the crowd.

Andrew raised his hands. "Hey, everyone. Thanks for coming today. We know how busy everyone is with the holidays right around the corner."

The crowd quieted and gave him their attention. Red camera lights blinked on, indicating they were recording.

"We really appreciate you being here to learn more about Radiant Records and celebrate with us. For those who don't know, I'm Andrew Grant, and this is Olivia Lovett."

"Hey, y'all." Olivia waved. "What we envision for today is a fairly informal Q and A session, where we tell you a little about our new label—and then we mingle and eat. Sound good?"

Some of the crowd clapped in response.

Andrew took over again, just as they'd rehearsed. "About a year ago, Olivia approached me with the idea of starting a record label that nurtures young artists and lets them flourish in today's industry. It took several months of convincing for me to say yes. She's persistent, I tell you." He nudged her with his elbow. "This summer, I finally came to my senses and saw what a great team we'd make. Olivia will take her own experience as a recording artist and work with our artists to prep them for tours, albums, press interviews, photo shoots, and the like. Very hands-on. As the president, I'll be doing a lot more behind-the-scenes business work."

Olivia leaned closer to the microphone. "Which basically means the boring stuff."

The crowd chuckled.

Andrew delved into a few more particulars of how the label would run and their vision for their place in the industry. "And now, we'd like to introduce you to the starting line-up for Radiant Records: Nick Perry and Ellie Evans." He stepped aside, and Ellie and Nick waved. "You may have seen these two playing around town, but it won't be long before you hear them on the radio and see them on your TV screens. We guarantee it."

"That's right. We plan to get their first singles recorded in the next month, with forthcoming albums due out in the springtime." Olivia angled her body, so she could smile at Ellie and

Nick, then returned her gaze to the cameras. "Remember today, folks. You're witnessing history."

Hidden by the podium, Andrew's hand snatched Olivia's and squeezed, as if to agree with her statement. When he released it, her hand felt suddenly cold.

She gave brief bios on Ellie and Nick. "Now we'd like to open the floor for some questions."

A perky brunette with a mole just above her lip raised her hand.

"Teresa, how about you?"

"Olivia, I'm sure I speak for all of us when I say you were a wonder to behold on stage. Will you be making a comeback on your new label?"

Olivia had expected this question, but the reality of hearing it aloud felt like a stone had smacked her between the eyes. "Thanks for your sweet words, Teresa. Actually, I have recently discovered, through several consultations, that my voice will never be the same."

As she spoke, the door to the restaurant opened and closed. A latecomer, no doubt, though Olivia couldn't see who—only a tuft of red hair. Probably Amy Jones, a producer at WYOT. She hadn't RSVP'd, but she was notorious for being late.

Olivia refocused on answering Teresa's question. "I can't sing anymore—at least not like I used to—and am discovering a new love in mentoring young artists."

Teresa nodded sympathetically and then scribbled something on her notepad.

But Olivia didn't want the attention to be on her and what couldn't be. Today was all about possibilities. "Who's next?" She and Andrew answered a smattering of other questions about the label, Ellie, and Nick.

Someone even asked for a small performance.

Olivia turned to see what Ellie and Nick thought of an impromptu concert.

Both agreed.

"All right, folks, let them get their guitars ready. We've got time for one more question before we show you what the future of Radiant Records looks like. Or rather, sounds like."

"I have a question." Bright-red nails struck the air as a hand shot up in the middle of the crowd.

Olivia couldn't see who the hand belonged to, because the woman was blocked by a taller gentleman.

"All right, go ahead."

The woman stepped into view. Her red hair was thin but big, teased up, so curls formed around her face, which was caked in makeup. The woman's neon-orange dress hugged her hips and featured a plunging neckline that left nothing to the imagination.

Olivia inhaled a quiet gasp. It couldn't be. She leaned against the podium for support.

"Are you planning to make Ms. Ellie Evans into the next Olivia Lovett?"

She hadn't heard the voice in years, but it clawed at her subconscious, rattling against her heart and inciting in her the desire to run and hide. "I-I don't understand the question." How she forced the words out, she'd never know.

Mama placed her hands on her hips, and a sneer lifted her lips to the side. "Is she gonna be the Celibate Country Queen 2.0? Little Miss Perfect? All the things you supposedly were?"

Andrew cut in to reiterate their vision for the label, but Olivia was already stepping from the podium, issuing her apologies. She raced down the hallway, barely making it to the restroom before vomiting up her breakfast.

24

Fourteen years ago

I still can't believe how much my life has changed in just nine years. Ever since I got to Nashville, I've had one goal. To forget.

And the best way to do that is to change everything about myself and my life. To throw myself into my work.

When I stumbled off the bus in Nashville, fresh from Oklahoma, fresh from heartache, I started calling myself Olivia Lovett. It had a pretty ring to it—and sounded nothing like Marie Culloway.

After years of hard work as a waitress at two different cafés, I finally caught a break, singing in the park, of all places. My manager, Gary, found me there and set me on a road to success. He helped me get rid of my "hick ways"— enough to stay true to my country roots but without giving away that I came from a trashy trailer park with a mama who is now in prison.

Gary helped me get a record deal about a year ago, and since then, life hasn't slowed down— just the way I like it. I even went on a small tour with Katrina Beechy, who's been getting a lot of attention around here lately. I'm about to set off on my own tour to launch my new album.

Today, I'm getting ready for an interview with Kathy Truitt on *Nashville Insider*. It's a big deal, but I'm anxious to get on the road. I hate interviews. It's the only part of the job I don't care much for. They're too personal. I don't want to talk about my life.

As I stand just off the set waiting for my interview, I adjust my belt with the fake-diamond-studded trim and fluff my hair—the hair that I died blonde the week I got to Nashville. I catch the eye of one of the stagehands and abruptly turn away.

Guys tend to stare at girls in the spotlight, and I never want to attract that kind of attention. If it was up to me, I'd wear a shapeless burlap sack to sing my music. But the higher-ups would never go for that, so I just try to wear clothing that's not too tight or revealing.

Honestly, I can never imagine dating again. What if I get close to someone—maybe even close enough to want to marry them—and they find out about my baby girl? Who would want a wife who can't be a mom, who, by all appearances, wanted to be a country music star so badly she ran off and left her daughter?

All these years, I've been afraid Ben would find me. And now that I'm on TV, the likelihood is even greater. Part of me fears that day like the plague.

The other part of me . . . well, the other part of

me wishes that the day would come. I've thought about going back, but I promised I wouldn't.

At least Mama hasn't found me yet. She might spill my secret to the world. Then everything I've worked so hard for—the life I've created, though it's based on lies—would come tumbling down around me.

She'd relish that.

"You're up." The stagehand presses his hand into the small of my back, and I force myself not to recoil from his touch.

Instead, I grin and whisper my thanks as I head onto the set.

Kathy Truitt stands to greet me. She's poised and refined, with kindness in her blue eyes.

She hugs me, and we sit on two overstuffed chairs facing each other.

"It's an honor to have you here today, Olivia. You've taken the country music world by storm with your latest single, 'By My Side.'"

"Aw, thanks, Kathy. But the pleasure is truly all mine." That's it, remember to be charming and, above all, genuine.

Kathy asks a bunch of questions about my upcoming tour and what inspired the album. I can handle these—professional with a touch of personal. Nothing to worry about.

But then, she veers off course. "So, Olivia, we've all been wondering. Do you have a special man in your life?"

Not an unusual question to ask a musician. I've got the perfect answer primed on my lips. "No, not yet." I'm the only one who knows *not yet* means *never*.

"What's stopping you from finding love? Surely it's not your looks or lack of talent. You must have several admirers."

I blush and get back on track. Hopefully, my answer will satisfy her. "I just haven't found the one yet, and don't intend to waste my time on any frogs in the meantime."

"Wise girl. You're building quite the reputation for yourself as Nashville's good girl—no partying, no drinking, no dating. Many are calling you the rising Celibate Country Queen."

I wave my hand to ward off the nickname, keeping the smile plastered to my face. If only they knew the truth. "I'm hardly a queen of country. The greats—Dolly, Loretta, Patsy—those are the queens."

"All the same . . . what's your reason for staying out of the scene many performers find themselves falling into? Is it religion? Something else?"

I cough. What can I say? Not the truth. "I guess I'm just trying to focus on all the blessings in my life right now. And yes, I have faith. God and I are real close." Well, at least that's not a total lie. God and I were close—once upon a time, until I broke all his trust in me. But I'm trying to find my way back to him. I'm no fool. I know he's given me a second chance, and I intend to prove I deserve it.

"That's wonderful. If only more young women were like you."

If Ben is watching this, he's probably laughing his head off. Or stewing in anger. The irony—that any young woman would want to be like me—must be killing him right now.

If they knew the truth, they'd realize I'm a pauper in a princess's disguise.

25

Maybe if Olivia avoided her long enough, Mama would disappear altogether.

Olivia waved to a few producer friends before they left the restaurant. The launch party was winding down. Everything had gone smoothly—perfect, really, except for the one glaring blight on the day.

Mama had swooped back into Olivia's life, and that was never a good thing.

Olivia peered behind her.

Mama sat at a booth by herself, her legs crossed, top foot swinging as she hawk-eyed Olivia. She wasn't leaving, was she?

Olivia should march over there, demand to know what was going on, and get this over with. But she couldn't. Not yet.

Instead, she scurried toward the kitchen, through the revolving door.

Rachel was bent at the waist, looking through a low cabinet for something.

Several servers made their way in and out of the kitchen, clearing dishes and packing away any leftovers that remained.

"Rach."

Rachel straightened, Styrofoam to-go containers in hand. "What's up?" She waved the containers in the air. "You and Andrew should take some of the appetizers home. How'd it go? I was stuck back here all afternoon."

"Good."

Her friend cocked her head. "Then why does your voice say different?"

Olivia nodded toward the large pantry, where the dry items were stored. "Can we chat?" She tried to keep her tone light in case any servers happened to be listening in.

"Sure." Rachel handed the to-go containers to a young waitress. "Delia, please fill two containers with an assortment of leftovers."

Rachel led Olivia out of the main hustle and bustle and into the pantry.

Back here, the light was dimmer, the air filled with fragrant spices like garlic salt and onion. Olivia's foot tapped the ground, anxiety jolting through her nerves. "My mom is here."

"Wait, what? Explain."

"She just showed up. Asked a question in front of everyone, clearly meant to test or embarrass me. Or both." She relayed the details of her mother's presence at the press conference and launch party. There, she'd lurked on the outskirts, her eyes always watching Olivia.

"What do you think she wants?"

"Probably money, but I can't be sure."

"I guess you'll have to ask her."

Olivia slumped against the pantry wall. "That's

what I'm afraid of. I haven't seen her in twenty-three years. Talked to her on the phone a handful of times, gotten letters—but seeing her is different. It makes me feel like I'm a kid again. I feel . . . powerless."

"You can't let her do that to you."

"I don't have a choice. It's how I feel."

Rachel reached out and rubbed Olivia's upper arm. "You may not have a choice in the way you feel, but you do have a choice in the way you react. Who knows? Maybe she's here to apologize for the horrible way she treated you when you were younger."

"Given the manner of her re-entry to my life, I highly doubt that."

Her friend shrugged. "Still, you never know. Perhaps God's giving you a chance to redeem the past."

"How do you redeem something so . . ."

"So messed up?"

"Yeah."

"You don't."

Olivia scrunched her nose. "But you just said—"

"I meant that you yourself don't. God does. He's the great Redeemer, remember? He redeems us from our sins. That means it's possible for us to move past . . . well, the past. He'll give you the strength you need to make strides forward."

"I moved forward a long time ago. I left Oklahoma and never looked back."

"Was that really moving forward? Or just running away?" Rachel held up her hand to ward off Olivia's protest.

Olivia shut her mouth.

"I'm not judging you either way. I'm merely saying, give your mom a chance. She may surprise you."

"It seems I won't have a choice. About talking to her, at least. She's still hanging around out there and, if I know her, won't be leaving until she tells me what's on her mind."

"Well then, go." Rachel turned Olivia toward the open pantry door and gave her a push. "I'll be praying."

Olivia's heart tap-danced in her chest. Maybe Rachel was right. Maybe Olivia and Mama could find a way to reconcile despite everything that had happened between them.

Maybe pigs could fly too.

Oh, that kind of thinking wouldn't help. Olivia shook the doubt from her mind and left the kitchen, returning to the main restaurant area.

"Was wondering where you ran off to."

She spun to find Mama against the wall outside the door, as if she'd been crouching like a lioness hunting its prey. Up close, her face appeared gaunt, and her makeup couldn't completely hide the dark circles under her eyes. Her eyebrows were plucked stick thin and penciled lines filled the void. Tiny wrinkles around her lips protruded as she frowned.

"Hey, Mama." Olivia's glanced around the room, which was practically empty by now.

Andrew was engrossed in conversation with someone. Ellie and Nick stood off to one side, talking with Allan Hubbard, a local radio host. Nobody seemed to notice Mama and Olivia.

Good. "Let's go talk." Without waiting for Mama to say anything else, Olivia led her down the hall to the room where she and Andrew had held auditions only seven or eight weeks ago. So much had occurred since then.

Mama flounced inside the room and planted herself on the edge of a table.

Olivia closed the door quietly behind them. For a moment, she couldn't bring herself to turn around—to face the woman who'd been the cause of so much pain. But eventually, she did. "Why are you here, Mama?"

"Always one to cut right to the chase, aren't you, Marie?"

"My name is Olivia now."

"You can't change who you are, girl."

"I can try." Olivia crossed her arms over her chest. How could Mama make her feel two inches tall, especially since Mama stood a good foot shorter than Olivia?

Mama snorted. "Who you kidding? You're still

the same little girl who talked nonstop about leaving Red 'cause you was too good for all of us country hicks."

Olivia straightened, remembered what Rachel had said. She couldn't let Mama hold such power over her emotions. "Tell me what you want or leave, Mama. You can't talk to me like I'm a child. Not anymore."

Her mother studied her. Then she pulled her hands into her lap and quieted. Suddenly, she burst out laughing. "Sorry, old habits die hard, you know. I really am trying to be a better person. Learned a lot about myself in prison. As soon as I was released, I decided to come here and show you how I've changed. Got sober. Trying to get nicer too."

Olivia's first instinct was to lash out, but it could be that Rachel was on to something. Olivia inhaled and walked to the table. She eased herself up onto the edge next to Mama. Her feet dangled in the air.

The faint scent of cigarettes leached from Mama, covered generously by peach body spray.

"I could be nicer too, Mama." She nibbled the inside of her cheek. "I'm sorry I reacted the way I did to seeing you."

"I'm glad to hear you say that, sugar." Mama's voice was nearly unrecognizable. Maybe a softer side to her did exist. Maybe . . . " 'Cause I need your help real bad."

Hold that thought. "What kind of help?"

"Now, I just need enough money to get on my feet." Mama lifted the edge of her dress and scratched her inner thigh. "Don't have nowhere to live. They took the trailer a long time ago, you know."

Of course Mama was here to ask for money. Why had Olivia assumed anything different? Olivia opened her mouth to tell Mama in no uncertain terms . . . but then, Mama didn't know any better, did she? Olivia couldn't expect her to change all at once. Simply being here, wanting to change—maybe that was enough.

But money wasn't the answer. A roof over her head, where she could recover from prison and get to know Olivia again—that's what Mama needed. "I can't give you money, Mama. I'd worry you might go back to your old ways."

Mama jumped off the table and whirled. "I knew you'd say that." She stomped her foot and stuck her finger against Olivia's chest. "No matter what I do or say, you'll always think you're better than me. Don't forget, Miss Celibate Queen of Country, I know the truth about you. You're no more pure and righteous than the rest of us."

"I never claimed to be. The media claimed it for me."

"And you never bothered to correct them, did ya?"

"I—"

"Olivia?" A voice piped up from the doorway, where Ellie stood, a bit red-faced. "I'm sorry, I didn't know you were in the middle of something. I'll go."

"Wait. It's okay, Ellie." Olivia speared Mama with a look that demanded she be on her best behavior, if that was even possible. "What's up?"

Ellie fidgeted from one foot to the other, then strode forward, hand outstretched. To Mama. "I don't think we had a chance to meet at the launch party. I'm Ellie."

Mama looked taken aback, but shook Ellie's offered hand. "Jeanine. Her mama."

Olivia cringed. Why did she have to say that part? But she forced a smile. "That's right. She surprised me with a visit."

Ellie's apprehension turned to sunlight. "Oh, it's so nice to meet you. Your daughter is wonderful. She's been such an amazing mentor to me. I wouldn't be where I am without her."

With a hip cocked, Mama studied Ellie carefully. "It's nice to meet you too."

Ellie turned to Olivia. "Andrew was looking for you, and I saw you come back this way."

"You can tell him I'll be right out. Thanks, Ellie."

"No problem." She backed out of the room. "Hope to see you again, Jeanine."

With a swift flick of the wrist, Olivia closed

the door once more. "Mama, as I was saying—"

"Well, I'll be." Mama stared at the door as if still watching Ellie where she'd stood. "That's her, isn't it?"

A shiver raced up Olivia's spine. "Who, Mama?"

"Ellie. That's *her*."

"Yes, that's the girl I signed to my record label." Please, no.

Mama shifted her gaze to look straight at Olivia, and in that moment, Olivia knew that Mama knew. "Your daughter."

Olivia stiffened. The only way out of this was to lie. Mama couldn't know the truth. The risk was too great if she confirmed it. "That's ridiculous. She's a talented musician—"

"Don't lie to me, Marie. You think I wouldn't know my own granddaughter? She's got your ears. *My* ears. And there's just something about her . . ."

"It's not as if you paid much attention to her for the two weeks I had her. So no, I don't really think you'd know your own granddaughter." Olivia put her hand on the door handle, ready to escape. "Just leave it alone, Mama. This is none of your concern."

"Does she know?"

There was no use lying. Mama knew, and when Mama knew something, she sank her teeth into it like a rabid dog and wouldn't let go. Olivia sighed. "No."

"You gonna tell her?"

"No, I'm not."

Mama's eyes darkened, and she actually looked pained.

What did Mama care? It's not like she'd ever given a hoot about Olivia or Ellie before.

Then, a steely gaze came over her, and her painted lips compressed into a straight line. "Marie Culloway, you're many things. But I didn't raise no coward."

"You didn't raise me at all, Mama. The only reason I am the way I am—"

"Marie, here's what we're gonna do. You're gonna give me the money I need to get back on my feet. If you don't, I'm gonna tell that girl the truth." Mama pushed past Olivia, removed her hand from the door, and brushed it aside. "You have one week."

26

Nashville had come alive with the Christmas spirit. Ellie nudged Nick as they walked down the sidewalk, a brisk breeze causing her to burrow further into her peacoat. "Look."

Several city employees were decorating a giant Christmas tree in Walk of Fame Park, a few standing on ladders, winding tiny lights around and around, and some on the ground, sifting through large boxes of ornaments.

Ellie stopped. "There's something magical about putting up a tree, isn't there?"

Nick stuffed his hands in his pockets. "Yes, but I wish they'd wait till Thanksgiving was actually over. The turkey deserves a day of its own without Santa horning in."

Ellie laughed. "True. But to be fair, that's only two days away." Was it already the end of November? The last week had been a whirlwind. She and Nick had barely found time to fit in their date, thanks to interviews and other preparations for recording their upcoming albums.

But now that she was here, she didn't want to be anywhere else.

Nick pulled his left hand out of his pocket and wrapped his arm around Ellie's shoulders, warming her with his body heat.

Yes, nowhere she'd rather be at all.

They continued to stand still, watching the city employees work. Three middle-aged men strung garland and red bulbs around lampposts throughout the park.

Nick's hand dropped from her shoulder and grasped her fingers instead. "Come on." He pulled her toward the tree.

Ellie dug in her heels. "What are you doing?"

"You'll see."

Nick and Ellie approached the employees.

One woman looked up, a lime-green beanie tugged over her ears. "Can I help you?"

"We were just wondering if we could help."

Ellie looked at Nick. "We were?"

Nick winked. He turned his attention back to the woman. "What do you say?"

The woman chewed her lip. "We could get in trouble if something gets broken. But I don't suppose it could hurt to let you hang a few ornaments if you're quick about it." She indicated the box. "Be my guest."

"Awesome, thanks." Nick let go of Ellie's hand and squatted by the box. He grabbed the corner of her coat and tugged.

She lowered herself next to him. "This has to be the most interesting thing I've ever done on a date." Not that she'd had many. No guy had captured her attention the way Nick had.

"I'm an interesting guy."

"That you are." Ellie nudged him, and he toppled over. She giggled. "Oops."

He recovered quickly, laughing with her. "All right, let's find the coolest ornaments in here." They rummaged through the box. It was filled mostly with fancy glass ornaments that reminded Ellie of Grandma's tree at home. Grandma had only let Ellie help decorate a few times, but that was okay. It was the other tree that meant the most to Ellie.

Ellie sighed.

"Oh no. What's wrong?"

"Nothing, nothing." Ellie found an angel ornament and ran her fingers over the smooth surface of the figurine's face. "My dad and I had this little tree we'd decorate every Christmas. The ornaments were all of the ones I'd made him as I grew up. You know, Popsicle sticks with my school photo inside, that sort of thing. I haven't been able to bring myself to decorate it since he's been gone."

"Ellie, I'm so sorry." Nick sat back on his heels.

Behind them, one of the city employees hummed "Silent Night."

"I seem to have a habit of bringing back your sad memories. First the hospital, now this. We don't have to decorate this tree. This is probably the lamest date anyway."

"No, no. It's okay. It's a happy memory. I'm

glad for it." She placed the angel back in the box and pulled out a simple red-and-white candy cane ornament. Daddy had loved candy canes. Couldn't get enough of them. She'd hang this one in honor of him. "Do you have yours ready?"

Nick held a guitar ornament. "Figured this was appropriate." He stood and helped her up.

They sauntered closer to the tree.

Nick studied the tree for a moment, then selected a spot facing the road. "So everyone will see it."

Ellie hung her ornament next to Nick's. "Everyone, huh?"

They waved to the employees, then backed away to the sidewalk. The ornaments looked tiny on the fifteen-foot tree, nearly swallowed up by the branches.

Nick shrugged. "We'll know they're there, at least. We've left our mark. That's all that matters."

Ellie could hear cars speeding past on the street behind them, and people bustled by loaded down with shopping bags. The chatter of early diners filled the air as dusk began to fall and the lights popped on around the park.

"Is it all that matters, though?" Ellie hadn't meant to ask the question aloud.

"You don't think so?" Nick kicked at a pebble. "Ellie. Look down."

She did and saw an in-laid star and guitar

plaque with the name Vince Gill under her feet. She never got over seeing the stars along the Walk of Fame. "Sorry, Vince." Ellie knelt next to the platinum and granite surface. What would it be like to have a star here someday, where thousands could see it? To have a permanent place, etched in stone, where generations upon generations would know her name?

Where Marie Culloway could stand and see a visible reminder of what she'd given up so long ago?

Of course, given the fact her one lead— Olivia—had turned up empty, the chance of that happening was slim, but Ellie would fight with all her might to make it happen. There was still hope.

They followed the path, pointing out some of their faves. Finally, the line of granite stars ended.

Nick stopped abruptly. He stared at the concrete sidewalk, and a crazy grin came over his face. With a quick glimpse around the square, he turned back to Ellie. "I'll be right back."

"You're leaving me?"

"Yep, but not for long. I have to go buy something."

"Wait, seriously?"

He squeezed her hand and nodded. "Trust me." Then he headed out onto the crosswalk and rounded the corner, and Ellie was alone.

What in the world? She blew into her cupped hands, then stuck them back in her pockets.

She glanced toward the Christmas tree. Thousands of tiny lights danced from the branches.

Ellie lowered herself onto a bench. People hustled past, stepping on the stars beneath their feet as if they didn't even notice them. Ellie wanted to cry out, tell them to watch where they walked—but hadn't she done the same thing unknowingly? They really should have the spots cordoned off, giving the stars the respect they deserved.

Nick reappeared holding a plastic store bag. "See, I was only gone a couple of minutes."

Ellie squinted. "What's in the bag?"

"Chalk." Nick walked to the beginning of the sidewalk, next to the spot where the last star twinkled from the granite. "Stay there."

"Man, you're bossy." But Ellie did as he asked.

He pulled a piece of chalk from the bag, squatted, and started writing.

She tried to catch a glimpse of his drawing, but his body blocked her view.

Nick finally stood and dusted off his hands. Then he walked back to retrieve her. "Okay." He dragged her toward the sidewalk with the eagerness of a young puppy. Then he pointed to the sidewalk. "There."

He'd drawn a box with a star imitating the Walk of Fame plaques. His attempt at a guitar emblem was adorable, resembling what Ellie imagined a six-year-old capable of. She let out a tiny gasp at the words written on the inside of the star: *Ellie Evans.*

Sweet applesauce. She looked up at him. Instead of gazing at the star, he was focused on her. "Nick, thank you."

He took both her hands in his. His thumbs rubbed the top of her hands.

The rhythm mesmerized her.

"I wish you could see yourself the way I see you. You're already a star to me."

"Nick." She reached up to touch his cheek. "I don't deserve your faith in me."

"That's what I'm talking about. You do. Don't you know how amazing you are?"

Ellie coiled her hand around the base of his neck and tugged gently downward. She rose on her tiptoes and brushed her lips lightly against his.

He pulled her closer to him as he drew her deeper into his embrace.

When their lips finally parted, Ellie opened her eyes and stared into his.

For this perfect moment, she—Ellie "Evans" VanRisseghem—felt wonderfully and beautifully seen.

27

Nothing said Thanksgiving like the Macy's Thanksgiving Day Parade and time with friends. And Olivia was blessed to have both today. She snuggled into Andrew's couch and pointed at the screen. "Oh, look! It's a guitar-shaped float."

Andrew moved some pots around in his kitchen and poked his head through the open doorway. "Nice. Grace would love that one."

"It's a shame she has to work."

"Yeah, almost all the clerks had to work this morning. I guess people forget little things they need for dinner, like chicken broth or rolls. Thankfully the grocery store closes at one, so she'll be able to join us in a few hours."

"Thanks for having me today." Olivia pulled a blanket from the back of the sofa and arranged it around her legs. "Although most people have their heater on by now."

Andrew chuckled. The oven creaked open, presumably so he could peek at the turkey inside. "Mine's on. It's just set to sixty-eight degrees."

"No wonder I'm freezing."

"You'd think an Oklahoma girl like yourself would be used to the chilly air in the winter."

"You'd think a Florida boy like yourself wouldn't."

Despite the trials of the last week—ever since Mama had reared her head and demanded money Olivia didn't have—Olivia's heart felt light in this moment. Andrew had that effect on her. Her eyes flitted back to the television, where a huge Mickey Mouse balloon float filled the screen.

Andrew settled onto the couch next to her. He handed her a glass of something bubbly.

"Mimosas?" Olivia took the fluted glass from his hands. "What are we celebrating this early in the morning?"

"Time doesn't matter when it's a holiday." Andrew leaned back into his burgundy couch cushions. "And we're celebrating our first two contracted artists, a successful launch party, and every great thing that's to come."

"I'll drink to that." Olivia sipped the orange juice and champagne, and the bubbles tickled her lips.

Andrew grabbed the remote and turned the television volume down several notches.

The announcers' voices lowered to a rumble.

"Speaking of the launch party, where did you disappear to toward the end? Who was that woman with the red hair?"

Olivia choked on her drink. Some sloshed over the edge of the flute as she leaned forward to place it on Andrew's coffee table. She snatched a water bottle he'd given her earlier and took a swig.

"You okay?" Andrew scooted closer to rub her back.

"Fine, fine." She straightened.

His hand fell away.

Olivia turned toward him, swiftly feeling overly warm. She kicked the blanket off and folded her legs underneath her body. "Remember when I told you about my mom?"

"Of course." Andrew set his mimosa next to Olivia's.

"That was her."

His forehead creased. "Wow. How did it go? This was your first time seeing her in years, right?"

"In more than two decades, yes." Olivia moved her fingers over the ridges in the water bottle.

The plastic flexed and creaked.

"And let's see. How did it go? Well, she pretended to be nice. Then she asked for money, as I suspected she would. I was a fool to think she might have changed."

"I think it makes you an optimist, not a fool." Andrew placed his arm along the ridge of the couch. His fingertips were mere inches from her shoulder. "People *can* change, you know."

"You really think so?" The question raced out. Did she really think Mama could become someone different? No. But maybe Olivia could. Mama had told her she'd be a Culloway forever, but if Andrew believed people could change, maybe Olivia could fully believe it too.

Could . . . could she could even someday tell Ellie the truth? Be a mother to her? A vision swam through her mind, one of her and Ellie living in the same house, like Andrew and Grace did. Eating breakfast together every day. Fighting and laughing over the Sunday comics. Watching the Macy's Thanksgiving Day Parade on the couch in Olivia's living room, Chloe and Pascal curled at their feet.

Of course, if Ellie had inherited Olivia's lack of cooking skills, they'd order in for Thanksgiving. The thought brought a grin to Olivia's face.

"Penny for your thoughts." Andrew touched Olivia's shoulder, and his fingertips skimmed her arm lightly.

She glanced down at his hand, then up into his eyes. The depths of them . . . oh. He cared so much for her, didn't he? She didn't deserve his affection, but suddenly, on this day of thanksgiving, she was more grateful for it than he would ever know. Andrew made her want to be better—made her believe she *could be* better. All the reasons why they shouldn't be together just drifted away.

Olivia dropped the water bottle onto the floor. She reached for Andrew's hand as it caressed her arm. Surprise filled his eyes as Olivia moved closer, until their faces were only a mere breath away.

With his free hand, he smoothed the hair around her face, tucked a strand behind her ear, and studied her, as if asking permission.

Her heart pounded. She hadn't let a man this near since Ben all those years ago. What if—

And then Andrew kissed her.

She released her hold on his hand and wound both her arms around his neck. His lips caressed hers in the same gentle but firm way he had about his whole being. As he kissed her, his hand stroked her cheek—adoringly, like he cherished all that she was.

Finally, he pulled back, and Olivia's lips felt bereft, slightly swollen. She couldn't speak.

Andrew let several seconds pass before filling the silence. "You have no idea how long I've wanted to do that."

"Me too." The answer shocked Olivia, because until it had happened, she'd never known it was what she'd wanted. Had never let herself consider it, because she wasn't worthy of Andrew. But conceivably, like Andrew said, people really could change.

And maybe admitting that—believing that— was the first step.

Somewhere in the distance, a phone rang.

Andrew groaned. "I don't want to leave this moment, but it could be Grace on her break. She might need to ask me something."

"No problem."

Andrew eyed the blanket on the floor. "At least now I know a better way to warm you up than turning on the heater." He winked as he rose and headed toward the kitchen.

Olivia snickered. So much had surprised her lately, but perhaps God was orchestrating something she couldn't see. Maybe all she had to do was walk through whatever he placed in front of her.

Andrew's voice carried from the kitchen. It rose and fell, but it didn't sound like he was talking to Grace. In fact, he sounded irritated. Surely someone wouldn't be calling with business on Thanksgiving Day, would they?

Olivia stood and traveled through the open doorway.

Andrew leaned against the counter, one hand holding his cell, the other rubbing his forehead. He glanced up at Olivia. "Look, I have to go." He paused. "No, I don't think that's a good idea." Another pause. "Goodbye, Paula." He punched a button and set his phone hard on the counter.

The tile was cold beneath Olivia's feet, despite her wearing socks. "Everything okay?"

"Not really." Andrew frowned, then opened the oven again. He stood there for a moment, just staring at the turkey.

The smell of sage met Olivia's nose. She wandered toward him, unsure of how to behave now that their relationship had shifted. Should she comfort him with a hug? Did he want to be left alone?

At last, he shut the door and turned toward her. "Guess you might as well know."

Her heart skipped. "Know what?"

He turned to his granite-top island, where a bag of potatoes sat. Andrew untied the bag and reached inside, pulling out six spuds and placing them on the counter. "About Paula. My ex-wife."

Oh. "You've never said much about her." Olivia snatched up the potatoes and took them to the sink. She ran water over them and scrubbed the dirt away.

"And you've never asked. Which I appreciate. Because it's a somewhat painful situation."

"I get that. That's why I never mentioned my mom before." Olivia reached for a few paper towels and dried off the potatoes, then turned and placed them back on the island in front of Andrew.

"Thanks." He groped in a drawer and pulled out a peeler, nudging it across the island toward Olivia. He dragged his trashcan toward them, taking the first potato and a knife in hand. "Paula and I married young. We had Grace nine months later."

"Wow. That must have been quite a shock." Olivia seized the peeler and started on a potato.

"Definitely was. But it didn't take me long to

see Paula wasn't quite committed to the idea of being a mother. She wanted to spend long nights out with friends, and left me and Grace home alone. She'd come home drunk. Weekends. Weekdays. Didn't matter." Andrew's knife flew across his potato's surface so rapidly Olivia worried he'd lose an appendage.

"So what happened? Is that what led to the divorce?"

"No. Her leaving us when Grace was four months old did that."

Olivia's peeler slipped and skimmed her finger instead. She winced and set the potato down.

"You okay?"

"Mmm-hmm." Olivia stuck her raw fingertip in her mouth. Andrew's wife left them—just like Olivia had left Ben and Ellie. But the circumstances were different, right? Surely Andrew would be able to see the difference if she ever got up the courage to tell him.

Andrew sliced his potato and tossed the pieces into a pot. Then he picked up another. "It was rough at first. I mean, what kind of mother leaves her baby like that?"

A scared one.

"I sometimes wonder if she ever loved Grace, even a little bit."

She did. She had to. She was a mom. But the answer stuck in Olivia's throat, because she instantly pictured Jeanine Culloway. She was a mom, but that didn't make her a mother. But Olivia was different—wasn't she?

"Grace and I made it work. Then three months ago, out of the blue, Paula called me. She wants to see Grace."

Light fluttered through Olivia's soul. She pulled her finger from her mouth. It wasn't bleeding. "She had a change of heart?"

"I doubt it."

"Why?"

"Women like that—they don't change."

"But . . ." Earlier, he'd said people *could* change. Did he not really believe it? If not, what would he say about Olivia's past? About her present circumstances, now that Ellie had come back into her life? "Are you going to tell Grace her mom is asking to see her?"

"I can't." Andrew set down the knife and leaned forward with both hands touching the counter. "I can't take the risk that Paula will hurt Grace. Grace is happy as she is. She's content. She knows I love her. She doesn't need some woman who left her returning and confusing her." Andrew picked the knife up again. "After all, that woman is not really a mother. No woman who left her child for selfish reasons could ever truly be considered a mother."

He hacked away at the rest of the potatoes until the white flesh was mutilated beyond recognition. Then he dropped the pieces in the pot, drowned them with water, and set them on the stove to boil.

Olivia couldn't take her eyes off the gas flames as they leaped up, hungry for their task—devouring any hope the potatoes ever had of being whole again.

Olivia pulled into her driveway and her motion sensor lights flickered on. She parked and rubbed the back of her neck. The day had been . . . emotional, from one extreme to the next. She'd forced herself to enjoy the time with Andrew and Grace, eating turkey and pie, watching the Dallas Cowboys get whooped by the Redskins.

Now all she wanted was a hot bath and her bed.

She cut the engine and climbed from the car, hauling her purse and the bag filled with leftovers from the passenger seat. With heavy steps, she walked to the front door, readying the key for the lock.

"Marie."

Olivia jumped. The croak had come from the ground.

Mama sat huddled in the dark on Olivia's front porch. All she wore was a flimsy pair of pants, a thin zippered coat, and some shoes with the toe worn out on the right foot. She clutched a mostly empty bottle of Jack Daniels.

The ancient Chevy sedan parked out front must

be hers. How Mama could afford a car was a mystery. She'd probably sweet-talked some old chump back home into letting her borrow it.

"What in the world, Mama? You've got to be freezing."

"Just wanted to see my girl on Thankssssss-giving." Mama lifted the bottle and took a slurp, backhanding the liquid that sloshed down her chin.

Olivia hesitated. But she couldn't leave her outside in this condition. "Let's get you inside." She unlocked the front door and set her things on the entryway table.

The dogs careened toward her.

"Lay down."

They obeyed, but Pascal whimpered.

Olivia headed back out to Mama, whose head listed to the side. She squatted and heaved Mama up under the armpits. Her skin was cold to the touch.

"Watch it." Mama struggled against Olivia for a moment, then obliged. Her teeth chattered.

Olivia led her inside and to the gas fireplace, which she flicked on. Warmth flooded the immediate space. She found a thick blanket and draped it around Mama's shoulders. "I'm gonna go make you some coffee."

She snatched the bag of leftovers and carried it to the kitchen, then busied herself making a cup of joe. As it brewed, she placed her hands on the counter. How many times had she done this in the first sixteen years of her life?

Back then, the predominant emotion she'd felt was anger. Anger that Mama had to be this way. That she'd chosen this life. That she'd never found a way to clean up despite having a child.

But now?

Now she couldn't help but feel something akin to pity.

Olivia took down a plate and reheated some turkey, potatoes, and yams. The cinnamon-sugar blend on the orange vegetables filled the air, a reminder that things once destined to taste horrible could be made sweet.

God, Rachel reminded me that you can redeem things. I'm open to that if you are. Change Mama, Lord. Maybe if she found you, she could be different. Things between her and me could be different.

Olivia filled a mug with coffee and cream, then took it and the plate of food into the living room.

Mama hadn't moved. She stared into the flames. Tonight she wore no makeup. Liver spots dotted her neck and cheeks. Her hair looked like it hadn't been washed in days. Dirt caked her cuticles. Had she been staying in her car? Olivia had assumed Mama had some money for a hotel—but then again, how would she? She hadn't worked in years.

Of course, she'd somehow found spare change for alcohol. Like always.

Enough of that. Mama was here. Maybe it was desperation that had driven her to Olivia's porch, maybe it was something else. But Olivia couldn't let her freeze or starve.

"Here, Mama." She held out the plate of food and set the mug on the coffee table.

Mama's hand snuck out from the blanket, and she grabbed the cup, sipping furiously in spite of the hotness of the liquid. She put it down, clutched the plate of food, and shoveled bites into her mouth.

Olivia sat on the other end of the couch and waited in silence.

Pascal came and rested his head on her lap.

In no time, Mama finished her food. She set the empty plate and fork on the coffee table next to the mug, then tightened the blanket around her shoulders, watching the fire dance.

This quiet was so unusual for Mama. Was she working up a way to apologize, to tell Olivia that her threats had been empty, that she wasn't going to tell Ellie the truth after all?

I trust you, God.

Mama sniffled.

Were those tears running down her cheeks? She'd never been a weepy drunk.

Had prison done something to her, or was this the Lord at work?

"Mama?" Olivia reached out a hand to comfort her but withdrew before touching Mama. Who knew how she would react? Sympathy could send her back into her old self.

"Did I ever tell you why I hate Thanksgiving?" Mama's words were less slurred now, almost rhythmic.

She did? "No."

"I was eight. My daddy was a trucker and actually home for once."

Olivia straightened. Mama had never once mentioned her daddy. Olivia had just assumed he'd not been in the picture, like her own father.

"My mama was so happy she went out and bought a big turkey, bigger than we'd ever had before. I helped her baste it and made some stuffing from a box. Daddy seemed quiet all day, except for right before dinner was ready. He came bursting through the door, and he gathered Mama in his arms, and they started dancin' to Patsy's 'Crazy.' "

Mama hated that song. Something pinched in Olivia's gut.

"Then he swept me up, and we all three danced and giggled." Her tone was so mournful.

But why? It seemed like a great memory.

"Mama eventually shooed us out of the kitchen and finished dinner. It was the best feast I ever did eat."

Mama fell silent.

Should Olivia say something? She'd never experienced a moment like this with Mama. How was she supposed to react?

But Mama lifted her thumb to her mouth and started chewing on her nail. "I always wondered why that wasn't enough for him. Why we weren't enough."

"Why? What happened?" Olivia snapped her lips shut. She hadn't meant to shatter the silence with her own questions.

Mama reared her head and swiveled her neck toward Olivia, her features contorted in confusion—almost like she'd forgotten Olivia was there. Her eyes were glassed over and her lips trembled.

"Right after dinner that night, my daddy went straight back to his truck and shot himself."

Olivia woke with a start and rolled over in bed. The clock read five a.m. Had something woken her?

And where were the dogs?

Mama had cried herself to sleep on the couch last night, so it could be they were sleeping out there with her.

Olivia sat up and ran her hands through her hair. Had last night been real? Had Mama really come by and shared an experience from her past, one that had likely shaped the rest of her life? When she'd revealed the horror she'd lived through, so much about Mama made sense.

Olivia had never stopped to think much about how Mama's history affected her. She'd only known a little, had only met Grandma Loretta twice—but that was enough to know Mama's childhood couldn't have been a happy one.

But the fact Mama had come here last night and told her what she did—that had to mean she cared about Olivia, deep down. Didn't it?

Perhaps this was the beginning of reconciliation. She and Olivia could have a conversation today about Ellie and come to an understanding. Olivia would explain why she thought it was best to protect Ellie from the truth.

Chloe trotted through the bedroom doorway, Pascal on her heels. They were never up at this hour. Something was amiss. Was Mama okay?

Olivia stood and headed into the living room, but Mama wasn't on the couch. And she wasn't in the bathroom. With quick steps, Olivia peeped through the blinds on the front window. Mama's car was gone.

A strange mixture of sadness and relief assaulted Olivia.

It was too early to make sense of this. Olivia turned to go back to bed—but something caught her eye. Her purse sat where she'd left it on the entryway table, but now it sported an orange sticky note.

Olivia grasped the note and recognized Mama's scrawl. "Took your credit card as a down payment. Because I'm such a nice mama, you can have an extra week before I tell your daughter the truth."

Unbelievable.

No. Believable. Very believable.

How could Olivia have ever thought Mama had changed? And what was last night about? Was it all an act to get in here to grab Olivia's credit card?

Olivia crumpled the note in her hand and stalked to the still-burning fireplace.

Then she tossed it in and watched it burn.

28

Christmas music trickled from Bernadette's kitchen, though Olivia felt anything but festive as she took a deep breath and trudged through the doorway.

The kitchen was empty of all but Rachel.

Olivia didn't know whether to rejoice or moan. She needed Rachel's advice—again—but she wasn't sure she was ready to hear a lecture.

Rachel's gaze popped up from the salads she was plating. "Didn't expect to see you today." She sprinkled feta cheese over several plates.

"We have to talk. I tried your cell but called Matt when you didn't answer. He said you were working today."

Rachel made quick work of slicing a few pears before arranging them onto the plates. "Hadn't planned on working Thanksgiving weekend, but Bernadette offered double pay for some business luncheon."

"That's good, that's good." Olivia slid onto the stool opposite Rachel and tapped her fingers on the countertop. "Where's your staff?"

"It's a small luncheon, so I didn't really need anyone to help cook or plate. Just someone to serve." Rachel worried her lip. "Did I tell you I hired Ellie?"

Olivia's fingers stilled. "What? Why?"

"She came in here asking for a job, to make a little extra cash around the holidays. You know, before her contract really sets in. She has a lot of waitressing experience, so . . . you don't mind, do you?"

"No, no, of course not. It's not like I own her or something."

"I know, but . . . ."

"It's fine, Rach." Olivia threaded her fingers into a steeple and sighed.

Rachel placed the plates in the refrigerator, then wiped her hands on her apron. "You said you wanted to talk. I have some time before I need to start on the soup." She walked around the counter and settled onto the stool next to Olivia.

"I've made a mess of things, and I don't know what to do. There's Ellie, my mom. And oh, Andrew."

"Andrew? How does he fit into this?"

"He kind of kissed me yesterday. And I kind of let him."

Rachel leaned against the counter, an appreciative look on her face. "It's about time."

"You don't understand." Olivia buried her face in her hands and groaned. "At first, I thought things could work between us. But then, his ex-wife called, and apparently she left when Grace was a baby . . ."

A shadow of understanding passed over Rachel's eyes. "So you think he won't understand if you tell him about Ellie."

"I know he won't. Plus there's my mom, who, as you know, somehow guessed the truth when she saw Ellie. Last night, she showed up again. It was strange. First, she opened up about her past, but . . . suffice it to say, she ended by threatening to tell Ellie if I don't give her money. She gave me an extension, but I don't have any money, remember? So how am I supposed to keep her quiet? I want her gone, away from Ellie."

Rachel tilted her head. "You know my thoughts on that subject. If you tell Ellie the truth, your mom's threats are just that—threats. There's nothing she can say to hurt you, at least as far as Ellie is concerned." She reached for Olivia's hand. "She knows about Ellie now, so it's not like you're really protecting Ellie anymore. Just because you withhold the truth certainly doesn't mean your mother will."

Rachel was right, as always. At least if Olivia told Ellie the truth, Ellie would hear it from her—and not whatever lies Mama had concocted. Yes, maybe this could work.

But the phone conversation from a few weeks ago smacked Olivia's memory. She groaned. "If only I hadn't lied to her. Why did I have to tell her I didn't know Marie Culloway?"

"So you do know her?" A tiny voice rose from

the doorway, and Olivia spun on her stool. Ellie stood there in black pants and a purple shirt, her face devoid of all color. She folded her hands in front of her and stared at Olivia. "Why would you lie?"

Olivia stared at her daughter. How much had she heard? "It's not polite to eavesdrop." Oh, why was she scolding her? This was all Olivia's fault, not Ellie's. Ellie had never done anything wrong—not one thing. Olivia was the poor excuse for a human being. Her daughter was just a victim of knowing her.

Ellie sputtered for a response.

Rachel jumped in with a gentle reply. "Ellie, you're a little early for your serving gig. Why don't you go out into the restaurant? Olivia will join you soon."

Ellie nodded and backed out of the kitchen, eyes as big as saucers.

Rachel turned to Olivia. "You have to tell her the truth. Right now. That girl deserves to know."

"You're right." And she was. Olivia couldn't go on pretending, could she? It was time to come clean. "Pray for me, Rach." She slid off the stool and squeezed her friend's hand.

"Always."

Olivia nodded, then put one painful step in front of another. She pushed through the doorway and walked toward the booth her daughter occupied.

Other than two techs testing sound and lighting, the dining room was empty. Nothing could get in the way of Ellie learning the truth now. Nothing but fear.

Olivia slid into the booth across from her.

The young woman stared at the table, moving her finger along its edge in a small circle, lips flattened in a straight line. "I didn't mean to eavesdrop. I thought I'd show up early for my first day of work here and happened to hear you mention Marie Culloway." She looked up into Olivia's eyes, questioning. "So you *do* know my mother? Why would you lie to me?" Her voice cracked.

"Because . . ." *I'm her*. But the words wouldn't come. Silence fell.

"I don't get it. I mean, if you know her, why wouldn't you just tell me?" Ellie's gaze searched Olivia's.

Olivia looked away, toward the stage where she'd first heard her daughter play, where she'd first felt this girl would change her life forever.

If she'd known then what she knew now, would she have turned away?

Would that have been better?

Olivia picked at a cuticle on her right hand. "Why do you want to find her?" *To yell at her? To ask questions you could never possibly understand the answers to?*

Ellie's lip trembled, and her hands became

327

fists. "I don't know if I can put it into words, really. There are so many reasons. I want to know if I'm anything like her. If she ever . . ."

"If she ever what?"

"Regrets leaving."

The gentle whisper floated to Olivia's ears and pricked something deep in her soul. Look at what she'd done to this poor girl, without even meaning to. Hadn't leaving been best? Would stepping back into her life now really do any good?

The Bible said the truth could set one free— but what if it only put Ellie into greater bondage? What if the fact Olivia had known she was her daughter but had done nothing about it hurt her daughter more than she could ever recover from? And then there was Mama. Sure, Olivia could warn Ellie about her, but she couldn't demand her daughter not have a relationship with her grandmother. And Ellie would fall under her spell . . .

Maybe she shouldn't take the risk.

But Mama would tell if Olivia couldn't find a way to pay her off permanently.

A headache pounded against her temples. Maybe she should start out with a small slice of the truth and see how Ellie handled it. This was a lot to lay on her all at once. "I did know Marie Culloway, once upon a time. But I haven't seen her for a long time now." That much was true. Marie Culloway hadn't existed for over twenty-three years. Not really. Yes, she tried to creep up every now and then, but Olivia Lovett had become an expert at tamping her down and keeping her in her proper place.

The past.

"Did she . . . ever mention me?"

"Ellie." Olivia reached across the table, covered one of Ellie's fisted hands.

It relaxed beneath her touch.

"Your mother, she loved you. She thought about you constantly. She left because she couldn't see a way to keep you."

Ellie's brow creased. "Are you sure she didn't just come to Nashville to get away from me? Because I was too much of a burden, and she had dreams she wanted to pursue?"

"Never for a moment believe that." Olivia had to emphasize this point. In fact, she couldn't emphasize it enough. "Your mother grew up in a harsh home environment. She didn't know how to be a mother. She wanted the best for you. When she gave you up, she did the only other thing she knew to do. Move to Nashville to pursue a career, do her best to forget."

"Why would she want to forget me?"

"Oh, sweetie. Not to forget you. That would never happen. It never did." Olivia's throat thickened. "To forget that she wasn't enough for you. She wanted to be. She just . . . couldn't."

"I still don't understand." Ellie sat back for a moment, closed her eyes. "Do you know where she is now? There's so much I have to ask her."

Dismay overtook Olivia and she pulled her sweaty palms into her lap. What else would she ever be able to tell Ellie to help her make peace with the past, even if her daughter knew Olivia's true identity? Knowing the whole truth would never be enough for her. It wouldn't change anything—except harm the burgeoning relationship she had with Olivia as a mentor. And what if that in turn harmed Ellie's chances at becoming a successful performer? Finding out the truth could send her running back to Oklahoma. Who knew what would happen?

What if Olivia could find the money to send Mama away from Ellie? Maybe Andrew could loan it to her from his personal funds—then she could pay him back from her earnings once the label started making money. It could work. He might trust her enough to loan her the money without knowing the exact reason.

But she'd have to get Ellie to stop looking for Marie Culloway. And there was only one way Olivia could help Ellie to truly move forward with her life, follow her dreams, have a successful career. Olivia could give her that, even if it meant never having a true mother-daughter relationship.

This wasn't a white lie she could fix later. There'd be no coming back from this.

But all those years ago, Olivia had done the thing that was hardest—the thing that she knew in her heart was best for Ellie.

Even if it meant no Thanksgiving dinners together, not helping her choose a wedding dress when she got married, not being in the room when her grandchildren were born.

Her stomach twisted and she tasted bile. No matter what she did, she'd lose her daughter and Ellie's life would never be the same.

Sometimes the truth didn't set you free. It only hurt the people you loved the most and put them in the path of dangerous drunken mamas with a penchant for destroying hope.

Olivia scrunched her eyes shut and whispered words she could never take back—words that, hopefully, in time, would close old wounds and help her daughter live the life she deserved. "I'm sorry, Ellie. Marie died years ago."

She was an orphan.

The thought kept tumbling through Ellie's mind as she served Bernadette's luncheon guests, then as she waited in the kitchen for them to be finished. It replayed on a continuous loop in her brain until it had been stripped of all emotion.

She'd been so focused on that fact, she hadn't even thought to ask Olivia more questions. How did her mom die? When? Did Olivia have any pictures of her? There was so much she wanted to know. She'd have to think through all her questions and see if Olivia could answer any of them.

Something inside of her had been so sure she'd find her mother, that she would finally be able to ask her questions about why she'd left. Ellie *needed* to hear the words from Marie's own mouth. And until now, she hadn't known what her deepest hope was—that she'd find her mom, they'd work through all the junk from the past, and then they'd have a real relationship.

As much as everyone figured she would, she didn't resent her mom for leaving. And now, she'd never have an opportunity to tell her that. Not until heaven. And that was only if Marie had been a believer.

"Thanks for your help today, Ellie. You did a great job." Rachel pulled her apron over her head and hung it on a peg in the kitchen.

"I appreciate you hiring me." Ellie slipped her jacket on over her uniform, forcing a smile.

"Ellie." Rachel said the word hesitantly, cocking her head. "How are you feeling after your talk with Olivia?"

She blew out a breath and shrugged. "Numb, I guess. I didn't expect to hear that my mom was dead."

Rachel's face contorted. Was she shocked by the admission? Wasn't that why she'd asked Ellie how she was doing?

"I assumed you knew what we talked about."

"I thought I knew too. I'm sorry that you had to hear that, Ellie." Rachel's cheeks had turned crimson. She looked almost . . . mad.

"Did I say something wrong?"

"Absolutely not. I'm not upset with *you*." Rachel pulled her mouth into a tight smile and handed Ellie a Styrofoam container. "Leftovers. You won't have to cook dinner now."

Ellie thanked her and headed through the kitchen door, past the dining room, and out into the wind.

She was an orphan.

Man, why couldn't she stop the notion from pummeling her?

Clouds covered the sky, and a few rain droplets splattered the ground. Fitting.

Ellie walked toward her bus stop.

Across the street, a mom tugged a little girl by the hand as they tried to outrun the rain. The girl's laughter flitted across the road and smacked Ellie between the eyes.

She continued to place one leaden foot in front of the other. But she didn't want to go back to an empty apartment—Lena was spending another day with her family.

Ellie pulled her phone from her purse and

speed-dialed Grandma. She had to talk to someone who understood her, or she'd burst.

Voicemail.

Which left one option. She turned on her heel and traveled toward Nick's place. She'd been by yesterday to drop off a pumpkin pie after Thanksgiving at Lena's parents' house, so the directions were fresh in her mind.

When she arrived at his brick building, which was much nicer than her own, she pulled open the door and hurried out of the rain. Ellie took the stairs a few at a time, careful not to spill the container of Rachel's goodies. She got to apartment 306 and knocked.

It took a while for Nick to answer. His eyes were bloodshot and his curls in disarray. He wore a white T-shirt and basketball shorts. "Ellie? What are you doing here?"

"Hey." Had she woken him up? "Sorry. I can go."

"No, come on in." He tugged the door open wider. "I didn't mean to be rude. I just got some disturbing news and wasn't expecting to face anyone."

"Oh no." She slipped in through the doorway, and he shut the door behind her. "What news?" Ellie set her purse and the food container on Nick's kitchen table just inside the entrance.

He rubbed a hand over his stubbled jaw. Then he hauled her into an embrace. The top of her head barely reached his chin. Despite his disheveled appearance, he smelled fresh and earthy—like pine, maybe. For a moment, they held each other, and for a moment, all felt right with the world.

She was an orphan.

She pushed the thought away. Right now was about Nick. Something was wrong with him. Ellie pulled out of their hug, took his hand, and led him to the couch. "You're worrying me. What's wrong? Is it one of the kids from the hospital?"

"No. My mom was in a bad car accident."

"Oh, Nick." Visions of her dad pelted her: strapped to his hospital bed, scrapes and bruises littering his body, arms casted, head shaved from brain surgery, tubes everywhere. She shivered. Didn't want to ask the inevitable question. "Is she okay?"

Nick's breaths came heavy.

She tucked her legs to the side and leaned against him.

His breathing slowed, steadied. "I think so. It just really shook me up. She's conscious, and the doctors say she'll make a full recovery."

"That's awesome." He didn't know how lucky he was. "I'm sure it's hard to be so far away, though."

"It is. That's partially why I'm leaving."

She sat up. "Leaving?"

"Her recovery will be six weeks or longer, just in the hospital and rehab alone. She broke her hips, both legs, some ribs, and punctured her lung. And my dad is in China for work."

"Can't he come home?"

Nick's face twisted, darkened. "He could, but he won't. They don't have the best marriage, and work is so important to him. He basically told me it's my responsibility, as the oldest child, to come home and help out. Especially since I don't have a 'real job.' "

"That's awful." Ellie's brain worked overtime. "But what about your album? We're both supposed to start recording soon."

Nick sat forward on the couch cushion. "I just got off the phone with Andrew before you got here. He said we could arrange for me to record in Texas if need be. I don't know how long I'll be out there."

"It's nice he's being so flexible."

"Yeah."

"How do you feel about everything?"

"I'm angry at my dad, but what can I do? Mom needs me. My brothers and sisters need me. Only one other brother can drive. All the others need someone to shuttle them around, make sure they get to school and stuff."

"Hopefully it'll just be the six weeks." Ellie tried to lighten her tone.

"Yeah, hopefully." He stood and began pulling

coats from his hall closet, folding them, and placing them on his coffee table. "I called Lauren, and she's going to come help out when she's not working her shifts at the hospital."

Something funny churned Ellie's stomach. "Who's Lauren?"

And why had he called her before calling Ellie? Had he only told Ellie about this because she'd shown up?

Chill out, Ellie. He was merely trying to get everything squared away, right? That didn't mean anything.

Nick crouched and sifted through a box on the floor of his closet. "A friend from back home. She's a nurse."

Wait, he'd mentioned her before during one of their talks, hadn't he? "Isn't she your ex-girlfriend?" The question came out a lot whinier than she'd intended. What was wrong with her? She shouldn't be giving Nick the third degree. He was hurting.

Nick turned and stared at her. "Yes, we dated in high school."

"Oh." And they'd be spending a lot of hours together, taking care of Nick's family. Wouldn't that naturally rekindle their flame? Nick was a sweet guy. Any girl would want to be with him. Many girls did. All the fans who were always crowding around him after concerts, asking him to sign random parts of their bodies, flaunting—

No. She had to stop that line of thinking right now. She wouldn't be that jealous girlfriend. Not that Nick had asked her to be his girlfriend. Maybe she'd misread the situation.

"You have nothing to worry about. We're just friends."

But were they? Maybe he thought so, but what if he was wrong? What if he saw Lauren again and forgot all about Ellie? A hot flash flowed through Ellie from head to toe. "I know."

"You don't sound convinced."

"I am." She tried to force confidence into her voice.

"Why are you worrying about something like that at a time like this?" The sharpness in his tone shocked Ellie. "Seriously, Ell, don't you know how I feel about you?"

He sounded so exasperated with her. She had been wrong to even bring it up, especially right now. Neither she nor Nick had the mental or emotional capacity today to deal with this.

Her stomach threatened to toss the salad she'd snuck during her serving gig. She should go. "I'm sorry. I'll let you pack." Ellie stood, awkwardly pressing her clammy hands together. She rushed toward the front door, then turned. "I'm sorry about your mom, Nick. I hope everything goes well with her recovery."

He brushed his hand through his hair, groaned. "Sorry, I'm being a jerk. Come b—"

"It's fine." She snatched her purse and the Styrofoam container off of his table and flung open the door. Embarrassment tumbled through her with every step. Her eyes itched and burned. "I'll be sure to ask Andrew how your mom is doing."

Before Nick could say another word, she flew into the hallway and down the stairs. Dots of something slid from her cheeks, watering the linoleum under her feet. Was she—crying? Ellie froze on the bottom step. The container of food slipped from her hands, splattering roast and potatoes all over the floor.

Why now? What was it about this moment that had broken the dam inside of her and allowed the tears to finally flow free? Was it finding out her mom was dead? Hurting for Nick? Reliving the car accident that had taken Daddy's life? All of it?

Her life?

She couldn't stay here. But where could she go? How could she escape the grief?

"God, help." The two words were all she could muster. Ellie pushed through the apartment building door, her tears mingling with the pouring rain.

29

Two days later, Ellie stood at the counter of Starbucks. All around her, excited chatter filled the air. Students huddled together, studying; musicians hunkered down in small groups, chatting about the latest country stars; and there in the corner sat a mother and daughter, laughing over their drinks.

Ellie just wanted to get her coffee, head home, and work on some new songs for her album. Unless Olivia finally texted her back. She'd asked if they could get together again to talk about Marie, but so far, nothing.

"Ellie." The barista called out her name and slid a hot beverage across the counter.

Ellie reached for the cup and took a sip. Black coffee. No sugar, no cream. Plain and dark, just like this day. Like life.

This self-pity had to stop.

She turned her body away from the mother-daughter pair and ran right into . . .

Kacie Hayes!

"Sweet applesauce. I'm so sorry." Ellie steadied her hand to keep her coffee from sloshing out of the hole in her cup's top.

Kacie shrugged. "No harm, no foul." She

blinked and smiled. "Hey, I know you. Ellie, right?"

"You remember me?"

"Of course." Kacie rummaged through her purse and pulled out her phone. "You never did send me that demo, though. I was hoping to work you into my tour as a backup singer."

"Yeah, I'm sorry about that. Things have been crazy." Ellie fingered the lip of her lid. "I actually just signed with Radiant Records." The thought still sent flutters up her spine. With the quest to find Marie Culloway more or less over, she could focus every iota of energy on her career. And she would.

"Congrats. I hadn't heard. I've had my head buried under a rock trying to put the finishing touches on my album."

"It's definitely a busy time of year."

"Radiant Records. That's Olivia Lovett's new label, isn't it?"

"It is."

"The queen herself. You really must be amazing to have been noticed by her."

Heat filled Ellie's cheeks. She was nothing next to a performer like Kacie, whose latest single had topped the charts. This girl was a sensation and clearly going places. "I still don't know what she sees in me. I think one of these days she's going to wake up and realize she signed the wrong person."

"I seriously doubt it. Someone of Olivia's caliber wouldn't waste her time or money on an artist she didn't believe in." Kacie scrunched her nose and lightly chewed the tip of her manicured nail. "So listen. I have a lull in my schedule." She pointed to Ellie's coffee. "Are you headed out? Or would you want to join me for a cup o' joe?"

"Sure. I'd love to."

Kacie ordered while Ellie found a table next to a window overlooking the busy street.

When Kacie started to make her way over, a few people nudged each other and stared in their direction. They followed Kacie, asking for autographs and pictures with her.

The girl graciously complied.

Wow, what would that be like?

After Ellie had been sitting there watching for about ten minutes, Kacie finally pulled away. "I'm so sorry. I had no idea that would happen."

"Your fans really love you."

"They love the me they think I am." Kacie cocked her head. "I'm not sure we can have a real conversation when people are interrupting us, and they probably will if we stay here. Want to come back to my house and hang out?"

Ellie could always work on writing music later tonight. Besides, Kacie—Kacie's life—fascinated her. She could learn a lot from someone ahead of her in the industry. "Why not?"

Kacie's eyes brightened, and she led Ellie out the door. She pulled a set of keys from her purse. "You can just follow me over."

"I don't actually have a car. I usually take the bus."

"Hop on in." Kacie clicked the key fob, and the lights flashed on a hot-pink Mustang. Of course she had a convertible. The perfect car for a star.

Ellie opened the passenger door and started to climb inside. She hesitated at the pile of books in the passenger seat.

Kacie tossed her purse in the back and got into the driver's seat, then leaned over to grab the books. "Sorry." She threw them into the backseat. "It's a bit messy."

With a quick shrug, Ellie got in. Her shoes shuffled against several Taco Bell burrito wrappers.

Kacie groaned. "Guess you've discovered my guilty pleasure."

"I prefer the Double Decker Tacos myself." Ellie laughed.

Kacie revved the engine. "Just don't tell anyone, all right? My manager would flip, given my recent new gig as spokesperson for Real Way Organics." She left the parking lot and eased onto the street.

"That's right, I read something in this month's *Country Music Today* about how you only eat organic and are committed to a healthy lifestyle. Or something like that."

Kacie let out a snort. "Yep, my manager has created the perfect image for me. Too bad it's not true. I couldn't choke down a salad every day if I tried."

Ellie leaned back in her seat. "You know, I remember feeling guilty while reading that article. I think I was eating boxed mac and cheese."

"Don't feel guilty at all. Most of the stuff you read about me isn't true." Kacie drove a few blocks and then angled the car into a long driveway. She pulled through a gate and into a three-car garage. The engine died. "Home sweet home."

Ellie got out of the car and followed Kacie through a door and into a massive designer kitchen. She could see her reflection in the stainless steel appliances and ran her fingers along the smooth marble countertop.

Kacie hung her purse on a rack mounted to the wall and pulled open the fridge door. "Want anything else to drink?"

Ellie had finished the rest of her coffee on the way over. "Water would be great. Thanks."

Kacie tossed her a bottle, and they made their way into the living room.

A grand mantel with a stone fireplace took center stage in the room, and a wraparound couch and overstuffed chair gave it a homey cabin feel, despite the high vaulted ceiling. A guitar sat next to the sofa.

Kacie snatched it up and sank onto the couch. She plucked a few strings, not saying anything for a moment. Almost like she wanted to, but couldn't find the words.

Ellie sat on the floor, cracked the water bottle open, took a swig. Waited.

Her new friend's fingers stopped gracing the guitar strings. Kacie looked up. "Don't let them change you, Ellie."

"Who?"

"The industry. Olivia. Whoever." Music lilted on the air once again. "I've only just started in this business, and already I feel like I'm not allowed to show people who I am."

Ellie ran her thumbs along the ridges of the water bottle, creating lines in the condensation. "What do you mean?"

"Did you know I love to read? I'm actually a huge nerd. Science was my favorite subject in school. Before I got signed, I didn't know the difference between mascara and eyeliner. Seriously. And as previously stated, I'm a junk-food fiend. But no one knows any of that about me. When I get up on that stage, I'm just a creation named Kacie Hayes."

Why was this woman Ellie barely knew spilling her guts like this? Maybe she saw Ellie as someone who could sympathize. Or maybe she was simply desperate for a friend. Hard to believe someone like Kacie Hayes would be devoid of sincere friendships, though.

"I didn't realize." Ellie frowned. "But those things—your choice of entertainment, your love of junk food—they don't really define who you are as a person. When you get up on the stage, none of that matters. You can express yourself through your music."

Kacie pushed her lips into a sad smile. "Ah, but that's only if I have something to say. Which I don't."

"What are you talking about? I love your music." Ellie set the water bottle aside and pulled her knees up to her chest. " 'Those Wheels Keep Turning' is one of my favorites."

"But I didn't write it. Someone on my team did. Sometimes I fear I don't have anything substantive to say at all." Kacie's fingers stilled again. "But I have a feeling you do."

Sure, Ellie had lots to say. But getting it out, sharing the deepest part of herself, was a risk. She'd always equated performing with being seen—but what did she really want people to see? Wasn't an honest glimpse of herself better than the fake brand of "authenticity" Kacie sported? Ellie shrugged. "I've written my fair share of songs."

"Show me." Kacie held out her guitar to Ellie.

Ellie gripped the guitar arm and shifted the instrument into her arms. A new melody drifted from the recesses of her heart. Her fingers flew as if possessed, and words formed on her lips, from where, she didn't know. All the pent-up emotions from this weekend—the sorrow, the raw reality that her mom was gone forever, and with that, her chance at knowing some deeper part of herself—mingled into a song.

By the time she finished playing, her heart pounded. Where was she? Ellie glanced up and shook herself from a trance.

In front of her, Kacie wiped away a tear. "That, my friend, was beautiful."

Ellie cleared her throat. "It's nothing flashy or fancy."

"No. It's better. It's authentic. You have a gift, Ellie. People everywhere are just looking for something real, especially in today's world of plastic." Kacie placed her hand on the arm of the guitar, as if she drew strength from it, from Ellie. "Keep being you, and I promise, it'll be enough."

30

Lies had a way of souring even the most beautiful of days.

Olivia stepped from her sedan into the sunlight, the crisp air resonating with the coming Christmas season. Thanksgiving had only been four days ago, but everyone had made the switch from turkey to tinsel in two seconds flat. Too bad she didn't feel in the holiday spirit this year.

She pulled open the doors to the office complex—they'd been able to secure the great-deal-of-an-office after all—and trudged through the large foyer toward the elevators. Her flats squeaked against the waxed tile floors as she walked, something heavy in her steps. She entered the elevator and hit the button for her floor.

Her phone buzzed. Rachel. Again.

Olivia hit Ignore. Her friend had somehow found out she'd told Ellie that Marie Culloway was dead. And Olivia knew what Rachel would say if she answered.

Rachel wasn't the only one Olivia was avoiding. She hadn't returned Ellie's texts since telling her the news.

The fake news.

What could Olivia say in reply? Ellie wanted

to get together to discuss Marie some more. The thought of furthering the untruth with other details about Marie and her death . . . well, it just didn't sit well with Olivia. Not that lying in the first place did either.

It had been for Ellie's own good, right? Ugh. The more Olivia considered it, the more she questioned just whom she was protecting.

The elevator dinged and the doors slid open. She stepped out and headed toward her office.

Voices floated from the lobby as she opened the door.

Dread pricked her skin. Was that Mama? Olivia forced herself through the door—and stopped fast at the sight before her.

Ellie sat on the edge of a chair in the lobby's waiting area, hands tucked beneath her legs, engaged in eager conversation with Mama.

What were they doing here? And why was Mama talking to Ellie? Olivia cleared her throat, and both women looked up.

A smirk smeared across Mama's face.

Ellie popped up from her seat. "Olivia, hi! I just finished a quick meeting with Andrew and ran into your mother on my way out. She's been keeping me entertained with stories of you as a child."

As if Mama remembered anything from Olivia's childhood. The smile Olivia forced out was so tight it hurt. "Oh really? Imagine that.

Mama, could I speak to you privately, please? Ellie, I apologize. I know I owe you a text. Things have been crazy." And were about to get crazier.

Ellie glanced between Mama and Olivia. Her eyes hinted that she knew something was off, but her voice didn't waver. "I understand." She glanced at the clock on the wall. "I need to get over to Bernadette's to help Rachel set up for lunch anyway."

"Tell her I say hi." Olivia snatched Mama's elbow and led her to her office. She shut the door firmly behind them.

Mama shook free and rubbed her arm. "Ouch, Marie. You don't have to be so rough."

Olivia paced the room, then placed her hands on the desk and stared into Mama's eyes. "What are you doing here, Mama?"

"Can't a woman get to know her grand-daughter without someone jumping down her throat?"

Olivia wanted to gag at the syrupy words. She flexed her fingers. "We both know that's not why you're here." How naïve of her to hope Mama would leave Nashville on her own. "You gave me another week to sort this out. Even took my credit card as a 'down payment,' remember?"

"I changed my mind." Mama turned to the large window and ran a fire-red fingernail down the portion in front of her. A screech filled the silence. "Your credit limit on that card was a measly five hundred."

"It was a new card. And I don't like to live on credit. I've seen what that does to people." It gave them debts they couldn't pay unless they debased themselves in one way or another. Mama should get that.

Mama ignored her. "If I don't see more than that, I'm assuming that means you want the girl to know the truth." The screeching halted. "The truth that her mama is—"

"Enough." Olivia slammed her fist against the oak beneath her. "I thought by moving away, I'd be free of you. Of the poison you spew. Clearly, I was wrong."

Mama swiveled and something flashed in her eyes. She pointed a finger toward Olivia. "All I want is justice."

"Justice?" Pain radiated from the side of Olivia's hand, where it had connected with the desk. "What's justice got to do with any of this?"

"I want justice for all the arrogance you've shown over the years." Mama's voice punctuated the air. "I provided a roof over your head in whatever way I had to—you sneered in my face. I landed myself in prison because of it— you never came to visit me. I showed up needin' help—you tried to turn me away. Face it, Marie. You want to blame me for everything, but you'd be gettin' what you deserve if your precious reputation, all the lies you've built up around yourself, came a-tumblin' down."

"Mama . . ." Olivia sank down onto her chair, all fight leaving her body. Despite everything Mama had done, Olivia hadn't been perfect either. "I admit, I always wanted to be better than you, to be more than I could be livin' in Red."

"Finally, a lick of truth leavin' your lips." Mama folded her arms and leaned against the windowsill.

God, I'm so tired of this. But it'd been this way Olivia's whole life. Things would never change.

Or could they?

Rachel's remark from the record launch party rose to Olivia's mind: *"He's the great Redeemer, remember? He redeems us from our sins. That means it's possible for us to move past . . . well, the past. He'll give you the strength you need to make strides forward."*

She'd prayed for God to change Mama. But maybe the change had to start with Olivia. Could be that's as far as it would go.

Perhaps it was time at last for a real heart-to-heart. No barbs thrown in anger, but instead, a peace offering. Still, that started with complete honesty. And it would take all the strength she had. *Please, Lord. Help me say the right thing here.* Olivia tugged on a strand of her hair. "I know I didn't always handle things well. But, Mama . . . you hurt me, the way you treated me."

"Back to me. It's always my fault, ain't it, Marie?" Mama spit out the name as if it was a curse.

And for a long time, it had been. Olivia had done everything she could think to escape the curse of her name, her past. She'd run. She'd tried to ignore it. She'd wiped the red dirt of Oklahoma from her feet and baptized herself into a new way of living.

But she'd never faced it head-on. All of that could change right now. If she forgave.

Who was she kidding? That was no easy task. How could she forgive the woman who'd abused her and despised her since she'd been born?

She couldn't—not in her own strength.

Olivia inhaled a shaky breath. God had been gracious, forgiven her past. It wasn't right of her to deny forgiveness to someone else.

But oh, how she wanted to.

God, this is the hardest thing I've ever had to do, other than leaving Ellie with Ben. Make me strong. "Mama, I forgive you." The words trembled as they left her mouth.

"I ain't asking for your forgiveness, girl." Mama faced the window again. She lifted a shaky hand and patted the top of her over-sprayed hair, lips pursed in the reflection.

The same strand of pity that had sliced Olivia after seeing Mama four nights ago struck again. Mama could act tough all she wanted. There was something there. Something unsure. Something sad.

"I know you're not." A quiet niggling urged Olivia from her chair. God, perhaps. Because this was the answer. She had to move forward once and for all. She cautiously approached Mama and placed a hand on her shoulder. "And I need you to forgive me too. You're right. I have blamed you. But I can't keep making decisions and doing things based on the past. Based on you."

Mama turned and glared, shrugging away Olivia's touch. "Is that supposed to make me feel better?" She snatched her purse and dug inside till she came up with a cigarette and lighter.

"I'm not trying to make you feel better. I'm trying to make things right. Trying to say that, in the past, I made decisions out of fear. Fear that I'd end up like you. Fear that I could never escape you " Yes. With every word, this felt more right. "But by forgiving you and asking your forgiveness, I can finally start over. Be the person God wants me to be instead of the person I've felt I needed to be in order to cover up the past."

Mama lifted the cigarette, stuck it between her lips, and raised the lighter. She flicked at the lighter wheel numerous times, hands shaking as she tried to ignite the cigarette and couldn't. At last, she removed the cigarette and rammed it and the lighter back into her purse. "Where's the money, Marie?"

Olivia sighed, rubbed her fingers along her forehead. Some people would never change, but that wasn't Olivia's problem. She could only control her own actions. She softened her voice. "I don't have a lot of money to give you." She reached into her desk and withdrew her checkbook, writing a check for the exact amount in her checking account. Not much, but hopefully enough to get Mama off her back and away from Ellie. She held out the check to Mama, who took it, examined the amount, and scoffed.

"You're gonna have to do better than that."

"It's all I have, Mama." Even if she could get more from Andrew after talking with him, would anything ever be enough for Mama? She'd keep coming back, keep holding the truth over Olivia's head. Someday, Mama would carry out her threat, which meant Olivia needed to tell Ellie the truth. But how?

She'd pray. Figure it out. And then, ask Ellie for forgiveness too.

"Fine." After stuffing the check into her purse, Mama flung herself toward the door. She leveled a stare at Olivia. "Don't know what I ever did to deserve a daughter like you." With a twist, she flounced into the hall.

The rubber band around Olivia's lungs snapped

loose, and fresh air flowed through them once again. She slumped against the window and tried to still her hands. Mama's leaving, the angry words—nothing about that was new. Nothing except the way Olivia had handled it. With forgiveness.

She'd changed. Really and truly changed. Transformation *was* possible. The idea tasted sweet.

"Liv?" Andrew stood at the door.

"Come on in."

"Everything okay? I heard shouting."

"Mama was here."

Andrew crossed the room and wrapped her in a hug. "You okay?"

She held tight to his chest and breathed in the scent of him. In the past, she would have pushed him away, afraid. Afraid she could never be who Andrew needed her to be. Afraid she'd hurt him or his daughter. Afraid her past would haunt her forever.

But today was a new day.

She could never escape Marie Culloway, true. Olivia Lovett was built from the ashes of Marie. She'd needed her in order to become who she was today. But Marie's past didn't have to dictate Olivia's future.

And Olivia laid a kiss on Andrew's lips to prove it.

31

"No, no, no." Ellie threw the notebook across her room. It bounced off the wall and landed askew on the carpet.

"Whoa." Lena stepped through the doorway. "What did that poor notebook ever do to you?"

From her position on the floor, Ellie propped herself against her bed and sighed. "It's not the notebook's fault its owner is a failure when it comes to creativity."

Lena's eyebrow quirked. "Do I need to buy a cake for this pity party?"

Her roommate was right, though if anyone deserved a pity party right about now, it was Ellie. But Lena didn't know what Ellie had found out about Marie. Ellie hadn't even told Grandma and Grandpa, who'd returned her missed call from Friday. By the time they'd connected, Ellie was so drained of tears she couldn't bring herself to shed more by talking about it.

"Cake is always nice."

"Coming right up. Oh wait, I have to study for a big test a week before finals. Now me, *there's* someone to pity." Her roommate leaned against the doorpost. "I fully believe my Russian art prof is determined to kill me through excessive studying."

"You're almost done. Hang in there."

"Thanks." Lena snapped her fingers as if she'd just remembered something. "Be right back." She ran from the room and returned with a wrapped Twinkie in hand. "Next best thing to cake, right?" She tossed the package to Ellie.

"My fave." Ellie shook the sponge cake down into the bottom of the package. The cellophane crinkled against her fingertips as she ripped into the top. "Thanks."

"You got it, dude."

Ellie rolled her eyes.

"I'd stay and chat, but I have to meet Myra to study. Again. So whatever's wrong—you can do it!" Lena struck a cheerleading pose and wiggled her fingers in the air. Then she dashed off.

A few moments later, the front door squeaked closed.

Ellie pulled the Twinkie from its wrapper and bit into the soft cake. The cream oozed into her mouth from within the luscious dessert. If only all her problems really could be solved with overly processed snacks.

But the problem of Olivia just plain avoiding her questions about Marie—or so it seemed— was beyond her control. She'd kept her phone nearby since yesterday, when Olivia said she owed her a text. But so far, nada.

And the problem of coming up with new

material for her album could only be solved with hard work and some inspiration.

Ellie crumpled the Twinkie wrapper and tossed it aside. She hopped up, grabbed her Bible, and slid onto her desk chair. Maybe the Psalms would offer some inspiration. But after fifteen minutes, she'd only managed to read the same passage over and over again.

She needed to get out of her own head. Perhaps she could go back to the hospital, check in on the children in the cancer ward. Before he'd left, Nick had told her Brian was doing better, but that Cindy Lou Who had experienced some setbacks.

A familiar pang pierced her in the gut. She hadn't spoken with Nick since he'd left four days ago. What kind of friend was she that she'd not called to ask how his mom was doing? Things had been really busy . . .

No. She was still embarrassed by her jealousy, plain and simple. And with him gone, things were just easier. Less complicated. Or so she kept telling herself.

Ellie worried her lip, then snatched her phone and dialed his number.

"Hello, Nick's phone." A female. One of his sisters, maybe?

"Hi, is Nick there?"

"Who is this?" Was it her imagination, or did the girl on the other end sound slightly possessive?

"Ellie. Who is this?"

"Lauren. His girlfriend."

The Twinkie turned sour in her stomach. She tried to form words but couldn't.

"Can I give him a message?" Lauren asked.

"No thanks." Ellie punched the End button on her phone and set it on her desk. Her fears had become reality. She'd told herself she was wrong, that, sure, Nick was popular with the ladies, but he'd acted like he and Ellie had something special.

It'd been one date. One kiss. Apparently she'd let herself make more of it than it really was.

Then why did his rejection hurt so much?

Her phone vibrated against the wooden desk. Was Nick calling back?

Her pulse ratcheted, and Ellie checked the caller ID.

It was a number she didn't recognize.

"Hello?"

"Ellie, hey, it's Kacie."

Oh. Not Nick. "Kacie. What's going on?"

"Listen, I know it's super last-minute, but I just got asked to sub into a guest spot at the Opry tonight."

"What?" Sweet applesauce. The Grand Ole Opry was a place of dreams for every country musician. All the greats had played there and most were members. Performing as a guest was the first step toward induction. "That's amazing!"

"I know. I'm still in a whirlwind. I'm so nervous I've downed three burritos. Shh, don't tell."

"My lips are sealed." Ellie leaned back in her desk chair.

'I was wondering if you'd do me a huge favor. One of my backup singers is out of town, and I need a fill-in. I know you've got your own music going on, but you're familiar with my stuff, right?"

Ellie shot forward in her seat. A chance to perform on the Opry stage? Yeah, it was as a backup singer—but who cared. "I'd love to help out. I'll just have to check with my label, but I'm guessing it'll be fine."

"Great. We're running sound check at four. Text me back at this number ASAP if you can't make it. And wear denim." A muffled voice filled the background. "Gotta go. Thank you so much. I owe you big time. Bye for now."

"Bye." Ellie sat there for a moment, then sprang into action. She called the Radiant Records office and chatted with Andrew, who assured her she wasn't violating her contract. Then, after shooting Kacie a text confirming she'd be there, she flung open her closet and found the cutest thing she owned. An outfit Olivia had picked for her, surprise, surprise. After a quick shower and a flurry of makeup and hairstyling, Ellie hopped a bus to the Opry. She sent a text to her grandparents asking them to pray that her first Opry performance would be a success.

Ellie got off the bus and entered the theater, which generated a down-home feel despite its classy history. Of course, the large Christmas trees on either side of the stage and the extravagant boughs lining the walls of the theater brought extra elegance to the large room. She stopped for a moment to take it all in and ran her fingers over the nearest wooden bench, just one of the many filling the auditorium. From here, with the house lights on and tech crewmembers darting on and offstage, the Opry seemed like any other stage. But Ellie knew better. This was where history was made.

And she was making her own tonight.

"Ellie, over here." Onstage, Kacie caught Ellie's eye and waved.

Ellie moved toward her and the other backup singers, two girls in their twenties.

Kacie made introductions and cruised off to speak with her manager and some sound techs.

Ellie chatted with the other singers, and at four they ran through a sound check.

Could this really be happening? It was so much better than the Lizard Lounge.

Several hours later, Ellie waited in the wings watching Joey Lambert, an established favorite in Nashville. He rocked the crowd and they cheered in response to his tight jeans and swagger. Kind of like Nick.

Ugh. She didn't want to think about Nick.

Her gaze swept the backstage area till she found Kacie, standing in a darkened corner, wringing her hands together. Ellie headed over. "Need me to sneak you a burrito?"

Kacie laughed and threw her arms around Ellie. "See, this is why I love you. You're super talented, but you put me at ease too." Her eyes grew serious. "Thanks again for making it so last minute. I'm sure you had lots going on tonight."

"Yeah, I had a hot date and everything."

"You did? Oh no."

"Kidding. The date was with my bed." Ellie stuffed her hands into the back pockets of her jean skirt, the truth of the statement more painful than she wanted to admit. "I had the day off from label stuff. I'm happy to be here."

"I can't believe I'm so nervous. I should be more professional than this, you know? I've played here several times before." Kacie crossed her arms over her chest.

Joey's sexy tenor floated past them from the stage.

"Won't be long till you're up here. On your own, I mean."

"We'll see." Ellie threw her arm around her new friend. "For now, I'm just happy to be here for you."

Just then, Kacie's manager waved them over. "It's almost time." He kept his voice low.

Ellie followed Kacie and the other singers to the edge of the stage.

The last chord of Joey's song rang out, and the crowd cheered, a few high-pitched whistles and girly screams undulating throughout the auditorium.

Joey let his guitar hang around his torso and gripped the microphone. "Thank y'all so much for letting me play for you tonight. Seriously, such an honor. Now I have another honor—to introduce to you one of my personal favorite artists. She's young, her career's on fire, and so is she."

Kacie blushed. Ah, a crush, perhaps?

"Ladies and gentlemen, give it up for Kacie Hayes."

Kacie bounced onstage and waved to the crowd, a huge grin plastered on her face. The gold bangles on her wrist caught the light.

Ellie and the other singers subtly followed and took their places at three microphones set upstage left. Music filled Ellie's in-ear monitor, a cheerful number that had the audience on their feet instantly.

Kacie hugged Joey and thanked him, then snatched the microphone from its stand. "Hey, y'all! Put your hands together and help me have some fun."

The band let the music fly, and Kacie's voice rang out. Ellie and the other singers joined in during the chorus and bridge.

Kacie's hips swayed to the number as she sang about movin' on and movin' up, while she flirted with the lead guitarist. She moved effortlessly across the stage.

Ellie could never do that. She'd feel so foolish. So fake. But the bubbly onstage presence fit Kacie.

And that was okay, wasn't it? Because there was more than one way to be genuine. They had different styles, but they both were artists. They may attract different crowds, but that was all right too. After all, every kind of audience needed something spoken into their lives.

Ellie bounced along to the music, letting herself become so wrapped up in having fun that she forgot to be nervous. A grin overtook her.

The song ended. One more to finish the set.

Kacie fanned herself. "Whew, y'all are taking my breath away with excitement. I can't thank you enough for being so welcoming."

Some tweens in the front row cheered in response.

"I don't know if I'm allowed to do this. But right now, I've got a real treat for y'all. Instead of doing a second song, I thought I'd introduce you to a friend of mine. I'm going to help her sing one of her brand new songs. One she just wrote this week, in fact."

Ellie peered just offstage to catch the identity of the mystery singer, but only saw tech crew-members standing around.

"Friends, please help me welcome to the stage the one, the only, Ellie Evans!"

Where had she hidden the wrapping paper?

Olivia stuck her head under the bed and searched for the tub of half-used rolls of paper decorated with Santas and Rudolphs. It was too difficult to see, so she emerged and reached for her purse on top of the comforter and dragged out her phone. The flashlight app would reveal if her search was in vain. As she flipped to find the app, her phone chirped to life.

Andrew's name popped up on the screen.

"Talk fast. I have presents to wrap." Olivia's voice teased.

"Liv, are you listening to this?"

"Listening to what?"

"Ellie. At the Opry."

Olivia straightened. "What?"

"Didn't you get my message?"

"No, I didn't." She'd finished up her Christmas shopping and then come home. The phone must have been on vibrate, or she hadn't heard it.

"Kacie Hayes asked her to sing backup tonight.

And then she called Ellie to the front of the stage. She's performing right now."

"What?" Olivia's voice squeaked, then she leaped to her feet and ran to the living room. She turned on the radio set and flipped to 650 AM WSM. "I'll call you back."

Ellie's singing rose from the speakers and haunted the room like a ghost. The girl had so much talent—but this song was darker, deeper than any other she'd performed before. Gone was the pep, the songs about faith and love. Though beautiful, Ellie's song featured words of mourning. Sadness. Death. About having unanswered questions, with no way to resolve them. About looking for something and never finding it.

Like she'd gone looking for Marie and never found her.

This change in Ellie—it was all Olivia's fault.

The song ended to thunderous applause. Hands shaking, Olivia hit the Power button on the radio and sat in silence. She'd been praying nonstop since her encounter with Mama yesterday, yet no clear way of telling Ellie, "I lied to you," seemed right.

But she couldn't let Ellie keep thinking her mother was dead. It was clearly torturing her.

It was time. But first, Olivia needed backup.

She picked up her phone, dialed a number, and waited.

"Hello?" Pots and pans clanged in the background.

"Rach, it's me."

"Hang on, the kitchen's loud." Then Rachel's end of the line grew quiet. "Okay, I'm in the pantry. Nice of you to finally return my calls."

Olivia clenched the phone and blew out a breath. "I need to talk to you."

"Go ahead."

"In person." At Olivia's feet, Pascal whined in his sleep, and she absently patted his head. "I'm finally ready."

"Good." Leave it to Rachel to perfectly understand Olivia's meaning. "Denise can take over here for a little while. I'll be there in fifteen."

"Thanks."

Olivia busied herself by tidying the living room as she waited for Rachel to arrive.

When the doorbell rang, the dogs went wild with barking and charged the front door.

Olivia opened it to find Rachel balancing several foil-covered trays. "What's this?"

"Leftovers. Now help a girl out."

Olivia swooped in and grabbed the top few containers. Foil peeled back from the corner of one, and a heavenly aroma filled her nostrils. "Smells divine."

"It's just pot roast, potatoes, carrots, and some dessert. Nothing fancy." Rachel followed Olivia to the kitchen and set her trays on the counter. She opened Olivia's refrigerator door and began rearranging, making room for the trays.

Olivia put the trays she was holding on the island. "You didn't have to bring me food."

"It was no problem." Leaning over, head in the fridge as she moved stuff around, Rachel's words were slightly muffled. "You know Bernadette doesn't like leftovers lingering after special events like tonight."

Olivia stole a glimpse inside one of the smaller dishes and was rewarded by the sight of several brownies. She popped the edge off of one and slid the chocolate crust into her mouth. "What event were you catering tonight?"

"Some law firm's holiday party. A little soon if you ask me. We're not even quite done with November yet." Rachel snatched the trays from the counter and stuffed them inside the fridge, then closed the door and set her hands on her hips. "But I'm not here to talk about that, am I?"

"No." Suddenly, the kitchen felt stifling. "Let's take the dogs for a walk."

"It's chilly out."

Olivia walked to the front door and took the dogs' leashes down.

Rachel followed.

The golden retrievers bounded toward Olivia and sat obediently at her feet.

"Come on. You can't turn down a pouty puppy face."

Rachel rolled her eyes. "I guess if it's easier for you to talk while we walk, then fine." She took Pascal's leash from Olivia's hand and snapped it in place on his collar. "Lead the way."

Olivia stuck her phone in her back pocket and threw a coat on over her cable-knit sweater. She opened the door, and Chloe tugged her outside into the cold. Oops. Olivia should have grabbed some gloves. Oh well. They'd just have to walk quickly to keep the blood moving.

Rachel shut the door behind Pascal.

Olivia locked up. "Let's go this way." She and Chloe turned right. All of Olivia's neighbors had gotten into the Christmas spirit, making her own unlit home appear dark and foreboding.

"If I'm going to freeze my rear off, it'd better be for a good reason." Rachel hunkered down in her royal-blue jacket and tugged a beanie onto her head.

Olivia blew out a breath, and a puff of white shimmered under the streetlights. "It is." How to start? "I listened to Ellie sing at the Opry tonight."

Rachel whistled. "How did that happen?"

"I'm not quite sure. Anyway, the song she sang . . ."

"Yeah?"

"It was all about looking for something that

you can never find. Seeking and losing yourself no matter how hard you try."

"Sounds depressing."

"It was."

"Olivia, why did you tell Ellie her mother was dead?" Rachel's voice issued a soft scolding.

Olivia stuck her right hand in her jacket pocket to warm it. The leash scratched against her left palm thanks to Chloe's constant tugging.

The sound of a child's laugh carried out the front door of a nearby home.

"I tried to answer her questions about why Marie—I—left, but they didn't satisfy her. And then I thought I could maybe pay Mama off, get her out of Ellie's life for good. So I told Ellie that Marie was dead."

"I know I sound like a broken record, but you need to tell that poor girl the truth." Rachel frowned.

"I know." A breeze picked up and blew the tips of Olivia's hair up into her face. A strand stuck to her lips, and she peeled it away. "At the time, I really did think I was doing what was best for her."

"Really? You thought it was best for her to think her mother, the mom she'd spent years searching for, was dead?"

"Better she think that than have Mama shoved in her face. And better she think that than believe I didn't want her." Yes, that had been part of her motivation, hadn't it? "But what else would she think, since I knew her identity and didn't say anything?"

"Liv." Rachel's voice softened. For a moment, neither said anything, and all Olivia could hear was the sound of dog nails clipping against the sidewalk. "Are you sure you weren't just protecting yourself?"

Olivia tightened her grip on Chloe's leash. "I see now that's exactly what I was doing. Maybe that's what I did when I left her in the first place. I don't know."

"Then you have to fix it."

"How?" Fixing it meant she'd risk losing Ellie again. Or Andrew—potentially someone she could see herself with forever—not to mention everything she'd worked for. All of it would go down the drain. "I've been praying, trying to figure out the exact words to say. I keep coming up empty."

"You only need the truth." Rachel stopped and looped her free arm through Olivia's. "The truth will set you free."

"I don't see that happening. But it's the right thing to do. Even if I lose everything."

Rachel squeezed her arm. "Maybe you have to lose everything in order for God to finally restore you. God's ways aren't always what we'd choose." She pointed to a huge manger scene on a lawn across the street. "No one expected him to send the Savior of the world to earth as a baby. They expected huge displays of power and might, a warrior king who could defeat armies with the blink of an eye. And you know, Jesus could have done all that. But he didn't."

Olivia stared at the tiny baby in the hay. At the mother and father leaning over his cradle, at the donkeys and other barnyard animals surrounding the King of the Universe. A king who humbled himself. Died. So she could be free.

And what had she been doing? Letting herself remain in bondage to her past choices. It was time to break out of the chains.

"You're right. There's no telling what could happen." Perhaps Andrew and Ellie would forgive her. Maybe they could have a relationship after all. Either way, she had to do the right thing. Olivia bent down and petted Chloe's golden-red coat.

The dog's tongue lolled out the side of her mouth, and her tail wagged.

"I'll sit down and tell Ellie everything. And pray that God gives me the words to convey how very sorry I am."

"I'm proud of you, Liv. I'm aware it won't be easy."

"Thanks for speaking truth to me, even when I didn't want to hear it at first."

"What are best friends for?" Rachel stuffed her

hand back into her jacket. "Now, can we please go back to your place? I'm freezing."

Olivia chuckled. "Yeah, all right." Inside her back pocket, her phone buzzed. "Hang on." She pulled it out and answered. "Hello?"

"May I speak with Olivia Lovett, please?"

"This is she."

"Olivia, hi, this is Lance Hurley, the booking manager for *Nashville Insider*."

No way. "Hello there." At Rachel's questioning glance, Olivia held up her index finger to indicate she'd tell her soon.

"Listen, we've got a last-minute cancellation on the show this week and would love to book Ellie. Tomorrow, if possible."

"Tomorrow?" What timing! Perhaps they'd heard the Opry broadcast and recognized the girl's incredible talent. "I'm fairly certain she's free. We'll clear her schedule if not."

"Fabulous. We'd like you there too, of course."

"Why would you want me there?"

"It brings a wonderful angle to the show."

"I don't want to steal Ellie's spotlight." Olivia started walking toward home, and Rachel followed.

"You won't. We've even got time for her to perform a number." Lance paused. "I'm afraid I need an answer now, or we'll have to move on to our next alternate."

"No, no, of course. We'll both be there."

"Perfect. I'll have my secretary call you with the details in the morning."

Rachel's eyes lit up. "Well?"

"Looks like Ellie is going to be performing tomorrow on *Nashville Insider*." She couldn't keep the squeal from her voice. What a huge opportunity for Ellie. And Olivia was going to win the silly bet with Andrew—a tiny bit of silver in the stormy clouds that had lined her day.

"That's great." They arrived home and entered. Rachel unclipped Pascal. She squatted down and put her arms around him, burrowing her nose in his fur. Then she looked up, eyes filled with concern. "But when are you going to tell Ellie?"

"Don't worry." Olivia scratched Chloe's ears, then removed her leash. "I'll tell her afterward. I'd do it in the morning, but I don't want anything to distract her from this moment."

32

It made complete sense for Ellie to have a twinge of stage fright. But shouldn't Olivia be over this tingly feeling of anticipation mixed with dread by now? She tried to shake the nerves from her hands, while Margie, the makeup artist, applied more blush to her cheeks.

In the chair next to Olivia, Ellie stared at her reflection in the mirror.

A guy named Ramón fluffed her curls to perfection.

With a cute pair of white slacks, a black flowing tank top, and silver heels, Ellie looked every bit a star.

She was all grown up, and Olivia's heart swelled.

Kathy Truitt, the host of *Nashville Insider*, was about to make Ellie famous.

"You're as lovely as ever, darlin'." Margie patted Olivia on the shoulder and snapped the blush container shut. "I don't know how you managed to stay lookin' so young all these years without plastic surgery."

"I'm not that old, Margie." Olivia laughed. But forty was right around the corner, and she had the crinkles around her eyes to prove it. Still, the best part of her life was ahead, wasn't it? She had to believe it—or else she'd never get up the courage to tell Ellie the truth.

Perhaps that's what the nerves were all about. After this interview was over, she had to come clean.

"Olivia, what do you think?" Ramón swiveled Ellie to face Olivia.

"She's perfect."

Ellie flushed. "Do you really think so?"

"I wouldn't lie to you." The irony of Olivia's words hit her in the chest. She forced a smile. She needed to enjoy this last day with Ellie. Once she told her the truth, who knew if they'd ever speak again? "Now come on, we need to get miked."

She and Ellie hopped down from their seats and headed out of the dressing room toward the green room, where they were to wait their turn. The faint scent of lemon clung to the air. A few people stood in the corner of the cramped space, which featured two couches, a folding table with a bowl of fruit and a spread of crackers and cheese, and a large TV broadcasting the stage of *Nashville Insider*. It hadn't changed much at all since Olivia's last guest appearance.

What had it been? Four years?

The room might look the same, but nothing about Olivia's life did.

A woman with a clipboard and headset looked up. "Oh good. I need to chat with you both. I'm the floor manager, Felicia." She indicated one of the tech guys in the corner. "Isaiah will take you to get your mics on. You're last in the lineup of guests today, so once you're miked, just hang out back here. I'll come and get you when it's time. You can watch the first part of the show on the big-screen."

Ellie remained silent and wide-eyed as Isaiah led them down the hall to yet another room and helped them clip on their mic packs.

Olivia tried putting Ellie at ease, but the girl just smiled politely and remained stoic. Poor thing. "At least I'll be there to help if you get stuck."

That elicited a real smile. "That's true. I keep forgetting you'll be there with me."

Together they snatched two bottles of water, worked their way back to the green room, and settled onto a plush green couch in front of the giant flat-screen television. They said hello to the other two guests: a Grammy-winning song-writer, whose songs were being picked up by the likes of Tim McGraw and Carrie Underwood; and Jack Jones, a well-established singer, who'd been in the industry for ten years.

Olivia greeted Jack with a kiss on each cheek, and they caught up. Ellie made Olivia proud, holding her own in the conversation, acting like her nerves had never existed.

The show began, and Kathy Truitt was as

classy as ever, with her red shoulder-length bob and black tailored suit.

When Jack was onstage getting ready to perform his hit new single, Felicia strode in from the hall. "Olivia, Ellie. You're on in five."

Olivia nodded, then turned to Ellie. "Ready?"

Ellie bit her bottom lip. "I guess so."

"You guess?" Olivia patted Ellie's hand. This might be one of the last times that Ellie would let her close enough to do something like this. She pulled the girl into an embrace. "You've got this. Remember. I believe in you—I've always believed in you."

Ellie's breath shuddered out onto Olivia's shoulder, and her arms tightened around Olivia's waist. "I wouldn't be here if it wasn't for you. I know . . ." She trailed off.

Olivia pulled back, brushed Ellie's bangs out of her eyes, and smiled. "You know what?"

Ellie looked down at her feet. "I know it's not professional to say, but you're like the mom I never had."

Oh boy. A dam inside Olivia threatened to break, but she had to hold it together. She'd be out onstage, on national television, in a few minutes. How she'd longed, for so many years, to hear the word "mom" applied to her. And look what God had done—brought to her the one person she most wanted to hear it from.

And all of that might be over soon. But for

now, Olivia would cherish the moment. "I feel the same way." She brushed away a falling tear. "Let's get out there and kick some booty."

"Okay." Ellie nodded, squared her shoulders, and plowed forward, out of the room, down the hall, and to the wings of the stage.

Olivia followed.

Someone tapped Olivia on the shoulder.

She turned to find Andrew behind her. "They let you backstage?"

"What, you think you're the only one with sway around here?" He chuckled, then turned to Ellie. "Break a leg, Ellie."

"Thanks, Andrew."

He reached out to touch Olivia's elbow, then gently led her a few feet away and lowered his voice. "I just came back here to say you were right all along, Liv. You have an eye for talent, and I couldn't be more proud to be partnered with you. You did it. You got Ellie on *Nashville Insider*."

What would he say once he found out the truth about Ellie? About Marie? But she'd explain everything, in the right time. "Aw, you're sweet to say that."

"And"—he adjusted his glasses—"I guess this means you won our little wager. So I'll be prepping my voice for my fate. You will warn me before making me get up to do karaoke somewhere, though, won't you?"

She wanted to hold on to this camaraderie. Would Andrew forgive her for keeping secrets? He had to. Because, more and more, she had given pieces of her heart to this man. Olivia cleared her throat. "You don't have to get up and sing. We're both winners as far as I'm concerned."

"Fair is fair." Andrew checked his watch. "I'll be cheering you on from the audience." He leaned in, kissed her quickly, and left her breathless as he headed down the corridor.

From the stage, the last note of Jack Jones's song resonated, and the crowd cheered.

Kathy announced a quick commercial break, and Jack leaned in for a final cheek kiss and hug. Then he came off the stage, guitar in hand, and winked at Olivia and Ellie. "Knock 'em dead."

"We will." Olivia flashed Ellie the thumbs-up sign. "Ready?"

"Yes." The single word, spoken in quiet confidence, said so much about her daughter.

Onstage, Kathy geared up for the return from the commercial break. "Up next, we have one of the country's rising stars, accompanied by the former star who discovered her—and they've got some big news to share. Please welcome Ellie Evans and Olivia Lovett."

Olivia led the way, and Ellie followed. Both waved to the crowd as they approached Kathy. They exchanged hugs and settled onto a purple couch that sat center stage, next to Kathy's

384

overstuffed chair. The lights were so bright Olivia could barely make out the audience at first, but then her eyes adjusted.

Kathy leaned forward as the crowd quieted. "Olivia, it's so nice to see you return to *Nashville Insider*. What has it been, fifteen years since you first appeared on this stage?"

"That sounds about right. It's lovely to be here, Kathy. Especially since I have Ellie with me." She wouldn't let Kathy put all the attention on her. Not when this was Ellie's day.

"In fact, I think we have a clip from that first interview here today. Who'd like to see it?" At the crowd's cheering response, Kathy laughed. "All right, roll it, boys."

A much younger Olivia filled the screen behind their heads. As she and Kathy chatted about her reputation as the Celibate Country Queen, present-day Olivia leaned over to Ellie. "Sorry about this. Don't worry. I won't let her talk about me the whole time."

Ellie smiled. "I don't mind. I've never seen this clip. It's fun to see you at my age."

As the clip continued, Kathy bent toward Olivia and Ellie. "I'm so excited you've chosen to announce your big news on our show."

Ellie glanced at Olivia, eyebrows raised.

Olivia opened her mouth to ask Kathy what big news she meant when, out of the corner of her eye, she saw a flash of red.

Her eyes zeroed in on Mama, sitting in the front row, beaming like the Cheshire cat. Her nails gripped the handles of her purse, choking the life out of it.

Why would Mama be here? The reason couldn't be anything good. But before she could contemplate what it meant, the clip ended.

What was wrong with Olivia?

She'd been fine a second ago, and then her face had crumpled and all color drained from her cheeks. Ellie followed her mentor's line of sight—and saw Olivia's mother sitting in the audience. With her face twisted into a Grinch-like grin, she looked oddly triumphant.

Kathy's voice invaded her thoughts and plunked Ellie back into the present. "Olivia, I think most of our audience knows you were a recording artist until your vocal chords started giving you trouble a few years ago. How did that feel?"

Olivia snapped her happy mask back into place, as if no other emotion had ever been present. "Of course it was very difficult. But then a new dream arose—to create a recording label for new artists. And that's where Ellie comes in. When I heard her sing for the first time, I just knew she was the perfect artist for our label."

"Ellie, what did you think when Olivia approached you with a possible offer?"

"I thought she must have mistaken me for someone else."

The audience chuckled.

The sound sank into her soul, soothing the nerves threatening to burst through her skin. "I feel incredibly blessed to be where I am today."

"I feel the same way." Olivia patted Ellie's hand. "It was fate."

"Fate, indeed." Kathy's smile exuded grace and kindness. "It's amazing how things work out sometimes." She turned her body toward the audience. "Olivia and Ellie have some incredible news they'd like to share when we return from commercial break."

The red lights flicked off from the cameras.

Ellie scrunched her nose. That was the second or third time Kathy had talked about big news. Maybe there was something she didn't know about? After last night's Opry performance, Kacie had mentioned the possibility of taking Ellie on tour as an opening act, but would that warrant such hype? And how would Kathy know about that?

Apparently Olivia was confused too. She tilted her head. "Kathy, I'm actually not sure what big news you're referring to." Her mic was still on, and the audience seemed to collectively lean forward to listen.

Tiny wrinkles spider-webbed out from Kathy's

lips as she pressed them together. "I got a call from your office. Aren't you both here to announce that Ellie is your daughter?"

The audience seemed to gasp as one.

Wow. Someone had clearly gotten the wrong message. Ellie opened her mouth to correct Kathy, but something about the way Olivia's eyes widened in horror—it almost seemed like . . . but no way. What Kathy said couldn't be true.

Olivia pinched the skin on her wrist and flinched. "No, that's not what we came here to discuss."

Kathy motioned for the producer, who raced over, headphones pulled down around her neck. "Didn't you tell me we got a call from someone at Radiant Records yesterday?"

The woman squared her shoulders, confident. "Yes, a Jeanine somebody. She said Ms. Lovett and Ms. Evans were long-lost mother and daughter and were ready to announce it to the world."

What? Why would somebody say that—wait, Jeanine. That was Olivia's mother. Ellie's eyes scanned the audience, but the woman was now gone. Ellie sat there under the hot stage lights, and her gaze swung back to Olivia. She took in the subtle cleft in Olivia's chin, reached up and touched her own. The dimples—they were the same. How had she never seen it?

But maybe she had, deep down. The dream

she'd recounted to Lena came tumbling back into her memory.

"Is it true?" She had to force the words out, afraid to hear Olivia's answer but needing to say it all the same.

Olivia slipped a hand under the back of her shirt and turned off her microphone. She reached for Ellie's hand. "Let's go talk about this somewhere else."

Ellie yanked her hand away. "No! Is. It. True?" Her voice rang out through the studio, and she gritted her teeth.

The deafening sound of the crowd whispering and fidgeting grew louder.

Olivia closed her eyes for a moment. She opened them slowly, as if wishing all of this away. "Yes, Ellie, it's true. I am your mother."

Ellie had wanted to hear the words for so long.

Though not like this. Not in front of thousands of onlookers, who only saw a juicy scandal—not the ruins of her life.

Olivia . . . her mother?

"Ellie, honey. Let's get out of here and talk." Olivia's eyes pleaded with her. But no. She didn't get to plead anything, not after lying the way she had.

"You looked me in the eyes. Told me my mother was dead." Ellie held her breath until the weight of all her blood seemed to pound in her ears.

"I know. I'm so sorry." Olivia—Marie?—chewed her lip. She reached out to comfort Ellie but pulled back.

Ellie could almost feel the phantom touch on her skin.

"There's no excuse. But I was going to tell you the truth."

"When? On your deathbed?"

Olivia scrunched her eyes, as if in physical pain. "You have every right to be upset with me. To hate me."

"Don't make this about you." Ellie couldn't contain the words. She hated the angry bite to them, but had no power to stop them from spewing forward, numbing her lips. "I just . . . why?"

"There are a lot of reasons. At first, I was trying to protect you."

"By lying?"

"Can we continue this somewhere else? Please go with me. I'll tell you anything you want to know."

Ellie massaged her temples. The room seemed to spin—more like her whole world spun.

Several people had their cameras out, videotaping. The drama between Ellie and Olivia would hit YouTube within the hour.

Ellie refused to be remembered this way. The only thing that mattered was the music.

As Olivia opened her mouth to speak—who

knew what lies she'd spin now—Ellie held up a hand to cut her off. She turned to Kathy, whose eyes radiated surprise and apology.

"Kathy, I believe you wanted to hear a song?"

"Y-yes. Yes, of course." She turned to the cameras and indicated they should resume the broadcast. Kathy cleared her throat. "Welcome back, my friends. It seems we got a few wires crossed, and Olivia and Ellie have decided to withhold their news a while longer. But Ellie is here to grace us with a song. Please welcome Ellie Evans to the stage."

Without looking at Olivia, Ellie stood and strode to the side of the stage, where a bass player, keyboardist, electric guitarist, and drummer waited to play. She yanked her guitar from its stand, flung the strap over her shoulders, and plugged in the instrument. She headed to the microphone stand. "Hey, y'all! As Kathy said, I'm Ellie Evans, and I'm here to play a little something that will be featured on my upcoming album release."

If Olivia Lovett—her own mother—didn't want to see her, then maybe the rest of the world would.

Ellie fought the tears threatening to flow from her eyes. "One, two, three, four."

The band followed her lead and started playing.

She closed her eyes and belted out the words,

words she'd written weeks ago, before knowing the truth.

Happy words. Words of hope.

Lies, all of them. But at least she hadn't told them intentionally. She'd just been naïve.

The music flowed through the room, through her veins, and finally, all felt right with the world. She could ignore what had just happened. She simply had to keep moving forward.

But then she opened her eyes.

And realized that, while she poured her soul out in song, nearly everyone in the audience had their eyes fixed on the stage where Olivia and Kathy were. Ellie forced out each word. She tried to focus, but Olivia paced while the producer attempted to calm her down. Ellie swiveled her head slightly.

The backstage crew hustled and gestured to each other.

Her gaze roved back toward the audience.

People talked through her song. From what she could tell, not one person looked her way.

The whole world wasn't seeing her at all. The cameras were probably pointed at Olivia and Kathy, picking up any conversation there might be, Ellie muted or simply background noise.

Maybe that was all she'd ever be.

It was all she'd been to her father, God love him. He'd never been there when he should have been, to hear her sing or otherwise. Not when it had really mattered.

It was all she'd been to Nick, who'd found someone else.

And she'd clearly never been more than that to Olivia.

Olivia, who had run away to become a country star instead of raising her daughter.

Olivia, who had been willing to invest in her as a mentor but never as a mother.

In the middle of her song, Ellie stopped singing.

No one looked her way.

She unplugged her guitar and quietly walked from the stage, the band still playing her song without the words—as if they didn't even miss them.

Why had the studio suddenly grown quieter? Olivia ceased talking with the show's producer, who had been apologizing profusely for the mix-up. She turned her head, and the whole audience seemed to watch her. Olivia's eyes connected with Mama, who now stood off to the side of the audience.

Mama brushed her hands together, as if to say *I'm through with you,* and walked down the aisle toward the exit.

Relief flooded Olivia. Mama was finally gone for good.

Ellie. Her voice no longer punctuated the studio air. Olivia gasped as her daughter unplugged her guitar and headed offstage. "Ellie, wait." Olivia pushed past Kathy Truitt, their shoulders connecting, and stumbled on the smooth wood floor.

Kathy steadied her and rotated toward the audience. "That's all the time we have today. Thanks for joining us on *Nashville Insider*."

Olivia shoved away from Kathy. She couldn't let Ellie leave without talking—really talking, not fighting onstage for the world to see. Why was this happening when Olivia had finally decided to come clean and tell the truth? She could have handled Ellie's fury. Was prepared for it, actually. But now, she may have had a hand in tanking her daughter's career before it ever began.

Poor girl . . . had anyone listened when she'd performed? Or had the focus been solely on Olivia?

She'd stolen her daughter's spotlight.

Ellie disappeared backstage.

Olivia rushed to follow her.

A few sound techs blocked her way. "Ms. Evans asked us to not let you follow her," one of them said.

"Get out of my way. Please." Olivia tried to maneuver between them, but they moved with her, so she couldn't get through. What she wouldn't give to have superpowers about now, with the ability to fly over all their heads and get to her daughter, whatever the cost.

It couldn't be too late. It just couldn't be.

A woman with streaks of gray in her ponytail raised a hand to Olivia's shoulder. "Respect her wishes, honey. You won't get anywhere by pushing the issue. Give her space."

"But . . ." Too much space and Ellie might run away forever, beyond Olivia's reach. Though, perhaps that's where her daughter was always meant to be.

Only Olivia could have mucked this up so royally. She should have kept her distance from the beginning, especially when she learned the truth. She should never have attempted to be a part of Ellie's life. Not only had Olivia scarred her daughter, she'd also ruined Ellie's chances to be taken seriously as a musician. Made her look like a charity case instead of a talented performer. Created more insecurity in her than ever existed before she'd come back into Olivia's life.

Olivia nodded, neck tight, then walked out into another hall, dim with yellow light. She sank to the hard tile floor and put her head in her hands. Her cheeks brushed the soft fabric of her sky-blue scarf—one she'd bought on an outing with Ellie. Tears dripped from the corners of her eyes, down her chin, and she pulled her head up to wipe them away. But no. Each one represented a moment. The past, the present, the future.

They fell from her face onto the scarf, temporarily staining a mosaic of memories into the fabric, then slipping away into oblivion.

This was all she had left of her daughter. Because no way in the world would Ellie speak to her again. And Olivia deserved that.

It was the curse of being Marie Culloway. How stupid of her to think she could escape.

The door scraped against the floor.

Olivia pulled her eyes from their fixation on her scarf and caught Andrew scrutinizing her.

He squatted down next to Olivia. "Are you okay?"

What a wonderful man. She didn't warrant such care from him. She smudged away a few remaining tears and forced a sad smile. "I will be."

"Good." Andrew shifted and rose again, away from her. "Because I need you fully functioning before I lay into you."

Lay into . . . ?

"What were you thinking, Liv?" He paced, voice getting louder the nearer he approached. "You signed your own daughter to our record label without telling me? Not to mention, you have a daughter?"

"I didn't know it was her until that night at Lorenzo's. Once I found out, I considered retracting the offer. I didn't know if it would be a good idea to sign her."

"I could have told you no, it wasn't a good idea. But you had to keep me in the dark. Risk my reputation and my money, for what? Your attempt to make up for the fact you left your daughter to pursue your own career?" Andrew's eyes shone with hurt and betrayal. "I thought I knew you."

If only she could explain. Olivia rose and wobbled on leg muscles cramped from sitting in place for too long. "I didn't leave her for that reason. Try to understand . . ."

"All I understand is that you're not the woman I thought you were." Andrew clenched his fists at his side, then folded his arms across his chest. "In fact, you're more like my ex-wife than I ever thought you could be. Why do I keep falling in love with women who care nothing for their children?"

Love.

She knew he liked her, admired her, but love?

Warmth crept through her. Yes, love. And the thing was she loved him too, didn't she? Because the thought of losing him caused the warmth to turn cold.

"Andrew . . ." Olivia reached for him.

He pulled away.

That stung worse than if someone had slapped her. "Please. Let me explain."

"There's nothing you can say that will make what you've done okay, Olivia." Andrew pivoted toward the door. The angry tension melted from his shoulders and became a mournful slump. "I'll have my lawyers contact you about dissolving our partnership. I have no desire to continue working with someone I can't trust." He flung open the door and exited the way he'd come.

It didn't matter if he loved her. Love wasn't enough. He'd never be with her now that he knew the truth about who she was.

What had she been thinking? God couldn't redeem her past. In one fell swoop, she'd lost everything: the culmination of her life's work, the man she loved, the mother she'd never wanted, and the daughter she'd always wanted but could never have.

She'd never thought it possible, but today, her dreams had died for the last time. In fact, they'd withered away into nothing, with no hope of resurrection.

33

The alarm blared in Ellie's ear, and she buried her head under the pillow. Why had she bothered to set it at all?

It was just another Friday in her aimless life. People who were going nowhere didn't need to wake up at nine in the morning, now did they?

She slammed the snooze button on the top of her old-fashioned alarm clock.

"Ouch, poor clock." Lena stood in the doorway, framed by a shaft of light from the hall.

"It deserved that and more." Ellie's voice croaked from disuse. "How are finals going?" She hadn't seen her roommate in days—which was all well and good, because Ellie hadn't felt like talking since the *Nashville Insider* appearance over a week ago.

In fact, other than Grandma, the only other person Ellie had talked to was Andrew, and just to tell him she wasn't feeling up to recording her single as scheduled. He'd seemed super understanding, said to take her time recovering.

Lena flipped on Ellie's light, and Ellie recoiled like a vampire facing garlic. Her roommate laughed, came into the room, and sat on the chair at Ellie's desk. "Two down, two to go next week." Lena picked up a pencil and twirled it between her fingers. The left side of her hair stuck up at random angles, and the other side lay flat against her head. "I can't believe I only have one semester of college left after this. Then it's out into the real world. I can't figure out if I'm excited for the adventure or freaked out of my mind."

"The real world isn't all it's cracked up to be." Ellie rolled over, placed her hands on her stomach, and stared at the crack in the ceiling just over her bed.

It started in the corner and fissured out from there, with small branches along the main crack. Would one of those branches eventually cause a rift so deep the whole roof came tumbling down?

"How long have you been lying in that bed?" Lena frowned. "Have you even left this apartment since everything happened? Talked to anyone but me?"

"Not sure. No. And yes."

Right after the truth had been revealed, Ellie had called Grandma, then stumbled to get the story out through her tears. Grandma had listened while Ellie railed against Olivia. She'd offered to fly Ellie home or come to Nashville, but Ellie hadn't wanted to inconvenience Grandpa and her.

Truth was she wished Grandma *was* here right now, stroking her hair and telling her it would all be okay.

"Very descriptive answer."

"What do you want from me? It's early. And I don't have to work at Bernadette's today." Ellie yawned. "So I think I'll go back to sleep, thank you very much." She faced the wall and curled around her body pillow, hugging it to her chest.

But Lena couldn't take a hint. "It's not early. Ellie, you have to get up and go do something. Want to help me with my Christmas shopping today? I need a break from studying."

"No." Facing everything outside these walls was too much. What if someone on the street recognized her and asked her how she was handling the news that her mother was the great Olivia Lovett?

The sound of rustling caught her attention. She turned over and propped herself up on her elbow.

Lena held up lined notebook paper. "What's this?"

"Nothing." Only a to-do list, the one thing she'd managed to accomplish this week.

"Call Grandma. Get boxes from Mini Mart. Pack." Lena waved the paper around. "You're leaving?"

"I haven't decided yet." But she couldn't imagine staying in Nashville and continuing to pursue her dream, not with Olivia here. And she definitely couldn't work with her day in and day out at Radiant Records. It was easier to leave, wasn't it?

Lena set the paper on the desk again. "Nick has been calling nonstop for the last week."

"How did you know that?" Ellie hadn't had the strength to deal with her emotions regarding Nick on top of everything else. Every time his name appeared on her phone screen, she'd ignored it.

"Because somehow he found my number and started calling me. He's worried about you."

"He shouldn't be."

"I'm worried about you too."

"I'll be fine." Ellie sighed and slumped back down into bed. "I just need some more sleep."

"What you need is to call your mom and talk it out."

Ellie threw her covers to the side and sat up. "How can you say that after what she did? She humiliated me in front of the whole country. Lied to my face."

"I know." Lena's tone exuded compassion. "And that totally stinks. But you still need to talk it out. That's what moms and daughters do. They fight. Then they talk and work it out. Just look at me and my mom. We go round and round. We'll probably never see eye to eye. And yet, we're family. We belong together."

But Ellie and Olivia weren't truly family. Olivia had made that choice twenty-three years ago when she'd abandoned Ellie. And she'd made it again weeks ago when she decided to lie about it all.

"Why didn't my dad ever tell me?" She blurted the words out without meaning to. Ellie sighed. "He must have known my mom's identity."

Lena walked over and leaned down to give her a firm hug, then pulled back. "I don't know, friend."

"Grandma said he was probably just protecting me. Guess it makes sense why he never seemed to support me coming to Nashville, huh?" If only he was here to ask, to have an authentic conversation about the past. "I never should have come. Maybe it's best if I leave now."

"Don't give up. Give yourself time to heal. Then face it all head-on. If you don't, you'll always regret it."

Ellie didn't want to accept the truth in Lena's words. Perhaps she *would* regret it. But it would hurt too much to stay.

Lena gave her another squeeze and headed for the doorway. "Let me know if you change your mind and want to come shopping."

"Okay."

The pathetic word hung in the air like the last leaf on a decaying tree.

Where did she go from here? What did she do? Ellie sat on the edge of her bed. Her jumbled thoughts were interrupted by her buzzing phone.

She reached to hit Ignore, but something in Lena's words made her check the caller ID.

Nick.

She hadn't spoken to him since he'd left. After his new girlfriend had answered Ellie's call, Nick had phoned and left Ellie several messages, especially after she'd appeared at the Opry.

Why was he bothering to call her now that he was back together with Lauren?

Ellie let his call go to voicemail. He'd forget her soon enough.

After a few minutes, a message dinged, indicating she had a new voicemail.

Her finger hovered over the Listen button—but why torture herself? She should erase it.

Still, something in her couldn't deny she wanted to hear his voice. She lifted the phone to her ear and played it.

"Hey, Ellie, it's me calling for the hundredth time. I get it if you don't want to talk, but I'm really worried about you." He paused, sighed. "I can't presume to know how you're feeling, but based on past stuff you've told me, I've got to think you're feeling pretty crummy and invisible right now. I don't know what Olivia was thinking or where she's coming from in any of this. All I know is that you shine, Ellie. Not just because of your amazing gift for music. Because you're you. I know you can't see that, and that's too bad. But you know what? Maybe you care too much about what the world thinks of you. Maybe you're looking for affirmation and worth in all the wrong places. I don't know. On Sunday, our pastor preached from Genesis Sixteen. It made me think of you. Go read it. I think it might speak to you in this situation. Anyway, I miss you. Talk to you later. I hope."

The room fell silent as the message ended.

Hearing his voice sliced her, made her miss him something fierce, as if everything inside her had been carved away.

Yet there was something else. Nick had a way of challenging her, even when she didn't want to be challenged.

What could it hurt? She snatched her Bible from under a pile of music books on her nightstand and placed it on her lap.

The thin pages swished between her fingers as she moved to Genesis 16. Oh yeah, the story of Hagar, the slave who was ordered by Sarai to sleep with her husband, Abram, and then mistreated by her mistress for doing exactly as asked.

Despised. Expendable. Yep, Ellie could definitely relate.

As she read, something caught her attention—something she'd never noticed before. Hagar had run away but became thirsty in her travels and ended up at a spring. She must have been distraught, wondering where in the world she was going to go. And God sent an angel to guide her.

How nice would that be, to have someone show up and tell Ellie, "*This* is what you should do"?

Ellie continued reading. "She gave this name to the Lord who spoke to her: 'You are the God who sees me . . .' "

Her jaw slackened.

Her whole life, she'd wanted to be seen, so she'd performed. But God had seen her before she'd ever picked up that guitar, hadn't he? If he saw a slave girl in the middle of a desert, a girl who had been mistreated and tossed aside by her owners, who had nowhere to go, who was pregnant and alone, then he saw Ellie too.

And he not only *saw* Hagar. He provided a direction, a path for her. A path that had led to life. Which must mean he cared about what happened to her.

And if he cared what happened to Hagar, maybe he cared what happened to Ellie too. He saw everything. Maybe he'd even led her here, to this place, where she'd met Olivia. She'd started down this path, and he'd given her everything she had ever wanted.

The truth had been harder than she'd wanted it to be. So what?

Even if Olivia had never wanted her, God did.

Ellie's hands trembled as she closed the Bible and brought it to her lips. It wouldn't be easy, but she knew where God—the God who saw her—was asking her to go.

Just like he'd sent Hagar back to the people who had abandoned her, Ellie had to go back to her mom.

34

At least the rags had finally stopped reporting on the scandal.

Olivia pulled the brim of her baseball cap down over her eyes as she waited in line at the grocery store. Shouldn't have chosen a Saturday morning. Too many shoppers. She skimmed the magazines one last time, running her fingertips over the glossy covers.

Nope. No mention of how loser mother Olivia Lovett had abandoned her love child and run away to bigger and better things.

Funny thing was it was probably the truest thing the tabloids had ever printed.

The phone had finally stopped ringing too. Who knew her number was so easy to get?

"Ma'am?"

Olivia jerked her head to attention.

The teenaged clerk at the counter motioned her forward.

"Sorry." Olivia tugged her cap down farther and placed her milk, bread, produce, and other purchases onto the conveyor belt.

The clerk ran each item over the scanner, which beeped almost rhythmically.

Burl Ives serenaded customers with "Silver and Gold" from the speakers overhead, and the distinct smells of cinnamon and pinecones swirled together and saturated the air.

"Gotta get me some of this."

"Hmm?" Olivia snapped out of her thoughts.

The clerk held up a carton of eggnog.

"Oh. Right." Olivia may not have anyone to celebrate Christmas with—Rachel was leaving to visit her husband's family in Maine next week—but she could at least indulge in a few holiday traditions.

The clerk watched Olivia from the corner of her eye. She snapped a wad of gum, and it crackled. "You know, you look an awful lot like that country singer who was in the news recently."

"I get that pretty often." *Come on, hurry it up.*

"Can you believe that lady? Ran out on her kid and then pretended to be a saint for all those years?" The clerk finished ringing up the last item. "That'll be forty-three oh six. I feel so bad for her daughter. I mean, my dad ran out on me, but at least I didn't have to relive the whole thing on national television."

What could Olivia say? People would never understand. Olivia herself didn't know if she really understood her own actions all those years ago. All she could do was move forward, figure out where to go from here. She pulled her credit card from her purse and swiped it.

The clerk snatched the receipt from the printer.

"Thanks for shopping with us, Ms. L—" Her eyes widened and her gum fell out of her mouth.

Olivia grabbed the receipt and shrugged. Then she pushed her cart with a little more force than necessary out the door into the sunlight. After loading everything into her car, she headed home. Olivia pulled onto her street and approached her house.

Out front sat an unfamiliar blue car. Looked like a Lincoln Town Car. Strange. As she maneuvered her vehicle into her driveway, a woman opened the front driver's side door of the Lincoln and got out.

Olivia turned off her ignition, grabbed her purse from the passenger seat, and stepped out.

The woman, who sported slacks, a strand of pearls, and a stylish blonde bob, walked toward Olivia. Her heels clicked on the sidewalk. "Olivia Lovett?"

"Yes?"

The woman didn't appear to be a reporter. In fact, despite the polished look, the wrinkles around her eyes seemed kind. She stuck out her hand, as if an automatic response, but then withdrew. "I'm Leigh VanRisseghem." She tilted her head and worried her lip. "Ben's mother. Ellie's grandmother."

"Oh." Was she here to chew Olivia out? She probably had years of anger built up inside of her, and now that she knew Olivia's identity, she

411

was here to let it out. The groceries could wait. "Why don't you come inside?" Better to get yelled at where the neighbors couldn't hear.

"All right."

Olivia unlocked the front door and headed off Chloe and Pascal before they could lick Leigh to death. "Back. Go lie down."

The dogs obeyed.

"Good dogs." She turned to Leigh. "The coast is clear."

Leigh stepped inside and closed the door behind her. Wow. Ellie looked so much like her.

What if things had been different? What if Olivia had married Ben like he'd suggested, and they'd raised Ellie together? Ellie had raved about her grandma, how kind, how wise she was. Perhaps this woman could have taught Olivia how to be a mother. Maybe, with her influence, Olivia could have forgotten the hold Jeanine Culloway had over her and become someone worthy of Ellie.

She'd never know now, would she?

Suddenly the room felt overly warm. Olivia unwound her scarf and set it on the entryway table. She lowered the heat on the thermostat and motioned to the couch. "Please. Have a seat."

Ben's mom nodded and sank onto the couch cushions. She folded her hands in her lap and squinted up at Olivia. "Won't you join me?"

"In a minute. I'll make some tea." Because

that's what one did when one had an awkward guest.

"What I have to say won't take long."

"Okay." Olivia sat next to her on the couch, accepting her fate. She pulled one of the pillows onto her lap and ran her fingers along the fringe.

"Ellie knows I'm in town—she called me yesterday asking me to come as emotional support, and I got in last night. But she doesn't know I'm here yet." Leigh moved her thumbs back and forth over her folded hands. "I confess I've wondered about you over the years. Never did know how to find you, though."

Olivia loosened her grip. "Look, I know you must hate me—"

"I don't hate you." Leigh sighed. "I know I should have called first but was afraid you wouldn't see me."

"Probably not." Olivia forced a chuckle. "I'm kind of a coward like that."

"A coward? No, dear. That's just it. I came here because I wanted to thank you for being so brave all those years ago."

"Brave?" Surely this woman, more than anyone else, had a right to think horrible things about her—and she thought Olivia was brave? "I don't follow."

Leigh reached out her hand, and this time, took Olivia's in hers. "You gave birth at age sixteen to a beautiful, wonderful girl, when you could have ended your pregnancy instead. That's something to celebrate."

A sob rose in Olivia's throat. "But then I ran away and left her with you."

"Tell me, Olivia. Is it true what everyone else says? That you ran off to pursue your music?"

"No. Yes. I don't know." The sob burst through her vocal chords, vibrating in the air. "I mean, I thought I did it because I was afraid of ruining her. But what kind of mother leaves like that?"

Leigh smiled a sad smile, patted Olivia's hand. "One who was young and scared. Ben told me what you'd said. How you didn't seem to be in your right mind. Of course, I was angry at first. But then he told me about how abusive your own mama was to you. How you'd come from a rough home with no daddy and no one to protect you. And my heart just broke."

"It's no excuse for what I did." Olivia reached for the Kleenex box on her coffee table, snatched a tissue, and ran it under her eyes. How she hated to cry in front of strangers, especially this one.

"What you did was give your daughter the best life you thought you could." Leigh studied her. "Ben never told us your new identity, though I suspect he discovered it long ago. I'm guessing he was afraid that you had the means to reclaim Ellie if you wanted to. He always protected her at all costs. Even though he wasn't around as much as he wanted to be, my boy was a good daddy."

"I knew he would be." Olivia's voice trembled. For the few hours she'd known him, Ben VanRisseghem struck her as the kind of guy she could have married. Again, the what-ifs pummeled her. "I told him that, after I left, I wouldn't be back. I wouldn't interfere. There were times I had to fight to keep my promise."

"I admire that." Leigh squeezed Olivia's hand. "I've been praying for you all these years, Olivia."

"I didn't deserve your prayers." Olivia pulled away. Leigh's words were too much. She couldn't accept the woman's forgiveness or kindness, couldn't forget the pain her own sins had caused.

"What do any of us deserve, really?" Leigh pushed a strand of hair behind her ear.

Olivia studied her, heart warring with her head. When Olivia listened to the world, she felt like the worst person ever for abandoning her child. But deep down, she knew that Ellie had been better off with this wonderful woman than with sixteen-year-old Marie Culloway. "I'm not sorry." Her words surprised her, but their truth built her confidence. "That I left Ellie with you. She turned out amazing with you as a mother figure in her life."

Leigh uncrossed her legs and leaned forward.

"Ellie is a special girl. Always has been. She has the sweetest nature, and is so full of compassion and love for others."

"Something I'm sure she learned from you." Yes, Ellie radiated beauty from the inside.

"Maybe. Ben, God bless him, well . . . he was a good boy, but compassion was a little harder for him to master. So I venture to guess that she takes after her mama."

Mama. "That's one word I wish I could own. But we Culloways—we were never fit to be mothers."

Leigh looked Olivia square in the eyes. "Pardon me, but that's a load of malarkey. You are that girl's mother through and through."

"I wanted that to be true. Back then . . . and today. But don't you see? I've ruined it all." Olivia ripped the tissue in half.

White specks of fluff dotted the pillow in her lap.

"Maybe you weren't prepared to be a mother when you were sixteen. Like I said, it was a brave thing you did, giving her up when you believed it to be in her best interest." Leigh frowned. "But you should never let fear determine your destiny. The past is in the past. Your name, your upbringing—those things don't define you."

"I thought that was true, but then I wrecked Ellie's life. Just like I always feared I would."

"Because you lied. Not because of some

generational curse that prevents you from being a good mother." Leigh fingered the pearls at her throat, one at a time. "And you didn't ruin her life. Fact of the matter is God made you a mom. He's clearly calling you to be that in Ellie's life, or why else would she be here? And let me tell you what. God equips those he calls."

"I don't feel very equipped."

"Neither did Moses or Mary or Joseph, or any number of people in the Bible who were afraid of what God had called them to do. Things that seemed impossible. Things that *were* impossible, on their own. It was only through God's strength that they overcame their own weaknesses and performed miraculous feats of courage."

Could it be true for her?

Could she be the kind of mom who would make her daughter proud?

The mom who would bring good things to her daughter's life instead of ruin and heartache?

All things were possible with God, weren't they?

Mama's face flashed through Olivia's mind, callous laughter echoing as if Mama stood in the room with her. "I want it to be true. But I have a hard time imagining it."

Leigh put her hands behind her neck, unclipped her necklace, and let the pearl strand fall into her palm. Then she inched closer to Olivia, reaching out. She placed the necklace around Olivia's throat and snapped it into place.

The gems felt smooth against her skin. The necklace fit perfectly, almost as if it had been designed especially for her. Olivia reached up to touch the pearls. "I don't understand."

"My own mother gave me this necklace after Ben was born. She told me grown women wore pearls, and now that I was a mother, I was a grown woman, with new responsibilities and new possibilities." Leigh smoothed a tear from Olivia's cheek. "Honey, you've never had anyone believe in you, but let me be the first mom to tell you—I do. Being a mom isn't easy, but the number one rule is something I can see you've already got down."

Olivia's heart soared at Leigh's words. "What's that?"

"You love your child no matter what. And that never stops no matter how many miles separate you, no matter how many years it's been since you've seen each other, no matter who did what in the past."

"So what do I do now?"

"Go do what you were made to do. Be a mother to your daughter."

35

Grandma said the first step was always the toughest.

Ellie stretched out her arm and steadied her hand. Then she pushed through the front door of Bernadette's Café.

The strong winter wind blew it open forcefully, and a few tech guys lifted their heads as they set up for tonight.

And there Olivia sat, in the same place where she'd "discovered" Ellie.

After she'd made her decision two days ago to talk to Olivia, Ellie had started to chicken out. She'd needed Grandma. And Grandma had come, like she always did.

Whatever happened today, Ellie was blessed.

Ellie put one foot in front of the other and realized Grandma was most definitely wrong. Every step closer to Olivia—her mom—felt heavier and tougher than the last. She finally reached the booth. "Hi."

Olivia's hands were wound together on the tabletop. "Hi."

Ellie slid into the booth and folded her hands in her lap. She stared at a nick in the table that marred the smooth surface. "I guess I don't know where to begin." Gathering her courage, she glanced up at Olivia.

"How about with some hot chocolate? Or tea? Do you like tea? Coffee?" Olivia opened her mouth to say more, but snapped it shut.

"Tea sounds good."

"Be right back." Olivia left and walked into the kitchen.

While Olivia was gone, Ellie watched Jimmy and the other techs mess with the lights. First, the stage was cast in a warm yellow glow. Red took over, followed by green, then a cool blue. The warm yellow returned and settled into the cracks on the stage. The light coated every crevice.

Ellie imagined herself up there again, remembered how wonderful it had felt to receive the validation from the crowd's approving smiles, the cheers, the nodding heads.

But no. She'd decided—she didn't need to be up there ever again.

"Here you go." Olivia returned with two oversized mugs, the kind found in an artistic coffee shop where a person could cozy up in a corner. Then she pulled several packets of teabags from her pocket. "I wasn't sure what kind of tea you preferred."

"I'm not picky. But thanks." Ellie fingered the packets and finally chose a peppermint flavor, something festive to make up for her mood lately. She unwrapped the teabag and plopped it into the round brown mug. "What did you get?"

"Cappuccino." Olivia wrapped her hands around her blue mug. She moved it across the table to show Ellie a foam heart on top. "Made with love, courtesy of Rachel."

"That's sweet." Ellie inhaled the minty steam from her own mug. It hit her cheeks and heated her through. "You're probably wondering why I wanted to meet."

"I've got a pretty good idea." Olivia kept her gaze fixed on her cup. "But I'd like to hear it. Whatever it is."

"There's a lot I want to say. But mostly, I guess I just want to know why." Ellie's lip trembled. Ugh. This was her one chance to really hear the truth. She didn't want to be crippled by emotion. "Why you left me. And why you lied."

Olivia lifted the mug and took a long draught. She closed her eyes, almost as if she was savoring the sweetness, like she'd never have another cappuccino again. At last, she opened her eyes. "I have no excuse. Only reasons. And those reasons might not make any sense to you."

"Okay."

Olivia frowned, nodded. "I grew up in a small town. My mama was the local drunk. And harlot. I never knew my daddy. All I could think about when I was growing up was how I was going to get out of Red. Be somebody. Do something important. Because my mama made sure to remind me over and over again that I was a nobody and that I'd never be important. To anyone."

Ellie's mouth fell open. She'd known such love and tenderness from Daddy and her grandparents—especially Grandma. How would it feel to have had someone constantly putting her down instead of encouraging her? "That's awful."

"It was." Olivia shrugged her shoulders. "My mama was mean, especially when drunk. But the few times I met her mother, I knew where she'd gotten it. Everything she'd learned about being a mama, she learned from Loretta Culloway, my grandmother. She'd had my mama young, and my mama had me young. So, when I got pregnant with you . . ." Olivia's voice slipped, and her knuckles whitened as she gripped her cup.

Understanding dawned. "You thought you'd be a bad mother too?"

The slightest nod of Olivia's head was the only movement she made. "I didn't just think it. I knew it." Her eyes looked up, and she met Ellie's gaze. "My mama did a number on my self-esteem. She battered and bruised me. Not just physically, but in my soul too. I couldn't stand the thought of doing the same to you."

Tears welled in Ellie's eyes for the hundredth

time over the last week. "But you're nothing like that." She still didn't understand why Olivia had lied, but surely her intentions weren't mean and spiteful like Jeanine's seemed to be.

"I see more glimpses of Mama in me than I care to admit." Then Olivia was quiet for a few moments. "For what it's worth, I never wanted to leave you behind. It was the hardest thing I ever had to do. But I did what I thought was best for you at the time."

"How could it be best for me to not know my mother?" And there was that mixture of raw anguish and anger, of wanting to understand, of knowing the facts, but the facts warring with the desires of her heart.

Olivia sighed. "Like I said, I'm sure it doesn't make sense. When I look at my decision now, twenty-three years and a lot of grace later, I can see that my thinking was flawed. Maybe the way I left was wrong, but somehow God used it to give you a wonderful mother figure in your grandma. She came to see me yesterday, you know." A tiny smile.

"She did?"

"Yes. And she's fabulous. I'm so glad you have her in your life to support you through all of this."

"She sure is amazing." What would life have been like if Grandma hadn't raised her, if instead Ellie had grown up in a house with a drunk for a grandma and a young mother who didn't know anything about taking care of a child? Ellie shuddered. She'd had it good, despite everything. Maybe Olivia *had* done what was best for her all those years ago.

But that still didn't change the events of the past few months.

Ellie had to ask the question that weighed most in her mind, even if the answer hurt. "Once you found out I was your daughter, why didn't you tell me? Were you . . . disappointed?"

"Never." The word rushed out of Olivia's mouth. "Not for one moment since knowing you were mine did I experience anything but complete adoration of you. I love you, Ellie. I always have."

"Really?" Ellie's throat constricted.

"Yes. Really." Olivia pointed to the stage. "When I first saw you on that stage, I had the strongest sense that knowing you would change my life forever. You're special, Ellie. If I felt any disappointment, it was that I wasn't the mom I wanted to be."

"But to lie . . ."

"That was wrong. I was scared, plain and simple." Olivia reached across the table, stopping short of Ellie's hand. "Still am, in fact."

"I'm scared too." Ellie followed her whisper with a swig of tea.

"I know you might find it difficult, but I have

to ask anyway. Ellie, please forgive me for all the pain I've caused you. It was never my intention to hurt you. I regret that very much. But I don't regret that God brought you back to me. It's made me face the reality of who I am, and for that I will always be grateful."

"I . . ." Could Ellie forgive all the pain? What was God calling her to do? He'd sent Hagar back to Abram and Sarai, but what had happened after that? "I'll try. To forgive you."

But where did she and Olivia go from here? Did they talk occasionally? Send cards on the holidays? Pretend like this had never happened and continue on with their separate lives?

She didn't know exactly. But one thing had become clear to her.

Something had to change.

"I'm moving back to Oklahoma." Ellie blurted out the thought. She winced. What would Olivia think of that decision?

Was that sadness crossing Olivia's face? "What about your singing?"

"I'm leaving it behind." What else could she do? She didn't need the affirmation anymore. God would see her no matter what she did. Why take on the added pain of potential rejection—by Olivia and whatever crowd Ellie happened to be singing to?

Olivia seemed to contemplate Ellie's statement. "I admit . . . I'm tempted to let you."

What did she mean *let* her? "No offense, but it's my decision."

"No, you're right." Olivia drummed her fingers on the table. "But I can't allow you to go without telling you a few things. It would be easier, don't get me wrong. Easier to run away, to pretend I tried, to keep living life in fear. But I've made a decision too. I'm not gonna do what's easier. I'm gonna do what's right."

"And what's that?" The pulse in Ellie's neck picked up speed.

"I need to tell you that, if you want to stay, I'll help you with your career. *If* that's what you want. I'll fight to get the label going again. If that doesn't work, we'll call on my connections."

"Oh." Ellie lowered her gaze back to her mug, swirled the contents. "Is that it? You want to help me with my career? I've decided I don't want it."

"And why is that?"

"I was using it to get attention from people, from you. And God's shown me I don't need that."

"Ellie, look at me."

Ellie lifted her head.

Olivia's eyes pierced her with kindness—and love. "You are too talented to quit. I know it's your decision, but I don't think God would ask you to give up something you love. In fact, now that you know you don't need it to be happy or

426

content, you're ready for God to use you."

Was that true? Kacie's words flew back to her. *"People everywhere are just looking for something real, especially in today's world of plastic. Keep being you, and I promise it'll be enough."*

Singing made her come alive. And if she could share life with others simply by being herself, shouldn't she?

"I figured it'd be easier to quit. But maybe you're right."

This time Olivia did take her hand. She squeezed. "Just because something is easy doesn't make it right. Which brings me to my second point. If you'll let me, I'd love to be a mom to you. Not just a mentor. A mom."

Words Ellie had longed to hear—and now they were all hers to keep and cherish. But was it even feasible? "What does that mean? What does that look like?"

Olivia squeezed her fingers again. "It can look like however you want. But I was thinking you could stay in Nashville and move in with me. Or, if you really want to go to Oklahoma, I'll go with you."

"You will?" Olivia was willing to give up her whole life here and return to a place where she'd been Marie Culloway? To go from success and fame back to a place of bad memories and abuse? All for Ellie?

Tears shone in Olivia's eyes. "For you, anything. I love you, daughter of my body and my heart. And if you'll let me, I'd love to help you figure out where to go from here."

Ellie sat there, in a trance. It was too good to be true. But with God, perhaps all things really were possible, if only she could step out of the way and let him work.

But that would require forgiveness.

After all these years, the ball was back in her court. And she could choose to rail and be bitter, or accept what God had for her and move forward.

She gripped Olivia's hand. "I'd like that." She paused. "Because I love you too."

36

Now that she'd made things right with Ellie, Olivia had something else to do.

She reached out carefully, trying to balance everything in her arms, and rang the doorbell. Olivia stamped her feet in an attempt to ward off the chill in the early morning air. The temperature had plummeted recently, and snow was predicted sometime before Christmas, which was thirteen days away.

Andrew opened the door to his home, fully dressed for the workday. Was he meeting with his lawyers again? Interviewing for new jobs? A wrinkle fell across his brow. "What are you doing here? And what in the world are you holding?"

"Can you let me in first, and I'll explain everything? I'm freezing my rear off here."

He adjusted his glasses and considered her for a moment. Then he nodded and stepped aside.

Olivia darted in.

The fishing pole in her right hand scraped the top of the doorframe. She turned and whacked the entertainment center with a tackle box. "Sorry."

"Why don't you set that stuff down before you take out my TV?"

A twinge in Andrew's jaw sent hope reeling through Olivia. The fact he was nearly laughing at her was a good sign that perhaps their friendship wasn't truly over. "Okay." Olivia set the fishing pole, tackle box, sleeping bag, lantern, and knee-high water boots down on the ground near the entryway.

The price tag from the pole got caught momentarily on a button on her new waterproof jacket, and the pole whipped up and smacked her in the cheek.

She cried out in pain.

Andrew rushed to her side. "You okay?"

She held her hand across her right cheek and eye to cover the sting. "I think so."

He took her hand in his and lowered it from her face.

She breathed in his nearness. The concern in his eyes nearly undid her.

Andrew studied her face, running his fingertips lightly down her cheek. "It doesn't look too bad. Thankfully it missed your eye. Just got the eyelid."

"Good." Olivia could barely force out the word. She couldn't remove her gaze from him.

He cleared his throat, stepped back, and dropped his hand. "I'll be right back. Take a seat." He hurried from the room. The freezer opened and Andrew rummaged in it.

She lowered herself onto the couch. The

pain inflicted by the fishing pole was nothing compared to the ache in her heart.

The moment he'd realized he was touching her, he'd left. Would he ever be able to forgive her?

Probably. He was a good guy like that. But whether they could ever be friends again, or business partners, or more . . . that was another story.

Andrew re-entered, carrying a frozen bag of something. He handed it to her. Peas. "Put this on your face. I didn't have any raw steak."

"Peas are just fine, thank you." She pressed the pack against her cheek, and the cold seeped in, whisking away the sting. "Don't think I would have put dead cow on my body for any amount of money anyway." She attempted a chuckle.

Andrew leaned against the opposite wall, as far from Olivia as he could possibly be. No amusement lit his features. "Why are you here, Olivia?"

Olivia. Not Liv. She shifted the pack down slightly, so she could look at him with both eyes. "I came to apologize. I should never have lied to you."

Clumps of peas dug into her fingers. They burned and soothed at the same time.

He crossed his arms and said nothing.

She inhaled a greater breath. "It's no excuse,

but I was afraid. Afraid of my past. Afraid of being a mom. Afraid my mom would ruin Ellie. Afraid that you'd hate me when you found out. Whatever you might think of me, know this. I didn't abandon Ellie in pursuit of music. I've made mistakes, but I don't think that was one of them. I love her. I've always loved her." She paused.

He loosened his tie. "Go on."

"It kills me that I hurt you. That I hurt her. My lies finally caught up with me, and I have to live with the consequences."

A few drops of moisture dripped from the ice-pack onto her lap.

"I know it's a lot to ask for—your forgiveness. But that's what I want. And I know it's probably impossible to ask that we remain friends, and especially that we remain business partners. But, I'm still in this if you are."

Andrew frowned and lowered his gaze to the floor. "I don't know. Like I said at the TV station, I have to be able to trust whomever I'm in business with. You broke that trust."

"I know I did. But, Andrew?" She waited for him to look at her again. This next part would be hard to say. Here's where she might lose him forever. However, it had to be said. "I'm not like your ex-wife. I've made mistakes, but it's not fair to compare me to her."

He shoved his fingers under his glasses

and rubbed the bridge of his nose. Then he straightened and walked to the couch, sinking down onto the cushion next to her.

Her cushion rose slightly at the pressure.

"I know."

"So what do you think?" She wanted to reach out and grab his hand so badly. Instead, she strangled the bag of peas. "Is there any way you'll reconsider resuming our partnership?"

"Look, Olivia. I forgive you. I do. I can understand being scared and lying. The whole thing had to have been traumatic for you." He absently picked stray pieces of lint from the couch and flicked them onto the floor. "But maybe it's best if we go our separate ways."

Olivia tightened her grip and suddenly the bag of peas burst, sending little green balls flying through the air in every direction. She mumbled an apology and lunged to catch a few rolling from her lap. Waterworks threatened to escape her eyes. She loved this man, and her actions—nothing else—would be the cause of both their hearts breaking.

"It's fine. Just leave them. I'll pick them up after you go."

He wanted her gone. She couldn't look him in the eyes, could only nod. "Right." Olivia stood slowly, legs wobbling. She headed for the door, reached for the door handle.

"Liv?"

The sound of her nickname gave her pause. She turned slowly. "Yeah?"

Andrew stared at the pile of stuff by his front door. "What's with the camping gear?"

"Oh." The sight of her recent purchases was the last straw. Tears of rejected hope finally fell. "I thought we could go. Camping, I mean. You know. Even though you didn't win the bet. It was supposed to be a peace offering."

Andrew stared blankly at her. Oh, he thought her a fool. But then his mouth curved into the slightest smirk. "You want to go camping?"

She threw her hands on her hips. "Of course I don't *want* to go. That's what makes it a peace offering."

"I mean, you wanted to go now? In December?"

"Well . . ."

"When it's freezing outside?"

"I figured we'd wear layers." So that's why all of the stuff she'd purchased was on major clearance. Made sense now.

Laughter burst from Andrew's throat. "And where did you get all of this gear?"

"Some sporting goods place." She hesitated, then let a grin slip through her defenses. "Those salespeople probably loved me. They told me everything I'd need, and I just bought anything they suggested."

Andrew shook his head in awe. "I don't know how you do it."

"Do what?"

"Make me love you even more, just when I'm ready to let you go forever."

She inhaled a sharp breath, and her hand fell away from the doorknob. "What are you saying?"

Andrew strode forward. He slid his hands down her arms.

Despite the barrier her jacket created, she shivered at his touch.

"I'm saying I love you, Liv. And no matter how hard I try, I don't think I can live without you."

She threw her arms around his neck and let the tears—rejected hope turned to joy—fall fast and free. "Oh, Andrew. I love you too."

He leaned in and planted a kiss full of so many emotions it sent her spinning. He bent to her ear, the tickle of his whisper floating by. "Olivia Lovett, I don't care who you were in the past. Only who you are now. Will you be my partner, in business and in life?"

She pulled back and her eyes widened. "What do you mean?"

"I want you as my business partner again. We'll keep Radiant Records together."

"That sounds wonderful." She fingered the collar of his shirt. "Is that all you meant?"

"No. I also want you as my wife." He lowered himself onto one knee.

Oh, this man.

"Will you marry me?"

Olivia couldn't stop the smile that spread across her face. "That depends."

"Oh yeah? On what?"

"Are you gonna hold me to my offer to go camping?"

He rose up again and put his arms around her waist, pulling her close. "You bet your boots I am. Every year. But we can wait till summer."

"I guess I can live with that. As long as I'm with you."

37

If Ellie had asked herself six months ago what she'd be doing two days before Christmas, it certainly wouldn't have been baking sugar cookies with her mom and grandma.

And here she was, standing in Mom's kitchen, while Grandma taught Olivia her secret family recipe.

"One of the most important things is to make sure your butter is softened beforehand." Grandma held up a stick of butter. "Otherwise, it won't cream together with the sugar properly."

Mom raised her hand as if in a classroom. "And creaming together means what exactly?"

Chloe and Pascal lay at her feet, relaxed yet clearly waiting to see if anyone accidentally dropped something for them to snag.

Grandma smiled and glanced at Ellie. "You want to tell her?"

Ellie held up a hand mixer. "It means you put them in a bowl and mix them together until they become these little butter-sugar ball clumpy things."

"Thank you for such a precise definition." Mom laughed and threw her arm around Ellie's shoulders. "I should be embarrassed. My own daughter knows more about baking than I do.

My Christmas cookie tradition usually consists of bumming some off of Rachel."

"This year is all about new traditions, isn't it?" Ellie snuggled into Mom's embrace.

At times, it still felt weird to call her Mom and be affectionate. But they'd addressed that elephant and decided to ignore the awkwardness, knowing it would eventually fade.

"Definitely." Mom kissed the top of Ellie's head.

Across the kitchen, Grandma wiped her eyes. She'd told Ellie how proud of her she was for forgiving and moving forward. Had even helped her pack up her room and move her things into a spare bedroom at Mom's house earlier this week.

She'd felt bad leaving Lena without a roommate on such short notice, but her friend had been super supportive and quickly found a friendly coworker in need of a place to stay.

Ellie held out her hand to Grandma, and she rushed over to join the group hug. A tear dripped down Ellie's nose, and she sniffled. "I am so happy you'll be here for Christmas."

"Me too, dear. Grandpa is excited to fly in tomorrow." Grandma pulled back and snagged a paper towel off the counter. She handed it to Ellie and grinned. "Now, let's get going. These cookies won't make themselves."

Mom saluted. "Aye, aye, captain. I can't wait

to bake something that won't burn in my own kitchen."

"I don't think you give yourself enough credit." Ellie dumped the measured sugar and sticks of butter needed for multiple batches into a large bowl. This could turn into a late-night affair. She plugged in the mixer and held it out toward Mom. "You want to do the honors?"

Mom cocked a hip and leaned against the counter. "I think I'll watch the master at work. Wouldn't want to ruin the cookies in the very first batch."

Ellie turned the mixer on and dug it into the bowl, beating and watching as two separate ingredients became one entity. She turned off the mixer, dipped a finger in the light and fluffy goodness, and tasted the concoction. Ellie glanced at Mom as she did.

Mom just looked at her, smiling.

This was how life was supposed to be.

They finished mixing everything together, Mom even taking a few turns at the beater. After letting the dough chill in the refrigerator, they rolled it out onto the island countertop and used a variety of cookie cutters Grandma had bought—trees, bells, candy canes, Santas, and presents.

Once they'd placed all of the shapes onto cookie sheets, Grandma opened the oven.

A wave of heat hit Ellie's face.

Grandma put the sheets inside and shooed them away. "I'll keep an eye on these. Didn't you say you wanted to watch some Christmas movies or something?"

Sweet Grandma. Making sure that Ellie included Mom in some of her favorite traditions. Ellie nodded. "Come on, Mom. Let's go raid my DVD collection."

Ellie led Mom into her room, found the correct box, and opened the flap. She dug around and pulled out several of her favorites. "As a kid, I'd watch *Rudolph*, *Frosty*, and the Grinch over and over again." She held each up as she mentioned them. "It drove Grandma crazy. I'd even try to watch them in January and February. Thought maybe it would make Christmas come sooner."

Mom chewed her lip. "I'm sorry I wasn't there for that."

Ellie lowered the DVDs. "You're here now."

"Yes, I am." Mom snatched the movies from Ellie. "Would you believe that I've never seen any of these?"

"Are you serious?"

"Deadly."

"We need to fix that right away."

"Let's go."

They headed into the living room, where they'd placed a tree the day before. They'd gone together to the lot and chosen the perfect tree to represent their lives—one that started sparse

440

and slightly twisted at the bottom, but came to a beautiful point up top. The branches were firm and exuded a strength that didn't allow them to break, evidenced by the heavy snow it had endured the night before they'd bought it. It had been left out in the cold yet still weathered the storm.

And now, strung with cranberries and adorned with red and silver ornaments, it bloomed with festivity and love.

Ellie popped open the DVD player and stuck in a disc. "Ladies and—er, well, lady. I present for your viewing pleasure . . . *How the Grinch Stole Christmas*." She hit Play, and the movie began.

The dogs trotted in from the kitchen and settled at the foot of the couch. The scent of baking cookies drifted under Ellie's nose.

Mom pulled a blanket over her and Ellie as the Whos down in Whoville started singing.

The doorbell rang, and Chloe and Pascal leaped up, barking and running toward the door.

Mom glanced at Ellie. "You expecting someone?"

Ellie paused the movie. "No. Maybe it's Andrew."

"Maybe." Mom absently twisted the engagement ring on her left hand. "But I told him we were having a girls' night." She pushed the blanket aside, shushed the dogs, and headed for the door. After leaning over and peeking through the peephole, she looked back at Ellie and raised her eyebrows expectantly.

"What?"

"It's Nick."

"Nick?" What was he doing here? He was supposed to be in Texas taking care of his mom and siblings. With Lauren. As nice as his voicemail from two weeks ago had been, she hadn't gotten up the nerve to call him back. And things had been so busy . . .

Ellie pulled the blanket up to her neck, instant nerves making her regret the pizza she'd eaten earlier.

"Should I let him in?"

Ellie shrugged. "I guess."

Mom opened the door. "Nick! Great to see you. Come on in."

"Thanks, Olivia." Nick stepped through the doorway and pulled off his gloves as the dogs sniffed his shoes. "I'm sorry to drop by unannounced. Lena told me where you guys lived." Nick glanced around her and stared at Ellie. "I've tried calling you." His tone didn't sound angry. Just confused. Sad.

And those eyes . . .

Ellie cleared her throat. "Here I am."

Olivia patted Nick on the shoulder as she closed the door. "Can I get you something to drink?"

"I'm fine, thanks."

"Okay. I'm going to go check on those cookies." She walked out of the room, but not before sending Ellie some sort of silent communication with a look. What was Mom trying to say? Maybe someday Ellie would be able to read her better.

She couldn't wait.

Nick sat on the La-Z-Boy chair next to the couch. "Hey."

"Hey." Ellie lowered her gaze to her twisted hands. "How's your mom?"

"She's doing great, actually. My dad decided to come home, so he could spend Christmas with us."

"That's good." Silence rose between them until Ellie couldn't stand it anymore. "I'm sorry I didn't call you back. I was dealing with some stuff."

"Yeah, I saw. And it's okay."

She glanced at him. "Your messages were encouraging. I even read Genesis Sixteen. It helped."

"Good."

"Yeah." Pascal licked her exposed toes, and she tucked them underneath the blanket. "Why are you here, Nick?"

"I had to be sure you were all right."

"But Christmas is in two days, and you should be with your family."

"I wanted to be with you." Nick's hands tightened into fists, then relaxed.

That didn't make any sense. "How does Lauren feel about that?" Try as she might, she couldn't keep the twinge of jealousy out of her voice when she spoke his girlfriend's name.

"Lauren?" Nick reached up to scratch his head. "What does she have to do with any of this?"

"I know you two started dating again."

"What?" Nick rocked forward in the La-Z-Boy and put his hands on his knees. "Who told you that?"

"Lauren. I called after you left, and she answered your phone."

Nick groaned. "I don't know why she'd say that. It's not true."

It wasn't? Hope flitted through her chest. "But I thought . . ."

With a swift movement, Nick rose and was next to Ellie in seconds. He took her face gently in his hands. "How could I even contemplate dating someone else when I'm falling in love with you?"

Ellie closed the distance between them, and gave him a kiss filled with all the missing and the wanting and the wondering of the past month. She ran her hands through his curls and pulled back. "Sweet applesauce. I missed that."

"Me too." He kissed the tip of her nose.

She took a breath, searching his eyes. "And for the record, I'm sorta kinda falling in love with you too."

His grin flooded her veins with warmth.

And then his stomach gurgled. He laughed. "Sorry. I haven't eaten all day. I had to catch a last-minute standby flight to get here."

He'd done that on Christmas weekend, just for her?

Ellie grabbed his hand. "Lucky for you, we are decorating cookies. You down?"

"Sure."

"We could even make some and bring them tomorrow to the kids at the hospital if you're available."

"I'm all yours."

She liked the sound of that.

They wandered into the kitchen, where Grandma and Mom were testing a few cookies.

Mom waved hers in the air. "Look. They're not burnt!"

Ellie turned to Nick. "Mom's not the best baker in the world."

"I'd never know it." Nick squeezed her hand.

Ellie introduced him to Grandma, who winked at her when his back was turned and mouthed, *He's cute*. Ellie bit back a laugh.

Nick rubbed his hands together. "Now, Ellie said something about decorating these bad boys?"

Grandma pointed to several bowls of red and green frosting. "Go wild."

They spread wax paper on the kitchen table and

445

got out sprinkles, coconut shreds, mini chocolate chips, and rubber spatulas for everyone. Mom flicked on the radio, and "Count Your Blessings" from the movie *White Christmas* streamed from the small speakers. Grandma made hot chocolate, and they sipped from their mugs as they worked on their cookies, transforming the blank slates into whatever they desired.

Flakes of snow began falling at the window, swirling in thousands of intricate designs that could never be repeated, beautiful moments scattered across the wind, each one perfect and lovely.

The neighbor's icicle lights danced.

And Ellie's heart did the same.

38

Four months later

There isn't a better time for wedding vows than spring.

I hurry in white heels toward the bridal dressing room, tucked away on the other side of the church's massive garden. All around me birds chirp, singing a song of renewal, waking up anything still dead from winter. The sun radiates the perfect balance of light and heat. Flowers fling their fragrance at me—and I welcome it.

My name is Olivia Lovett. But I'm Marie Culloway too. I've finally accepted that I can be both. And today, I become someone entirely new.

Olivia Grant.

What a beautiful day for second chances.

I arrive at the bridal suite and step inside. It's small, with a charming wooden table and two chairs. The vintage wallpaper reminds me of something I've seen in an old BBC movie. I catch my reflection in the gilded mirror and press a hand to my chest.

"Oh, Mom. You look so gorgeous." Ellie comes behind me and hugs my waist, careful not to wrinkle my white gown. She lays her head on my shoulder.

We stare into the mirror together, my daughter's tea-length lilac dress fanning out from its empire waist, fading into my gown, getting lost in it.

I've never felt more myself. "Thank you, sweetie. So do you." I skim my fingers beneath my eyes. "You're gonna make me cry."

Tears poke through Ellie's lashes. "Join the club." She laughs. "Where did you run off to?"

"I'd forgotten this in my car." I hold up the pearl necklace Leigh gave me, the one that symbolizes my motherhood, my life before and after Ellie. My life now. "Help me put it on?"

Ellie reaches for the necklace and secures it around my neck.

It settles into the hollow of my throat, and I swallow.

"It's time, Mom."

I walk to the table, where two bouquets of cut wildflowers stand in a vase. I hand one to Ellie and keep the larger for myself. "Let's go."

We walk hand in hand through the garden, toward the wrought-iron gazebo. Strains of classical music float on the breeze, sweeping over us. Finally, we arrive at our destination. My breath hitches at the intimate setting— three rows of ten chairs each, split by an aisle decorated with rose petals.

Friends and family fill the seats, ready to

celebrate this new beginning with us. Rachel flashes a big grin from the front row. Leigh dabs her eyes with a tissue, while Nick stares at Ellie, something warm in his gaze.

Andrew stands up front in a tuxedo, looking as handsome as ever.

Grace stands next to him in a feminine black suit—his "best woman."

I grin.

I still can't believe he wants me, with all my baggage. But he's assured me he does.

The string quartet begins playing something by Bach.

Ellie turns to me. "Ready?"

"Ready."

We move together down the aisle and reach my groom.

The pastor clears his throat. "You may be seated. Who gives this woman to this man?"

Ellie squeezes my hand. "I do."

I hug my precious daughter, who releases me to Andrew. The love bounds between us all, a living, breathing thing. We exchange our vows, place rings on each other's fingers. And then my husband kisses me, and electricity charges the day.

After we're announced as man and wife, we greet our guests. Then we head to the reception area, round tables set in a separate part of the garden. Everyone settles in and begins enjoying their salads. After a delicious meal of filet mignon, which, I admit, I don't taste at all, Ellie comes to me and whispers in my ear. "It's time."

I nod, inhale. This is the moment I've dreaded. And longed for.

I take my dress in hand as I stand.

Andrew looks at me, a question on his face.

"It's a surprise." I follow Ellie to the small stage, where two stools and two microphones wait for us.

We both take our guitars from their cases and tune them.

Ellie and I take our seats. My daughter adjusts her mic. "Hey, y'all. If I could get your attention for just a minute. Thanks for being here on this amazing day for my mom and Andrew. Mom and I wrote this song for today, to celebrate new beginnings."

She strums the simple tune and starts singing the words we've strung together.

My vocal chords tighten. I haven't sung in public in so long. The doctor says I can't. And our practices didn't sound so great on my part. I could barely jump an octave.

So why am I up here? Why do I put myself through this?

I glance at my daughter, and I know.

This is the dream. My dream, for forever and a day. To do life, sing through life, with her by my side.

I open my mouth, and out flow the words. They're beautiful. And my voice—is this real? It's what it once was.

But no, it's more. Different. Richer. Deeper.

And I realize that, just when I thought I was finished for good, God's given me one more song to sing.

About the Author

Lindsay Harrel is a lifelong book nerd with a B.A. in Journalism and an M.A. in English. She lives in Phoenix, AZ, with her young family, and two golden retrievers in serious need of training. Lindsay has held a variety of jobs, including curriculum editor for two universities, medical and business writer, and copywriter for a digital marketing agency. Now she juggles stay-at-home mommyhood with working freelance jobs, teaching college English courses online, and—of course—writing novels.

When she actually has time to do other things, she loves to sing, read, and sip passion iced teas from Starbucks. She loves to watch God work in ordinary lives to create something extraordinary, and she writes to bring hope to those who may have lost it along the way. Connect with her at www.LindsayHarrel.com and any other place she hangs out online, including Facebook and Twitter.

Acknowledgments

As I've discovered—and keep discovering—this book-writing thing is no simple journey. There are so many people who have helped make this book a reality. Thank you to each and every one of them, including:

My ah-mazing agent, Rachelle Gardner, for believing in me when you didn't have to. There's no one I'd rather have with me on this journey.

My awesome publishing team at Ashberry Lane: Christina Tarabochia, Sherrie Ashcraft, Kristen Johnson, Rachel Lulich, Andrea Cox, Nicole Miller, and Amy Smith. Thank you for taking a chance on me (and on Olivia and Ellie too).

My writing mentors, Susan May Warren and Rachel Hauck, along with all the other My Book Therapy peeps (Beth Vogt and Lisa Jordan in particular) who encouraged me along the way. Your wisdom and all that you've poured into me over the years have made me not just a better writer—but a better me.

My GLAM girls—Gabrielle Meyer, Alena Tauriainen, and Melissa Tagg (the best craft partner in the world!). I just love you to pieces. Without you girls, i wouldn't know the meaning of true sisterhood. And ticks. I wouldn't know much about them either. *wink*

Other writer friends who have encouraged and spurred me on, including Tari Faris, Jessica Patch, Jill Kemerer, Katie Ganshert, Ashley Clark, Laurie Tomlinson, Ruth Douthitt, and so many others.

My mentors, Sue Sunderland and Roma Gavaza. Thanks for all the prayers. I wouldn't have survived without them.

My Palmcroft Five33 ladies—Rachel Edwards, Rachel Sloma, Naomi Fugit, Melanie Beem, Becky Getz, Brenda Perry, Tiffany Harding, and Elizabeth Honeycutt—for sharing this mommy-hood journey with me. Also, for listening to me blab nonstop about my dreams and never telling me to shut up.

My beta readers for the first book I ever wrote: You are all saints. Thanks for helping me become a better writer.

Chloe and Pascal, my very real golden retrievers, who inspired the fictional ones in this book. Your crazy antics make me smile.

My amazing family, especially my mother-in-law, Nancy Harrel, and stepmom, Kristin Walker. Thank you, thank you, thank you for watching Elliott so often, so I could pursue this dream!

My father, Kent Walker, for believing in me from a young age and instilling confidence in your diva child. You are the best daddy a girl could ask for, and I'm so glad you're mine.

My son, Elliott, for taking such good naps, so Mommy could write! And for being the world's most adorable toddler (okay, so I'm biased).

My husband, Mike, for not complaining when I spent so much money on books and writing conferences. Hehe. But seriously. You have loved me through all the ups and downs, and I am so blessed to be married to a man who believes in me and supports my dreams.

And finally, God. The idea that you died to save me is overwhelming in and of itself. But to allow me to live this life, doing something I love—you take my breath away. Thank you for loving me so lavishly.

Center Point Large Print
600 Brooks Road / PO Box 1
Thorndike, ME 04986-0001 USA

(207) 568-3717

US & Canada:
1 800 929-9108
www.centerpointlargeprint.com